ISBN 978-0-483-52783-6
PIBN 10636024

CLARISSA FURIOSA

A Novel

BY

· W. E. NORRIS

AUTHOR OF "BILLY BELLEW" "THIRLBY HALL"
"ADRIAN VIDAL" ETC.

NEW YORK
HARPER & BROTHERS PUBLISHERS
1896

By W. E. NORRIS.

BILLY BELLEW. Ill'd. Post 8vo, Cloth, $1 50.
MARCIA. 8vo, Paper, 40 cents.
A MAN OF HIS WORD. 4to, Paper, 20 cents.
ADRIAN VIDAL. Ill'd. 4to, Paper, 25 cents.

PUBLISHED BY HARPER & BROTHERS, NEW YORK.

CONTENTS

CLARISSA FURIOSA

CHAPTER I

DURING AN AUTUMN SESSION

THE House of Commons on a murky November evening
(at which time of the year the representatives of the people
ought to be much more pleasantly and healthily employed
than in endeavoring to force necessary measures down the
throat of an unsportsmanlike opposition) is indeed a melancholy spectacle for the sympathetic eye to gaze down
upon. But who, except a very ignorant and sanguine person, can expect sympathy to descend from the Ladies' Gallery, or the misery and iniquity of an autumn session to
be justly appreciated there? Miss Clarissa Dent, for example, craning forward with parted lips, and drinking in
every word of the really eloquent denunciation which a
famous Radical statesman was hurling at the government
of the day, had no idea that the orator was fighting a
losing battle very much against his will, nor any pity to
bestow upon the weary legislators beneath her, save upon
the few occupants of the front ministerial bench—who, to
be sure, seemed to be taking their punishment with amazing
apathy and indifference.

"How *can* they answer him?" she demanded, in an
agitated whisper, of her aunt, who was seated beside her.
"He hasn't left them a leg to stand upon!"

"Hasn't he?" returned the stout, lymphatic lady addressed. "I wasn't listening, and I am not sure that I

know what it is all about; but your uncle says the bill is perfectly safe, so it doesn't matter whether they can answer him or not. Most likely they can, though; for I believe Sir Robert Luttrell is to reply, and Sir Robert, your uncle says, is far and away the best debater on our side."

Clarissa scrutinized with increased interest the hat beneath which this champion of constitutionalism and the existing order of things was taking repose. There was not very much to be seen of the Right Honorable Sir Robert Luttrell, Chancellor of the Duchy of Lancaster, except his hat; for he had tilted it over his eyes, his head was thrown back, his closely trimmed gray beard was at right angles with the rest of his person, and, but for the slow, regular swinging of one long leg over the other, he might have been supposed to be fast asleep. But when his redoubtable antagonist sat down, amidst prolonged cheering, and when he himself rose, resting both hands for a moment upon the table, a keen, intelligent spectator, such as Miss Clarissa, was able to divine that the languid-looking elderly gentleman who was about to speak might prove sufficiently wide-awake for all practical purposes. His head was well shaped and well covered with curly hair, which was almost white; he was tall and spare; he evidently had been, and in one sense still was, extremely handsome; his dress showed signs of care, and there was a certain indescribable air of power about his pose and mien—arising, perhaps, from his being so obviously at his ease. The fighting man, whether friend or foe, is readily recognizable, and we mortals are so constituted that he commands our respect, not to say our love, whatever be his method of introducing himself to our notice.

Sir Robert Luttrell's method, it must be confessed, was a little disappointing, at the outset, to those who were unacquainted with him and it. His halting, hesitating delivery, the long pauses in which he indulged, and his frequent, deliberate consultation of documents were scarcely of a nature to provoke enthusiasm. But by degrees his complete mastery of his subject became more and more apparent; by degrees, too, the quiet style in which he made his successive points rendered it increasingly manifest that he had his adversary on the hip. The government of which he was a member was, for the moment, demanding an extension of powers in dealing with a disturbed portion of the United Kingdom, and he was able to show, not only that what was asked for was indispensable, but that the party in opposition had never even attempted to dispense with it. The political career of the far more eloquent orator who had preceded him had not been altogether free from inconsistencies, and to these Sir Robert drew attention in a dry, half-surprised, half-melancholy tone which delighted the House. He had the air of merely stating acknowledged facts and of inviting somebody to be so very kind as to explain how an honorable and right honorable gentleman had contrived, within the space of a few months, to perform that strange gymnastic feat known as turning his back upon himself. 'It is not likely that his speech affected a single vote, or that he had any expectation of its doing so; yet he scored a triumph which was tolerably sure to be taken note of in the constituencies, and even within the walls of the House he gained one more enthusiastic adherent.

"That was perfectly splendid!" Clarissa exclaimed, after Sir Robert had resumed his seat. "I almost suspected myself of being a Radical half an hour ago, but now I haven't the slightest doubt that I am a Tory. He was absolutely convincing! Didn't you think so, Aunt Susan?"

"I dare say he was," answered fat Mrs. Dent, with a yawn; "he is said to be a very able man. It is a great pity that he is so extravagant; for I believe it has come to this now, that office is almost a necessity to him, and of course the other side must have their turn *some* day. I am sorry to take you away, dear, if this sort of thing amuses you; but your uncle is leaving, I see, and I promised that we would drive him home."

The majority of the members were leaving; for the debate could not be brought to a conclusion that night, and it was just then being continued by a long-winded, obstructive person to whom nobody cared to listen. Mrs. Dent and her niece, after finding and entering their carriage, were soon joined by a dapper little elderly gentleman in a very expensive fur-lined coat, who put his shrewd, pleasant, smooth-shaven face in at the window for a moment to say:

"I'll be with you immediately; I want just to say a word to Luttrell."

This was Mr. Dent, of the famous banking house of Dent & Co., member for a metropolitan constituency, and a man entitled, on many obvious grounds, to the respectful esteem of his fellow-lawgivers. That he enjoyed the friendship and esteem of Sir Robert Luttrell was a circumstance hitherto unknown to his niece, who had but recently taken up her abode under his roof, and her own esteem for Uncle Tom was considerably enhanced when, bending forward, she saw him holding that eminent statesman by the elbow. Presently the pair approached the carriage, talking in low tones as they advanced, and then Mr. Dent said:

"Clarissa, Sir Robert Luttrell wishes to be introduced to you. He is kind enough to say that Lady Luttrell will accept you as a substitute for your aunt at dinner next Thursday."

Sir Robert took off his hat, and, while expressing his regret that Mrs. Dent's state of health compelled her to avoid heated rooms, declared himself very grateful to her niece for consenting to undergo the tedium of a solemn political dinner.

"Politics and politicians don't interest young people," he remarked, with a shrug and a laugh. "For the matter of that, I don't know that they would interest old people if we had anything better to be interested in. Is this your first visit to the House of Commons, Miss Dent? How bored you must have been!"

"Indeed no!" exclaimed Clarissa. "This was my first visit to the House of Commons, but I hope it will not be my last; for the newspapers give one no idea at all of what a debate really is. Your speech made me see quite clearly how shabby and insincere the opposition are, and I should think it must have made them feel ashamed of themselves too. In future I shall always beg Uncle Tom to get me into the Ladies' Gallery if there is any prospect of your speaking."

She turned red (but the darkness concealed her blushes) after making this flattering statement. She was entirely without experience of the customs and conventions of high society, and it occurred to her too late that for a mere schoolgirl to address so very great a man as Sir Robert Luttrell in that way might savor of impertinence. Sir Robert, however, seemed to be quite pleased.

"The leaders of the opposition," he answered, "are, I am sorry to tell you, dead to all sense of shame; but I, who belong to the party of simplicity and rectitude, am by no means impervious to compliments, and you have paid me the prettiest compliment that I have received for many a long day, Miss Dent. How much nicer you are than your uncle, who won't even give me credit for being serious!"

The truth is that he was not very serious; and doubtless that was why, notwithstanding his conspicuous abilities, he was not, and never would be, the chosen leader of an extremely serious nation. Mr. Dent, on the way home, explained to his niece in a few pregnant words how it was that Sir Robert's disabilities outweighed his abilities.

"It is his misfortune to be dangerously clever, and his fault that he is incurably indolent. No Conservative administration could be formed without him, and no department could be safely intrusted to him. As Chancellor of the Duchy he is the right man in the right place; but that office can't always be kept open for him, and it is only £2000 a year, instead of £5000, which he wants, and thinks he ought to have. One foresees the day when he will be driven to accept a peerage—as a preliminary step to figuring in the Bankruptcy Court."

"Oh, Tom, you would never let it come to that!" exclaimed Mrs. Dent.

"My dear, what a shocking and unauthorized assertion!

Your words seem to imply that I myself am desirous of
obtaining a peerage, and that I should hesitate at no pecuniary sacrifice to gratify my ambition, whereas you ought
to know that I am quite the most unambitious politician
in Great Britain."

"You are ambitious for your friends, Tom, if you are
not ambitious for yourself, and I am sure you will not
allow the Luttrells to be ruined for want of a little ready
money."

"Ah, you flatter me, my dear Susan, you flatter me! It
is the business of a banker, I admit, to lend money ; but it
is likewise his business and his duty to do so upon unim-
peachable security.   After all, I am not Rothschild, nor
is our good friend Sir Robert essential to the greatest happiness of the greatest number.   Let us endeavor to take a
sane and philosophic view of what can't be helped, bearing always in mind the great truth that nothing matters
very much."

The foregoing dialogue conveyed no distinct impression
to the mind of Clarissa, who—eager though she was to acquire information, and prompt at assimilating it when
placed before her in the form of definite facts—was as yet
easily puzzled by innuendoes.   An orphan, who could
scarcely remember her mother, and whose father had been
a grave, stern man of business, approachable only at meal-
times during the holidays, she had, during the first eighteen years of her life, been about as solitary a human
being as could have been discovered in England or out of
it.   She had cried on leaving school, although she had had
but few friends there ; she had cried when her father died
suddenly, although he had given her so little cause to lament him ; there was in her a fine large store of affection
ready to be lavished upon somebody and hitherto unclaimed
by anybody.   Of this a considerable portion was now overflowing upon her uncle and aunt, who had taken her to live
with them in Portland Place, and who, indeed, were showing themselves very kind to her, having no child of their
own.

"It is a thousand pities, not to say ten thousand pities," Mr. Dent remarked, when his younger brother's death cast this fresh responsibility upon him, "that Clarissa is not a boy. Still, being what she is through no fault of her own, she must be made the best of. With care and good management, we may, I trust, restrain her from eloping with the butler."

Mrs. Dent would have been horrified at the bare suggestion of anything so improper and improbable if she had not been accustomed to the very extraordinary things which Tom was in the habit of saying.

"You see," he added, by way of explanation, "she has a bias towards eccentricity. Or, rather, you don't see it, but I do. I detect it in her eyes and the arrangement of her hair, as well as in her speech every now and then. However, she is still quite fluid, so to speak, and it is your obvious duty, my dear, to run her into a nice, trustworthy, conventional mould."

Poor Mrs. Dent, who had for many years been an invalid and who was entirely devoid of experience in the training of the young, protested plaintively against so startling a representation of her duty to her neighbor; but she was partially reassured by her husband's next remark.

"Your diffidence is becoming, Susan, and not altogether misplaced. What should console you is that the task of moulding Clarissa is only too likely to pass into other hands before long, and it will be for me, I am afraid, to say into what hands it shall or shall not pass. I feel strong enough to beat a domestic servant, but the Lord knows whether I shall have the strength and wisdom to make a judicious selection among the fortune-hunters who are sure to come buzzing round her presently!"

Clarissa in a few years' time would enter into undisputed possession of the fortune which she had inherited from her father. This, it was generally understood, would be a comfortable though not a large one; but as Mr. Dent, who was his brother's sole executor, had maintained a discreet reserve upon the point, nobody knew for certain what the late junior partner's interest in the banking business had amounted to. In any case, suitors were not likely to hang back; for the girl was decidedly pretty, notwithstanding her somewhat angular figure and the awkward habit of poking her head, which her school-mistresses had been unable to correct, and which she herself excused on the plea of short-sightedness. Her fluffy flaxen hair and the blue eyes (often screwed up) in which her uncle had pretended to discern indications of dawning eccentricity were well enough, her complexion was really admirable, her nose and mouth did not sin against received rules, and she had a double row of excellent white teeth which were displayed every time that she spoke.

"They are displayed a little too much," the family physician said, when, for certain reasons, he had been requested to make a careful examination of the young lady; "it is a sign of a delicate constitution, and I think she will require watching. Her lungs are sound, and the cough which alarms you does not mean much—for the present. At the same time, I would not let her catch cold, if I were you. Why not take her abroad for the winter?"

There were several reasons for disregarding this very inconvenient piece of advice, one of them being that, although an active member of Parliament may succeed in finding a pair, it is not always possible for a busy banker to absent himself from his affairs for several months together, while another was that foreign habits and foreign cookery were abhorrent to Mrs. Dent. However, the doctor did not insist, and Clarissa, for her part, was not conscious of having anything the matter with her beyond a troublesome little cough. What she was conscious of— and had sufficient cause to be—was an exuberant vitality, an immense curiosity respecting the outer world, of which she had hitherto seen so wonderfully little, and, just now, much exultation at the prospect of dining with a Cabinet Minister and meeting all sorts of interesting people at his table.

People are apt to be interesting, or the reverse, in exact
proportion to their novelty or staleness. Sir Robert and
Lady Luttrell, who had been entertaining members of Parliament and the wives of members of Parliament for very
many years, probably thought that the party which assembled at their house in Grosvenor Place on the succeeding
Thursday was composed of units duller than ditch-water;
whereas Miss Dent, as soon as she had heard the names
of her fellow-guests, felt it a privilege and an excitement
to be even in the same room with them. She was very
prettily dressed on that occasion, economy in the matter
of dress being quite unnecessary so far as she was concerned; she was more or less aware of looking her best;
she was too unaffectedly modest to be shy, and it is, therefore, not surprising that she produced a decidedly favorable impression upon those who saw her for the first time.
Her hostess in particular (for the reasons above specified,
no doubt, and because Clarissa's conversation and manners
were so unlike those of the ordinary fashionable young
woman of the day) took a fancy to her at once.

"My dear," she said, speaking with a very slight foreign
accent and laughing in response to a somewhat *naïve* ejaculation of the girl's, "it is charming of you to thank us,
but you will soon discover that it is we who ought to be
thanking you for having brought a little brightness into
our dreary gathering. My son—who is the only creature
present, except yourself, with any pretension to youth—
will tell you what terrible affairs our dinner-parties always
are. Oh yes; it is true that there are some great men in
the room; but, between ourselves, it is not very difficult
to be great, and it is very easy to be wearisome. Not that
I wish to disgust you with all these old gentlemen. If you
are able to find them admirable and awe-inspiring, so much
the better for you."

Lady Luttrell was a Frenchwoman by birth, but had
lived long enough in England to have acquired many of
our habits, as well as a perfect command of our language.
Clever, vivacious, and still retaining a fair share of the

beauty for which she had been famous towards the middle
of the nineteenth century, she was, and always had been,
of considerable assistance to her husband in a social sense.
Probably at the bottom of her heart she loved the land of
her adoption better than that which she made a point of
visiting every winter, but with which she had few remaining ties; probably, also, her great popularity was due to
the fact that she not only liked us, but had assimilated our
little ways.   It is scarcely possible for a foreigner to be
really popular in English society until he or she has made
that inferential acknowledgment of our superiority to other
nations.   For the rest, she was a woman of the world, and
an extremely agreeable and kind-hearted one; so that Clarissa, who prided herself upon being a little bit above narrow racial prejudices, had every right to be charmed with
her.

The comparatively juvenile statesman who escorted Miss
Dent to the dining-room was spared any painful intellectual effort in seeking for subjects of conversation suitable
to his neighbor, his whole time being taken up in replying
to quick, eager queries, some of which had the privilege
of amusing him mightily.   He could not—or, at all events,
he said he could not—enlighten her as to the policy decided upon at a Cabinet council which had been held that
day, nor had he very much information to impart respecting the special department which he himself represented
in a subordinate capacity; but he was able to tell her who
the distinguished personages in her immediate vicinity
were, and he was likewise able to gratify her curiosity with
regard to the one individual present who was distinguished
from the rest of the company by virtue of possessing no
particular distinction.

"Don't you know Guy Luttrell?" he asked.   "I thought
you were a friend of the family.   Your uncle is, anyhow,
and I dare say he has a pretty accurate notion of how much
Master Guy has cost an indulgent father.   Oh yes, I suppose
he is rather good-looking; most people call him so.   I don't
think I very much admire that type of man myself.   One

foresees that he will be fat before he is middle-aged. He has been a bit of a *mauvais sujet*, I believe."

"I should say that he was very good-natured," Clarissa remarked, scrutinizing the heir of the Luttrells through her glasses.

"They always are; that is one reason why they are always so expensive. And Sir Robert can't very well afford an expensive son in these hard times, poor man! Guy began life in the Guards, and amused himself very satisfactorily for a year or two. Then an end had to come to that, and he exchanged into some line regiment or other; since which he has been doing A.D.C. work in various places. He is said to be on the lookout for an heiress now, and I am sure he will have no difficulty at all in finding one. Why is it, Miss Dent, that your sex invariably prefers scamps to sober, irreproachable, hard-working fellows like me?"

"I can't think," answered Clarissa, absently.

She was still engaged in endeavoring to take the measure of Captain Luttrell, who might be a scamp, but who had not so very much the appearance of being one. Tall, broad-shouldered, and fair-complexioned, with a light mustache which did not conceal his well-shaped mouth, he was no bad specimen of the better class of contemporary British warriors. In features he was not unlike his father, whose trick of keeping his eyes half closed he had also inherited; but Sir Robert's eyes, when open, were seen to be bright and iron-gray in color, whereas Captain Luttrell's were sleepy and blue. Moreover, the younger man had a narrower forehead, a flatter top to his head, and somewhat more fleshy cheeks than the elder. These trifling indications of inferiority did not prevent him from being pleasant to look upon, nor did they cause Clarissa to modify the favorable judgment which she was disposed to pass upon him. To be sure, she had not the faintest idea of what a "scamp" meant, and assumed that Guy Luttrell had done nothing worse than spend rather more money than he had in his pocket.

Later in the evening he was introduced to her by his

mother, who said, "Guy, I have been telling Miss Dent that she ought to come south with us this winter and get rid of her cough. Can you not manage to sing the praises of Pau for once, in spite of your being such a John Bull ?"

Captain Luttrell, smiling sleepily and gazing down upon Miss Dent from the height of six feet two inches above the level of the floor, remarked that Pau really wasn't a bad sort of place, considering that it labored under the disadvantage of being situated in France. "There's hunting of a sort, and shooting, if you don't mind going up to the mountains for it, and game of various kinds, if you're fond of 'em. I don't know any place out of England where you're so little bothered with beastly foreigners. We have a villa there ; at least my mother has, for it belongs to her. Has she been asking you to stay with her ? Upon my word, I should go if I were you. You'll find it ever so much more like home than Cannes or Mentone, or some vile hole of that kind."

Clarissa laughed, and replied that if there was any place like home she was not at all likely to make its speedy acquaintance. Lady Luttrell had very kindly offered to take charge of her in the event of her being expatriated by the doctor ; but she feared her cough was not nearly bad enough to afford her an excuse for accepting the invitation.

"Ah, well, that's one way of putting it, of course," Captain Luttrell observed. "I suppose what you mean is that you ain't going to leave England unless you're obliged; and there I'm altogether with you. The worst of it is," he added, sighing heavily, "that we poor wretches of soldier-officers *are* obliged. It won't be many months before I'm sent out of the country, I'm sorry to say."

"But not to the South of France, I presume ?" said Clarissa.

"Oh dear, no ! to a very much more objectionable part of the world than that. I assure you, Miss Dent, that I sometimes think we pay far too high a price for the honor and glory of being a big empire."

He sat down and proceeded, after a leisurely fashion, to

pour his personal and professional grievances into a partially sympathetic ear.   Clarissa was of opinion that a soldier ought not to make quite such a fuss about incidental hardships; yet, when her uncle came to take her away, she had decided in her own mind that Captain Luttrell was a lovable, if not precisely an admirable, fellow-creature, while she could not but be flattered by the kindliness of her hostess, who, on wishing her good-night, said :

"Now, mind, I carry you off to Pau with me before the end of the year—*c'est entendu!*   If your uncle makes difficulties, we will call in the doctors and stop his mouth."

"It is not impossible," Mr. Dent remarked, dryly, as he seated himself in the brougham beside his niece, "that your uncle might make difficulties if such a project were seriously put forward.   What else am I here for ?"

But the significance of this query was lost upon the unsuspecting Clarissa.

CHAPTER II

HACCOMBE LUTTRELL

THE grand but somewhat inhospitable coast-line which extends from Hartland Point to the Land's End is indented here and there by estuaries and natural harbors which look useful enough to a landsman's eye, but which sailors know better than to run for under stress of weather if they can possibly help it. Many a good ship has gone to pieces on the treacherous bars which must needs be eluded before those smooth and sheltered waters can be reached; and although it is possible to make Haccombe Harbor when a fresh gale is blowing from the W.N.W., no Haccombe man can see a vessel endeavoring to perform that feat under such circumstances without regrets, which are naturally intensified if he happen to be a member of the life-boat crew. Towards the end of November or beginning of December, however, a few weeks of hazy calms and light easterly breezes are not unfrequently accorded to mariners, and it was at that quiet, rather melancholy season of the year that Sir Robert Luttrell was pacing up and down the broad terrace which fronted his house, throwing occasional absent-minded glances at the dim silver-gray expanse of water beneath him.

"Yes," he said, with a sigh, in answer to an observation which had just been made by his companion, "it is a beautiful old place, and any man might be proud of owning it, provided that he had money enough to keep it up. When you have to be perpetually cutting down expenses right and left, you begin to feel that some luxuries are scarcely worth what they cost. I suppose I ought to do as others do, and let the house to some confounded brewer, or—or— "

" Or banker?" smilingly suggested Mr. Dent, who, clad in a gray suit and with his hands in his pockets, was the recipient of this slightly petulant outburst on the part of an old friend. "No, my dear Luttrell, I do not rise. I have become rich, it is true ; but my life has been spent in a groove which I hope to run down quite smoothly and pleasantly until my death. At this time of day it would upset me dreadfully to jerk myself out of it and begin to play at being a country gentleman. As for cutting down expenses, it really does seem to me—"

"Ah, my good fellow," pleaded Sir Robert, throwing up his hands deprecatingly, "please don't say that again ! It seems to you that half the servants might be dismissed, and half the house shut up, and half the amount of cham- pagne drunk, and so forth, and so forth ! But you don't know what you are advising me to do ; you don't know what the irresistible dead weight of established custom is. Some people, perhaps, have strength of mind enough to make everybody about them miserable ; I haven't. I do what I can and hope for the best, while fully anticipating the worst. *Après moi le déluge!* Guy, I dare say, will sell the place when he succeeds me—always supposing that the place remains his to sell."

Haccombe Luttrell, the imposing gray-granite mansion towards which Sir Robert's back was at the moment turned, had been for some three centuries the abode of his progen- itors ; but as the entail had been cut off, the chances of its passing into the possession of his posterity were a little doubtful. Nobody knew this better than Sir Robert's banker, former schoolfellow, and trusted adviser, who turned to gaze silently at the weather-worn façade, with its ivy-clad walls and mullioned windows, and who drew his hand several times reflectively over his smooth-shaven cheeks and chin.

"Why don't yóu send him to America, Luttrell ?" he asked presently.

" Who ?—Guy ?—what do you mean?" returned the other, with a touch of irritability. " How the deuce can I send him to America ?—and why the deuce should I ?"

" It was only a figure of speech. America, of course, comes to us, like Manchester and Liverpool and other places where wealthy men produce wealthy daughters for the benefit of impoverished land-owners. But that appears to be the sole solution, doesn't it ?"

" So Lady Luttrell says ; but it is one thing to lead Guy to the water and another to make him drink. He isn't very fond of drinking, you see—at least, not of drinking water."

Mr. Dent shot a quick, inquiring look at the speaker. " I thought that was a thing of the past," he said.

" Oh, well, I hope so—yes, I think so. He isn't quite so young as he was, and in some respects, no doubt, he is a reformed character. But I very much doubt whether anything in the world will ever induce him to marry an ugly girl. You wouldn't think," added Sir Robert, wistfully, "that that fellow would be so abominably hard to please ; but he is."

" We all become hard to please the moment that we are urged to consult our own obvious interests," remarked Mr. Dent, a little sententiously. " If we didn't, we should mar the perversity of the whole scheme of human destiny— which would be a very great pity from a spectator's point of view. Is your son to accompany you to Pau this winter ?"

" He won't accompany us ; he may come out for a week or two after Christmas, but it is quite uncertain as yet, I believe, whether he will give himself the trouble or not. Why do you ask ?"

" As if you didn't know ! In all truth and sincerity I am grateful to you and Lady Luttrell for your kindness to Clarissa ; I think she ought to spend the cold months in a milder climate. I don't see how we could take her abroad ourselves, and if we accept your invitation on her behalf, we shall do so with a full sense of the obligation under which we are laid. But—"

"Rubbish about obligations!" interrupted Sir Robert. "If it comes to that, I am far more deeply indebted to you than you are ever likely to be to me. We shall be only too delighted to have the society of your niece, who seems to me to be a charming young lady, and with whom I notice that Madeline has already struck up a friendship. For goodness' sake, don't talk as though any trifling service that it may be in our power to render you could be compared with all that you have done for us!"

"Banks have no feelings," returned Mr. Dent, rather dryly; "we help others in order that we may help ourselves; it is a pure matter of business."

"I wasn't speaking of the bank, my dear fellow; I was speaking of you personally."

"Then you were speaking of a business man who is commonly considered to have a pretty clear idea of what he is about. You haven't much to thank me for, and I was going to say just now that I should have nothing to thank you for if this Southern trip were to have the results which Lady Luttrell anticipates and desires. I agree with you that Clarissa is charming; but she is at present quite raw, and what she will be like when she is ripe I can't pretend to foresee. All I know is that I am responsible for her until she attains her majority, and that it would never do for me to let her espouse a man whose motives, from the nature of the case, could hardly be regarded as above suspicion. I am sure you will forgive my bluntness."

For a moment the expression of Sir Robert Luttrell's face seemed to imply that that confidence was not altogether warranted. He was by nature proud; in his heart of hearts he thought that his son was a sufficiently good match for any banker's niece, and he did not quite like to be accused of harboring ulterior designs when his only intention had been to do a good-natured thing. But Dent was too old and too good (possibly also too useful) a friend of his to be snubbed; so he laughed and replied:

"I must decline to hold myself answerable for any notions or wishes that Lady Luttrell may have taken into

2

her head ; but I quite see the reasonableness of your fears,
and I will make a point of speaking to her upon the subject. I will even tell Guy, if you like, that Miss Dent
must be regarded as forbidden fruit."

"Thank you, no," said Mr. Dent quietly; "I doubt whether that would have the desired deterrent effect. If you
mention my niece to him at all, it would be more to the
purpose to state that she will probably not be a rich woman, though I dare say she will be comfortably provided for.
He might do very much better, both as regards fortune
and as regards compatibility of tastes. But the simplest
and most satisfactory solution of all would be to prevent
him from joining you at Pau this winter."

" Very well; I'll do my best. Only you ought to be
aware by this time that I never can prevent things from
happening. Isn't it the lifelong experience of every good
Tory that things always do happen in spite of us ? And,
talking of the impossibility of preventing things, what is
to be done about those mortgages ?"

The conversation now assumed a character more interesting to those engaged in it than relevant to the progress
of the present narrative. Mr. Dent, in response to a somewhat pressing invitation and in obedience to the behests
of the doctor, who thought that a change to the mild
climate of the west of England might take Clarissa's cough
away, had brought his niece down to Haccombe Luttrell,
and proposed to leave her there for a week or so after his
own return to London and business. As has been seen,
he had some misgivings about the advisability of allowing
her to proceed to Pau with her new friends and his old
ones ; yet he was scarcely prepared to place his veto upon
a project which had so much to recommend it, and for
the time being he had matters to discuss with Sir Robert
which claimed his whole attention.

The discussion proved—as, under certain circumstances,
financial discussions are very apt to prove—inconclusive
and unsatisfactory, one party to it having only the distasteful measure of retrenchment to advocate, while the

other was anxious to get ready money upon the best terms obtainable and with as little waste of time as might be. Neither of them, perhaps, was very sorry to be interrupted by the precipitate arrival of a dark-haired, blue-eyed maiden of fourteen, who clutched Sir Robert by the arm and gasped out, breathlessly:

"Father, we all want to go fishing, and old Abraham says there's a nice breeze outside, and mother told me to ask you whether I mightn't have a holiday. Paul is coming and so is Miss Dent, and Mademoiselle would be very glad to have a free afternoon to write letters. You could come too, if you liked—both of you."

"Thank you very much, my dear," answered Sir Robert, laughing; "but so far as I am concerned, I have no hesitation in saying that I should *not* like to be as sea-sick as you will certainly be when you get out into that easterly roll. Dent, unless I am very much mistaken in him, shares my affection for the firm land. Well, I suppose you may have your holiday, if your mother sees no objection. Paul must take the tiller, though, and the sheet is not to be made fast, and you are not to jump about—mind that!"

The girl endeavored not to look more compassionate and disdainful than she could help; but her efforts were not crowned with complete success. "I *have* been out in a boat once or twice before now," she remarked, "and I haven't been sea-sick for nearly two years; still, I won't forget to give your orders to the others."

Then she flung her arms round her father's neck, kissed him on both cheeks, called him an old dear, and ran back towards the house, making a liberal display of thin, lanky legs, to announce that the proposed expedition had received the sanction of the head of the family.

"That child," remarked Mr. Dent, as he gazed meditatively at her retreating form, "is going to be a very beautiful woman one of these days, Luttrell."

"Do you think so?" said Sir Robert. "Yes, I dare say you are right. Madeline is like her mother, who also was a very beautiful woman in days which don't seem so

very long ago.   Oh, I know what you are thinking; that
is what everybody thinks about girls who are blessed with
good looks; and I suppose, taking everything into consideration, we ought to be especially thankful that she is likely
to command such a high price in the matrimonial market.
All the same, I prefer, with your permission, to thank
God that she has still three or four more years of childhood before her."

"Don't quarrel with me for saying things which I
haven't said or even thought," pleaded Mr. Dent, laying
his hand upon his friend's shoulder.   "Take me to see
your Jerseys now, and we'll forget all disagreeable subjects.
One consolation is, that, do what we will, we have precious
little power over the destinies of other people."

The destinies of Clarissa Dent and Madeline Luttrell,
which will be unfolded in due time for the benefit of such
readers as may have patience enough to follow them, were
not greatly affected for better or for worse by the events
of that mild, still day of early winter, and it is only worth
while to chronicle these for the sake of showing how Clarissa (then a very impressionable young woman) fell to
some extent under the influence of the Reverend Paul
Luttrell.   Paul, who was Sir Robert's second son, would
doubtless have developed into an ornament of the royal
navy had he not, immediately after passing out of the
Britannia, surprised and vexed his parents by announcing
his unalterable determination to proceed to Oxford and
take holy orders.   His will being a great deal stronger
than theirs, he had carried his point and was now curate
in a London parish; but he had lost neither his love for
the sea nor his rudimentary knowledge of seamanship; so
that old Abraham Lavers, who was generally held responsible for the safety of such Haccombe Luttrell visitors as
cared to go out fishing, never hesitated to let the parson
sail the boat when the latter formed one of the party.   In
matters pertaining to dogmatic theology, however, Abraham—being himself a Bible Christian—was less docile,
and it was seldom that he and "Master Paul" met with-

out a prolonged desultory argument which left each dis-
putant very much where he had been at starting.

Clarissa, sitting in the stern while the boat stole out towards the open sea before a faint easterly breeze, listened
with interest and curiosity to statements of the unswerv-
ing attitude of the Established Church as regarded Baptis-
mal Regeneration, and to what Noncomformity had to urge
in opposition to that doctrine. The tall, broad-shouldered
young clergyman, whose gray eyes were clearer and whose
face was more powerful, if less handsome, than his brother's,
had upon the whole the best of the argument, she thought;
but her sympathies were rather with the gray-bearded old
fisherman, who certainly contrived to put his case in a
forcible and homely fashion rather difficult to controvert.

"Church 'ere, Church there, 'tis Scriptur' or the Pope
o' Rome we'm bound to foller, sir, you may depend," he
wound up by declaring; and although the young man
laughed good-humoredly, Clarissa half suspected that he
changed the subject because he had no convincing retort
ready.

The remaining members of the expedition—a lively,
smartly dressed, and rather pretty young matron, a girl of
masculine appearance and manners, and a couple of gilded
youths—were fully occupied with one another; Madeline,
busily baiting hooks, was engaged in earnest conversation
with Mr. Lavers's grandson, a long-legged, sheepish-look-
ing boy, whose dialect was barely comprehensible to unaccustomed ears. When old Abraham stepped forward to set
a head-sail, the Reverend Paul remembered his duty to his
neighbor, and began:

"I hope you don't mind a little bit of a lop. We sha'n't
find the sea quite as smooth as it looks after we get out beyond the point."

"I daren't boast," answered Clarissa, smiling. "I have
crossed the Channel four times in a steamer without any
catastrophe; but that is all the experience I have ever had
of the sea. Lady Luttrell was saying that you once intended to be a sailor; what made you change your mind?"

"Perhaps you would hardly understand if I were to tell you," the young man replied.

"Perhaps not; still you might try, if you didn't mind. It would give us something to talk about."

"Yes; but I don't very much like talking about it as a mere subject of conversation. It is tremendously important and serious to me, you see—the one serious and important thing that there is, in fact. However, I am not as cowardly or as shy as I was once upon a time, and, whether you ask out of idle curiosity or not, I will answer your question."

He did so in clear tones and in very unambiguous language, confessing the faith that was in him, with perhaps just a shade of defiance at first, as was not unnatural, considering that the language which he used was pretty sure to be stigmatized as cant by those who sat near him and who might be expected to overhear some of it; but gradually he warmed with his subject, and the girl whom he addressed, at all events, was not disposed to laugh at him.

"You are very fortunate to be able to believe like that!" she remarked, with a sigh, when he paused.

"There is no great difficulty about believing," he answered; "people believe all manner of absurdities, real and apparent, such as that it is unlucky to upset the salt or to walk under a ladder; the difficulty is to act up to one's belief. That is why so many civilized persons, who really can't be accused of incredulity, find it very comfortable and convenient to call themselves agnostics."

"I don't call myself by any name so grand as that," said Clarissa, meekly; "only I can't quite manage Noah's ark and Jonah's whale and Joshua's moon and Balaam's ass. I wish with all my heart that I could; but it really isn't in my power."

"Now, sir, if you'll just bring her 'ead round to the wind and ketch 'old of this 'ere line, we'll see what we can do," called out old Abraham; and as lines were given to the rest of the party, and Madeline, in a high state of excitement, placed herself close to Miss Dent, chattering volubly, well-worn subjects of controversy fell for the time being into abeyance.

The boat was rising and falling gently upon the long Atlantic swell, which—perhaps because it was so long—disturbed nobody's internal economy. Full justice was presently done to the contents of the luncheon-baskets, a very fair take of fish was secured in the course of the afternoon, and when the waning light gave the signal for a prolonged beat back towards harbor, Clarissa had as yet obtained no opportunity of ascertaining how much or how little her reverend neighbor believed or deemed it essential to believe. But after land had been reached, and the others had started in couples to walk up to the house, and she, lingering behind for a few minutes in the falling dew and the semi-darkness, had been caught up by Paul, he said, as if their conversation had only just been interrupted:

"The legends or poems or dreams of which you speak have so little to say to Christianity that you would never break your shins over them unless you secretly wished your shins to be broken. In the matter of belief, all that can be required of you is that you should be able to repeat the Apostles' Creed."

"And what about the Athanasian Creed?" Clarissa inquired.

"Well, there are clauses in it which I do not repeat myself; and although that may be unorthodox, my rector and my bishop wink at such unorthodoxy. Once grasp the truth and you will see the insignificance of details. Only, when you do, you will find yourself involved in considerable difficulties with regard to conduct."

"Why?" asked Clarissa.

"Because you are young, because I understand that you are rich, or going to be, and because our creed compels us to be perpetually doing things that we don't want to do and leaving undone the things that we should like to do."

"I hope I shall always do what I believe to be right," Clarissa declared, with a fine confidence in herself which appeared to have the effect of amusing her companion.

"I'm sure I hope you will," he answered, laughing a little ; "but it doesn't quite follow as a matter of course that what you believe to be right will be right, you know. Anyhow, if you should ever feel a wish for a word of ghostly counsel from a person who may at least claim to be tolerably free from prejudice and bigotry, a line addressed to me here will be forwarded to the Bermondsey lodgings which I usually inhabit."

In this manner were laid the foundations of a friendship which did not remain without eventual sway over Clarissa's wayward career.

CHAPTER III

LADY LUTTRELL'S boudoir was the prettiest and pleasantest room in a very pretty and pleasant house. Charmingly furnished, facing due south, fronted by a space of sunk flower-garden, beyond which the landlocked bay and wind-swept promontories of Great and Little Haccombe Head could be descried, it was warm in winter, comfortable all the year round, and reserved, by tacit understanding, for its proprietress as a quiet haven of retreat into which no unauthorized person might presume to penetrate. Sir Robert was authorized, but did not abuse his privilege. So unusual a proceeding, indeed, was it on his part to intrude upon his wife after breakfast—at which hour she was supposed to be occupied in interviewing the house-keeper or in reading and answering letters—that when he appeared abruptly on the day following that dealt with in the last chapter, her ladyship exclaimed, in apprehensive accents :

" Robert !—is anything the matter ?"

Many things had been the matter of late in a household where normal expenditure largely exceeded normal revenue, and where, owing to causes with which all owners of land are sadly familiar nowadays, revenue was becoming more and more abnormal in its insufficiency every year. But Sir Robert, it seemed, had not come to groan and grumble, as he sometimes did, or to suggest measures of retrenchment which he never would have consented to put into practice. He only said, as he sank into a low chair beside his wife's writing-table : " Dent has to go back to London to-day."

"Yes, I know," answered Lady Luttrell, looking but
partially reassured; "he took leave of me just now. Does
he—does he make difficulties?"

"About money, do you mean? No, he doesn't make
difficulties; that would really be a work of supererogation,
considering what a fine crop of them already exists. But
he said a word or two about that girl and her coming to
Pau with us which I must admit he was justified in
saying. One does feel that it wouldn't be pretty to take
unfair advantages. Personally, I am as innocent as the
driven snow; I don't even know whether Guy means to
come out after Christmas or not; but I am afraid Dent is
not very far wrong in suspecting you of having a scheme
in your mind, and I want to tell you, before it goes any
further, that I couldn't countenance anything of the
sort."

Easy-going Sir Robert seldom expressed himself in such
peremptory terms; but when he did, it might be taken as
certain that he meant to be obeyed. Lady Luttrell, throwing up both her hands, which were small and white and
sparkling with jewels, hastened to repudiate the intention
so gratuitously ascribed to her.

"What an idea!" she exclaimed. "You, who know
how fastidious Guy is, ought to know that it would be
quite hopeless to select a bride for him. The mere fact of
my having selected Miss Dent would be enough to set him
against her; but I should never dream of selecting Miss
Dent, who is neither beautiful nor witty nor *mondaine*.
What chance could she have of attracting him?"

"I call her pretty, and Guy is approaching the age at
which one ceases to be attracted by the special fascinations
that you mention. I agree with Dent that the simplest
plan would be to give him a hint that his presence at Pau
will not be essential to our happiness this season."

"That would be a very sure way of making him resolve
to join us; of course he would wish to discover what reason
we could have for behaving so unnaturally. After all, the
poor girl cannot be prevented from meeting young men

sometimes. Since Mr. Dent is so easily alarmed, I wonder that he should have said nothing about Paul, whose attentions were quite assiduous last night, I noticed."

"Oh, well, Paul is vowed to celibacy, I suppose, like the rest of the High Church young parsons of the period."

"My dear Robert, how little you know of your own sect! Paul is what I believe you call Broad Church—which means that he recognizes no ecclesiastical authority at all, and is removed by leagues from the High Church people, who have the affectation to claim the title of Catholics. Yet it stands to reason that there cannot be more than one Catholic Church, and—'

"Yes, yes, my dear," interrupted Sir Robert hastily; "your position is unassailable; I am sure I have admitted that scores of times. All the same, there is no danger of Paul's wanting to marry Miss Dent, while there might quite conceivably be a danger of Guy's wanting to do so."

But Lady Luttrell, who had a feminine capacity for opportune irrelevance, persisted. She did not, it may be presumed, wish to enter upon any further discussion of a possible event which might help to set the family on its legs again, and she knew very well how to drive her husband out of the room. Herself a stanch adherent of the Church, whose fold she had not been asked to quit at a time when mixed marriages were rather more common than they are now, she had for many years counted upon Sir Robert's indifferentism, and had used every effort to make a convert of him; but, whether through indifference or through a very clear understanding of the disadvantages under which Roman Catholics still labor in this country, Sir Robert had stood to his guns, stipulating that the two boys should be educated in the faith of their forefathers. Madeline he had graciously conceded to her mother (because it really does not so very much matter what a girl's religion may be), while for himself he only pleaded that he might be allowed to hold his own unobtrusive opinions in peace. Lady Luttrell had long since abandoned all hope of him; nevertheless, she was aware that she could at any time put him to flight by drawing her theological sword from its scabbard, and it suited her to do so now.

Clarissa, meanwhile, had been saying good-bye to her uncle, from whom she was sorry to part, although it cannot be pretended that she was at all unwilling to be left behind by him. It had been arranged that she was to stay for another week or two where she was, and then, after a halt of a few days in London, to proceed to the South of France with the Luttrells, for the benefit of her health and the enlargement of her experience and ideas. Naturally enough, the prospect pleased and excited her; naturally enough, she preferred glimpses of the outer world and the society of people some of whom were distinguished and some young to the comparative solitude of Portland Place and a daily drive round the Park in a closed carriage with Aunt Susan. If she felt some faint twinges of compunction, they were speedily allayed by Mr. Dent, who said:

"My dear girl, you owe us no apology; on the contrary, it is we who ought to be begging your pardon for committing you to the care of strangers rather than sacrifice our own comfort and convenience. Come back to us in the spring without a cough and without—well, let us limit ourselves to saying without a cough—and we shall feel infinitely indebted to you as well as to Lady Luttrell."

Clarissa did not wonder for more than a minute or two after her uncle's departure what he had been going to say, but had refrained from saying. Her thoughts were at that time rather less bent upon matrimony than those of most girls. She considered it not impossible that she might marry some fine day; but she was in no hurry about it, and the shadowy hero who arose before her mental vision at odd moments was all the more unlike Guy Luttrell because he did not in the least resemble any human being who has ever trod this earth's surface. He did not even bear much resemblance to the Reverend Paul, although she liked Paul and had arrived at the conclusion that he deserved her sincere respect.

For the matter of that, she liked the Luttrell family

tutti quanti—Sir Robert, in spite of his inherent levity, which often puzzled her; Lady Luttrell, with her pretty French gestures, her quick intelligence, and her kindly, motherly ways; most of all, perhaps, Madeline, who had taken one of those sudden, intuitive fancies to her which children sometimes do form for their elders, and who made her the recipient of numerous unsolicited confidences.

"What a pity it is that you are not poor, Miss Dent!" the girl exclaimed one day. "Then you might be my governess, instead of that horrid old Mademoiselle Girault, and you could live with us always!"

Clarissa said that would be very nice, but could not go quite the length of wishing to be a governess. Whether she was rich or poor she hardly knew, never having had occasion to think about money or to realize how very important a factor wealth is in human happiness. It was Paul who, meeting her one evening on his return from shooting (for he was a very fair shot, and saw no necessary incongruity between a double-barrelled gun and a parson's white dog-collar), thought fit to read her a short homily upon that subject, and to warn her, not very obscurely, of the dangers to which those who possess wealth and those who would fain acquire it are alike exposed.

"It is your misfortune," he remarked, as he strolled along beside her, with his gun over his shoulder, in the gray twilight, "that unless you begin by distrusting most people a little, you will probably end by distrusting everybody altogether. You will have experiences—rich men and women invariably do have them—which will astonish and disgust you, and then, with your impulsive disposition, you will be apt to jump to wrong conclusions. If I were you I should keep cool, try to make as much allowance as you can for temptations which you yourself can't feel, and bear in mind always that human beings are neither angels nor devils."

"I don't know why you should call me rich and impulsive, and imply that I am an idiot into the bargain," said Clarissa, who, if she took after her fellow-creatures in being

neither angelic nor diabolic, took after them also in entertaining a decided objection to being preached at on week-
days. "Uncle Tom tells me that I shall be tolerably well-
off when I come of age; but does it follow as a matter of
course that I shall be afflicted with disgusting experiences?
I suppose what you mean is that somebody will want to
enrich himself at my expense, and that my opinion of the
entire human race will be lowered in consequence. Impulsive and ignorant as I am, I really do think I have just
sense enough to be able to distinguish between black and
white—perhaps even to pardon a black sheep for wearing
the fleece that nature has given him."

"Don't be too sure," returned Paul, not a whit disconcerted. "It is easy enough to forgive a professional thief
for picking one's pocket; it isn't so easy to forgive one's
friends for being a little short of wholly disinterested in their
friendship. I don't say that you, as a considerable heiress
(which of course you are, or will be), cannot have any disinterested friends; that is the very thing that I am afraid
of your being driven to assume. But I do say that you
will need a lot of circumspection, and a pinch of philosophy besides. People may be very kind and very fond of
you for your own sake; yet it may be uncommonly hard
for them to refrain from breaking the tenth commandment
sometimes."

Clarissa stopped short and scrutinized her mentor as
narrowly as the faint remnant of daylight would permit.
"When you say 'people,' do you mean your own people?"
she asked. "You sound to me as if you did—and I don't
think it is very nice of you."

This time Paul did feel somewhat confused; for, as a
matter of fact, he had been thinking about his own people,
and had wished, if possible, to convey a hint to Miss Dent
which might avert the necessity for subsequent excuses and
palliations. But it is so seldom possible to convey such
hints that a wise man and one who would fain keep out of
hot water does not attempt the task. This man, by virtue
of his youth, and in common with other members of his

sacred calling, had a noble disdain for the perils of hot water; yet he could not quite screw himself up to the point of saying, "My mother is one of the best of women; but we are horribly hard up, and she knows how essential it is that my brother should marry money. Therefore she will do all she can to marry you to my brother, who isn't a bad fellow in his way, but who has lived a life which will certainly make you think him a bad fellow when you have heard all about it."

This being a speech forbidden by considerations of filial and fraternal affection, the Reverend Paul Luttrell had to take refuge in feeble subterfuges and safe generalities, which did not deceive his hearer. It was not that the motives of one individual, or of half a dozen individuals, in particular for making a friend of her were likely to be of a mixed character; it was only that wealth, like beauty or wit or any other personal gift, constituted an attraction which those who possessed it would do well to take into account. "In short, if one doesn't expect too much of poor human nature, one avoids laying up disappointments and disillusions for one's self. I know by experience how many rich men are turned sour and stingy, and take an absurdly distorted view of the world, simply from being so constantly pestered for loans or donations."

Clarissa, deeming it highly improbable that Sir Robert or Lady Luttrell would pester her in the manner described, perceived that Paul's object was to set her on her guard against some other peril which he did not care to specify, and no very extraordinary amount of insight was required in order to conjecture what that peril was. But supposing a fond and anxious mother did wish her eldest son to make a good match? That was surely a pardonable aspiration, the discovery of which (if indeed it existed) ought not to turn anybody sour. Moreover, there could be no opportunity for its fulfilment, since Captain Luttrell, according to his own statement, was about to proceed on foreign service.

"I won't forget your advice," she said, laughing, "and

I will try to suspect people of liking me—when they do like me—because I shall have a small fortune of my own in a year or two. But I really cannot allow you to deprive me of all feelings of gratitude or to prevent me from enjoying myself at Pau this winter. I suppose you can't have the slightest idea of how I am going to enjoy it all. Very few girls of my age, I should think, have seen so little as I have."

She had, in truth, seen next to nothing of this world and its inhabitants. Enclosed within the four walls of a boarding-school, or spending a few weeks of seclusion at some British or foreign watering-place with her silent father, who had been wont to leave home in holiday time, but who had hated making new acquaintances, she had derived such information respecting men and things as may be derived from books, and no more. Now she was to be introduced—so, at least, both Lady Luttrell and Madeline assured her—to a gay and lively society, some foretaste of whose manners and customs had been afforded to her by her stay at Haccombe Luttrell and her observation of her fellow-guests; she was going to a land of sunshine and beautiful scenery, with exceptional opportunities of mixing with the French as well as the English denizens of the place; she was as full of curiosity and joyous anticipation as if she had been six years old and on her way to her first pantomime. Upon the whole, therefore, her clerical adviser might almost as well have held his tongue, and probably if he had not been so young a man he would have done so. As it was, he was conscious of having failed, and only remarked, cheerfully :

"Oh, I hope you'll enjoy yourself, and I quite think you will. What with dancing and hunting and lawn-tennis and one thing and another, Pau is what most people consider a very enjoyable place. Personally, after having tried both, I prefer Bermondsey; but that is because—luckily for me—I am one of those queer beings who prefer work of any kind, however discouraging and repulsive, to perpetual play."

CHAPTER IV

THE CHÂTEAU DE GRANCY

Some of us, when we hastily turn our backs upon the fogs and frosts of our native land and fly southwards, in the wake of the swallows, as fast as a not very well organized service of express trains will carry us, yearn for a sight of liquid blue skies, of palm-trees and olives and aloes and even of white, dusty roads—dissatisfied unless such evidences of a really warm climate greet us at our journey's end. But a large proportion of the English people who are sent abroad every winter by the doctor's orders care not one jot for these things, preferring to find, during their temporary exile, a somewhat improved reproduction of what they have left behind them; and that is why the department of the Basses-Pyrénées continues to be, as it has been for half a century or so, the favored recipient of British guineas. The truth is that Pau is not much more Southern in appearance or vegetation than Devonshire; and if spring sets in a little earlier in those latitudes than it does in ours, the vicinity of the mountains is apt to bring about frequent returns to winter, provoking melancholy comparisons between the heat of a coal fire and that which poor shivering mortals are able to extract, with the aid of the bellows, from a pile of damp logs. However, there is a very good English club at Pau, and polo is sometimes played on the Haute Plante, and golf and cricket and lawn-tennis are always obtainable; so that when to these advantages are added a pack of hounds, and places of worship suited to every shade of religious opinion tolerated by the hospitable Anglican Church, it must be acknowledged

3

that the place does its best to be endurable. Moreover, the view in fine weather of the wooded hills beyond the valley of the Gave, and the purple summits and snowy peaks in the distance, is something worth travelling a long way to enjoy.

The Château de Grancy, which stands on the eastward side of the town and, facing due south, commands that charming prospect, had for many years been the property of Lady Luttrell, who was once upon a time the beautiful Mademoiselle de Grancy, and who, on the death of her parents, had inherited the family dwelling, together with a modest fortune in hard cash, not one franc of which now remained to her. The house had scarcely more claim to be called a *château* than have certain Irish mansions to be known as castles, and, like them, it stood in somewhat conspicious need of repairs ; yet its rooms were lofty and spacious, the cracked plaster of its walls was for the most part concealed by creepers, the garden, though untidy, was full of flowers, and the general aspect of the place was sufficiently bright and home-like to explain the affection which had always been entertained for it by the Luttrell family.

Such as it was, it drew warm expressions of admiration and delight from Clarissa Dent, whose good fortune it was to form her first impression of Pau on one of those brilliant, cloudless December days a yearly half-dozen of which would make the fortune of the locality, if it were not already made.

"But you must not suppose that we always look like this," Lady Luttrell felt bound in honesty to caution her young friend. "As they say here, *il faut que l'hiver se fasse,* and your aunt was quite right to make you bring your furs with you. Still I am glad that you should see what we *can* do in the way of weather and scenery when we are upon our good behavior."

She was in reality pleased and flattered by the girl's un-affected enthusiasm ; for she loved the scenes of her own half-forgotten girlhood, and returned to them every year with an increased sense of relief and thankful escape. Life in England had come to mean for her perpetual anxiety, perpetual vain efforts to make both ends meet, perpetual doubts whether the political game, with its enforced hospitalities and its terrible uncertainties, was worth the candle. What rendered Lady Luttrell so popular as a London hostess, and had been of no slight assistance to her husband during his public career, was her gay, light-hearted manner, and the few suspicious persons who, after she had welcomed them with such affectionate cordiality, accused her of being a humbug, were probably far from imagining how accurate their criticism was. If we were not all humbugs, in the sense of wearing the mask of comedy while engaged upon a somewhat tragic performance, social intercourse would become too depressing to be kept up.

When in winter-quarters, however, there was no need for pretence on the part of this harassed lady, and the hospitality which she freely dispensed and accepted was a genuine satisfaction to her. Elaborate dinner-parties she left to the rich Americans who at that time were beginning to establish themselves as leaders of Pau society ; occasional informal dances did not cost much, and the hosts of visitors, indigenous and exotic, who besieged the Château de Grancy were a good deal less hungry and less exacting than those who honored Grosvenor Place and Haccombe Luttrell with their company. They are also a great deal more entertaining, being of diverse nationalities and representing amongst them the manners and customs of almost every European race. Frenchmen, Spaniards, Russians, Poles, Italians, and even here and there a German, mingled with the predominating British contingent upon that neutral ground—a little surprised, perhaps, to find themselves rubbing shoulders with one another, yet well-bred enough to accept the situation in a spirit of temporary fraternity —and Sir Robert, who was an excellent linguist, stood upon a pinnacle of public favor nearly as high as that occupied by his wife. As for Clarissa, after a fortnight of what seemed to her to be an unceasing flow of gayety and dissipation, she felt as if she had obtained the experience of an ordinary lifetime; and indeed the fact was that she did see and converse with a large number of people.

"I can't understand what you mean when you say that you come here for rest," she remarked to Sir Robert, for whom a constant source of amusement was provided by the freshness of her ideas and language. "I should have thought this daily and nightly racket would have tired you out. To me, of course, it is delightful; but that is because I have never been through anything the least like it before."

"By the time that you have reached my age, my dear young lady," Sir Robert replied, "you will probably have discovered that nothing is so tiring as solitude. When one is alone, one begins to reflect on one's sins and sorrows, which is a very dismal thing to do; in a crowd one finds oblivion, and that is another name for rest. Besides, I can say what I like out here, whereas at home I must always bear in mind that the person to whom I am talking is as likely as not to communicate my interesting remarks to the newspapers and get me into no end of a row with my colleagues. You yourself constitute the chief responsibility that weighs upon me just at present. I tremble to think of what your uncle would do to me if you were to lose your heart to one of the handsome foreigners whose society I observe that you select by preference."

She was in no danger of adding to the list of Sir Robert's troubles in that way, although it was true enough that she endeavored, as far as her limited powers of conversing in French would allow, to exchange ideas with dwellers upon the Continent rather than with her own countrymen and countrywomen. She had already an insatiable thirst for information, an ardent desire to get at the meaning and origin of phenomena, which led her to grasp every opportunity that appeared to be within her reach. In later life this tendency was productive of much vexation of spirit to herself and others; at that time it did no harm to anybody, while it conveyed to her the pleasing, but erroneous, impression that she was in a fair way towards finding out all about it.

For the rest, she could not have been better placed, so far as the forming of impressions, erroneous or otherwise, went, than she was in that house; for the Luttrells knew everybody, and everybody else into the bargain, their position in the English political and social world enabling them to disregard the precautions with which less distinguished people felt bound to hedge themselves about. Damaged reputations contrived without much difficulty to effect an entry into the Château de Grancy; enriched London tradesmen, wintering abroad, enjoyed there the privilege of an introduction to their customers; and if some straitlaced ladies lamented that dear Lady Luttrell's receptions were not a little more select, it had to be admitted that they were often extremely amusing. Just before Christmas Madeline was set free by the departure, on leave of absence, of stern Mademoiselle Girault, her governess, and then it was that Clarissa was for the first time persuaded to mount one of the wiry little horses of the country, who, she was assured, was so quiet that no ill could possibly befall her so long as she remained upon his back.

Clarissa was no horsewoman; but as her education had included a few dozen riding-lessons, she achieved some preliminary excursions without mishap, and soon felt sufficiently sure of herself to accompany Sir Robert and Madeline to a near meet, although it was understood that she was not to attempt to follow the hounds. Sir Robert, whose half-hearted efforts at economy did not go to the length of preventing him from bringing a couple of English hunters out to Pau for the short time that he spent there every winter, would not permit his daughter to risk her neck in that way, despite her urgent entreaties.

"No, no, my dear; wait till you are married," he said. "Your husband, if you select him carefully, may be one of the many men who approve of hunting ladies; your father isn't. Besides," he added, on the particular occasion in question, "you can't desert Miss Dent, for whose

prudence and safety we have all made ourselves responsible."

Sir Robert perhaps meant that he did not care to sacrifice
his chances of seeing a run by accepting responsibility for
anybody's prudence and safety but his own in the hunting-
field.   As he jogged along beside the two girls on that fine
morning, keeping as clear as he could of the throng of
vehicles which were proceeding towards the same trysting-
place, he may have been thinking how sadly brief his holidays were and how necessary it was for him to make the
most of them.

"You are fortunate young people," he remarked presently, with a sigh; "nothing to do but to amuse your-
selves and bask in the sun till you are tired of it!   How
would you like to be under orders to return to London in a
week, as I am, with a Lenten penance of routine work and
interminable, obstructive jabber before you?"

Clarissa thought she would like nothing better than to
share in administering the affairs of a great empire; but
Sir Robert assured her that he was blessed with no such
privilege.

"The great empire blunders along somehow or other
with a loose rein; the sole concern of the modern statesman is to secure votes, and you can't conceive what a dull,
dreary game that is!   It is a thousand times better fun to
gallop after a bagged fox."

That form of sport was soon accorded to him, and as
Clarissa and Madeline, in obedience to instructions, turned
their horses' heads homewards, the latter remarked confidentially:

"I didn't say anything to my father about it, for fear of
his beginning to fuss, but I shall get Guy to take us both
out with the hounds when he comes.   I know that little
horse of yours can jump, because I've tried him."

Clarissa was gazing at the faint outline of the distant
Pyrenean range, between which and the high, level land
over which they were riding a thin veil of haze was spread;
the occupants of returning equipages were nodding and

waving their hands to the two girls; a few non-hunting equestrians, overtaking them, drew rein to inquire whether Miss Dent's card was quite full for a ball which was to take place that evening; life, for the moment, seemed so pleasant and beautiful and exhilarating that it left scarcely anything to be desired—assuredly not the advent of Captain Luttrell, who might prove a disturbing factor in the situation.

"Is your brother coming out, then?" she asked, after a time.

"Yes, thank goodness!" answered Madeline. "Mother had a letter from him this morning, and he is to be here in about a fortnight, she says. You met Guy in London at dinner, I know. Didn't you think him awfully good-looking?"

"I thought he was good-looking," answered Clarissa, without enthusiasm; "but it doesn't really matter very much what a man's looks are. His conduct is so very much more important."

"But he *is* good-looking," persisted Madeline. "Besides which, he is the best rider, the best shot, the best dancer—in short, the best all-round man you ever met in all your life. If that is what you call conduct, you may put Guy at the top of the class."

Clarissa explained that the accomplishments enumerated did not, in her opinion, come quite under the head of conduct. What was required of a man, and especially of a gentleman, was that he should be strictly honorable; that he should be distinguished, so far as his abilities enabled him to be so, in his profession; that he should be free from vices, and that he should be a good son and a good brother.

"Well, he is a first-rate brother, anyhow," Madeline declared. "He is always ready to do what I ask him—which is more than can be said for Paul, who, between you and me, is an awful prig. I don't know much about it, but I suspect Guy has been rather a naughty boy sometimes, and I like him all the better for it. Anything is better than being a milksop. Don't you think so?"

Perhaps, at that period of her life, Clarissa was a little inclined to think so; but she felt it right to preach a very different doctrine to her juvenile companion. Anybody, she pointed out, can be as wicked or as careless or as selfish as you please; nothing is more easy. The hard matter is to have a high standard and to act up to it. Not, to be sure, that it was any concern of hers whether Captain Luttrell's standard was a high or a low one.

"But I want you to like him," the child said; "I don't want you to decide whether he is as sure of going to heaven when he dies as Paul is. It seems to me that very few really nice people will go to heaven, and they say that no heretics will; but I don't quite believe that, do you? Of course you can't, as you are a heretic yourself."

Clarissa, not feeling competent to tackle so abstruse a question, and being more than a little doubtful as to what her own religious convictions were, changed the subject. "Suppose we canter on," she said. "I dare say I shall like your brother, and I dare say it won't break his heart if I dislike him. What I am quite certain of is that I shall not join you if he takes you out hunting. The bare thought of jumping over a bank or a ditch makes me cold with fright."

Madeline, as she had intended to do, protested vehemently against such groundless pusillanimity, and embarked upon a prolonged narrative of her personal early experiences in the saddle, the upshot of which was that, so long as you sat tight and left your horse's mouth alone, you could do anything. The theme being one upon which she was fond of dilating, it lasted her until the outskirts of the town were reached, when she so far remembered what had started it as to add:

"But Guy will teach you more in an hour than I could in a month; he knows everything that there is to know about horses and riding, and he has won lots of steeple-chases. And he isn't a bit conceited about it, either. The wonder is—and it just shows how good he is—that he should come out here to see us when he might have ever so much better fun by spending his leave in England."

"His self-sacrifice seems to be duly appreciated, at all events," remarked Clarissa, dryly.

But it was not in the least appreciated by his father, who, on returning home that evening, mud-bespattered, contented, and comfortably weary, was made acquainted in an off-hand, casual manner with a piece of news which Lady Luttrell had not judged it opportune to impart to him before he set out.

"Upon my word," he ejaculated, "this is a little too bad!—though I am bound to say that it is only what I expected. No sooner will my back be turned than the mice will begin to play; my express injunctions will be set at naught, and I shall be made to break faith with a friend to whom I am under the greatest obligations! The whole plot, of course, is absolutely transparent, and the whole blame, of course, will be thrown upon me. This is the reward that one gets for being a slave to one's queen and one's country!"

"What plot and what blame?" the innocent Lady Luttrell wanted to know. Was it possible that, in spite of what she had said to him in England, Robert still set her down as a vulgar, foolish match-maker, and imagined her capable of such a *bêtise* as to summon Guy to the South of France in order that he might cast himself at Miss Dent's feet?

Robert replied that it was possible—not only possible, but actual. "Although I beg to withdraw the adjectives, which are of your selection, my dear, not mine. There is nothing vulgar in being a match-maker, nor, in the majority of cases, anything foolish. In this instance, as I ventured to tell you before, there appears to me to be a certain lack of decency; but that must be between you and your conscience. Every fair-minded person (but where is one to look for a fair-minded person?) will allow that I ought not to be held answerable for what may take place after my public duties have compelled me to quit the scene."

"But you are a monster—a veritable monster!" cried Lady Luttrell. "May one not be permitted to embrace one's son before he is ordered off to a pestilential climate from which he will perhaps never return ?"

"All right," answered Sir Robert; "I am a monster. None the less so, no doubt, because I have been unable to prevent the ill-timed embraces of which you speak. All the same, I'm hanged if that fellow shall ride my horses to a standstill! I shall send them back home at once by long sea."

But Lady Luttrell knew very well that he would not do that. Why should he, considering that it would be out of the question for him to hunt any more that winter ? She likewise knew, and was glad to know, that her husband would trouble her with no further remonstrances, while her own conscience had nothing whereof to accuse her. There were, of course, desirable possibilities connected with Guy's visit to Pau; but the control of these must be, and should be, left in the hands of a beneficent Providence.

CHAPTER V

GUY BEHAVES VERY WELL

FINE weather cannot last forever anywhere, and if it lasts for three consecutive weeks in the depth of winter, in latitude 43° N. and within a short distance of a lofty range of mountains, those who have enjoyed it ought certainly not to grumble when it breaks. However, they always do grumble, and on a certain January afternoon the language used respecting the climate by the frequenters of the English Club at Pau was becoming too forcible for exact reproduction. A little knot of them had collected beside one of the tall windows of that rather handsome establishment, and they were gazing out indignantly at the driving rain, the muddy Place Royale, and the drenched, draggled passers-by.

"About the biggest fraud in Europe, I call it !" said one malcontent. "Why the deuce people who have comfortable homes of their own in England should come out here to be soaked to the bones and chilled to the marrow the doctors alone know ! I'm bound to go wherever they choose to send my wife; but I shall tell them pretty straight what I think of *this* place when I get back."

"You won't make 'em feel ashamed of themselves," observed his neighbor, gloomily. "My belief is that they shunt the lot of us because they don't want us to die upon their hands, and because they know that this sort of thing is enough to kill a horse."

"It *does* kill a horse," chimed in a third; "anyhow, it has pretty well killed mine, I know. What else can you expect where there are no decent stables to be had for love or

money? Well, I shall know better than to hire an infer-
nally expensive house for six months in such a vile hole
again—that's one thing!"

"Oh, come!" protested brisk, bald-headed little Colonel
Curtis, who, in his character of a resident at Pau, felt these
remarks to be more or less personally offensive; "you can't
expect to get a rainless winter nearer home than Nubia.
Why don't you to go to Nubia?—and be hanged to you!
What I maintain is that Pau isn't to be beaten in Europe.
Just you try the Riviera, and see how you like the *mistral!*"

"At least one may count upon meeting one's friends at
Cannes," growled Mr. Samuels, a black-bearded, over-dressed
Hebrew who, having made an enormous fortune in the cot-
ton trade, had espoused an earl's daughter and basked habitually in the smiles of highly placed personages; "one
doesn't feel like an outcast and an exile there."

"Of course," said Colonel Curtis, with deadly calmness,
"I can't tell how you would feel, or how you ought to feel,
in decent society, Samuels, and I don't pretend to know
who your friends may be; but I do know that our visitors'
list this winter includes representatives of the best blood in
England."

He proceeded to enumerate these distinguished beings,
recovering his good humor a little as he did so; for he
loved both his adopted place of residence and the aristocracy of his native land, and it gladdened his heart to think
that the former should be patronized in such respectable
numbers by the latter. "And then there are the Luttrells,
whom we have with us every season," he concluded. "I
suppose even Samuels would deign to shake hands with a
Cabinet Minister—that is, if the Cabinet Minister had no
objection."

A good-natured bystander, perceiving that the atmos-
phere was highly charged with electricity, and that there
would be a row presently unless somebody intervened, was
disinterested enough to start one of those subjects which
are always sure to promote general harmony.

"The Luttrells are pretty nearly broke, I hear. Is it

true, colonel, that they have sent for Guy to marry him to that girl who is staying with them? And will she really have twenty thousand a year? Somebody told me, the other day, that she will come into any amount of money " when her uncle dies."

Colonel Curtis, charmed at being referred to as an authority upon matters of social importance, forgot his incipient quarrel with the purse-proud Jew and assumed an air of judicious reserve.

" It is quite impossible to say," he replied, " what Miss Dent may or may not be worth eventually. Her father, as I dare say you know, was very well off; her uncle, whose wife is an invalid, may live for another twenty or thirty years—in fact, I believe he is a trifle my junior—so that there is the possibility of his marrying a second time and having children. I don't care to chatter about the family affairs of an old friend like Lady Luttrell; but it stands to reason that she would not be very sorry if her eldest son were to take a fancy to a young lady whose prospects are, to say the least of them, hopeful."

" Especially as, by all accounts, her eldest son has not shown himself a particularly hopeful specimen so far," remarked one of the colonel's hearers. " Had to leave the Guards in rather a hurry, hadn't he?"

" He has given his parents some anxiety, no doubt," answered Colonel Curtis, who was barely acquainted with Guy, and knew no more of the inmates of the Château de Grancy than everybody in Pau knew; " but there is nothing against his character—nothing at all. He has sown his wild oats, that's all, like the rest of us—like the rest of us!"

The little man twirled up his mustache, sighed retrospectively, swayed from his toes to his heels, and endeavored, not without success, to look as if he had been a sad dog once upon a time. As for Guy Luttrell, his claims to that distinction were tolerably notorious, and people who were in smart society, or who wished it to be believed that they were, had to prove their intimate acquaintance with his peccadilloes, real and suspected. For the next ten minutes, therefore, these unoccupied gentlemen forgot to curse the rain, and were as happy as if they had been an equal number of the opposite sex round a tea-table or a wash-tub.

Their pleasant talk was interrupted by the subject of it, who strolled into the room and asked whether anybody was going to play pool; whereupon it appeared that everybody was. It likewise appeared that everybody was overjoyed to see Captain Luttrell, who was addressed affectionately as "dear old chap," and who (although he had chanced to overhear a word or two which had not been intended to reach his ears) smiled very good-humoredly upon the company. It was his nature to be good-humored, and uninvited familiarity seldom or never produced the effect upon him which it does upon more highly strung, nervous temperaments. If he had been asked for his candid opinion of the half-dozen men who presently adjourned with him to the billiard-room, he might perhaps have pronounced them to be "rather cads," but it is much more likely that he would have called them "very good sort of fellows." In any case, they contributed to his amusement for the next hour and a half, and, being by far the best player present, he won all their money.

Darkness had fallen upon the dismal scene outside when he got into his mackintosh, turned up his collar and his trousers, and splashed along the ill-lighted Rue du Lycée towards his mother's villa, where he had now been domiciled for several days. He meditated, as he went, upon many things—among others, upon the words above alluded to, of which he had been an unintentional hearer, and which had not caused him any surprise. Of course those fellows guessed, of course everybody must guess, what his people wanted him to do, and why they had been so anxious that he should spend a part of his leave in their midst. The governor, to be sure, had seemed to dissociate himself from the excellent scheme, and had gone off home, with the air of washing his hands of all responsibility; but that, as Guy smilingly reflected, was apt to be the governor's little way, both in public and private life.   Sir Robert loved to pose as the victim of circumstances — especially when the circumstances were not of a nature prejudicial to his own interest.

Sir Robert's son had inherited a fair share of the paternal characteristics, and he knew it.   He also knew that it was almost his duty to marry money and would unquestionably be his pleasure, provided that the thing could be done compatibly with the ill-defined principles which ruled his life. Yet, by reason of those same ill-defined principles, he did not as yet see his way to making love to Clarissa Dent.   It would be too easy and (to give, with suitable apologies, his own mental phrase) "too damned unfair."   He must be pardoned for assuming that feminine affections are very easily won : we all generalize from personal experience, and Guy's personal experience had rendered it impossible for him to arrive at any other conclusion.   And the memory of such numerous experiences, the feeling that, although still young, he was a hundred years older than this recently emancipated school-girl, made him hesitate and scruple to lay siege to her innocence.   There was not much in his past career of which he repented, save his foolish endeavors to live at the rate of three or four times his income ; his impression was that he had been neither more nor less of a sinner than other men ; but he had the instincts of a gentleman, which often crop up in the most unexpected quarters and at the most unexpected moments.

Thus, when he reached the Château de Grancy and found nobody but Clarissa in the drawing-room, he carefully abstained from behaving as habit and the situation would have prompted him to behave.   He stood for a moment, with his back to the fire, facing the girl, who had rather reluctantly laid down her book on his entrance, and all he said was :

"I suppose it's about time to go and dress.   There are some people coming to dinner, aren't there ?"

"I believe so," she answered ; "and then we are to go on to a ball.   At least, Lady Luttrell and I are going ; I don't know whether we are to be honored with your company or not."

"Nor do I," said Guy. "My mother tells me that I have been asked; but I'm not quite so keen about balls as I was in years gone by. I'm afraid you wouldn't promise me a couple of dances by way of inducement, would you?"

That was a perfectly harmless speech to make, he thought —the sort of speech that one could hardly avoid making, under the circumstances—and of course he did not really care a straw what answer he received. Nevertheless, he was just a shade mortified on being told that Miss Dent was afraid she couldn't. It was possible that she might have one square dance left; but, as far as she could remember, she was already engaged for the whole evening.

"What!—eighteen or twenty dances booked in advance?" he exclaimed, with raised brows. "Far be it from me to dispute your right to form arrangements of that kind, but—aren't they rather unusual?"

"I don't know," answered Clarissa, meekly; "you must be a far better judge of what is usual than I am. But it seems to be the custom here to take time by the forelock, and although I am not at all a good dancer, I generally find at a ball that my card is almost full for the next one before the evening is over."

"That," observed Captain Luttrell, "proves one of two things: either you are a much better dancer than your modesty will allow you to admit, or else you must be extraordinarily popular on other grounds. One sees the other grounds," he added, politely; "*ça saute aux yeux*, as they say here. Still, I should suspect you of being a first-rate partner into the bargain."

The girl was really very pretty, he thought to himself, as he surveyed her with a semi-paternal smile, and derived some inward amusement from noticing how her color rose at his commonplace compliment—not strikingly so, perhaps, in the ordinary sense of the term, yet attractive and rather distinguished-looking, with her fluffy hair, her eager, short-sighted eyes, and her parted lips. As a matter of

fact, Clarissa, for whom the climate as well as the amusements of Pau had worked wonders, was looking quite her
best at that time. She had almost lost her troublesome
cough, she was in high spirits, the world was going well
with her, and she was full of good-will towards the world
at large. Of that good-will, however, she had no super-
abundance to bestow upon Captain Luttrell, who, ever since
his arrival, had thought fit to talk to her as though she had
been a little girl of Madeline's age, and by whom she did
not quite see why she should be patronized. So she somewhat ostentatiously stifled a yawn and reopened her book,
while he, taking the hint, presently strolled out of the
room.

Lady Luttrell, as has been mentioned, did not give formal dinner-parties during those winter months when she
was supposed to be, and supposed herself to be, practising
economy; but this did not prevent her from continually
asking a few friends to dinner, and that evening she had
seven of them, French and English, most of whom were
going on later to the entertainment for which Clarissa was
so fully engaged.

Madame de Malglaive, a stern, rather forbidding-looking
lady of pious life and strictly Legitimist principles, who
had been young in the distant days when Lady Luttrell
had been Antoinette de Grancy; her son Raoul, a slim,
handsome, dark-complexioned youth, fresh from Saint-
Cyr; the Vicomte de Larrouy, a brisk, good-humored,
talkative Béarnais who carried his fifty-odd years lightly,
and who, after many seasons of cosmopolitan life at Pau,
had learned to speak a species of English, of which he was
extremely proud; stout Lady Chiselhurst, the wife of one
of Sir Robert's colleagues, with her marriageable daughter—
these, together with a secretary of embassy, caught on his
passage to Madrid, and a young American, reputed to be
possessed of enormous wealth, constituted one of those incongruous little assemblages which Lady Luttrell loved to
collect round her oval table. She understood very well,
too, how to entertain them and help them to entertain one

another when they had little or nothing in common;∼for she was blessed with that talent as a hostess which is inborn, unteachable.

Clarissa, placed between Raoul de Malglaive and the transatlantic millionaire, might have found some difficulty in talking to either of them, had not each been started on the right path by a dexterous, unobtrusive hint. As it was, Mr. Ingram, the American, was able to discourse, with satisfaction to himself and his neighbor, upon English country life, which it appeared that he had enjoyed exceptional facilities for studying, while young De Malglaive, who was at first disposed to be somewhat shy and silent, became quite loquacious as soon as he was given to understand that he might express himself in his own language, and that Miss Dent was particularly eager to hear anything that he could tell her respecting a French military career under the Republic. He was a simple, modest sort of boy, conveying, with his great serious brown eyes and his slightly sombre cast of countenance, the impression that there was more in him than appeared on the surface, inclined to be modern, for the rest, in ideas to which he did not dare to give explicit utterance within earshot of his mother, and more than once put to silence and confusion by a glance across the table from that redoubtable lady. Clarissa liked him better than the correct, self-satisfied Mr. Ingram, who, despite certain disparaging criticisms which he thought fit to bestow on us as a nation, paid us the compliment of patronizing our tailors and affecting a passable imitation of our colloquial methods. He spoke French fluently, and bent forward several times to address a few words to M. de Malglaive, which showed how conversant he was with the lessons of the recent autumn manœuvres, but which were not very cordially responded to. Perhaps it takes several generations of easy circumstances to develop a human being capable of appreciating the beauty and necessity of minding his own business.

But the conversation was for the most part general, and turned, after a time, upon the ball whither everybody present was bound, with the exception of Madame de Malglaive, to whose rigidly exclusive visiting-list wealth was no passport.

"I have not the honor of knowing her, this Meestress Breeks," she said, with a slight upward movement of her shoulders; "she belongs to a world which I have never cared to frequent. For you, my dear Antoinette, it is quite different, no doubt; you are, so to speak, compelled to know everybody, and you have, besides, a charming young lady to amuse. It is, perhaps, also different for Raoul, of whom I do not desire to make a hermit. From all that I hear, you will be magnificently entertained."

"So I am assured," said Lady Luttrell. And then— possibly by way of exhibiting a discreet danger-signal to her friend—she made haste to add : "Mrs. Briggs is a compatriot of yours, Mr. Ingram, so of course you know all about her. I met her once or twice in London last spring, and thought her charming; but one sees so little of anybody in London."

Mr. Ingram thought it probable that Lady Luttrell had seen as much of his fair compatriot as he had done. He, too, had been granted the privilege of an introduction to her in London, where she mixed with the best society, having the requisite means for doing so. She was not, he continued, with a faint smile, in New York society; but he presumed that that was of no consequence.

"Not the smallest," said the diplomatist, laughing. "We don't know what New York society means, and we don't want to know On the other hand, we do know what the best of good champagne is, and we flatter ourselves that we can estimate the value of a pretty and lively woman as well as anybody."

M. de Larrouy told the company, with legitimate pride, that he could boast of being numbered among Mrs. Briggs's intimates. In fact, he was going to lead the cotillon for her that evening, and, although he was bound to secrecy respecting details, he might mention that it would surpass anything of the kind which had hitherto been witnessed in Pau.

"You will say that I am a little too old for a leader of cotillons; but what would you have? It is true that I have led hundreds in my day, and that I may claim to possess a little more experience than younger men. *Enfin!*— since madame was pleased to insist!"

He was evidently enchanted with the honor which had been conferred upon him, and could not resist whispering a few confidences to Lady Chiselhurst, who pressed him for further information. "Bracelets with real jewels for the ladies, scarf-pins in fine pearls for the men—but I beseech you not to betray me; I should never be forgiven!"

Lady Luttrell's guests departed almost immediately after dinner, and when her own carriage was announced, Clarissa was helped into it by Guy, who had put on a hat and a fur-lined coat.

"So you are coming, after all?" she said.

"Oh yes," he answered; "I couldn't hold out against the prospect of being presented with what old De Larrouy calls a 'fine pearl' pin. Besides, it will make me feel quite young again to see him leading a cotillon, as he used to do when I came out here from Eton for the Christmas holidays. I would ask you to dance it with me, only I feel sure that you must have promised it long ago to some more worthy partner."

"Not so very long ago," Clarissa replied. "If you had asked me before dinner, I would have given it you with pleasure; but now I am pledged to young M. de Malglaive, who quite admits that he is not at all a worthy partner. It seems that he has only been to one ball before in his life, and then he had the misfortune to tumble down. So he has rather distrusted himself since."

Lady Luttrell, from the corner of the carriage, in which she was by this time ensconced, exclaimed: "My dear child, you must not think of spoiling your enjoyment for the sake of a boy like Raoul! Tell him to find somebody else—or to stand and look on."

But Clarissa did not think it would be fair to hurt the

poor fellow's feelings in that way, and Guy displayed no overwhelming anxiety to cut him out.

"I will stand and look on, as befits my years," said he. "Perhaps, if you are very generous and I am very lucky, one of the 'fine pearl' pins may be bestowed upon me by you. Outsiders, you know, are allowed to take part in the cotillon when any lady is compassionate enough to select them."

"To hear you talk, one would think that you were a middle-aged man!" exclaimed his mother, half-laughing, half-vexed. "That is a poor compliment that you pay me, to make me out so old."

He was still young; but without any affectation he felt almost old enough to be Miss Dent's father, and dancing, of which he had been passionately fond in years gone by, had ceased to be a form of exercise that he cared very much about for itself. When he entered the fair-sized, brilliantly lighted, and exquisitely decorated rooms in which the hospitable Mrs. Briggs was receiving her friends, he was quite content to station himself in the background and watch the more or less graceful performances of other people. As a matter of fact, he had to dance, because his skill was notorious, and sundry old acquaintances were present whom he could not ignore; but during the greater part of the evening he cheerfully accepted the position of an interested spectator.

He accepted it, that is to say, with such cheerfulness as might be attained to by one whom the scene inevitably reminded of irrevocable follies and neglected opportunities. Another opportunity—possibly a final one—was now, he strongly suspected, being offered to him; but really he could not take advantage of it. Yet, if he had been a little younger, and if she had been a little older, and if things had been rather different! . . . For indeed Clarissa, dressed in the pale shade of pink which became her best, was looking charming that evening, and he noticed also that she had allowed her modesty to get the better of her veracity in stating that she was not a good dancer. More than once he was greatly tempted to approach her *per obstantes juve num catervas;* but, not without a sense of conscious virtue he abstained. It was safer to flirt with pretty, vivaciou little Mrs. Briggs, who, whether she was in New Yorl society or not, was quite at home in that of the Europeai aristocracy, and who, like all her countrywomen, had plent: of amusing and original things to say. There was a Mr Briggs somewhere or other, busily engaged, no doubt, ii amassing the dollars which his wife expended so freely; bu apparently he had no taste for foreign travel.

After partaking of a supper upon which he felt justi fied in warmly complimenting his hostess, Captain Luttrel could do no less than comply with her request when sh begged him to select a partner for the cotillon from amonɡ a bevy of disengaged and not very attractive damsels whon she pointed out to him. Nothing if not good-natured, Guʏ chose the least promising-looking of these, and it may b hoped that he made her happy. At all events, he mad her dance, which was in itself no mean achievement, anc he overcame her shyness by talking to her as if he hac known her all his life. Meanwhile, he himself was verʏ well amused in watching the evolutions directed by th evergreen M. de Larrouy, who had invented several entirelʏ new and original figures for the occasion, and who wa: skipping about with all the agility and enthusiasm that h had been wont to manifest in the good old days when ther had been an emperor at the Tuileries and a *préfet* belong· ing to the fashionable world in the Basses-Pyrénées.

Clarissa, seated at the opposite extremity of the lonɡ room, raised her glasses more than once to see how Cap· tain Luttrell was getting on with his rather clumsy part· ner, and was moved to genuine admiration of him by whaɩ she saw. Whatever he might be, he was kind-hearted anc a gentleman, she thought; and she said as much to younɡ De Malglaive, who responded, with becoming humility:

" He resembles you, mademoiselle; he takes pity on th universally rejected."

Perhaps it was because she felt it incumbent upon heɪ

to reward, as far as she could, so much unselfishness that Clarissa, when M. de Larrouy's artistic figures had been concluded and Mrs. Briggs had come to the front with her bracelets and her scarf-pins, tripped across the polished floor to bestow the latter form of decoration upon a gentleman who declared himself honored beyond his most extravagant hopes. And then, for the first time in her life, she found out what waltzing can be made to mean.

"That was perfect!—absolutely perfect!" she exclaimed when, after a couple of turns round the room, Guy relinquished her to her partner. "You dance so beautifully that I almost believe I have been dancing beautifully myself!"

"You may quite believe it," said Guy, laughing; "it happens to be the truth."

"Ah, no! I am a very poor performer at my best; only I am certain that with you I should never disgrace myself. I suppose it is very greedy of me," she added, after a moment's hesitation, "but—do you think you could manage to give me just one more turn before we go?"

"I should rather think I could, and would! Don't you see those bouquets and bracelets which are just about to be distributed? I assure you that you are the only person here who will get the chance of refusing mine."

Now, it is doubtless a small thing to be able to dance well, and no very great thing to be a good-natured sort of fellow; yet the judgments that we form of our fellow-creatures and the judgments that they form of us are largely dependent upon trifles. Lady Luttrell would not have been dissatisfied at the end of the evening if she had known how well disposed Clarissa was towards her scapegrace of an eldest son, nor perhaps would she have thought it necessary to say, as she did on the way home:

"Guy, you are too lazy for anything! I bring you here on purpose to amuse this poor child, and you never dance with her once until the cotillon is almost over! I am ashamed of you!"

"Miss Dent will tell you," answered Guy, "that I took

the very first opportunity I got, and made a few more for myself afterwards; I am now the proud possessor of a pin which I shall cherish to the end of my days, in memory of the best partner I have ever encountered, or am ever likely to encounter."

Clarissa said nothing; but her fingers closed upon the bangle which encircled her wrist and which to her also had acquired a certain value as a memento. But it was not of the generous Mrs. Briggs that she expected that ornament to remind her in years to come.

CHAPTER VI

THE UNHEROIC HERO

WELL disposed as Clarissa was towards Captain Luttrell, and pleasant though the recollection of Mrs. Briggs's ball had been rendered for her by its concluding episodes, she was as far from any idea of falling in love with him as he was from realizing her conception of a hero of romance. The beautiful, talented, and intrepid being who was destined to conquer her heart (always supposing that Providence should see fit to throw him in her way) was a figment of the imagination, constructed out of the old-fashioned novels which she had been allowed to peruse at school, and was extremely unlikely to be met with in real life. Indeed, it may be surmised that if such a person, or anybody at all like him, had come into existence, he would have been knocked on the head in early youth by some benevolent but exasperated lover of our fallen race.

Nevertheless, Miss Dent liked Guy quite well enough to be a little annoyed by the obvious indifference with which he regarded her. He paid her compliments, it was true, made pretty speeches about her dancing, and professed himself eager for the repetition of the great pleasure which she had been pleased to grant him; but he had the air of talking rather in joke than in earnest, and he did not take the trouble to attend any of the parties which followed in quick succession upon the heels of that already described. In short, he conveyed to her the impression that in his eyes she was a mere schoolgirl, like Madeline; and such a view was, to say the least of it, unflattering.

"I do think, Guy," said his mother, one evening at dinner, "that you are the most unsociable person to have staying in the house I ever knew or heard of! What with the hunting, which you always pretend to despise and the club, where, I suppose, you gamble and lose your money, one sees literally nothing of you from morning to night!"

Guy, who had been following the hounds all day in pouring rain, and had come home pleasantly tired, laughed with his customary good-humor.

"I should have thought," he answered, "that you and Miss Dent would be grateful to me for taking myself off. What is to be done, when it rains, in a house where there is no billiard-table? While this weather lasts the only way in which I can make myself of use is to exercise the governor's horses for him; but as soon as the sun comes out again I shall be ready for picnicking or lawn-tennising or anything else you like. Not that I believe the sun ever will come out again."

There really did not appear to be much prospect of it. Old residents were saying, as old residents in winter resorts always do say when the inevitable spell of cheerless wet and cold sets in, that they had never in all their experience seen anything like it before; poor Colonel Curtis had been having such a bad time of it at the club that he was fain to shut himself up at home and sadly tap a falling barometer every half-hour; while Clarissa, among others, was beginning to feel a little bit ill-used.

"But not by me, I trust," said Guy, after she had made a somewhat disconsolate remark to that effect. "If you think, as my mother seems to do, that I have been neglecting my duties, and if I can be of any service by staying at home to-morrow and holding a skein of wool for you to wind, you have only to speak the word."

"No, thank you," answered Clarissa, with just a touch of snappishness; "I have no use for wool, and I am afraid I should have no use for you, either."

"But you will when it clears up and when he takes us both out hunting," said Madeline; "you will find him of

the greatest use then. Guy has taught me almost all that
I know."

But Captain Luttrell did not respond to this leading observation, nor could he be persuaded to accompany the
ladies to the house of a neighbor, where there were to be
tableaux vivants that evening, followed probably by an informal dance. He was so awfully done, he pleaded, and
thought he caught a bit of a chill, too. If he might be excused for that once, he really would go with them next
time. Evidently the prospect of another dance with Miss
Dent was not alluring enough to compete with a comfortable arm-chair and a cigar beside the fire.

Now, if all this was, as has been said, a little annoying to
Clarissa, it was not of supreme importance, Captain Luttrell
being, after all, no more than a pleasant acquaintance, of
whom she would willingly have made a friend, had he been
disposed to meet her half-way. But some days later a very
disagreeable incident occurred, and one which she had difficulty in forgiving, although he was in no way to blame
for it. Climatic conditions had by that time altered considerably for the better, and the only reason why Clarissa
was not out riding, on such a beautiful, sunny afternoon,
with Guy and Madeline was that the former had in a somewhat marked manner refrained from urging her to accompany them. He was going, he had said, to put his young
sister through a course of schooling which, he was afraid,
would bore Miss Dent, and he expressed no sort of anxiety
to undertake the education of a second pupil. Miss Dent,
therefore, having decided to remain at home, had established herself with a book in a sheltered corner of the garden, where it was quite warm enough to sit out-of-doors
and read, supposing that she wanted to read—which she
didn't.

She had been gazing abstractedly for some little time at
the distant mountains, all glittering and glistening with
freshly fallen snow, when the sound of approaching footsteps and high-pitched French voices roused her from
her day-dream. It was Lady Luttrell and Madame 'de

Malglaive, who were engaged in conversation, and she
held her breath, knowing that she was hidden from them by
an intervening belt of evergreens and having no particular
wish to be dragged from her retreat. Thus it came to pass
that, without the slightest intention of playing the eavesdropper, she distinctly heard Lady Luttrell say:

"My dear, you do not understand our English customs.
With us marriages are not arranged; we only try sometimes
to bring them about, and in this case we are not trying at
all. Sir Robert has scruples, which you will think absurd,
and which I myself think rather absurd. Still I am compelled to respect them."

"It is a great fortune," said Madame de Malglaive,
gravely; "you will be inexcusable if you allow it to escape
you. The more so as it seems to me that the girl—"

"Ah, yes!" interrupted Lady Luttrell; "this is the provoking part of it! I, too, have noticed that she has a decided *penchant* for Guy; but I am not permitted to lend a
helping hand to events, and even if I were it would be useless, I fear. You know—or perhaps you do not know—
what Guy is! No consideration of wisdom or prudence
will ever induce him to do what he does not want to do,
and it is only too evident to me that he has taken this poor
child *en grippe*. Yet she is neither plain nor stupid; he
might do a thousand times worse, and no doubt he will.
Enfin!—une affaire manquée, that is all that one can say
about it."

Madame de Malglaive, apparently, had something more
to say about it; but, as the two ladies had now turned
their backs and were walking away, her remarks did not
reach the ear of the indignant listener. Indignant Clarissa could not help being, nor was she at all mollified by
having been made aware of Sir Robert's honorable scruples. This match, it seemed, had not, according to Lady
Luttrell, been "arranged," but it had certainly been desired; and now that it had to be regarded as "*une affaire
manquée*," the kindness and hospitality of which she had
been the recipient ought not to be further trespassed upon.

Her first impulse was to go back to the house, despatch a telegram to her uncle, and announce on the morrow that, since she was perfectly well, there was no longer any necessity for her to remain abroad. But, fortunately, she had just enough of common-sense to restrain her from making herself so ridiculous. She saw that she would not be able to change all the plans that had been made for her without an explanation, and to give the true explanation of her departure would be a little humiliating ! Moreover, Lady Luttrell, who had a perfect right to wish that her son should make a good marriage, had, after all, been guilty of no sin. With a slight effort, pardon might be granted to that anxious mother ; but at Clarissa's age one is not quite sufficiently heroic or philosophic to pardon a man for behaving as Captain Luttrell had deemed it indispensable to his safety to behave. That he should have "taken her *en grippe*" was a matter for regret, no doubt; still he was very welcome to his likes and dislikes. "But really," said Clarissa to herself, "I think he might have waited to find out whether he was in the smallest danger from me before giving himself so much trouble to keep out of my way."

Consequently, from that day forth Guy was made to understand very clearly that Miss Dent found him a bore. She did not always answer when he spoke to her; she often seemed to be unconscious of his presence, and would yawn wearily on being reminded of it; she curtly declined to join him and his sister in their rides, and once, when she had hesitatingly consented to give him a dance, she unblushingly threw him over in favor of Mr. Ingram. That this method of treatment should have imbued Captain Luttrell with a strong desire to kick Mr. Ingram, as well as with an increased appreciation of charms which other men besides Mr. Ingram appeared to find potent, was scarcely surprising. But it did not spur him on to place himself in open rivalry with those more favored persons. From the first he had determined to adopt a magnanimous course so far as this wealthy and altogether inexperienced young woman was concerned ; since she was pleased to spare him all effort by metaphorically trampling upon him, so much the better! He therefore effaced himself, with a smile upon his lips and not much more of wounded vanity in his heart than was to be expected of one who had hitherto had every reason to believe that he was irresistible.

"Clarissa," said Madeline, suddenly, one afternoon, "why do you hate Guy? Oh, you needn't deny that you hate him; I have seen it for ever so long, and I can't make it out! What can he possibly have done to offend you?"

Madeline, by Clarissa's request, had ceased to address her as "Miss Dent." An intimacy had sprung up between them which, notwithstanding the slight disparity in their years, had become very close, and was destined to prove enduring. Already they had, or pretended to have, no secrets from one another; so that now, while they were strolling down one of the shady paths of the park on their way to the Plaine de Bilhères, where they were to witness a golf competition in which Guy was taking part, it was almost a question whether honesty and the claims of friendship did not demand a simple statement of the truth. Clarissa, however, after a brief inward debate, contented herself with replying:

"What rubbish! I don't hate your brother a bit; I don't think enough about him to hate, or even dislike, him. Very likely if he was *my* brother I should admire him as much as you do. As it is, he seems to me to be a very— what shall I say?—ordinary sort of person."

"He is *not* ordinary," cried Madeline, firing up, "and I don't for one moment believe that you think he is! Why, there is nothing that Guy can't do better than other people! —riding, shooting, fishing—"

"Oh yes, and dancing too," interrupted Clarissa, with a laugh. "I dare say we shall have to congratulate him upon having won this golf-medal, or whatever it is, into the bargain. Only all that doesn't strike me as making him such a very extraordinary being. A golf-medal isn't quite the same thing as the Victoria Cross, you see."

"How can he help it if he has never been given a chance

of fighting ?" asked Madeline, pertinently. "I am quite sure that he will never hesitate to risk his life, whether he gets the Victoria Cross for it or not. You are not going to call him a coward, I hope ?"

Clarissa disclaimed any idea of bringing so offensive an accusation against Captain Luttrell. No doubt he would fight as well as another in case of necessity ; but she confessed that he did not give her the impression of a man who was likely to do anything foolhardy. He was rather too sensible and too self-indulgent for that, she thought.

Madeline, who was a somewhat hot-tempered young person, looked for a moment as though she resembled her brother in respect of entire readiness to show fight ; but, instead of doing that, she burst out laughing, and made one of those shrewd observations whereby children not unfrequently astonish their elders.

"If you had not assured me that you had never been in love in your life, Clarissa," said she, "I should suspect you of being a little bit in love with Guy."

Such a silly speech merited no rejoinder and received none. Clarissa contemptuously raised her chin a couple of inches, changed the subject, and took care to talk so fast that her juvenile companion had no chance of reverting to it until they had descended to the long, level expanse of waste land known as the Plaine de Bilhères, which has been utilized for purposes of recreation by cricketers, lawn-tennis players, and golfers ever since Pau became an English colony.

Immediately on their arrival they were accosted by Mr. Ingram, who was a golfer of some proficiency, and who, it appeared, was on this occasion playing with and scoring for Guy.

"You are just in time to see us start on our second round," he said ; "perhaps you may care to walk with us for a few holes. Oh no ; you won't put us off. My nerves are warranted to stand anything ; and if they weren't it would make no difference, for our steps have been dogged all along by a crowd of people who have never witnessed anything like Luttrell's driving before. Just look at them !"

Clarissa looked at them, and could scarcely restrain herself from joining in their low, awestruck murmur of admiration when Guy carelessly stepped up to his ball, and with a swift, full swing of the supple club, sent it soaring away into space. Mr. Ingram's performance was of a more modest, but perhaps equally useful kind.

" I am the tortoise and Luttrell is the hare, you know," he explained to Clarissa, who was walking forward beside him, while Madeline had joined her brother. "I can generally catch him up when it comes to short play, and we were all even at the end of the first round, you know."

Mr. Ingram seldom failed to end his sentences with "you know," being under the impression that it is customary to do so in the best English society. His attentions to Miss Dent, which had latterly been conspicuous, were due, it may be conjectured, to a clear comprehension of what is customary all the world over. He was not in the least smitten with the reputed heiress, and was fully persuaded in his heart (not, it must be owned, without reason) that the standard of beauty, elegance, and attractiveness was far higher among his own countrywomen than elsewhere ; but he was all the more willing to bestow a temporary patronage upon Clarissa because he suspected that that overbearing, free-and-easy fellow Luttrell did not like it.

Clarissa, in common with the rest of the throng of spectators, followed, for the next half-hour or so, the vicissitudes of a game which is, perhaps, of all games the least interesting to look on at ; but then, to be sure, she was not looking at it very much. Her eyes wandered continually to the distant, sun-smitten mountains, from the snowy Pic du Midi de Bigorre in the far east to the Pic du Midi d'Ossau, a sort of miniature Matterhorn, which rises almost directly south of Pau. Her thoughts, too, wandered a long way from the level, calm discourse of Mr. Ingram, who was playing very nicely and who seemed to be getting a little the better of his more showy antagonist. But if the progress of this contest failed to excite her, an incident presently occurred which, while it lasted, was too exciting to be pleasant.

"Thunder!" exclaimed Mr. Ingram, lapsing suddenly into an idiomatic form of speech which it was his usual effort to avoid, "that boy is going to be drowned!"

Clarissa followed the direction of his outstretched finger, and saw for a moment a round, black head and a pair of small arms flung up above the waters of the neighboring Gave. That stream, swollen by the recent rains and still more by the subsequent melting of the snows, had acquired the dimensions of a broad and turbid river. It was evident that the urchin, stooping to fish out a golf-ball, driven thither by some erratic player, had lost his footing and was now in imminent danger of losing his life into the bargain. Cries of consternation arose on all sides; half-a-dozen men, including Mr. Ingram, ran hastily towards the bank, and stood there in attitudes expressive of the indecision that they probably felt. But Guy Luttrell, who had his coat off in a twinkling, was evidently not afflicted with a malady which is only too apt to debar the majority of us from proving how brave we really are. Clarissa, holding her breath, saw him plunge into the water and saw him immediately swept down-stream by the rushing current. Then he disappeared behind a jutting promontory, overgrown with osiers, and she, together with the rest of the spectators, started off as fast as her legs would carry her to witness the sequel.

They were not quite in time to witness what, as Guy afterwards admitted, had been a very near approach to a catastrophe. When his friends caught sight of him, some two or three hundred yards beyond them, he was already ashore, with his half-drowned burden, and had sat down to recover the breath of which he found himself somewhat short. It was, in truth, rather luck than skill that had saved him; for he had been carried out into mid-stream, and would probably have been whirled on until his strength gave out but for the topmost branches of a fallen tree,

5

which he had just succeeded in clutching. But he did not at the time think it necessary to mention these details.

"Oh, *I'm* all right!" he said, laughing, in answer to the sympathetic inquiries which were presently showered upon him. "I'm not so sure about this little beggar, who must have swallowed a gallon of dirty water, I expect. Does anybody know where he lives?"

The boy, whose business in life it was to carry clubs, was well known to several of the bystanders, and he was at once removed to a neighboring cottage, where restoratives were employed with satisfactory results. But this occupied some little time, and Guy was repeatedly implored not to stand about any longer in his dripping clothes.

"Very well," he said, at last; "I'll be off, then. No; I don't want a lift, thanks. The best thing to do when you are wet through is to trot home on your own feet."

So he departed at a trot, after declining Mr. Ingram's offer of an overcoat, and remarking that he was afraid his late antagonist must be allowed to walk over for their match.

"Not that I acknowledge myself beaten," he added. "We'll fight it out some other day."

Assuredly he had not been beaten. On the contrary, he had gained a victory which he had been free from any intention of winning, and of which the vanquished person was as yet hardly conscious. Only, when Madeline asked, triumphantly, "How about Victoria Crosses *now?*" Clarissa was fain to eat humble pie.

"I apologize," she answered. "I didn't think he had it in him; but I was wrong. It just shows the necessity of putting one's neighbors to the test if one wants to find out what they are."

And then, with a cruelty which nothing but extreme youth could excuse, she turned to Mr. Ingram, who was escorting the ladies home, and remarked: "I suppose the rest of you were not ambitious of being decorated with Victoria Crosses or even with Humane Society's medals."

"I am not an ambitious man," replied Mr. Ingram, composedly; "my little part in life has to be played without accompaniment of drum and trumpet. But there is this to be said for me, that I am not jealous, and my congratulations to your friend Luttrell are soured by no *arrière pensée.*"

Perhaps Mr. Ingram had slightly the best of it in that small passage of arms; but Clarissa, not entirely taking his meaning, enjoyed the satisfaction of believing that she had administered a rebuke in a quarter where it seemed to be deserved.

CHAPTER VII

WHY NOT?

NONE but the brave deserve the fair, and while youth lasts we are all of us, whether fair or unfair, prone to fall down and worship courage. In this our instincts do not lead us very far astray; for, in truth, the first and foremost thing required of a man here below is that he should prove himself a man. As time goes on, to be sure, we learn (among many other distressing and disheartening things) that physical valor may coexist with various reprehensible and even despicable qualities; but if Clarissa Dent had believed that, she would not have been the generous and impulsive being that, happily for herself, she still was. Generosity forbade her to withhold the tribute of her unstinted admiration from a man who had risked his life to save that of a fellow-creature, and if Captain Luttrell had given her some cause for personal dissatisfaction with him, none the less was he a hero of the loftiest order.

However, he had no notion of so regarding himself, and he made very light of the afternoon's adventure when Clarissa met him again at the dinner-table.

"One isn't drowned so easily as all that," he said, in reply to his mother's reiterated ejaculations of thankfulness and dismay; "if I hadn't been reserved for some other fate, the Haccombe Bay lobsters would have made a meal of me long ago. Don't you remember when old Abraham and I got capsized, and were three hours hanging on to the bottom of the boat before they could pick us up? That was a very different thing from being ducked for a few minutes in a muddy stream. Of course I knew it would be all right, or I shouldn't have jumped in."

He could not possibly have known that it would be all right, and Madeline felt it due to him to point out that he could not. Clarissa held her peace, perceiving that he did not wish his exploit to be magnified; but, naturally enough, her esteem for him was enhanced by this becoming display of modesty.

It may have been imagination, but she could not help thinking that he was even less desirous than usual of talking to her that evening. At any rate, he addressed his conversation almost exclusively to his mother and sister, and immediately after dinner he went off to the club. Could it be that he was under the impression—the false and ridiculous impression—that she was disposed to become enamoured of him, and that that dramatic incident had completed the conquest of her young affections? Clarissa's cheeks burned as this extremely odious and unwelcome surmise forced its way into her mind.

No, if Guy had been under the above impression, and if he had wished to cure Miss Dent of a misplaced attachment (but, as a matter of fact, this was not so), he could hardly have adopted a more foolish course than that which he was actually pursuing. It is not by ostentatious neglect that wounds of the heart are healed over or interest diminished, and, whether Clarissa liked or disliked him, it was inevitable that she should think a good deal about him that night—particularly as she could not get to sleep. Thus it came to pass that Clarissa's thoughts, in which repentance, mortification, and wonder were about equally blended, took the final form of self-examination. Possibly it was not then, possibly it was not until some days later, that she admitted to herself in so many words what a humiliating misfortune had fallen upon her; yet there must, no doubt, have been some unacknowledged reason for the fact that her pillow was moistened with her tears.

This was her first experience of what, in after-years, impressed her more powerfully than anything else in life—the

inequality of the sexes and the systematic injustice with
which the so-called weaker sex is treated by the stronger.
For a man to fall in love, without hope or prospect of return, is unlucky for him, but has never been held to be in
any way disgraceful; whereas a woman, who is just as
much a human being as he, becomes an object of universal
ridicule and contempt for doing the very same thing, although she cannot help it. It is commonly asserted, to be
sure, that she ought to be able to help it; but that is only
one among the very numerous absurd assertions to which
upholders of conventionality are wont to commit themselves.
Clarissa, as soon as she knew for certain that she loved Guy
Luttrell, tried to believe that she was not the least ashamed
of doing so, and, notwithstanding her ill success in this gal-
lant endeavor, she contrived to hold her head quite as high
as usual when he was present.

But although there might be nothing disgraceful in loving a man who disliked her, and who had the additional
bad taste to show that he was a little in fear of her advances, disgrace of the deepest kind would, of course, be
involved in giving him any ground for supposing that such
was the case. Clarissa, therefore, began to treat Captain
Luttrell with a disdainful coldness which, as she was rather
glad to notice, was neither lost upon him nor enjoyed by
him. She declined, with quite uncalled-for asperity, to
profit by the lessons in equitation which he kindly offered
to give her; when, on several successive occasions, he asked
her for a dance, she had an excuse, which was obviously a
mere trumped-up excuse, ready for him; she displayed a
marked preference for other people's company as often as
he made his appearance, and more than once she was downright rude to him.

"In all my experience," remarked Mr. Ingram, who was
an intermittent and amused spectator of these tactics, "I
have never seen a young lady give herself away so absolutely
as Miss Dent is doing. It's pathetic, you know, and Captain
Luttrell ought to be ashamed any way. Because he either
has ordinary intelligence or he hasn't. If he has, it's too

bad of him to hold back any longer; and if he hasn't —
But I can't believe that you Englishmen are really as dense
as you sometimes look."

"Guy Luttrell is not generally considered to be a fool,"
returned Colonel Curtis, somewhat nettled by this attack
upon his fellow-countrymen. "He is a gentleman, if you
understand what that means, and he may feel bound to
'hold back,' as you call it, from an heiress who is under
his mother's care just now."

Mr. Ingram confessed that such an explanation of Captain
Luttrell's apparent insensibility did not strike him as particularly plausible; yet the colonel was not very far off the
mark, and Guy, whose experience had been rather longer
and more varied than that of the young American, would
have known very well what interpretation to place upon
poor Clarissa's behavior had he been in a position to judge
her dispassionately.

By degrees, however, he had arrived at the discovery
that he was no longer able to survey Miss Dent from a
wholly dispassionate standpoint. Ill-conceived as her efforts to show him that he was by no means a *persona grata*
to her had been, they had nevertheless proved successful,
and he was now compelled to acknowledge to himself—not
for the first time—that his susceptible heart had passed out
of his own guardianship. No better reason, of course, could
have been afforded him for beginning to lay siege to the
heiress, nor any better excuse supplied for the abandonment of his self-denying ordinance; but, as he was really
and truly in love, he was precluded from detecting the obvious, and he quite believed that he was, from some cause
or other, repugnant to Clarissa. Under all the circumstances, therefore, he could but congratulate himself that
his leave of absence and his sojourn at Pau were alike drawing towards a close.

"Aldershot is about the most detestable spot in England,"
he told his mother one day; "but to Aldershot I must go,
preparatory to embarking for some still worse spot out of
England. Time's pretty nearly up, too."

Lady Luttrell broke out into lamentations which Clarissa
could not help thinking were partly addressed to herself.
"Don't speak of it! I can't bear to think of your being
packed off to India in a horrid troop-ship, and banished
from us for no one knows how many years! What a wretched
thing it is to be short of money! And what a stupid arrangement it seems that the people who have the money are
almost always those who don't know how to make a sensible
use of it!"

Well, if this was meant for a reproach, it was scarcely
merited, and if Lady Luttrell's manner had become a trifle
less affectionate of late, that was only because she so entirely
misapprehended the situation. Clarissa, unluckily for herself, was blessed with no saving sense of humor; otherwise
she might have taken some comfort to her sad heart from
a contemplation of the perversity and incongruity of things.
As it was, she only felt sore and incensed against Lady
Luttrell, who ought to have known, if anybody did, why
the miserable money which her *protégée* did not want could
not be expended upon the desired object of sparing a reluctant soldier his turn of foreign service. She was likewise
exceedingly sorry for herself, seeing before her a prospect
of perpetual spinsterhood and perpetual yearning for what
could never by any possibility be hers. She was, in short,
if anybody likes to call her so, a sufficiently silly and sensitive young woman just then; only, as the majority of us
have been quite equally silly at one period or another of our
lives, we may perhaps allow her the benefit of extenuating circumstances. After all, youth and the follies of youth are in
most cases of very brief duration, while in some they are
altogether harmless. Clarissa was destined to commit far
more foolish actions before the close of her earthly career
than the shedding of frequent secret tears over a volume of
lovelorn and pessimistic poetry.

Little, indeed, did she know or guess about the follies of
Guy Luttrell's youth, of which it cannot be said with truth
that they had been harmless either to himself or to others.
In her eyes he was a modern Bayard—the embodiment of

that non-existent personage whom she had sometimes pict-
ured to herself as her possible future husband—and nothing
but the fear of betraying so portentous a secret gave her
strength to continue being as uncivil to him as she was.

Winter was a thing of the past—or, at all events, appeared to be a thing of the past—when the date fixed for
his departure drew so near as to be but four-and-twenty
hours distant.   The beech-trees in the park had donned a
thin spring livery of tender green; the snows were shrink-
ing higher and higher up the flanks of the purple mountains; Lady Luttrell was beginning to groan over the
necessity of feeding hungry Conservatives in London soon
after Easter, and the return of Mademoiselle Girault had
long ago restored the unwilling Madeline to her studies.
Clarissa, thus left a good deal to herself (for the Lenten
season was observed somewhat strictly at the Château de
Grancy, and afternoon engagements had ceased to be either
numerous or pressing), had wandered out, towards the
hour of sunset, along the Promenade du Midi, past the
statue of Gaston de Foix and so down to the Basse Plante,
where she had paused to drop her elbows upon a low wall
and gaze, with wistful, short-sighted eyes, at a prospect of
which the beauty and the soft, varied coloring never palls
upon appreciative beholders.

"I will lift up mine eyes unto the hills from whence
cometh my help"—the words came suddenly into her mind
and passed her lips in a whisper, although she had no idea
of what their dead-and-gone writer had meant, nor any distinct conciousness of how they could be made to apply to
her own case.   Yet, when we are unhappy, the calm stead-
fastness of the everlasting, unchanging mountains has a
soothing influence upon us—perhaps because it reminds us
of our personal insignificance and of the pettiness of the
little evanescent troubles which wrinkle our foreheads and
turn our hair gray.   Everything, of course, is relative, and
Clarissa's troubles were doubtless as important or as unimportant, so far as she was concerned, as the rise and fall
of empires: such as they were, she felt at least better able

to bear them in the free air and encircled by that solemn, silent pageant of Nature than within four narrow walls. The sun had not yet sunk low enough to redden the distant peaks; but the Gave beneath her, the rounded, wooded hills, and the windows of the Jurançon houses opposite were flooded and glowing in crimson light, and as she looked down upon that ruddy stream, shrunken now and intersected by broad stretches of gravel, her thoughts naturally reverted to a certain afternoon when it had been a wide, rushing river, and when a very brave man had not hesitated to cast himself into it. Well, somebody else had taken an equally reckless plunge at that self-same moment, and was likely to be punished for her imprudence with infinitely greater severity than he; but what then?

"I hold it true, whate'er befall;
I feel it when I sorrow most;
'Tis better to have loved and lost
Than never to have loved at all,"

murmurs poor Clarissa; and really there is not the slightest reason to laugh either at her or at her quotation. But Captain Luttrell, stepping briskly homewards and catching sight of that solitary, pensive figure, must needs break in upon her musings with a piece of singularly ill-timed jocularity:

"Hullo, Miss Dent! Composing a sonnet to the dying day? Rather a dangerous thing to do in these latitudes. You'll get such a chill presently, if you don't mind, that you'll be apt to follow the day to its grave before the sonnet gets into print."

Clarissa started and flushed. "How I hate people who make one jump!" she exclaimed, irritably.

"I apologize. But I am no worse off than I was before; for it is some little time already since you began to honor me with your hatred, isn't it?"

"I am sorry that you should think so," answered Clarissa, recovering her dignity and her composure. "You are quite mistaken, as it happens. I am glad to say that I do not hate anybody in the world, and I can't imagine why you should suppose that I have any feeling so strong as that about you."

"We'll substitute antipathy, then; though I'm not sure that I shouldn't prefer hatred, of the two. Anyhow, you are about to be relieved of my unwelcome society, so I dare say it doesn't matter much. All the same, since we are upon the point of parting, and since it is not very probable that we shall ever meet again, I wish you wouldn't mind telling me what it is that you find so obnoxious in me."

The odd thing was that this question was put in perfect good faith, and it was perhaps even more odd that Guy had not put it earlier. The reader, however, has already been made acquainted with some of his reasons for preserving an abnormal reticence, and if he now felt justified in giving expression to his natural curiosity, that was only because he was genuinely convinced that Clarissa Dent was an abnormal woman. The normal woman, as he could not but be aware, not only liked but adored him.

"I find nothing obnoxious in you," was the gratifying reply that he received. "It would be rather more to the purpose if I were to ask you—but really I don't care to know. As you say, we are not very likely to meet again; so it doesn't signify."

A colloquy initiated after that fashion could hardly terminate without some further clearing of the ground. Guy and Clarissa paced slowly, side by side, down one of the shady by-paths of the park (although that was not their way to the Château de Grancy), and, after a vast deal of circumlocution which it is needless to report, each offered the other a sufficiently pretty apology. There had been some misunderstanding, it appeared : Captain Luttrell did not in the least dislike Miss Dent, and nothing had been further from Miss Dent's intention than to snub Captain Luttrell.

"Well, I'm glad we are going to part friends, anyhow," the latter concluded, with an air of cheerful acquiescence, "and I am glad we have had this little explanation. By

Jove! how cold it gets the moment the sun has gone down! Won't you let me help you on with your cloak?"

She handed him the wrap which she had been carrying over her arm, and he placed it round her shoulders. He was so experienced in the performance of such small services that he ought to have been less clumsy about it; but somehow or other a hitch occurred in the operation. With an impatient murmur she turned her face towards him as he stood behind her; he saw that her eyes were misty with tears; she saw that his brows were drawn together, and that his lips were quivering—and then, all of a sudden, there was no more necessity for explanations. Verbal explanations are, at best, but sorry expedients, something unspoken almost always lurking behind them; but the language of the eyes does not deceive; nor, to be sure, is it very often intended to do so when the eyes in question happen to belong to two lovers.

"And, after all, why not?" Clarissa was saying, joyfully, about a quarter of an hour later. "Why should we not do what everybody wants us to do?"

"Upon my word, I don't know," answered Guy, laughing. "Except, of course, that I am not, and never shall be, half good enough for you."

CHAPTER VIII

THE OPPOSING FORCES

THERE were perhaps several considerations, in addition to that modestly instanced by Guy Luttrell, which rendered his betrothal to Clarissa Dent a proceeding of doubtful wisdom; but Lady Luttrell only realized one of these, and could not be so ungracious as to allude to it in the fulness of her joy at the tidings imparted to her. For the rest, her conscience accorded her plenary absolution. She had done nothing at all to promote or encourage this match; she had quite made up her mind that it would never take place, and neither Sir Robert nor Mr. Dent could justly reproach her if two young people who were admirably suited to one another in every respect had seen fit to astonish her beyond all measure by calmly announcing that they had exchanged vows of eternal fidelity.

"My dear child," she exclaimed, enfolding Clarissa in a tender, maternal embrace, "I can't tell you how happy you have made me! There is nobody—I can truly say *nobody* —whom I would rather welcome as a daughter-in-law, and, fastidious as dear Guy is, I am quite sure that he could not have made a better choice."

Considering that the bride-elect was, or was going to be, a rich woman, while the expectant bridegroom could hardly be quoted at a high figure in the matrimonial market, there was a hint of patronage about this speech which might have amused some people. But it did not amuse Clarissa, who was disposed to accept her new-found happiness in a spirit of becoming humility, and who thought Lady Luttrell very kind.

For the matter of that, everybody was very kind. Madeline, of course, was overjoyed; but it was scarcely to be anticipated that Madame de Malglaive, Mr. Ingram, and others would hear the news so early as the very next morning, and would hasten, without a moment's loss of time, to offer their heartfelt felicitations. As Guy had not informed any of them, it must be assumed that somebody else had done so, and probably somebody else had deemed it expedient to do so; but Clarissa did not object. She was only too happy that all the world should know how happy she was.

One sad but altogether inevitable drawback to her happiness was that Guy was compelled to leave her by the night mail for England. His leave was up; there would have been no time to communicate, even if there had been any use in communicating, with the authorities, and all that could be said was that their separation would not be a very prolonged one. Moreover, Aldershot is within easy reach of London.

"I shall write to you every day until we meet again," Guy promised, "and you must write to me, too. And then —well, there's no reason for a long engagement, is there? I suppose it wouldn't do for us to defy popular superstition by being married in May, but what do you think about June?"

He really did not imagine that there was anything to be urged against a speedy marriage, or that any obstacles were likely to be placed in the way of it. His father, he naturally presumed, would share his mother's satisfaction; he foresaw no opposition on the part of Mr. Dent, whose ambition ought to be pretty well gratified by an alliance with the Luttrells, and as for the honorable hesitation which he had felt at the outset, that troubled him no more. Why, indeed, should it? He was going to marry Clarissa because he loved her, not for the sake of her fortune, the amount of which he had not even had the curiosity to inquire; he would not insult her by referring to the subject; nor, he was very sure, did she require to be told that he was an honest man. There were plenty of other things which she did require to be told, and plenty which he required her to tell him ; so that the entire afternoon was occupied in an interchange of questions and answers which were delightful to the persons concerned, but which may safely be left to the imagination of readers who have been, or are destined to be, somewhat similarly circumstanced.

"Isn't it terrible," exclaimed Clarissa, as they sauntered slowly up the garden in the fading light of evening, "to think that we were within a hair's-breadth of never understanding one another at all !"

Guy agreed that it was, but was of opinion that the fault had not lain with him. How could he possibly have divined the truth when she had lost no opportunity of showing that she positively detested the sight of him ?

"I was sitting just over there," continued Clarissa, pointing tragically towards the fatal spot, "when I overheard your mother telling Madame de Malglaive that you had 'taken me *en grippe.*' I don't like to think about it even now."

"Then we won't think about it," returned Guy, who had already been informed of the dismal episode alluded to. "We'll think about the present and the future and forget the past. I have always found that that is the best plan."

It was, at all events, a plan which he had always adopted and which has its obvious advantages. He was not dishonest ; he had confessed, on being interrogated, that Clarissa was not, strictly speaking, his first love ; but he had added, with a firm conviction of his own veracity, that he had never really and seriously loved any other woman before. And that assurance had sufficed for her. Does not everybody in the world make one or two false starts ? Had not she herself, when at school, cherished a fugitive fancy for an emaciated and eloquent curate ?

Lady Luttrell, Madeline, and Clarissa drove down to the railway-station with Guy to see him off, and, as the occasion was not one that called for tears or fears, the whole four of them were in the best of good spirits. They were to meet again soon—in a few weeks, indeed, for Lady Lut-

trell said it was high time to be thinking about a move
northwards, now that the cold weather was quite over and
done with.

"I have written to Robert," she told Clarissa, after the
train had steamed away, "and I suppose you also have sent
a letter to your dear, good uncle. It is just possible," she
added, presently, "that they may not be quite as delighted
with our news as they ought to be; parents and guardians
are apt to be so cautious and fussy. But you must not
mind that; I will undertake to say that everything shall
be arranged and agreed to as soon as I reach London."

"I don't see what difficulty there can be about it," answered Clarissa, with a slight touch of incipient combative-
ness in her tone.

She did not, in truth, see what difficulty could arise.
Guy had made his choice, she had made hers, and nobody
had either the right or the power to stand between them;
it was as simple as that. Lady Luttrell, however, saw
plainly enough that there were breakers ahead; and she
was scarcely surprised, though she was a little annoyed,
when the post brought her, in due course, a very sharp
epistolary rebuke from her absent lord.

Sir Robert begged to say distinctly that he must wash his
hands of the whole business. At the same time, he must
express his regret that, in defiance of his clearly worded
wishes and instructions, his wife should have thought fit
to lend herself to what had all the appearance of being "a
put-up job." He had seen Guy and he had seen Dent.
"The former, to whom I ventured to give my opinion of
the part which he has played in this rather discreditable
affair, made out, I am bound to admit, a fairly good case
for himself; the latter, I am glad to tell you, acquits me of
any complicity in it, but of course refuses his sanction to
anything of the kind. He is writing, I believe, to his niece,
and will, no doubt, explain to her, as he has already explained to me, that, so far from being an heiress and a free
agent, she will for some years to come be entirely dependent upon him. I gather, indeed, that there is no certainty

about her ever coming into more than a very moderate fortune. One would have thought that a woman of the world would have taken the trouble to ascertain the details before placing herself and others in so ambiguous a position; but I am afraid, my dear Antoinette, that you will continue to despise prudence and discretion till the end of the chapter."

This was not a very pleasant letter to receive; but Lady Luttrell, little as she deserved to be scolded, had fully anticipated a scolding. What disquieted her a good deal more than Sir Robert's censure was his surprising assertion that Clarissa was neither an heiress *in esse* nor *in posse;* and thus it was that her ladyship passed through half an hour of painful suspense, which she had some ado to restrain herself from cutting short by going up-stairs and knocking at Miss Dent's door. But at the expiration of that interval the girl entered the room, holding several sheets of closely written note-paper in her hand, and looking, upon the whole, less perturbed than might have been expected.

"I have had letters from Guy and from Uncle Tom," she began. "I am sorry to say that they are rather unsatisfactory—at least, Uncle Tom's is. He writes in a way which I am sure is meant to be kind; but he says he cannot approve of the engagement and must forbid it. It seems that, by my father's will, I shall only have such money as he may choose to allow me until I come of age, and he says Guy has not enough to marry upon. Then he goes on — oh, here it is: 'I need hardly add that I should not feel justified in providing you with the means of making a marriage which, for various reasons, seems to me most unlikely to insure your future happiness.' But of course he can be no judge of that."

Lady Luttrell wrinkled up her brows in distress. "Certainly he has no right to say anything so rude and so false," she declared. "Still, if he really has the power that he claims—and I suppose a man of business, like Mr. Dent, must know what he is talking about—"

6

"Oh, he has the power to stop my allowance for a few years to come," said Clarissa, composedly; "but I should hardly think that he will exercise it when he finds that I am quite determined.   I am not in the least afraid of poverty, you see; so that the prospect of being poor for a time doesn't affect me, one way or the other."

There was a look of quiet obstinacy about the set of the girl's lips which Lady Luttrell had not noticed there before, and which would have been reassuring if it had been possible to count upon the obstinacy of another important person concerned.

"My dear," she said, affectionately, "I do so thoroughly sympathize with and admire you! You are quite right to disregard threats which I don't think that your uncle ought to address to you without condescending to give reasons, and which I agree with you that he can scarcely be so foolish and so ill-natured as to carry out.   After all, his control over you and your money must soon cease. And—and what does Guy say about it?"

Guy, it appeared, had said just what a gentleman and a disinterested lover might have been expected to say.   Interviews with his father and with Mr. Dent had failed to convince him that he had anything to repent of or regret; although he admitted that, from their point of view, they were entitled to make some of the accusations that they had brought against him.   His own point of view was that when two people loved one another, they were bound to say so, and his experience was that they invariably did.   Temporary lack of means, temporary banishment to garrison life in India, temporary worries and discomforts—all these were, no doubt, drawbacks which neither he nor Clarissa had foreseen and which he could not ask her to face without due consideration.   Personally, he might be disposed to make rather too light of them.   For the rest, he placed himself unreservedly in her hands, assuring her that he would bow to her decision, whatever it might be, and that the only thing which no decision could alter or diminish was his entire devotion to her.

Lady Luttrell breathed more freely after listening to these very noble sentiments. She was strongly of opinion that the drawbacks alluded to would not have to be faced, and that the difference between legal authority and practical ability to exercise it could be brought home to Mr. Dent. Can a guardian absolutely prohibit the marriage of his ward? Lady Luttrell was not sure; but she had very little doubt as to the feasibility of coercing guardians. And what nonsense it was to pretend that Clarissa's fortune would be a modest one! Must she not, in any case, succeed eventually to the wealth of her childless uncle, who was known to be a very rich man? These thoughts passed rapidly through the mind of a lady who was not in reality as mercenary as she may appear to be, and who fully meant what she said when she exclaimed:

"Dearest Clarissa, I cannot regret that some obstacles have been placed in your path; because they have been the means of proving to you, as nothing else could have done, how indifferent dear Guy is to questions of money. We old folks, of course, have to consider them, and I frankly own that I should have been alarmed if he had proposed to marry a pauper. But it so happens that he is not going to do that, and I am confident that I shall soon be able to make your uncle see reason. Only perhaps, as this fuss has been raised, we had better lose no more time about returning home. It is always easier to arrange matters by word of mouth than by letter."

Nature or Providence, as has already been mentioned, had not seen fit to endow Clarissa with any comforting appreciation of the humorous side of things; so that she did not find this innocent speech half as amusing as it really was. She replied, quite gravely:

"Guy does not mind marrying a pauper, and it seems to me that that ought to be sufficient. I should think that when Uncle Tom is convinced that we have made up our minds, he will allow me enough to dress upon—which is all that I shall ask him for. But even if he refuses, it will make no difference."

"Oh, we must not be too peremptory," said Lady Luttrell, laughing; "we must not have family quarrels when there is so little necessity for them.   Write to that troublesome old uncle of yours; tell him that we are coming home, and that I insist upon keeping you with us in Grosvenor Place for the first few days.   In that way I may contrive to have a talk with him before you meet and to smooth his feathers down, instead of ruffling them up, as I am afraid you would be inclined to do.   Leave him to me, and everything will soon come right, you will see."

Within a week Lady Luttrell, whose energy and resolution were generally equal to any emergency that might arise, had broken up the Pau establishment, had despatched the heavy luggage and some of the servants by sea from Bordeaux, and was herself *en route* for London, accompanied by her daughter, her young friend, and such attendant domestics as she considered indispensable.   Of her husband's opposition in the task which she had taken in hand she had no great fear, while what she knew of Mr. Dent encouraged her to believe that, like the majority of his sex, he would sacrifice a good deal for the sake of a quiet life. She had at first entertained some secret apprehensions respecting Guy; but since Guy seemed disposed to stand to his guns, victory was to all intents and purposes assured.

CHAPTER IX

MR. DENT'S TERMS

"You do not convince me," remarked Mr. Dent. "Lady Luttrell does not convince me. Even the young man himself does not convince me; though I make you welcome to the admission that he has established a title to my respect which I did not think that I should ever be called upon to bestow in that quarter. After hearing you all at full length and holding my own tongue quite short, I still remain of opinion that this marriage would, at best, be a very hazardous experiment."

He was sitting in the spacious but rather gloomy library in Portland Place, the four walls of which, had they been endowed with ears and the power of articulation, could have reported many shrewd and sensible sayings of his; for he was a man of no small influence in the political and financial world, and all sorts and conditions of his fellow-countrymen were wont to seek interviews with him. But shrewdness and common-sense were likely to prove of little avail in the present instance, and his niece, who had been permitted by Lady Luttrell to return to the shelter of his roof that day, only laughed.

"As if every marriage was not a hazardous experiment!" cried she.

"Well, but one endeavors to minimize the risk; or, rather, one would if one could. After a London season or two you would know a great deal more than you know now, you would have met a great many more men than you have met yet—"

"And I should have lost the only man in the world whom

I can ever wish to marry," interrupted Clarissa. " Don't
you understand, Uncle Tom, that that is the beginning
and the end of the whole question? You may not like it—
though why you should dislike it I can't imagine—but what
has happened has happened, and cannot be helped."

" *Reste à savoir*, as Lady Luttrell might say," returned Mr.
Dent, with a smile. " You can't marry your Guy without
my consent, remember, for the very prosaic reason that
there won't be money enough. Upon that point Sir Robert
and I have exchanged confidences which leave us quite of
one mind. And although I cannot expect you to believe
me, it is nevertheless a fact that things which have been
done are frequently undone."

"I shall be my own mistress in three years," said Clarissa,
her countenance darkening somewhat; " but I suppose you
hope that he will have forgotten me by that time."

Then, all of a sudden, her eyes filled with tears, her lips
quivered, and she hurriedly snatched a handkerchief out of
her pocket.

" Oh, why should you wish to be so cruel to us !" she exclaimed. " What harm have we ever done you ? Why can
you not let us be happy together in our own way ?"

Mr. Dent rose and laid his hand gently upon his niece's
shoulder. "My dear," answered he, "I can't tell you why.
There are reasons—your inexperience is a very obvious one
—but it would be useless, or worse than useless, I dare say,
to mention them all. Sir Robert will tell you what occurs at
a Cabinet council when an intelligent minority chances to
be in the right. The intelligent minority bows to the mis-
guided majority and hopes, against hope, for the best. I
take it that that is my present rather unenviable position."

Clarissa flung her arms round his neck. "You consent,
then !" she cried, joyfully ; " I was sure you would !"

" Ah, well !—upon conditions. First of all, let me explain
to you that the estate left by your poor father was of such
a kind and the directions of his will were so worded that I
cannot possibly say now, nor shall I be able to say until the
time comes for handing your fortune over to you, what it

will amount to. During the interim there is an invested capital, of which I am to allow you as much or as little of the interest as I may think fit. At present this produces, I find, eight hundred pounds a year, or thereabouts—which, of course, is not a large income. Not large enough, I mean, to enable you to support a husband."

"Surely it is not usual to talk about wives supporting their husbands!" interpolated Clarissa, without a smile.

"It is not usual to talk about their doing so; yet they are often expected to do it. And that is my humble little point. I am not going to provide Guy Luttrell with the means of throwing up his commission; I am not going to add to your income; I might even retain the whole of it and allow it to accumulate for your ultimate benefit if I chose. But as you are evidently in earnest, and as he assures me that he is, that amount, and no more, you shall have for the next three years. Guy has his pay and an allowance, which I suspect is not a very magnificent one, from his father. Consequently, if my terms are accepted, you and he will have to follow the drum on foreign service, and for some time to come you will not be much, if at all, better off than your neighbors. It remains to be seen whether these terms will be accepted or not."

They were, at all events, instantly and unhesitatingly accepted by Clarissa, whose demonstrations of joy and gratitude her uncle had some temporary difficulty in repressing.

"Don't be in such a desperate hurry," he pleaded; "you have certainly nothing to thank me for, and it may turn out that you have nothing to rejoice over. Here is the unvarnished truth: I am rich and childless; I could easily afford to give you what you want and what, I suppose, the Luttrells hope for. But, rightly or wrongly, my wishes and views are opposed to yours in this matter; so I have decided as I have told you. I shall not budge from the position that I have taken up; let us hear now what the other side has to say."

"If by 'the other side' you mean Guy, I know very well what he will say," Clarissa declared, confidently.

Had she not, indeed, already received assurances from him which forbade her to entertain the shadow of a doubt upon that point? During the *pourparlers* which had been carried on between Sir Robert and Lady Luttrell and Mr. Dent, the upshot of which had been but partially divulged, her lover and she had stood aside; but there had been no faltering in the resolution of either of them. Guy, to be sure, had generously refused to hold her in any way bound to him, and had confessed and impressed upon her that her uncle's consent must be a necessary preliminary to their marriage; but not for one moment did she believe that he would allow such considerations as had just been specified to separate them. To suppose that he would was tantamount to supposing that he had never really cared for her at all—which was manifestly absurd.

When, therefore, she set forth to keep a certain appointment, her heart was light and her spirits as joyous as the sunshine of that spring afternoon, which had triumphed over the London mist and smoke and was reminding many a prisoner in the vast, dirty city of green fields and budding woods and clear streams far away. Seated in a closed carriage beside her somnolent aunt, who was to drop her in Grosvenor Place before taking the three customary turns round the Park, which represented Mrs. Dent's daily share of fresh air and exercise, she rehearsed by anticipation the imminent colloquy. Guy, who was to be up from Aldershot for the day, would meet her with an air of suppressed eagerness and interrogation, and with his eyes a little more widely opened than usual; Lady Luttrell and Madeline would seize her and guess her news before she had time to speak; and then, no doubt, it would be admitted on all hands that she had been justified in boasting of her ability to vanquish Uncle Tom. For the fact was that these good people had not succeeded in getting anything in the shape of an answer out of him, save that he would say what he had to say to his niece, and to nobody else; nor had Clarissa been relinquished to his guardianship without grave apprehensions, numerous injunctions, and even a few tears.

"How happy we are all going to be !" the girl could not
help ejaculating, as she sat upright and looked out through
the carriage-window at the passing stream of vehicles and
brisk pedestrians. It seemed to her that everybody and
everything had suddenly assumed a sympathetic mien of
joyousness, appropriate to the occasion.

"Well—perhaps," agreed Mrs. Dent, somewhat dubiously.
And then, raising her head a little from her cushions and
smiling kindly enough upon her young neighbor : "I am
sure I hope you are, my dear. I should have thought that
your uncle might easily have made you all a good deal happier; but he says he has his reasons, and he generally knows
best."

Now, if one of Mr. Dent's reasons for acting as he had
done had been to impose a test upon Guy Luttrell which
would cause that ease-loving fellow to jib, he would have
been compelled to acknowledge the futility of so cynical a
calculation had he witnessed the meeting which took place
a few minutes later between his niece and her betrothed.
For no sooner had Clarissa been admitted into Sir Robert
Luttrell's house than Guy stepped quickly forward and
drew her into the library on the ground floor, whispering,
as he did so :

"Tell me first !—whether you bring good or evil tidings.
I don't want to hear them in the presence of a third person."

He was a good deal agitated—more agitated than she
had ever seen him before ; his brows were slightly contracted, his lips twitched, and the hand that grasped hers
had lost its accustomed cool firmness. Looking into his
face, she saw, with a glow of joy at her heart, how he loved
her and feared to lose her, and she could not resist the
temptation of prolonging those delicious moments by holding him in suspense.

"Well," she answered, slowly, "I don't know that my
tidings ought to be called exactly good. That will be for
you to say after you have been told what they are."

But of course there was but one verdict for him to pronounce; and he pronounced it with such fervor, with such exuberant and boyish glee, that she was fain to burst out laughing and crying simultaneously while she listened to him.

"Eight hundred a year!—why, it's positive affluence! Add that to my own little pittance, and we shall be able to live like fighting-cocks out at Colombo, where the regiment is to go in the autumn. Dear old boy!—may his shadow never grow less! I had fully made up my mind, do you know—and so had the governor—that he didn't mean to have me at any price. I say, Clarissa, would you kindly excuse me if I jumped over the table once or twice? Unless I can let off steam somehow or other, I won't be answerable for the consequences."

He actually did it (and it was no easy thing to do either), springing and alighting with the grace and dexterity of a trained athlete, while she exclaimed, through her laughter and her tears, "Oh, Guy, how *can* you be so silly! What would the Pau people, whom you were too lazy to dance with and who always accused you of giving yourself airs, think if they could see you now!"

"They would think, my love," he answered, as he paused beside her, panting a little, "that nobody in the wide world has so good a right to jump for joy as I have at the present moment."

And, with that, he broke forth into passionate language which has been used a thousand times before and will be used a thousand times again—language which had the charm of complete novelty for its hearer, if not for its utterer, but which neither of them, it is to be feared, could recall at this time of day without some retrospective embarrassment. Presently he was seized with abrupt misgivings. Had he, after all, any business to accept this great sacrifice on the part of the woman whom he loved? Was she quite sure that she was prepared to brave expatriation and a tropical climate and a host of minor discomforts? Ought she not, perhaps, to take a few more days for reflection and consideration?

Her answer was what he must have expected, although he had not spoken insincerely. At the bottom of his heart there may have lurked a vague impression that he, too, was about to make a sacrifice; that he might, if it had so pleased him, have secured a wealthier bride, have remained in England among his friends and amused himself far better than he was likely to do in Ceylon. But nothing resembling this took definite shape in his thoughts. He was perfectly happy; he was going to be united to the girl whom he adored; old Dent had behaved like a trump, and he would not change places with any man living.

It was reserved for Lady Luttrell to detect and point out, later in the day, the shadows which flecked an otherwise sunny prospect. Not in the presence of Guy and her future daughter-in-law did she embark upon so ungracious a task; to them she was as affectionate and congratulatory as they could have wished her to be. She even sent a kind message to Mr. Dent, although she was extremely angry with him. But to her husband she could not help avowing that things had not gone quite as she had desired and intended them to do.

"One hardly knows what to think about it," she said, anxious lines appearing upon her forehead. "It is a genuine love-match, and that is so far satisfactory; yet eight hundred pounds a year seems very little, and we are given no idea of how much more there will be. I suppose Mr. Dent must have counted upon our refusing his offer. Considering what he owes to you, it is scarcely pretty of him to treat us in that way."

Sir Robert, who had returned from the House of Commons tired and sleepy, was moved to mirth by this last remark. "Dent may be pardoned," said he, "if he is of opinion that I owe him considerably more than he owes me. For my own part, I stand amazed at his good nature; for I think, as I have told you all along, that he has a pretty strong case against us. We, of course, protest that we are blameless, that we never coveted his niece's fortune nor laid plots to gain possession of it, and that we really couldn't foresee the sudden descent of Cupid upon the scene. Very well ; he takes our word for that—which is more than I should have done if I had been he—consents to a marriage which he doesn't like, promises that the girl shall have the full income to which she is entitled, and—proceeds to button up his pockets. To me that appears such handsome behavior that I declare I shall not know which way to look the next time I meet him."

"But he will not always keep them buttoned !" protested Lady Luttrell. "Surely you do not mean that, Robert !"

"I mean," answered Sir Robert, "that Dent has an absolute right to do as he pleases with his own ; I mean that all manner of unexpected contingencies may arise—that his invalid wife may die, for example, and that he may marry again. I mean that some people are too clever by half, and that other people are not necessarily heiresses because their deceased father has had a certain amount of interest in a banking business. I mean that Miss Clarissa is a charming young lady, that Guy is at least as lucky as he deserves to be, and that it will do neither of them the slightest harm to spend the first years of their married life in an inexpensive colony. Finally, I mean that nothing of all this has been my doing, that I decline all responsibility for the consequences, and that I am now going to bed."

But this was putting the case at its very worst ; and in the course of a day or two Lady Luttrell was able to feel almost, if not entirely, contented with her son's bargain. It was a great pity that he should be driven out of his native land, it was a great pity that so much needless mystery should be made respecting Clarissa's ultimate inheritance, and it was not very nice of Mr. Dent to allude to certain episodes in Guy's history which might have been matched in the history of no matter what young man of the world ; still, when all was said, much cause for thankfulness remained. A more richly dowered girl than Clarissa Dent might perhaps have been discovered ; but it did not by any means follow that Guy would have deigned to espouse her, while it was tolerably certain that he must eventually succeed to the wealth of his uncle by marriage. Then, too, there was the comfort of knowing that the young people were honestly, not to say absurdly, enamoured of one another; and this was really a great comfort to her ladyship, who loved romance, so long as it could be brought into line with reason and prudence.

As for Mr. Dent, it may be assumed that he was not overjoyed when his niece returned, with sparkling eyes and a becoming flush upon her cheeks, to tell him that everything was settled; but he only raised his shoulders slightly and remarked:

"So be it! You have troubles before you, my dear; but you would have had troubles before you in any event, and neither I nor anybody else could have preserved you from them."

The Reverend Paul Luttrell was of a different opinion, and as he was a man who seldom hesitated to express any opinion that he might entertain, he rated his parents soundly for the part that they had taken in this affair, and told his brother, in so many words, that he ought to be ashamed of himself.

"But, my dear fellow," objected Guy, after listening patiently and good-humoredly enough to a recital of the causes which should have sufficed to debar him from any attempt to win the affections of a mere child, "you make no allowances for human nature. As it happens, I scrupulously abstained from attempting to win her affections—not for the reasons that you give, which, with all due respect to you, I think are rather rot, but because I didn't like the idea of grabbing a big fortune. I couldn't help loving her, and I suppose she couldn't help loving me. Was I to turn my back upon her and take to my heels, after I had discovered the truth, merely on account of the possibility that she may become rich some day? She isn't rich now, you know."

"No; not on that account, but on account of what you are pleased to call 'rot.'"

"What extraordinary beggars you parsons are!" exclaimed Guy, throwing up his hands; "you are always preaching forgiveness of sins; but deuce a bit will you forgive, or believe a man when anybody else would understand, as a matter of course, that he is going to turn over a new leaf!"

"*Litera scripta manet,*" returned Paul, somewhat doggedly. "I don't doubt your intention to turn over a new leaf; but how would you like your wife to run her eye over the old ones?"

"I shouldn't like it at all," Guy confessed, laughing a little, "and I don't suppose she would find them edifying or profitable reading either. Parson as you are, you must know as well as I do that precious few men reach my age without having passed through some little experiences which are best forgotten. So don't be an ass, old man; and, for goodness' sake, don't go and make Clarissa miserable by telling her tales out of school."

Paul could not and did not do that. He confined himself to reading Miss Dent a brief lecture upon the duties and trials of matrimony, the necessity of giving and taking, bearing and forbearing, and so forth—all of which struck her as a little commonplace, though doubtless well meant. But when he went on to say that all would depend upon whether she took the Christian view of marriage or regarded it merely as a social contract to be dissolved at will, she made so bold as to inquire what he was driving at.

"Are we not going to be married in church?" she asked.

"Oh yes; and you are going to be married by me, I believe. But many people are married in church who afterwards appeal to the Divorce Court, and a still larger number live more or less avowedly apart because, as they allege, they 'can't get on together.' I want you to realize that, however convenient such arrangements may be, they are opposed to the Christian doctrine."

"Well," answered Clarissa, after considering for a moment, "I won't argue the point; for nothing can be more certain than that I shall never wish to make an arrangement of that kind."

CHAPTER X

CAPTAIN AND MRS. LUTTRELL

IF, as certain competent judges are wont to affirm, happiness in some shape or form be of necessity the object of every human being's aspirations and efforts, Clarissa Dent's triumph over such apprehensive well-wishers as her uncle and the Reverend Paul Luttrell must be pronounced to have been complete; for unquestionably she was as happy as any girl could be during the six weeks which followed the public announcement of her betrothal.

"And that, after all," Mr. Dent was fain to acknowledge, with a smile and a shrug, "is the main thing. What an old brute you would think me if I were to warn you that you must not expect these halcyon days to last! Moreover, you wouldn't believe me, and I should be quite sorry if you did. Let me, instead, give you a time-honored piece of advice, which I am sure you will act upon, and recommend you, now that the weather is so nice and sunshiny, to make hay and gather roses."

She was very ready to do that, and roses in ample quantities were scattered upon her path. The Luttrell family—pleased, upon the whole, with the turn that affairs had taken, sanguine as to eventualities, and really attached to their future relative—did all they could to render a London season pleasant for her, and of course they could do a great deal. The responsibilities of chaperonage—which, indeed, she was not in a state of health to assume—were taken off Mrs. Dent's shoulders; Clarissa was given opportunities of meeting the most distinguished men and women of the day, which, with her eager craving to see what everybody and everything were like when surveyed at close quarters, she appreciated to the full; and what was highly satisfactory was that among all the great personages who seemed to enjoy talking to her she could not discover Guy's equal. She amused him not a little by telling him as much.

"If you only knew what a commonplace, every-day sort of fellow I am!" said he. "Not that I want you to know. For that matter, I dare say a good many people would laugh if I were to give them my opinion of you, though I defy anybody to call you commonplace."

He was, in truth, proud of her, of her social success, of the ease with which she comported herself in no matter what situation, and of her personal beauty, which, as is so often the case, had developed amazingly under the influence of her heartfelt contentment. Moreover, he was very deeply in love.

It was in the month of June that the marriage took place, with every desirable accompaniment in the shape of costly wedding-gifts, fashionable guests, music, flowers, and strips of crimson carpet. The young couple departed to spend a brief honeymoon in the Isle of Wight, and as they drove away, Mr. Dent, who chanced to be standing at Sir Robert Luttrell's elbow, remarked:

"Well, you have done it now."

"Don't say *I* have done it," protested that eminent statesman; "it really isn't fair to say that I have done it. From first to last I never had a finger in the business, and you yourself admitted that I had done what in me lay to keep faith with you."

"Then I will say that *we* have done it. Likewise *they* have done it. I don't know what your sensations may be, Luttrell, but I feel very much as if I had just slaughtered a poor little lamb. Oh, it's all right; it was quite inevitable; lambs must be killed, and butchers are useful, respectable members of the community. But Nature never intended me to be a butcher, and that is why I am afraid I shall have no appetite for dinner to-day."

"What the deuce are you talking about, man?" asked Sir Robert, wonderingly and a little resentfully. "Do you think that my son is going to ill-treat your niece?"

"One hopes not; one doesn't quite see why he should, and one remembers that he has the average share of good qualities. Only he is no more like what she thinks he is than that very admirable painting of a little boy in frilled drawers is like the right honorable gentleman the present Chancellor of the Duchy of Lancaster—and sooner or later she is bound to find that out."

"You might say the same of any man in London whom she could have married," observed Sir Robert, still slightly ruffled.

"Very likely. After all, I may be disquieting myself in vain; for women seldom or never take things as one expects that they will take them. Added to which, as I said just now, it couldn't have been helped."

If any discoveries of a painful or startling nature awaited the bride, she certainly had not made them when, a month later, she arrived at the small furnished house near Aldershot which had been prepared to receive her. To Madeline, in the absence of any confidential friend of riper years, she had written several long letters from the Isle of Wight, describing her perfect felicity and extolling her husband's goodness, his chivalry, the marvellous modesty and simplicity of his character. It was never Clarissa's way to keep silence when under the sway of emotion.

The little Aldershot house, for which Guy had many apologies to offer, she pronounced charming. Of course it would have been ridiculous to waste money upon furnishing an abode which they would have to quit so soon, and she rather enjoyed the novel sensation of being compelled to consider ways and means. It looked delightfully snug and cozy, she said.

"Oh, well—it's hideous, to tell the truth," Guy answered, with a rueful little laugh; "but I dare say it can be made to do for the time, and there wasn't much choice. We'll make ourselves more comfortable when we get out to Co--

lombo. Now the next thing will be that you will have to be introduced to the ladies of the regiment, whom I don't know particularly well myself. I'm afraid you are sure to hate them."

But Clarissa was not in the mood to hate anybody, nor, so far as she could judge, did the ladies who made haste to call upon her deserve detestation. They were perhaps a little dull; they did not seem to have much to say upon topics of general interest, and a certain subdued defiance was noticeable in the manner of all of them. But Mrs. Antrobus, the colonel's wife, a tall woman with a hook nose, a harsh voice, and a candid style of expressing herself, explained this latter phenomenon.

"You find us a bit standoffish, eh?" said she, in response to a remark which Clarissa certainly had not intended to convey that impression. "Well, you mustn't be surprised at that, and it won't last any longer than you choose. We aren't going to be patronized, that's all; and when a man leaves the Guards to join the Cumberland Rangers, we don't think he is performing such a wonderful act of condescension that he need give himself airs upon the strength of it. Your husband, as I dare say you know, has done scarcely any regimental duty at all as yet, and the idea seems to be that he is inclined to turn up his nose at his brother officers. I'm bound to say that I haven't observed this myself; still it's just as well to warn you at starting that that sort of thing is very bad form and is sure to be resented. So I hope, for your own sake, you won't go in for it."

Clarissa mildly disclaimed, on Guy's behalf and on her own, any desire to act in the manner described; but she was not greatly fascinated with Mrs. Antrobus, who, after putting a few direct, abrupt questions as to the state of Sir Robert Luttrell's and Mr. Dent's respective finances, concluded her visit by remarking:

"Well, I don't suppose you will be with us long; but I dare say you will get on all right, if you can manage to bear in mind that we consider ourselves as good as anybody."

Guy was much diverted by the report which was subsequently given to him of this rather formidable lady's warnings.

"So they suspect us of being haughty, do they ?" said he. "I am not sure that it isn't a useful sort of reputation to have—for you, I mean; because you probably won't care to be very intimate with these women. The men are as decent a lot of fellows as one could wish to meet. Perhaps I ought to dine at mess every now and then, though."

He took care to display sociability in that particular every guest-night, and it may be presumed that the sacrifice did not cost him any very serious amount of personal inconvenience. Popular Guy Luttrell had always been and was always sure to be ; while Mrs. Harvey, Mrs. Durand, and the rest of them soon found themselves sufficiently at ease in his wife's presence to chatter freely, after the manner of their kind, about their babies and about small garrison scandals.

To Clarissa they and their subjects of conversation were, it must be owned, altogether unimportant. She had at this time merged her identity in that of her husband, on whose account she was beginning to dream ambitious dreams, and whose retention of his present undistinguished position she thought, with Mrs. Antrobus, would probably not be protracted. Brave, soldierly, and gifted (as she had persuaded herself) with talents far exceeding the average, he might aspire to something a long way above the reach of the Major Harveys and the Captain Durands with whom he was for the moment associating. Already by anticipation she saw him conferring lustre upon an ancient name by rising to the rank of general in early life. Others, whose inferiority to him required no demonstration, had achieved this, and why not he ?

"But I don't think Captain Luttrell is a very keen soldier, is he ?" objected Mrs. Harvey, to whom Clarissa was encouraged, one day, to confide something of these visions of military glory. "His heart isn't in it, like the heart of my poor, dear old Jack, who is sure to be laid on the shelf before long."

Mrs. Harvey was a quiet, dowdy little woman, with a large family, a small income, and a sad, yet resigned, conviction that nobody in the world was quite so badly off as she and her Jack.

"I don't say so in a disparaging spirit," she hastened to add; "of course your husband has many interests in life besides soldiering, and it stands to reason that he will leave the army when he succeeds to his property, if not sooner. What is very serious earnest to us can only be play to him, you see."

Clarissa declared that she was certain Guy did not regard his profession in that light.

"Ah, well!" sighed the elder woman, wistfully, "he can afford to regard it in what light he pleases. If he chooses to take it in earnest, his father's influence, no doubt, will be powerful enough to do almost anything for him; but I should have thought, like most other young men of fortune —and I'm sure one can't blame them!—he did not regard anything as particularly serious except play."

To speak of Guy Luttrell as a young man of fortune was scarcely accurate; but it was only too true that he greatly preferred play to work, and there was one form of play to which he was more addicted than his wife had as yet had occasion to discover. Of this she was made aware, after a fashion which distressed her not a little, at a ball given by one of the cavalry regiments stationed in Aldershot at that time. She had been spending a most enjoyable evening and had danced a great deal with her husband, who had gladdened her heart by assuring her that he would never, if he could help it, dance with anybody else; but as there were one or two ladies present with whom it was quite imperative upon him to dance, he had left her for a time in the supper-room, and thus it was that a fragment of dialogue which ought to have been conducted in lower tones reached her ears. Two resplendent young officers, standing side by side and sharing a bottle of champagne, were discussing some third person, whose name did not immediately transpire.

"Oh yes; very good chap, but an awful gambler! Shouldn't wonder if he were to come a regular howler one of these fine days. Loses his money like a man, though; I must say that for him."

"Ah, so I hear. He was playing poker at our mess the other night and dropped a pretty tidy sum before he went home, I believe. It got too hot for me, I know. Didn't he have the name of being rather a thirsty soul, too, when he was in the Guards?"

"Well, yes; there was a row about it on one occasion, some years ago, I think. I forget exactly what happened; but he was over head and ears in debt at the time, and, what with one thing and another, I fancy he got a hint to go. However, he is supposed to have turned over a new leaf now; so I dare say he'll be all right."

"H'm! his father is hardish up, by all accounts."

"What, old Luttrell? Yes, very likely; but Master Guy has married a woman with a pot of money. If she's a sensible woman she'll put him on a liberal allowance and keep the key of the cellar."

"I'll be hanged if I'd allow my wife to treat me like that!"

"Oh, I expect you would, and I'm sure Luttrell will. Any woman could ride him in a snaffle bit—let alone a sensible one."

"For how long?"

"Well, until he met another woman, I suppose. But he isn't exactly a colt nowadays, and it will be his wife's own fault if she lets him get out of her hand."

The two good-humored calumniators—if calumniators they were—moved away, leaving a woman who was, unfortunately, far more sensitive than sensible to ruminate over their careless words. Clarissa was certainly not happy in the character of an involuntary eavesdropper, and now—as once before in the garden of the Château de Grancy—she lacked the requisite wisdom to disregard what she had had no business to hear. When she and her husband returned home, Guy, who could not help noticing how pale, silent, and depressed she was, implored her vainly for some little time to tell him what was the matter; but she could not go to sleep with such a heavy weight upon her mind, and she ended by relating the whole episode—not without tears.

For a moment Guy looked grave; but then, somewhat to her surprise and chagrin, he began to laugh.

"So you thought you had married a tippling gamester, did you?" said he. "Oh no; things aren't quite so bad as that, though I must plead guilty to having played poker with those fellows when I was asked and to having lost my money. It wasn't a very formidable sum, as far as I can remember, and you yourself can bear witness that I came home sober. But look here, Clarissa—rather than that you should cry about it, I'll cheerfully promise never to touch a card again. I don't much want to take the pledge, and I don't think it is exactly necessary; still, if you insist—"

Clarissa, seized by a sudden access of shame and remorse, jumped up and laid her finger upon his lips. "Don't say such things!" she exclaimed. "I knew that what those horrid men said couldn't be true, and I wouldn't for the world make you promise to give up a single one of your amusements; only—well, I suppose I ought not to have listened at all."

"It's a good rule not to listen when one's friends are being discussed," agreed Guy, smiling. "I always think I know as much about my friends as I want to know, and if there's more to be discovered, I'd rather find it out for myself than hear it from other people. One either trusts a man or one doesn't, you see. If one doesn't, he is hardly what you could call a friend, is he?"

Clarissa hung her head. "Have I behaved as if I distrusted you, Guy?" she asked, in a quivering voice.

"No, indeed you haven't, my love!" he exclaimed, taking her in his arms and kissing her. "You have trusted yourself to me, and I hope you will never have reason to repent of your bargain. Of course I am not as young as you are—I only wish I were !—and if I could begin my life over again I should leave undone a good many things that I have done ; but that's impossible, so there's no use in worrying about it. As for gambling and drink, you may make your mind easy ; I'm ready to forswear them both, if you wish."

" Oh, but I don't !" protested Clarissa ; " I never meant that."

" Well, then, I'll forswear excess. Now are you contented ?—and may we dismiss the subject ?"

She could not but reply gratefully and penitently in the affirmative. There was something more which she had thought of mentioning—something about Guy's alleged proneness to be led by women—but, after what had passed, she felt that it would be unworthy and humiliating to make further demands upon his forbearance. Besides, what could he have told her ? As he had said, one either trusts a man or one doesn't.

CHAPTER XI

SOME GOOD DAYS AND A BAD ONE

IT was in the month of October that Guy Luttrell and his wife left London for Brindisi on their way to join the Cumberland Rangers in Ceylon. Not altogether for nothing, even in these democratic days, is one the eldest son of a Cabinet Minister, and it had been found practicable to spare both Clarissa and her attentive husband the horrors of a troop-ship voyage. It might have been found practicable—or so, at any rate, Lady Luttrell had hoped—to spare them the trials of exile into the bargain ; but Mr. Dent had not appeared to understand certain thinly veiled hints to that effect, and had contented himself with handing his niece a check to defray the cost of the overland journey. Clarissa, for her part, did not dread exile, nor was she able to mingle her tears with those of her mother-in-law and Madeline when the time came to say farewell. Setting aside the circumstance that she wanted to see something of the world in a geographical as well as a social sense, she was still in that state of selfish beatitude which is apt to characterize the newly married, and which renders them, while it lasts, such extremely poor company for other people.

"Do you know," she said confidentially to Guy, when at length they stood, beneath a cloudless blue sky, upon the deck of the P. and O. steamer which was to conduct them to their destination, "I am rather glad to think that we have several years of foreign service before us. I feel as if I should have you more to myself in that far-away place than I should if you were within reach of all your gay friends at home."

"Well, if you're glad, I'm glad," he responded, cheerfully.

As a matter of fact, he thought that there was only one country worth living in, and, fond as he was of sport, would a thousand times rather have shot partridges and pheasants in England than elks and elephants in Ceylon; but he was of a contented, philosophical disposition, besides being anxious above all things to give pleasure to the woman whom he loved. For her sake he had given up a good deal, and was prepared to give up more, if need should be. In deference to her prejudices he had eschewed gambling and had almost eschewed backing horses; he was honestly desirous of proving himself a model husband, nor could anybody deny that his conduct, so far, had been above reproach. Consequently the withering sun of the Red Sea blazed down upon two happy mortals whom their fellow-passengers pronounced to be singularly unsociable, and who had no querulous complaints to address to the captain.

And when—a little to Clarissa's regret—there came an end to days and nights of steaming across the wide Indian Ocean and she obtained her first view of the exquisite island which was to be her temporary home, the last thing that could have entered her mind would have been to complain of such a destiny. There are, of course, people —and even a good many of them—who complain loudly of an enforced residence at Colombo; but then they know what the tropics are, and have ceased to be enchanted by sights, sounds, and scents which are full of wonder and delight for the new-comer. Clarissa, too, was to weary, in process of time, of perpetual summer—to gaze with languid indifference at tall, graceful palms, feathery bamboos, marvellous flowering shrubs, and gorgeous creepers, to sicken at the fragrant odors of the sunset hour, and to long for the gray skies, the keen air, and the comfortable coal fires of an island less favored by Nature. *Tout passe, tout lasse;* but a merciful Creator has hidden the future from us; and so, unless we are very unlucky indeed, we all get a fair share of good days in the course of our little lives.

Now, the days which Captain and Mrs. Luttrell spent in

setting up and garnishing a charming abode for themselves within easy distance of the barracks were altogether good days. Guy secured without difficulty (for the question of rent was not, after all, a very important one) a spacious, one-storied dwelling, situated in the so-called Cinnamon Gardens—a broad, flat expanse of many acres, covered with bushes of the shrub which, under the old Dutch rule, used to be jealously protected as a chief source of revenue, but which has ceased to be cultivated, now that government monopolies are no more. The house, surrounded by a wide, cool veranda, the pillars of which were concealed in luxuriant wreaths and festoons of climbing plants, satisfied Clarissa's soul; and if she expended a good deal of money in adding to its beauties, there was no great harm in that, seeing that a considerable balance still remained in her hands out of Uncle Tom's check.

"This is an improvement upon Aldershot, isn't it?" she exclaimed, exultantly, on the first evening when she and her husband dined together in their new abode, after quitting the rather noisy hotel where they had been sojourning; and Guy could not but agree that it was.

"If one is to be buried alive, one really couldn't wish for a prettier grave," he had the generosity to add.

But they were in no danger of being buried alive, and although Guy, with his limited notions of what constitutes society, would not perhaps have allowed that such a thing could exist in Ceylon, social intercourse was accorded to the young couple in doses almost too large to be conveniently swallowed. The governor and his wife, who had received letters from the home authorities, showed them much hospitality; other officials followed suit; what with polo, cricket matches, informal race-meetings, dinners and dances, Clarissa's engagement-book soon became so full that she began to sigh for rest and would fain have declined a few invitations.

"Well, I don't think it would be prudent to start doing that just yet," Guy said, when consulted upon the point. "We shall only make ourselves unpopular if we do, and it's a pity to be unpopular. Later on there may be reasonable excuses, you know."

There was going to be an excuse; of that the young wife was aware, and the thought of what was coming affected her nerves and her spirits sometimes. But as yet she had mentioned this to nobody but her husband, who made light of it, assuring her that it was the greatest mistake in the world to take time by the forelock in such cases. The fact was that he enjoyed seeing people, and she felt that it would be unpardonably selfish to condemn him to the life of solitude which would have better suited her own tastes.

Looking back—as she often did afterwards—upon those weeks and months of wellnigh uninterrupted gayety, she had difficulty in recalling the precise moment at which it began to dawn upon her that her tastes and Guy's were essentially dissimilar. Some differences of opinion, which could scarcely be called quarrels, she did remember. At the time she penitently attributed them—with reason, it may be—to an irritability of temper on her part which was something new to her and which she could not always control. It was certain that Guy was very patient and very forgiving. But he did not hesitate to leave her for a week at a time when an opportunity offered of joining in a shooting expedition; his leisure hours were chiefly spent in playing polo or educating a couple of young horses which he had bought; he could not make himself domestic, he could not pretend to take an interest in the books which she devoured so eagerly; still less could he discuss theology with her, as she sometimes essayed to lead him into doing. In the matter of religion Guy's notions were beautifully simple. He neither thought much about it nor practised it himself; but he was convinced that sceptics were a bad lot, while scepticism in women shocked him almost as much as downright immorality—possibly even a little more.

"You shouldn't let your mind run upon such questions," he said, reprovingly, to Clarissa; "once you start upon that line you can't tell where the deuce you'll stop. It would

look awfully bad if you gave up going to church just because there are some things that you can't understand.
If it comes to that, who *does* understand them ? Of course
I don't set up to be an authority; but—but there's the
Church, you know, and the early fathers, and all those
learned old chaps. Don't you think it's a little bit arrogant to assume that they have been telling lies for the last
eighteen hundred years or so ?"

There was no rejoinder to be made to so highly orthodox
a method of dealing with an incipient unbeliever, and from
that day forth Clarissa had to confide her doubts and per-
plexities to the birds, the flowers, and the waving trees that
stood her in stead of human company when escape from
human company was practicable. She loved her husband
as much as ever; but her respect and admiration for him
were, unfortunately, on the wane.

As time went on a lull supervened in the gayeties of
Colombo. The governor had gone up to Kandy, official
entertainments were at an end, and the excuse for retirement, of which mention has been made, had so far ceased
to be a secret to the ladies of the Cumberland Rangers that
Mrs. Luttrell was enabled, without giving offence, to absent herself from their daily gatherings on Galle Face, that
long and broad esplanade which the society of the place
frequents in the cool of the evening, and where great rollers,
thundering in from the Indian Ocean, bring fresh breezes
and a smell of the sea with them.

"Not that I consider it very wise of you," Mrs. Antrobus said, in her abrupt way, one day.

Despite her bluntness and occasional rudeness of manner,
Mrs. Antrobus was a kind-hearted woman, and Clarissa,
who had grown accustomed to her ways, was never very
sorry to see her marching up the garden, swinging her
sunshade upon a long forefinger.

"You see," the good lady went on, "I have had a considerable experience of men, and you mustn't mind my
telling you that the best of them want watching. As for
your husband, I think myself that he is a very good fel-

low; but anybody can see with half an eye that he is just the sort of man to get himself into scrapes when there are pretty women about. I dare say you wouldn't consider Mrs. Durand pretty—"

"Mrs. Durand!" interjected Clarissa, in accents of disdainful surprise.

"Oh, *I* don't call her pretty; but she's pretty enough for the purpose and silly enough for anything! Just now she has taken it into her empty little head that your husband admires her, and she is as pleased as Punch in consequence. Likewise she is laying herself out to attract him."

"Really she is most welcome," Clarissa declared, with her chin in the air.

"Well, then, my dear, she oughtn't to be. I don't say that this present flirtation is likely to lead to any harm; only if you let him begin he'll go on—mind that. Tell me to mind my own business, if you like—you won't offend me—but take the advice of a woman who has knocked about the world and kept her eyes open, and don't you be deterred by false pride from making rules while you have it in your power to make them. You can mould your husband now; you won't be able to mould him a year or two hence."

There might be some truth in that; but Clarissa could not condescend to profit by counsels which struck her as vulgar, coarse, and founded upon a complete misconception of the only attitude which a wife could assume with dignity. Colonel Antrobus, who was notoriously under the thumb of his authoritative spouse, was a submissive husband, no doubt; but a woman who respects herself does not care to have a submissive husband. If he cannot behave himself properly unless her eye is upon him, he must behave improperly; it is absolutely essential to their common happiness that she should be able to trust him, and Clarissa, as may be remembered, had made up her mind to trust Guy.

When she was once more alone, therefore, she contrived to laugh—though not very heartily—at the well-meant warning with which she had been favored. Mrs. Durand!—a common, flashy woman, who wore jewels in the daytime, addressed young subalterns by their surnames, without any prefix, and smoked cigarettes publicly in order that she might earn the proud distinction of being called fast!—it would indeed be a sorry compliment to Guy's taste to suppose him capable of being fascinated by such a charmer. She had half a mind to tell him, as a good joke, when he came in, of the susceptibility with which he was credited; but, upon second thoughts, she decided to say nothing about it. The joke was not such a very good one, after all.

Assuredly it was not in consequence of what Mrs. Antrobus had said that Clarissa was prevailed upon, on the following Sunday, to join a luncheon-party at Mount Lavinia which, as she was informed, was to be graced by Mrs. Durand's presence. Mount Lavinia, situated at a distance of some seven miles along the Galle road, is a favorite place of resort on the first day of the week with Colombo residents, and Guy mentioned casually, one evening, that he had promised to drive thither with "the Durands and one or two other cheery people."

"I wish you would come too," he added; "but I suppose there would be no use in asking you to do that."

There would not have been much use in so doing (for she dreaded the heat and fatigue that the excursion would entail) had he not seemed to take her refusal rather too much for granted. As it was, she was tempted—just by way of watching the effect of her reply upon him—to say, "Oh, I don't know; I think I should rather like it."

But, although she had not really intended to go, she could not back out of it when his face lighted up with unmistakable pleasure, and when he exclaimed, "That's first-rate! We'll put the bay pony in the cart, then, and drive over together, like Darby and Joan. You'd rather do that than go in the wagonette with the others, wouldn't you?"

It was, at all events, not unpleasant to be made aware of his own implied preference, and if Clarissa had not enjoyed that Sunday drive, she would have been hard to please. But she did enjoy it to the full, the conditions being in all respects as favorable as could be desired. The heat was not too oppressive; the way along the broad, red road, between the thundering surf and the still lagoon which adjoins Colombo, presented a series of stationary or moving pictures which gladdened the eye with their rich, varied coloring. The groves of cocoa-palms, the vivid green paddy-fields, the marvellous flowering trees—golden, scarlet, orange, and white; the graceful, feminine-looking Singhalese, walking bareheaded, their long, glossy hair gathered into a tight knot and fastened by a tortoise-shell comb; the turbaned Tamils; the palm-thatched carts, drawn by small, humped-necked bullocks—all these, if they had no longer the first charm of novelty for Clarissa, still sufficed to rejoice her heart.

"I remember," said she, "one day when I was at Haccombe Luttrell a groom passed us on the road, exercising a big chestnut mare of your father's. The mare was very fresh, and she stopped for a minute to kick so furiously that I made haste to scramble up a bank and get out of range of her heels. A laborer who was on the other side of the hedge popped his head up and stared. Then he turned to me, and, jerking his thumb towards the mare, remarked, with a grin, 'I reckon her's glad her's livin'.' Well, that is just how I feel now. I am glad I'm alive!"

Guy was delighted to hear it, and said so. A tropical climate did not produce quite that effect upon him, nor could he comprehend why beautiful scenery or brilliant colors should be exhilarating; but that his wife was enamoured of existence was all the better news because she had scarcely seemed to be so of late. He drew his whip across the pony's flanks, laughing contentedly.

"I knew it would do you all the good in the world to come out of your shell for a few hours," he remarked.

It was certainly doing her good; although she read what was in his mind, and realized, as she had recently learned to do, that she must suit her conversation to him if she wished

to spend a happy day. But that, for the moment, seemed
to be no such hard matter. Lovers—and lovers these two
still were—can always find one engrossing subject to talk
about, and the fact is that Guy and Clarissa talked about
little or nothing else while the fast-trotting little pony drew
them towards Mount Lavinia a long way in advance of the
heavier equipage which contained their fellow-excursionists.

When the wagonette drew up in front of the hotel, its
occupants found a lady who was in the best of good-humors
waiting to receive them. It must be owned that Clarissa
did not always exert herself to be agreeable to the Mrs.
Harveys and Mrs. Durands, with whom she had so little in
common; but on this occasion they profited by the good-
will which she entertained towards the world at large.
The luncheon-party proved a complete success, and Guy,
for his part, noted with some satisfaction that his wife was
doing her best to make it so.

The subsequent proceedings, unluckily, proved less successful and less satisfactory from Clarissa's point of view.
She had supposed that, after a reasonable delay for coffee
and cigarettes, she would be allowed to resume her seat in
the pony-cart; but it appeared that so speedy a return to
Colombo had never been contemplated by the organizers
of the jaunt. One by one—or, rather, two by two—the
lunchers strolled out of the room, Guy pairing off with
Mrs. Durand, and when Clarissa ventured upon some
tentative suggestion as to its being nearly time to make a
start, the lady whom she addressed exclaimed :

"Bless you, no !—not for the next three hours. We're
all going to sit upon the beach and throw stones into the
sea until the sun goes down. You aren't afraid of mala-
ria, are you ? I can lend you wraps, if you forgot to bring
any."

It was a bore, but there was no help for it; so Clarissa
accepted the escort of Major Harvey, a dull, lean, lanky
man with a very long mustache, and walked down in his
company to the beach, where neither Guy nor Mrs. Du-

rand was to be seen. There, with patient impatience, she
sat for what seemed to her an interminable length of time,
while her companion confided to her some of the sorrows
of an impoverished married man. Major Harvey, she
gathered from his own account of himself, had once been a
bright ornament of society, a distinguished sportsman and
athlete, and (as was only to be expected) something of a
lady-killer; but now, alas! he had neither money, leisure,
nor time to do himself justice. Everything had to be sacrificed to the children, who were "tumbling over one another
like rabbits." Mrs. Luttrell might take his word for it that
precious few men would be such fools as to marry if they
could only foresee what awaited them.

"I should have thought that Mrs. Harvey had at least as
much to complain of as you can have," Clarissa remarked
at last.

But indeed she was scarcely listening to him, and had
not yet acquired the habit, which in after-years became a
second nature to her, of plunging into the fray on behalf
of her own sex upon the slightest provocation. What preoccupied and annoyed her was that, although, as has been
mentioned, the party had split up into couples, and although some pronounced flirtations were being carried on
in her immediate vicinity, Guy and Mrs. Durand had apparently thought fit to seek a more sequestered spot in
which to exchange ideas. She was not jealous—how could
she possibly be jealous of that woman!—but she felt that
Guy was making himself and her a little ridiculous; nor
was her vexation diminished by certain jocose comments
upon his prolonged absence which presently began to make
themselves heard.

However, there was worse to come. The sun was upon
the point of sinking, the brief twilight would soon give
place to night, the wagonette and the pony-cart were drawn
up in readiness with lighted lamps; yet the assembled company was still short by two of its proper strength. Messen-
gers were despatched in quest of the truants, and returned,
having failed to discover them; everybody was showing

8

signs of impatience, while one person was becoming seriously uneasy. Only Captain Durand, to whom such experiences were perhaps no novelty, remarked philosophically that he was sure it would be all right.

"Luttrell will drive Katie in the pony-cart, if Mrs. Luttrell doesn't mind coming with us."

"I really think it would be best," said Mrs. Harvey. "I don't want to hurry anybody, but I am afraid I *must* get back to the children, and it isn't as if there could be the least cause for alarm. The pony goes so much faster than these poor old horses that Captain Luttrell will be certain to overtake us soon."

Clarissa, with a smile upon her lips and something not unlike rage in her heart, assented; and a very miserable drive back to Colombo she had. Her fellow - passengers, it was true, refrained from humorous remarks; but that scarcely mended matters, since it was obvious that they did so out of sheer pity for her. Moreover, the pony-cart did not catch up the wagonette.

Clarissa had reached home, and was noting the near approach of the usual dinner - hour with mingled wrath and apprehension, when the crunching of wheels upon the gravel made her aware that she might safely indulge the former sentiment, if she chose. Guy hurried in, full of apologies and looking very like a naughty schoolboy.

"So awfully sorry you had to drive back with those wearisome people! I'm afraid you must have been cursing me. The fact is that we walked on and on, without thinking of looking at our watches, and then—"

"It does not in the least signify," interrupted Clarissa, coldly; "I can quite understand your having forgotten what time it was in such charming and refined company."

"Come, Clarissa, you surely don't think that I prefer Mrs. Durand's company to yours!"

"I am afraid the others must have thought so, and that was not very pleasant. However, nothing of the kind will occur again; for your excursions will be made without me in future. So, as I say, it doesn't in the least signify."

Her intention, of course—whether she knew it or not—was to provoke one of those quarrels, followed by an explanation and a reconciliation, which all women love and all men abhor; the very last thing for which she was prepared was that her husband should ignore the challenge. Yet that was just what he did. With a half-deprecating glance at her, he murmured something about running off to change his clothes, and promptly suited the action to the word. On his return he seemed to have forgotten that anything was amiss; throughout the dinner he talked pleasantly, if somewhat more volubly than usual, and immediately afterwards he departed for the barracks, whither, as he alleged, duty summoned him.

Clarissa, as soon as she was alone, sank down into a chair, covered her face with her hands, and sobbed bitterly. It was no exaggeration to say that she would have submitted to insult and cruelty rather than to such a method of treatment. All was over, she felt—the dream was at an end. Possibly Guy loved Mrs. Durand, possibly he loved nobody: what was beyond a doubt was that he no longer loved his wife, or he never could have behaved as he had done.

CHAPTER XII

SEVERAL MISTAKES ARE MADE

SIR ROBERT LUTTRELL, who was a man of experience, had often been heard to declare that anything on earth is better than a row; and possibly his convictions in that respect had been transmitted, together with other desirable and undesirable inheritances, to his eldest son. At all events, Guy would have thought himself a very great fool if he had made any further allusion to an unfortunate occurrence which Clarissa appeared to have dismissed from her mind. In reality there are, of course, exceptions to every rule. Thunder-storms clear the air, wars prepare the way for prolonged periods of peace; even domestic broils may be preferable to polite estrangements. On the other hand, it is not to be denied that those who value liberty and a quiet life can very often obtain both by obstinate, selfish good-humor, and from the day of that ill-fated expedition to Mount Lavinia Guy at least enjoyed the privilege of being his own master.

The privilege was one which, as a matter of fact, he did enjoy and make the most of. He was not much at home; he spent a good many hours in the society of Mrs. Durand, who rather amused him; he soon managed to persuade himself that Clarissa liked solitude, and was as well satisfied with their actual mode of life as he was.

"I hope you don't find this sort of thing awfully slow," he said to her once, with a solicitude which he not unfrequently displayed, and which, if he had only known it, was infinitely more distressing to her than the neglect to which she was becoming habituated.

"Oh no," she answered; "I have plenty of books to read, thank you."

Guy seldom opened a book. Lazy though he was by temperament, it was incomprehensible to him that history, philosophy, poetry, or fiction could form any substitute for an active share in the drama of existence. Still he was generously willing to make every allowance for diversity of tastes, and he deemed it not unnatural that, under all the circumstances, his wife should feel unequal to social exertions.

For the rest, she had a few friends : among others, Lady Brook, the governor's wife, a quiet, delicate, rather melancholy woman, the greater part of whose life had been spent in colonies, which she did not like, and in enforced separation from her children, whom she adored. This middle-aged, prematurely gray-haired lady, having taken a fancy to Clarissa, asked her, soon after the new year, to spend a week at Kandy, where the governor was then residing, and Guy (whose military duties detained him at Colombo) joined with Mrs. Luttrell's medical attendant in urging her to accept the invitation. A little change was just what she wanted, they both declared. So, although she herself was of opinion that what she wanted was not so much a little as a great change, and that the latter was unobtainable, she yielded to their entreaties and went.

The Pavilion, as the governor's residence at Kandy is called, is a less spacious and imposing edifice than the Queen's House at Colombo; large entertainments are less obligatory there, and as Sir George Brook was away on a tour to the more distant districts of the island during Clarissa's stay, she had a quiet, pleasant time of it in the company of her hostess. With the place itself she was enchanted—as indeed all who have seen it must be. Situated some two thousand feet above the level of the sea, it can boast of a climate in many respects superior to that of Colombo, while retaining the luxuriant tropical vegetation in which Clarissa had not ceased to delight. The slim, lofty palms, the green, wooded hills, the purple mountains in the distance, and the red-roofed Bhuddist temples, reflected on the placid surface of the lake, near to which the Pavilion stands, did not fail to charm her; every turn of the winding roads drew a fresh cry of admiration from her during her drives with Lady Brook, who smiled rather sadly and said:

"Yes, it is very lovely; but I often think how gladly I would exchange it all for some grubby little house in South Kensington. In a few more years, I am thankful to say, George will be able to take his pension, and then, I hope, we shall never stir out of England again."

"But won't he be rather sorry to have come to the end of his career?" Clarissa asked.

"Ah, there it is! Perhaps he will enter Parliament, though; and then, you see, he is not as young as he was. For a young man, of course, it is everything to have a career—and to be interested in it. Otherwise they are so apt to get into mischief."

"I suppose they are," agreed Clarissa, pensively.

She had already discovered—and the discovery was most distasteful to her—that Guy was not particularly interested in his career. It might be that he had also got into mischief, or was likely to do so. If Lady Brook had meant to convey something in the nature of a hint (and very probably she had, being acquainted with the Luttrell family, and being likewise of necessity acquainted with the gossip of the community which her husband ruled), she was too discreet to over-emphasize it. Shy by nature, and trained to excessive caution by her many years of official life, she would have felt it impossible to offer advice to the young wife, save in general terms.

In general terms, however, she took occasion more than once to state what, according to her notions, a wife's duties were. She was quite old-fashioned; her notions differed completely from those which her hearer was gradually forming; her standpoint as regarded the relations between her sex and the other was one of convinced and contented inferiority. But she was so kind, so simple, so far from presuming to dictate or rebuke, that no one could wish to dispute with her. Moreover, there were other subjects upon which she was able to speak with authority; and Clarissa, who was rather badly in need of a friend at the time, was thankful enough to have found one whose dispositions were thoroughly maternal. Her visit to Kandy was prolonged from a week to a fortnight—Guy, whose permission was asked by post, offering no objection—and when she returned to Colombo she was in noticeably improved health and spirits. She even brought back with her a stock of good resolutions; for she had been a good deal influenced, if not exactly convinced, by the precepts of her gentle hostess. Without admitting that woman's sole mission in life is to bring up children and study the comfort of a husband, she nevertheless perceived that woman's happiness is in a large measure dependent upon her tacit adoption of some such system.

Now, Guy Luttrell, to do him justice, was the easiest man in the world to live with, and it may be added that he asked nothing better than to live upon terms of amity and affection with his wife. Any little sacrifice that he could have made to please her—such as, for example, the relinquishment of his intimacy with Mrs. Durand—would have been cheerfully incurred; still one does not (or, at any rate, he did not) make sacrifices without being asked to do so; so that, in the course of the months that followed, Clarissa found more than one opportunity of trying her good resolutions by a practical test. Upon the whole, however, those months were not unpleasant to her; nor, during the last weeks of the period, had she to complain of any lack of care or sympathy.

When, early in May, her baby was born, and mother and infant were pronounced by the doctor to be going on as well as possible, Guy drew a long breath of relief. He had been more apprehensive than he had cared to avow, and now that his mind had been set at rest, he could not permit considerations of petty economy to deter him from despatching needlessly diffuse telegrams to anxious relatives at home. The anxious relatives would perhaps have

been rather better pleased if he had been able to announce
the birth of an heir to the family honors and estates ; but
he himself was very well satisfied with his little daughter,
to whom in due course was given her grandmother's name
of Antoinette, and whom he did not find nearly as repulsive as the generality of the human young. Soon after
Clarissa's recovery, which was a speedy one, it was thought
advisable that she should be removed to a less relaxing climate ; and Lady Brook, who was deeply interested in babies
and mothers, having kindly offered the use of the governor's cottage at Nuwara Eliya to Mrs. Luttrell, Guy obtained a few weeks' leave in order to escort his charges
thither.

There cannot be many places within the tropics where a
complete change of climate is so easily obtainable as in
Ceylon, or where the ascent to a height of six thousand feet
above the sea can be accomplished in a luxurious railway-
carriage. The travellers reached their journey's end to
find themselves in a fresh, verdant, mountainous district,
the temperature and scenery of which might have reminded
them of Scotland in summer but for the masses of scarlet
and crimson rhododendrons which were just then in full
glory. They were even likely erelong — so the servants at
the Queen's Cottage assured them—to renew acquaintance
with a genuine Scotch mist ; for the southwest monsoon
was nearly due, and rainy days are the rule rather than the
exception at Nuwara Eliya. For the time being, however,
the skies were clear, the air was crisp and bracing, and the
pretty, English-looking garden had already nooks and corners admirably adapted to the requirements of a convalescent. Clarissa was very happy there with her baby and
her temporarily domesticated husband, who had few temptations to quit her side. At certain seasons of the year this
high sanatorium is thickly populated, and the inhabitants
entertain one another with much vigor ; but just then everybody had gone down to Kandy or Colombo ; even sport
was not to be had in the neighborhood without preparatory
arrangements which Guy was too indolent to undertake,

and so the Luttrells practically had the place to themselves, with undisturbed enjoyment of their own company. It was a sort of pause—a truce, as it were—in their lives, which one of them at odd moments felt to be only a truce, but which, for all that, was restful and delightful.

When at length the rain began to fall it descended in such earnest that for three days in succession Clarissa was confined to the house; although Guy paddled out in a mackintosh and shooting-boots, because, as he said, one really couldn't sit in-doors from morning to night.

"Of course you can't," his wife agreed, compassionately, "and I don't see how you can stay any longer here, either. It is different for me; I have baby, and books to read, and letters to write; and Lady Brook told me I might use the house as long as I pleased. So I think, if you don't mind, I should like to remain where I am for another week or ten days. But you must go back to Colombo and—and amuse yourself."

He protested a little, but his scruples were not very difficult to overcome. It would certainly be a pity for Clarissa to leave her present quarters prematurely, seeing that she had derived so much benefit from the change to the hills, and that the baby appeared to be thriving. On the other hand, he supposed he ought to be thinking of a return to the regiment. Not, to be sure, that he was very much wanted, so far as the discharge of routine duty went; but a *gymkhana*, he explained, was to be held at Colombo in a few weeks' time, and he had promised to ride in it.

"And I fancy I shall about win, if I can begin schooling the pony at once. At present he knows nothing at all."

"Oh, you are not going to ride one of your own, then?" asked Clarissa.

"No, not one of my own; he belongs to—to another fellow," Guy answered, rather hurriedly.

What would have been the use of telling her that the pony was the property of Mrs. Durand? She might not have liked it if he had, and they had been getting on so comfortably of late without any mention of Mrs. Durand's

name. So Guy departed on the morrow, and Clarissa was
left to her baby, her books, and her meditations—which
latter were cheerful or the reverse, in accordance with the
mood in which she chanced to be. She had wit enough
to perceive that, by a little judicious closing of the eyes
and by acquiescence in the waste of her husband's career,
she might lead as happy a life as falls to the lot of most
women; but at the bottom of her heart she was becoming
more and more conscious that she would be able to do
neither the one nor the other. Consequently, there seemed
to be breakers ahead.

An occasional fine day, sandwiched in between many wet
ones, prevented her from growing weary of her solitude,
and a reluctance to resume regular habits would probably
have detained her indefinitely at Nuwara Eliya if Lady
Brook had not expressed a wish by post that she should return to Colombo.

"I am sure," that kind and sagacious lady wrote, "you
have been long enough alone now, and I think you ought
to see our *gymkhana,* in which your husband, I am told,
is to take part. Besides, I have something to say to you
which may concern both you and him."

A few days later Clarissa, having regretfully discarded
the warm English gowns which she had been wearing, and
having resumed a garb more suited to the steamy heat of
the Singhalese capital, called at the Queen's House, where
she received the communication which Lady Brook had
been instructed not to commit to paper. The Governor-
General of India, it appeared, would shortly be in want of
a new aide-de-camp, and Sir George Brook had reason to
believe that he could secure the berth for Captain Luttrell,
should the latter care to accept it. There would be drawbacks, no doubt; but these, in the opinion of Sir George
and Lady Brook, would be more than counterbalanced by
contingent advantages.

"It is not as if there could be any question of your being separated from your child," Lady Brook said; "she is,
fortunately, far too young for that to be necessary. And

Sir George thinks that this appointment would give your husband opportunities of getting on which he could never hope to obtain while he remains with his regiment."

In short, Clarissa was urged to use her influence with Guy, whose consent to act in furtherance of his own interests seemed, for some reason or other, to be considered doubtful. Lady Brook was kindly and affectionate, but scarcely explicit. She told her young friend how sorry she would be to lose her, and how much she hoped that they might meet again in England; she did not tell her—how could she?—what Sir George, a rather bluff, peremptory personage, had said upon the subject—"The fellow had better be got out of the place; he's doing no good here. Running after some woman, I hear, and not unlikely to make a fool of himself and bring about a scandal. It wouldn't be the first time, you know. Probably he is too lazy to jump at a chance which most men would be glad enough to have; but I should think you might do some good by having a little talk with his wife."

Clarissa was somewhat mystified, divining that there was more than met the eye in this sudden eagerness for Guy's promotion; but her own slumbering ambition on his behalf was awakened, and she readily undertook to convey to him the informal intimation with which she was charged.

"Not good enough, my dear," was the unexpected reply that she received from her husband that evening, after giving him a full account of Sir George and Lady Brook's benevolent designs. "I have done A.D.C. work more than once, and I know only too well what it is. A bachelor may stand it, and even enjoy it, for a time, if he's young enough: a married A.D.C. is a sort of contradiction in terms — as I suspect you would be the first to discover, supposing that I were such an ass as to take this billet. But I'm not."

"You must not think of me at all in the matter," protested Clarissa, eagerly; "what can a little temporary discomfort or inconvenience signify? My one wish is that you should rise in your profession, and they say you are

sure to do that by getting upon the Governor-General's
staff."

"Do they, really? How very little they must know
about it! To begin with, I haven't passed the Staff Col-
lege; secondly, no amount of backstairs influence could
shove me into one of those appointments which crowds of
more capable men are tearing and rending one another to
seize; thirdly and lastly, I really don't care a pin about
rising in my profession."

"I think you should be ashamed to say that!" said Clarissa, flushing suddenly.

"Ah, my dear girl, you are ambitious and I am not;
that is the difference between us. But even if I were as
ambitious and unscrupulous as—shall we say the majority
of successful soldiers?—I shouldn't advance in the slightest degree towards the rank of field-marshal by transport-
ing you and the baby to Calcutta or Simla. No; I think
we will leave well alone. Ceylon is not Paradise, I grant
you; still there are worse places, and, after all, we aren't
going to end our days here. If you can stand it for another year or two, so can I."

She was as unable to shake his resolution as she was to
make him lose his temper; although, truth to tell, she said
some things, in the course of the discussion which followed,
that would have tried the tempers of most men. He was
amused by her vehemence, he was flattered by the exaggerated estimate which she had formed of his military capacities; but—he did not want to go to India, he was not
ambitious, and there was an end of it.

"One would think that you had some special reason for
wishing to stay in Ceylon!" she exclaimed, at length.

He did not look at all guilty; he did not seem to understand (nor in fact did he understand) what she meant; but
when, at the *gymkhana* on the following day, she saw him
win a race very cleverly on Mrs. Durand's pony, and when
she had to listen to the audible comments of Mrs. Antrobus and other ladies round about her, certain nascent suspicions of hers received ample confirmation. Before the

day was over she was sent for by the governor's wife, who asked :

" Well, have you spoken to Captain Luttrell ? Would he be willing to go ?"

" Yes, I have spoken to him," answered Clarissa, quietly ; "but he is not willing to go. He thinks we are very well where we are."

" But you know, my dear," remonstrated Lady Brook, after a brief scrutiny of her neighbor, who was peering with short-sighted eyes at the paddock, where Mrs. Durand could be discerned in animated conversation with Captain Luttrell, " I am afraid that is rather a mistake."

" I dare say it is," Clarissa agreed ; " only there is never much use in warning people that they are making mistakes, is there ? I have made mistakes myself, in spite of having been duly warned."

She might have added that she was likely to make a good many more ; but, not having carried self-knowledge quite to that pitch, she only expressed her gratitude to Lady Brook and the governor for their well-meant intentions, and began in a vague way to formulate inward intentions of her own which would have astonished Guy beyond measure had they been imparted to him.

CHAPTER XIII

RAOUL DE MALGLAIVE

SOMETIMES, as everybody is aware, great events take place and complete changes are brought about within a few months; sometimes nothing particular happens during a much longer period. At any rate, there are years, and even successive years, when the ceaseless work of time is carried on so imperceptibly that middle-aged people are apt to doubt whether it is being carried on at all. Young people, of course, can hardly add so large a number as three to the tale of their years without consciousness of having taken vast strides towards the grave; but Sir Robert and Lady Luttrell, sitting side by side on the terrace of the Château de Grancy, one mild spring afternoon, neither looked nor felt much older than when we saw them last on Guy's wedding-day, three years before. Their history, like that of the country which one of them had been doing his best to serve, had been agreeably uneventful; and if Sir Robert had intermittent worries now, he had had intermittent worries then also. As a matter of fact, his financial situation had altered considerably for the worse; but he only thought about his financial situation when he could not help it.

"So," said he, handing back to his wife a letter which she had given him to read, "they will be in England again almost as soon as we are. Dear me! it seems only the other day that they left."

Lady Luttrell sighed. "Yes; and yet they may have had time to become unrecognizable. Not Guy—he sounds just the same, and I am sure he will be just the same; but sometimes I am a little frightened about Clarissa."

"Frightened about her or frightened of her?" Sir Robert asked.

"Both, perhaps. She is so self-willed and, in many ways, so different from the rest of the world! Her letters tell me nothing; but she is more communicative with Madeline, and she seems to have put ideas about marriage into the child's head which I am not at all sure that I like. And now that she has five thousand pounds a year of her own to do what she pleases with—"

"Ah! that is serious, no doubt. I was delighted when Dent told me that her fortune reached that figure; still, when one remembers that very ill-advised measure the Married Women's Property Act, and when one thinks of what an extremely annoying thing it would be for Guy to lose five thousand pounds a year, one understands your alarm. But I gather that they are perfectly good friends now. That silly quarrel, a year or two ago, about some officer's wife to whom Guy was supposed to have been too attentive—as if he weren't sure to be attentive to every woman who crossed his path!—has quite blown over, has it not?"

"Oh yes, that has quite blown over," Lady Luttrell answered. "Clarissa was altogether in the wrong, and I dare say she is ashamed now of having talked about anything so ridiculous as a separation. I certainly shall not allude to it when we meet. But what I heard of her from dear Lady Brook, who was a most kind friend to her while Sir George was governor of the island, makes me a little uneasy. I should not so much mind her being irreligious—"

"You wouldn't, eh?"

"No; because heretics, after all, have no real religion to lose, and there is more hope of bringing an unbeliever than a self-satisfied Anglican, like Paul, to the only true faith. But these notions which she seems to have taken up about the rights or wrongs—I can't remember which it is—of women may get her and all of us into trouble, I am afraid."

"I don't see why they should. You won't accuse her of differing from the rest of the world in that respect, anyhow. It is quite the custom nowadays to entertain such notions—and nobody is a penny the worse. Human nature remains what it always has been and always will be; social necessities continue, and will always continue, to demand very much the same code of laws. Why shouldn't Clarissa amuse herself, like the others, by talking nonsense? I dare say it keeps her out of worse mischief. Added to which, I take it that Guy has no objections."

Lady Luttrell was not so sure of that. It did not seem to her certain that Guy's patience—which she believed to have been sorely tried—would hold out forever, and what she knew of her son led her to fear that he would hesitate less than his duty to his family required him to do about sacrificing £5000 a year. What could not be denied or doubted was that Captain Luttrell and his wife had failed to hit it off together. It was all very well to say that they were good friends; but would they remain friends now that they were about to return to England, and that the fortune of one of them would perforce render the position of the other, as captain in a line regiment, somewhat anomalous? Clarissa, in short, was mistress of the situation, and it was, in Lady Luttrell's opinion, a most undesirable thing that so young a woman should be mistress of any situation.

"I wish the poor dear little boy had not died!" she sighed. "It was so dreadfully sad, their losing him just after his birth!"

"Well, yes; but not so sad as if he had lived for a year or two," said Sir Robert, "and one may anticipate that there will be another boy—or other boys. Meanwhile, there is Netta, whom you ought to be longing to embrace."

"Of course I am longing to embrace her, dear child! Still she isn't quite the same thing as a grandson. For obvious reasons, not quite the same thing to us, and not quite the same thing to her parents, for reasons which I am sure you wouldn't understand."

"I am afraid I hardly follow you, my dear," answered Sir Robert, with a slight shrug of his shoulders.

It did not, in truth, occur to him that, given certain

circumstances, a woman will sacrifice herself for the sake of a son, but not for that of a daughter. He knew that Guy's chance of ever taking up his residence at Haccombe Luttrell was but a slender one; he did not know—as his wife did—that Clarissa had more than once given expression to subversive views respecting the sanctity of the marriage tie, and he was less eager than he might have been under happier conditions to see a healthy grandson progressing towards maturity. For the rest, he hated few things so much as contemplation of the future, and he changed the subject by inquiring:

"What has become of Madeline?"

"I thought you knew," answered Lady Luttrell, "that she had gone out riding with a large party of them—M. de Larrouy, young De Malglaive, and I forget who else."

"And no chaperon?"

"I believe there is a national chaperon, though her name does not come back to me at this moment. But, as far as the management of horses is concerned, Madeline can take better care of herself than anybody else could take of her."

"That may be; but I should have thought that a girl with eyes like hers—not to mention her nose, mouth, and chin—might have required a little supervision in matters not connected with the management of horses."

Lady Luttrell made an eloquent gesture. "What would you have? I cannot keep her under lock and key; I cannot get upon the back of a horse myself; and, supposing the worst to come to the worst, Raoul de Malglaive is rich, or will be. I really don't think that we risk very much by allowing the child to enjoy herself in the way that gives her the most enjoyment."

"It is the very deuce," observed Sir Robert, musingly, "to have a Roman Catholic daughter! There are so few Englishmen of means and position who belong to what you call the only true faith. Yet there are some, and I wonder that you haven't begun to fix your gaze upon them. Surely young De Malglaive does not realize your conception of a brilliant *parti!*"

9

"Oh, I only mentioned him because, as far as I can remember, there is nobody else who could possibly be dangerous. And he is not really dangerous at all. From what his mother tells me, he has been, and still is, a *viveur ;* he will not marry for a good many years to come, and when he does he will marry somebody of her selection. As for Madeline, she is imbued with Clarissa's ideas—which, they say, are the modern ideas. They are ridiculous, if you like; but they will at least preserve her from dreaming of falling in love with a dissolute Frenchman."

"I am delighted to hear it," answered Sir Robert. "Come, *ma mie*, let us go in-doors to our tea, and be thankful that we were born such a long time ago. We may have been fools in our youth, but I cannot think that we were ever quite so idiotic as the young men and women of to-day."

One of the young women of to-day, in the person of the beautiful Miss Luttrell, was at that moment cantering over the *coteaux* near the village of Jurançon in the company of a young man who differed less from his progenitors than she did from hers. Raoul de Malglaive, during the comparatively brief space of time which has been mentioned, had developed from a raw boy into a terribly experienced and rather melancholy man of the world. In the matter of refined vice no surprises remained possible for him, nor much excitement ; he had seen and learned what almost all young Frenchmen and not a few young Englishmen of his rank see and learn ; he had acquired a reputation of which he was not particularly proud, and with which, oddly enough, his strict old mother was not precisely dissatisfied. By her way of thinking, a De Malglaive owed it to himself and his ancestors to earn a reputation of some kind, and every De Malglaive whom she could remember had left the record of a stormy youth behind him. It was the family tradition to bid adieu to youth and storms at the proper season, and she had no doubt that Raoul would prove faithful to it erelong by suing for the hand of the suitable young lady whom she already had in her mind's eye. But among the suitable young ladies (for there were several of them) Miss Madeline Luttrell was not included. Beauty, Madame de Malglaive may have thought, is a questionable advantage in a wife; fortune is not to be despised, and foreign blood is likely to prove a serious drawback. If poor, dear Antoinette Luttrell—of whose pecuniary circumstances her old friend was quite well informed—was contemplating anything of that sort, disappointment awaited her; an Anglo-French alliance did not commend itself favorably to Madame de Malglaive.

Her son, however, dutiful though he was, and something of a fatalist into the bargain, was not to be trusted quite so implicitly, not to say disdainfully, as this imperious lady trusted him. The recent renewal of his intimacy with Madeline, whom he remembered as a mere child, and whose striking beauty astonished him almost as much as the ease and freedom of her conversational style, had brought to him a multitude of sensations so complicated and unprecedented in his experience that he was half afraid to analyze them. That she had been living and growing while he had been similarly occupied in Paris and elsewhere was a matter of course, no doubt; but it is always a little surprising to those who have grown up to find that their contemporaries have not remained at a standstill during their absence. And so, riding alongside of her in the waning light of that still afternoon—the remainder of the company being some hundred yards or so ahead—it came naturally enough to him to remark, with a faint sigh:

"You are not what you used to be, mademoiselle."

The observation was directly provoked by something that she had just said about her sister-in-law, but the thoughts which gave rise to it had a somewhat wider significance.

"None of us, except M. de Larrouy, are what we used to be," answered the girl, laughing. "M. de Larrouy, I am sure, will still be leading cotillons when I am purchasing spectacles and thinking about marrying my daughters; but other people have to change with the times. You yourself, for example—you are no longer the shy

young man who was so grateful to poor Clarissa for dancing
with him, are you ?"

Raoul, with a slight smile, admitted that he had ceased
to suffer from *mauvaise honte.* " But why do you call Mrs.
Luttrell 'poor' Clarissa ?" he inquired.

" Have I not been telling you all this time ? She is to
be pitied ; she is altogether in the right ; she is not happy,
and I can see by her letters, though she never says it in
so many words, that Guy is to blame for her unhappiness.
When she comes home we shall hear more, perhaps ; but
I suppose the truth is that Guy is like other men."

" You would prefer him to differ from other men, then ?"
said Raoul, interrogatively.

He understood what she meant ; but it seemed to him
so strange that a young lady should converse upon such
subjects, and the mingled candor and ignorance with which
she had already alluded to them had such a queer sort of
fascination for him that he affected bewilderment for the
sake of leading her on.

" It is not a question of what I should prefer," she answered. " When I last saw my brother I was still in the
school-room, and I confess that at that time he realized my
ideal of what a man ought to be. I am not sure that he
would realize it now, and I am quite sure that he does not
realize Clarissa's ideal. Did you ever hear our English
proverb, 'What is sauce for the goose is sauce for the
gander'? Clarissa has taken that as her motto."

" It is a device which may lead her into numerous combats," M. de Malglaive remarked, with his grave smile.

" It is not the thought of combats that is likely to alarm
her. Also, in our language, 'fight' rhymes with 'right.'
You, of course, are on the side of the men—you may even
have excellent reasons for being on their side—but you will
admit that the two sexes are not treated with equal justice.
Why should you be allowed to do, and perhaps admired
for doing, what is considered utterly disgraceful in us ?"

The audacity of the question was atoned for by the manner of its utterance. This young girl, with her violet eyes,

her dark hair, her creamy complexion, and her perfectly modelled figure, was so lovely that she had a right to say what she pleased; and if her speeches sometimes sounded rather startling to French ears, the innocence and good faith with which they were made were obvious. That, however, did not make it any easier to reply to them, and M. de Malglaive was fain to fall back upon time-worn generalities. Men were men; women were angelic or diabolic, as the case might be; he feared that if Mrs. Luttrell proposed to inaugurate a social revolution, she would incur some unpleasant experiences without attaining her object.

"It is true that I do not know how much or how little she may have to complain of."

"Nor do I," Madeline confessed; "but I know—because she is always telling me so in her letters—that she thinks there ought to be no difference between men and women, and that there would not be any difference if men had not made laws for their own advantage. The divine law, she says, is the same for all."

"But I understood that she had discarded divine authority."

"Not altogether. She has discarded Christianity, I am afraid; but other people, who continue to call themselves Christians, may have done that, perhaps, without having had the honesty to say so."

Raoul de Malglaive, who presumed that this allusion was meant for him, rode on for fifty yards or so in silence.

"My mother says," he remarked at length, "that it is possible to be a very good Christian and yet to neglect the practice of religion. It might be more honest to tell her that I have doubts about the miracles of Lourdes; but that would make her very unhappy, and, when all is said, how do I know that she is mistaken? Will you take me for a profound hypocrite if you see me kneeling by her side before the Grotto to-morrow?"

The girl turned her head a little to scrutinize her questioner. He was very handsome, and he sat his fidgety chestnut mare well. His clear olive complexion, his large, soft brown eyes, and his somewhat sad cast of countenance did not seem to belong either to a hypocrite or to a debauchee; yet, if certain informants of hers were to be believed, he had assuredly proved himself no saint.

"You will please your mother by kneeling down, and you cannot do much harm to yourself or anybody else," she answered. "You might even profit by being in that attitude to ask for what I am sure you must want."

"Oh, if I were to ask for what I wanted, and if, by a miracle, I were to get it," returned the young man, laughing, "a very costly *ex voto* would soon be added to the collection of the Blessed Virgin. But you mean," he continued, becoming grave again, "that what I want is faith. Happy those who possess it! You are of that number, are you not, mademoiselle?"

He put the question with a certain subdued eagerness, for he had all a Frenchman's horror of freethinking women, and he was proportionately relieved to hear her reply, tranquilly:

"I do not even know what doubt means. It seems to me that if I ceased to be a Catholic, I should cease to be myself."

Raoul's sigh was expressive rather of satisfaction than of regret. He was half inclined to beg that, since she had that happy certitude, she would remember one who was less fortunate in her prayers, when she saved him from the risk of appearing ridiculous, which, in common with the majority of his compeers, he dreaded beyond everything, by asking:

"But what is it that you want so much?"

He could not possibly tell her; he had only just begun to tell himself, and he shrank from even hinting at a secret of which he felt sure that he had not the faintest suspicion. The advent of M. de Larrouy, who came trotting back to meet the couple, relieved him, however, from the necessity of making any reply.

M. de Larrouy, brisk and energetic as of yore, had instructions to give relating to the expedition to Lourdes which he had organized for the following day, and in which a large number of persons less pious than Madame de Malglaive were to take part. Some would go by rail; some by road, in a *"breack à quatre chevaux";* a few had expressed their intention of riding the whole way. But, as the distance there and back would be little less than fifty miles, so much fatigue and so early a start could not be recommended to Miss Luttrell. "Our young friend here, whose cavalry training has accustomed him to live in the saddle, can please himself."

Raoul observed that he was at home for a holiday and that he was not desirous of riding his only horse to a standstill. The break would suit him very well, and he ventured to recommend it to Miss Luttrell, as preferable to a hot, dusty railway-carriage.

"As you like, *mon garçon,*" the cheery little Vicomte replied; "there will be room for everybody."

Then he went on to explain the programme for the day—the breakfast, which he had taken care to order in advance, the visit to the famous Grotto and the church, the subsequent *promenade dans les environs,* the return by moonlight, after a rather early dinner. "It will be ravishing!" he declared; and Raoul was quite inclined to hope that it would.

Soon the Château de Grancy was reached, and Raoul, taking leave of Miss Luttrell and of the other ladies and gentlemen to whom he had not spoken much during the ride, turned his horse's head towards his mother's abode, which was situated about a quarter of a mile away. He did not hurry himself, having many things to think about — especially things which Madeline Luttrell had surprised him by saying in the course of the afternoon. Had she really meant what she said? Had she known in the least what she was talking about? The first question might, perhaps, be answered in the affirmative; the second, no doubt, in the negative. Yet, fantastic though her sister-in-law's ideas appeared to be, so far agreed with them that he would have given a good deal to obliterate the last three years of his life. When one is in love for the first time—such was his condition, and he knew it—one would fain be able to offer what one hopes to receive. But that could not be. It was pleasanter to remember, among other speeches which Miss Luttrell had made, that she had once inadvertently called him "Raoul," as she had been wont to do in the days of their childhood, and that she had colored ever so slightly after that little slip of the tongue. By way of acknowledgment, he murmured "Madeline" more than once under his breath before he rode into the great, echoing stable-yard where a groom was awaiting him.

CHAPTER XIV

THE PILGRIMS

LONG ago—so long ago that the existing generation has had time to forget all about him and the social conditions with which he dealt—a charming French poet wrote "Les Confessions d'un Enfant du Siècle." The century which was then in its youth has now reached extreme old age; Alfred de Musset and his contemporaries are clean out of date, and their mantle, such as it was, has fallen upon persons at whom it is not yet permitted to smile; but now, as then, a Frenchman who dreads ridicule (and there is nothing on earth that a Frenchman dreads so much) is bound to belong to his epoch. He must, of course, be very wicked; but he must no longer be romantic; above all, he must clear himself of any suspicion of being *naïf*. His sins are to be committed coldly and deliberately; he must believe in nothing, beyond the somewhat obvious fact that it is pleasant to gratify the demands of the senses. The day is possibly coming when somebody will discover that what is really difficult, and therefore entitled to admiration, is self-control, and that courage—the one virtue which still continues to hold its own—can scarcely exist without it; but that desirable era does not at present show symptoms of dawning.

Raoul de Malglaive had so far justified his claim and ambition to be accounted a *fin-de-siècle* young man that during his few years of military service in Paris and its vicinity he had spent a youth of the kind commonly described as stormy. The so-called storms had left him calm (to the enhancement, of course, of his reputation); but he had seen and experienced almost everything that there is to see or experience—aided considerably, no doubt, by his handsome face and by his ability to throw away a good deal of money. What he had never experienced until a filial visit to Pau brought him once more into relations with Madeline Luttrell was that love which, let us hope, comes to every decent man once in his life, and which, among the other sufferings which it is sure to entail, is apt to make him ask himself mournfully whether he is a decent man at all. It is not necessary to enter into details respecting Raoul's acquaintance with the feminine variety of human nature. If he held no very high opinion of women in general, the fault was scarcely his; nor had he ever doubted that there were a few rare women—his mother, for example —of whom the world was not worthy. Only he had always been under the impression that they must, in the nature of things, be ignorant of that circumstance, and that was why some remarks of Madeline Luttrell's had brought home to him a painful and disquieting conviction of his personal unworthiness. Entertaining the views that she professed to entertain, was she not more than likely to turn away in disdain and disgust from one whose record was so very far from being immaculate as his?

Madame de Malglaive, who was pretty well informed as to that record, and who never made any allusion to it, would have been capable of reassuring him if, by an impossibility, he had applied to her for consolation. She was a hard, stern, strict old woman, with a very soft place in her heart for the son whose extravagant tastes she had gladly pinched herself to gratify; she thoroughly understood the temperament which he had inherited; she knew, or thought she knew, that youth must have its fling, and she had no fears for the future. As regarded her own sex, she would have declared confidently that every woman prefers a man who has a few sins to repent of, and she was a firm believer in the old saying that a reformed rake makes the best husband. However, it by no means entered into her plans to bring about a project of marriage between her son and Miss Luttrell, the latter being, as she had long ago ascertained, absolutely without *dot* or prospect of any.

When Raoul entered her large, ill-furnished, dimly lighted *salon* just before the dinner-hour, and when, with the old-fashioned respect which she liked him to observe, he had kissed her hand, she had a few disparaging remarks to make about the Luttrell family, to whose villa, it appeared, she had paid a visit that afternoon.

"Riddled with debts, I am told, and living, as they have always lived, far beyond their income. That poor Sir Robert will be almost ruined when he goes out of office, I believe, and Heaven knows whether anything remains of Antoinette's fortune! Add to that the inconceivable folly of their son, who, after marrying a rich woman, is bent, it seems, upon providing her with an excuse for divorcing him! It is impossible to feel any sympathy with people who manage their affairs so badly."

Later in the evening she spoke in terms scarcely less contemptuous of Madeline.

"The girl is pretty—even beautiful; but Antoinette will find that there will be very great difficulty in arranging an alliance for her. It is not only that her father is prepared to give her nothing, but one looks forward; one sees the whole family on straw; one says to one's self—I presume, at least, that all prudent parents, even in England, would say to themselves—'This will not do! Our son must not be exposed to the risk of having to provide for his wife's relations!'"

"In England," Raoul remarked, "alliances are not arranged as they are with us. Marriage there is an affair of inclination."

"So they pretend; but, having seen many English people here and having observed their ways, I remain of opinion that Miss Luttrell is in danger of ending her career as an old maid. For her sake, as well as for her mother's, I trust that I may be mistaken. *En somme!*—the question is one with which we can be in no way concerned."

The last words seemed to be spoken with intention; but

Raoul was not sure that they were so, nor was he inclined to pursue the subject further. His love for his mother had always been largely seasoned with fear; he suspected that she had already decided in her own mind who his future wife was to be, and he saw no use in entering upon argument and possible strife while it still remained so very doubtful whether Madeline would have anything to say to him. He himself had a tolerably strong will, and, like most persons whose will is strong, he was averse to stating what he meant to do before he was in a position to do it.

Madame de Malglaive was much pleased to hear that her son proposed to join in the expedition to Lourdes which, so far as she was concerned, partook a little of the nature of a pilgrimage. Many and many a time had she visited the hallowed scene of the apparitions, praying fervently for boons which had not always been granted, and she was never unwilling to return to the charge. It mattered little to her whether her companions were believers, like herself, or whether—as the greater part of them would probably be on the present occasion—they were mere sightseers. She had not even had the curiosity to inquire of whom the party was to be composed; all she knew was that she was to journey by rail with the Luttrells and a few other elderly friends, and all she was anxious to know was whether Raoul would arrive in time to walk with her to the Grotto before the midday *déjeûner*.

He assured her that he would not fail to give her that satisfaction, adding, with something like a pang of remorse at his heart when he saw her hard face become bright and tender, "As for that, I will place myself on my knees beside you, *ma mère*. It can do me no harm; perhaps—who knows ?—it may even do me some good."

" It is for you that I shall pray, my son," the old woman murmured.

But indeed he did not require to be told that she would do so, and it made him sorry to think that her supplications would be thrown away. She was very good and very forbearing with him upon the subject of religion, which she seldom or never made a subject of discussion. Her hope, as well as her belief, was that he would be converted in due time, just as she hoped and believed that he would end by marrying in accordance with her wishes and abandoning certain habits which ought to be abandoned at a certain age. She did not realize how grave his case was, or that, notwithstanding his youth, he had already arrived at the point of wishing with all his heart to believe in accepted dogmas, and being altogether incapable of the feat.

But of course it was neither of his mother nor of the difficulty of dispensing with the reasoning faculties that Raoul was thinking when he found himself, the next morning, seated opposite to Madeline Luttrell in the "*breack à quatre chevaux*" provided by M. de Larrouy. The weather was perfection, with just enough of nip in the breeze which blew from the mountains to temper the heat of the sun; the cosmopolitan company was a merry one; Madeline, dressed in a well-fitting costume of creamy white serge, was looking lovely; the four good little horses trotted up hill and down at a pace which might have suggested to their owners that, with such treatment, they would not be good little horses much longer, and Raoul's spirits, which had been somewhat depressed at starting, rose with each successive kilometre. The conversation was perforce general; yet he managed every now and again to exchange words and looks with his opposite neighbor which did not relate to the general conversation. He could not help feeling that there was a sort of tacit understanding between them; he could not help hoping, though he kept saying to himself that there was as yet no shadow of an excuse for hope.

"I am going to the Grotto with you and Madame de Malglaive," Madeline announced, when he helped her to descend, on arriving at their destination.

The travellers by rail were waiting for them in front of the hotel, at the door of which the break had come to a standstill; it was rather late, and most of the party were hungry. M. de Larrouy had intimated that breakfast was

the first event upon the programme; but Raoul had mentioned in an undertone that he was bound by a promise to
his mother, and Miss Luttrell, it appeared, meant to witness his fulfilment of the same.

"To see a sceptic asking for a miracle?" Raoul inquired,
smiling faintly.

"I shall not see you at all; I shall be saying my own
prayers. But I should think that if anybody is in need of
a miracle, it must be a sceptic. Ask for it, at least—that
will be a first step. Did you never hear of the blind Protestant who came here and recovered his sight?"

He made no answer. He had not heard of that remarkable case; nor, if it had been ever so well authenticated,
could he have hoped that his own mental vision would be
dimmed thereby. There are patent, inexorable facts to
which it would be very comfortable to be blind, but which
cannot be ignored when once they have been looked in the
face; and indeed it was no miracle that Raoul was disposed
to crave of compassionate Heaven — although, when he
thought of what he had been and of what Madeline Luttrell was, that seemed to be the most fitting name for it.
He gave his arm to his mother (who, for the sake of claiming that support, sometimes pretended to be in need of it),
and they walked together down the broad, gravelled promenade which skirts the Gave de Pau and leads to the won-
der-working source. Only Lady Luttrell and her daughter followed them, everybody else having yielded to the
paramount claims of appetite and the representations of
M. de Larrouy.

"So much the better!" Madame de Malglaive said.
"Now we shall be alone; for I do not count Antoinette
and *la petite*, who will not have the bad taste to intrude
upon us."

Her confidence in the discretion of the two ladies named
was not misplaced. They dropped upon their knees presently in front of the famous cave where a peasant child
once saw visions which have brought so rich a harvest to
others, and they did not turn their heads to look at Ma-

dame de Malglaive, who assumed a similar posture a few
yards to the rear of them, or at Raoul, who knelt at his
mother's elbow.   The young man watched these three
worshippers with a yearning to be able to join in their devotions which was the more pathetic because he was so
terribly conscious of its absurdity.   There was something
that he wanted very much, something that he would fain
have prayed for, something that, for all he knew to the
contrary, the mysterious Creator of this planet, with its
manifold intricacies and complications, might be pleased
to give him, if properly approached; but how could he
address his request to the alleged human mother of that
Deity—symbolized here by a vulgar image and surrounded
by the grateful offerings of those who had attributed their
recovery from disease to her intercession?   It might be
true that she had interceded on behalf of those sufferers;
it might be true that she had appeared to Bernadette Sou-
birous; it might even be true that she had made that as-
tounding announcement, *"Je suis l'Immaculée Conception"*
—the most improbable things may be true when once the
domain of the supernatural has been entered, and it seems
certain that the superstitious are both happier and better
people than the incredulous.   Only, as Raoul could by no
means conquer his incredulity, there was nothing for him
to do but to sigh and hold his peace.

As he knelt there, silent and sad, his eyes wandered
hither and thither—from the Grotto, blackened by the
smoke of thousands of tapers, to Lady Luttrell and her
daughter, whose backs were turned towards him, to his
mother, whose thin lips moved incessantly, and then to
the hills and woods and mountains which had looked down
for years upon the growth of this gigantic, touching illusion, and which would some day, no doubt, witness its
decadence and extinction.   "But we shall all be dead by
that time," he thought, "and it will not signify in the
least to us or anybody else whether we have been disappointed or gratified by our short lives."

But while our short lives last the difference between disappointment and gratification is of the utmost importance; and so it happened that a day of which he had expected no great things became one to be marked forever with a white stone in the memory of this half-hearted philosopher. For whether the piety of his three companions was real or simulated (and he had no reason at all to doubt its reality), it was, in the case of one of them, discarded as lightly as an opera-cloak when she had finished her prayers, and she entered into conversation with him on the way back to the hotel after a fashion which dispersed all the gloomy forebodings that had begun to possess his mind.

"Do you care about trotting round at M. de Larrouy's heels and being shown the various objects of interest?" she asked, incidentally. "If you don't, we might perhaps give the expedition the slip and stroll down the banks of the river after breakfast. I never can enjoy myself in a crowd."

She was given to making speeches of that kind—speeches which, coming from the mouth of a Frenchwoman, would have gone near to scandalizing him, but which were so evidently uttered without *arrière pensée* by her that he was half-delighted, half-discouraged by them. A girl, whether English or French, does not extend such amiable invitations to a man whom she loves, he thought.

However, he was thankful to be granted the privilege of her undivided attention upon any terms, and, as matters fell out, that privilege was obtained easily enough.

The excellent *déjeûner* ordered by M. de Larrouy had reached its last course by the time that the four belated suppliants reached the hotel; Sir Robert Luttrell, accompanied by a Russian ex-diplomatist who was of the party, had already wandered out-of-doors with a cigar, and such members of the heterogeneous gathering as still lingered at table were being reminded by their active cicerone that there was not a great deal of time to be lost.

"But how late you come, my dear ladies!" he exclaimed, throwing up his hands as our friends entered the room. "I should be desolated to hurry you; but if we are to visit the church and the old town, and to drive a few miles up the valley towards Argelès, we must positively make haste! I thought that those who did not hold to joining in the drive would perform their devotions in the course of the afternoon."

"I am sure that neither Madame de Malglaive nor I hold to being driven anywhere," answered Lady Luttrell, "and the younger people can catch you up at the church, if they want to catch you up. Please, go away, all of you; if you have left us something to eat, we shall console ourselves for being abandoned."

The truth was that Lady Luttrell was free from fears respecting Raoul. He was not at all the sort of young man whom Madeline was likely to fancy; and even if she should fancy him, worse calamities might happen. He was well-born, well-to-do, and, as Sir Robert had said, there are so few eligible Catholics in England! Although, therefore, their meal was hurried through, and although the subsequent ascent to the Basilica was made with all possible speed, she did not keep a very vigilant eye upon her daughter, nor was she much disquieted when, on rising from the *prie-dieu* chair which she had drawn up beside that of her old friend before the altar, she found that Raoul and Madeline had vanished.

"They will have followed the others," she remarked. "Come, let us look for a sunny corner somewhere where we can sit down and rest. I begin to find that excursions are a little fatiguing."

Madame de Malglaive looked rather grim, but said nothing. She had the advantage of her former schoolfellow in knowing quite definitely what she wanted and what she did not want. She did not, for instance, want her son to marry a portionless foreigner, and she was comfortably convinced of her power to prevent him from doing so.

It may be that Raoul would have been uncomfortably convinced of the same thing, had he been able to flatter himself that he had surmounted the initial difficulty of winning Madeline's love; but, in spite of all the successes

10

that he had had, he was not a vain man, and he was satisfied, for the time being, to know that the girl whom he
adored was animated by friendly feelings towards him.   It
was she who had suggested in a whisper that they should
not linger to examine the countless votive offerings in the
Basilica, which neither of them saw for the first time ; it
was she who led the way out into the open air and down
the colossal stairs to the banks of the river ; beyond a doubt
his society was pleasant to her, and to be aware of that was
surely to be aware of a great stroke of good-fortune.

At certain times of the year privacy is not to be had at
Lourdes or its immediate neighborhood ; but the season of
the great pilgrimages had not yet opened, and only some
half-dozen motionless, mournful petitioners occupied the
open space in front of the Grotto when Madeline and Raoul
passed by on their way to the banks of the Gave.   Presently
they were as completely alone as if they had been on an
island in the South Pacific, and Madeline, pausing upon a
grassy bank which overlooked the stream, said :

"Suppose we sit down ?   This is what we should call in
England a hot summer day."

He assented, wondering a little at the matter-of-course
way in which she treated a situation which for a young girl
of his own nationality would have been totally impossible.
He misunderstood neither it nor her ; he knew—or, at all
events, he had been assured—that the great liberty accorded
to Anglo-Saxon maidens is productive of no evil results ;
yet Madeline Luttrell, who had a French mother, always
talked to him in French, and this latter circumstance added
a certain undefinable flavor of piquancy to the conversation
that ensued.

"You look upon England as your country;" he said, interrogatively; "you do not often care to remember, perhaps, that you are half French ?"

"On the contrary," she answered, "I often think that I
am more French than English, and that is just how my
mother feels ; although in some ways she has become absolutely Britannic.   We are subjects of the queen, our lives

are spent in England; but it is to France that we come for our holidays, and it is in France that we are happiest. I suppose our hearts really belong to France."

This was good hearing, and Raoul thought of gently insinuating that since Miss Luttrell had not yet espoused an Englishman, she might yet be destined to take up her permanent residence in the country of her heart; but she did not allow him time to risk a possible indiscretion.

"Very soon our holiday for this year will be at an end," she remarked; "London is filling, and Pau is putting up its shutters. And you?—what will you do after everybody has gone away?"

"Oh, I shall return to the regiment; what else is there for me to do?" the young man replied. "It is not too gay, life in the regiment," he added, with a sigh.

"Indeed? I thought, from the reports that I have heard of your life, that it must be extremely gay."

He answered with some earnestness that reports about other people's lives were seldom or never true. For his own part, he detested the existence in which most of his brother-officers delighted. He had seen enough of it; he would be glad to forget it; there were only two things for which he really longed—active service, or else a quiet life on his own property in the Basses-Pyrénées with—with some congenial companion.

"You may have both," she returned; "neither sounds so improbable as to demand miraculous intervention — which I think you said yesterday that you would have to ask for, if you asked at all. By the way, did you ask for anything at all this morning?"

He shook his head gravely. "When I ask, mademoiselle, it will not be to the Blessed Virgin, who, I fear, would turn a deaf ear to me, that I shall address my prayers. In any case, they are not very likely to be heard."

She threw a quick side-glance at him and changed the subject, without perceptible embarrassment. His meaning could hardly be doubtful to her; but it was evident that she did not wish him to say more, and he had not confi-

dence enough in himself or his chances of success to
insist.

They sat for the best part of an hour there above the
hurrying stream, and their colloquy, which related chiefly
to Raoul's military experiences and his desire to strike a
blow for France in some remote quarter of the globe (since
there seemed to be so little hope of a European conflagration), would scarcely have disquieted Madame de Malglaive,
had she overheard it. It is true that, every now and again,
a swift interchange of looks occurred which that quick-
sighted lady might have deemed alarming, not to say reprehensible.

Sir Robert Luttrell, who chanced to be strolling that
way, ruminating over the imminent dissolution of Parliament and the possible discomfiture of the Conservative
party, was scarcely better pleased than Madame de Malglaive would have been when an abrupt turn in the path
brought him face to face with his daughter and the young
Frenchman.

"Hullo !" he exclaimed, rather sharply ; "why aren't you
driving with the rest of the party ?"

"Because we thought it would be so much pleasanter to
take a walk," answered Madeline, rising leisurely to her
feet. "Won't you come with us ?"

Sir Robert grunted. "I think we had better get back
to the hotel," he answered. "We are to dine in the middle of the afternoon, I believe."

So the trio retraced their steps, and Raoul understood
that there would be no more private converse with Miss
Luttrell for him that day. He had not, perhaps, made
a very brilliant use of his opportunity ; but there was a
humble little wild-flower in his pocket which she had been
playing with and had dropped within his reach. He fancied that she must have seen him pick it up.

CHAPTER XV

MATERNAL AUTHORITY

On the following morning Raoul de Malglaive, with a cigarette between his lips, was wandering meditatively along the devious and somewhat carelessly kept paths which intersected his domain. The property was his; but he had never assumed the management of it, leaving that, as in the days of his childhood, to his mother, who was an excellent woman of business, and who was indeed at that very moment closeted with the family lawyer. At eleven o'clock precisely she would sit down to breakfast, and would then be joined by her son, such having been the custom of the house ever since Raoul could remember.

The young man's musings were less sad than his face, which wore its habitual expression of grave melancholy; for, although he had had a tedious drive home on the preceding evening—owing to Miss Luttrell's parents having, for some unexplained reason, required her to return with them by train—the memory of that walk and talk by the banks of the rushing Gave still remained with him, and served as the foundation for a whole row of aerial castles. He could not help thinking that Madeline understood; and if she had not encouraged him, she had at least not done the reverse. Unhappily, there was much connected with his recent history which she could not understand, or could understand only after a very vague fashion; and that was why care and regret bore him company on that still, warm, brilliant morning. Unlike Guy Luttrell, who was of opinion that nothing is more simple than to pass a sponge over the records of the past; unlike his own mother, whose belief in the whitewashing remedies prescribed by the Church knew no limits, he felt that a man is composed of what he has been just as much as of what he is, and that the man whom he had been could ever deserve to be Madeline's husband was impossible. Yet we all, in the course of our lives, obtain both good and bad things which we have not deserved, and it was, after all, in no despairing mood that Raoul re-entered the house to bestow ' his accustomed respectful salute upon the lady who ruled there.

Madame de Malglaive took her place at the table, laying down a sheaf of documents beside her plate. "Now that these affairs are concluded," she remarked, "I can give myself the little change which I always find that I require at this time of year. I think of going to Saint-Jean-de-Luz to-morrow." She added, with her keen old eyes fixed upon her son's dismayed countenance, "It is, of course, understood that I do not force you to accompany me."

It was very well understood by him, and probably also by her, that he would be compelled to do so. He had only a few weeks at his disposal; he knew that every day of those weeks was precious to the old woman whose speech was so seldom affectionate, but whose love for him had been evidenced by a generosity which had been ill requited, so far; to take her at her word and let her depart without him would be out of the question. He only ventured to ask whether there was any need for such precipitation.

"I have already telegraphed to the hotel for rooms," Madame de Malglaive answered, inflexibly, "and, as you know, I never change my plans."

"Nor your opinions?" suggested the young man, smiling faintly.

She shook her head. "It is true that I do not often change them; but then I do not form them hastily. If you could come with me to Saint-Jean-de-Luz—but I will not insist."

Raoul rose and stood, with his hand resting upon the

back of her high chair. "Do you know that you are asking a good deal of me, *ma mère?*" said he, in a low voice.

She turned her head and looked up at him, all the hard
lines disappearing from her brows and cheeks as she did so.
But apparently she decided not to say what she had been
going to say.

"No, no," she answered, brusquely, "I ask nothing.
Saint-Jean-de-Luz is dull; Pau is perhaps amusing; you
must not be the slave of my convenience. Nevertheless,
it is becoming too hot here—the sea air is more healthy—
it would be better—"

She paused abruptly, and Raoul, after a moment of silence, only said : "*C'est bien, ma mère;* I will accompany
you."

"It will be better, my son; believe me, it will be better,"
the old lady returned.

That was all that passed between them; but there was
no need for further words. If Madame de Malglaive did
not readily change her plans or her opinions, her son was
of a somewhat similar temperament in that respect; but he
had not as yet the right to say that he had formed the plan
which she evidently meant to oppose; so he swallowed his
disappointment. A thoughtless son he had often been in
the past, but he had never deliberately given his mother
pain.

Madame de Malglaive could not, and indeed did not,
suppose that Raoul would be guilty of such a breach of
good manners as to omit paying a visit of adieu at the
Château de Grancy; yet she made no mention of her own
intention to proceed thither, which was carried out early
in the afternoon. She happened to have heard that Sir
Robert and Madeline were engaged to attend a large luncheon-party, so that she was not surprised to find Lady Luttrell at home and alone. That, in fact, was just what she
had hoped for.

"I come to embrace you before leaving," she announced
at once. "We start for Saint-Jean-de-Luz to-morrow, and
I fear that this house will be deserted before we return."

It may have been something of a disappointment to her
to note that her old friend's ejaculations of regret did not
partake of the nature of consternation. She was not an
ill-natured woman ; but she was persuaded that the Luttrells wanted to marry their daughter to her son, and she
would not have been sorry, in declining the unspoken suggestion, to administer to its originators that rap over the
knuckles which their cool presumption seemed to merit.

"I am so sorry," Lady Luttrell remarked, tranquilly,
"that our stay at Pau is nearly at an end for this season;
but my husband ought really to have returned to his duties before now, and I suppose, as you say, this house will
very soon be closed again."

Madame de Malglaive's eyes wandered round the room.
"It is a good house," said she—"solidly built and standing in an advantageous position. What a pity that it should
remain shut up for so many months together, and that it
should suffer, as it must do, from the damp ! Nevertheless, I consider that it is well worth the sum at which M.
Cayaux values it, and I am glad to have been able to place
my money upon such good security."

Lady Luttrell was visibly disconcerted. She had found
it necessary to raise a certain amount upon mortgage, and
just before Madame de Malglaive's arrival she had heard
from her local man of business that her wishes had been
complied with ; but she was not anxious to advertise the
circumstance that she was in pecuniary straits, and she could
not keep herself from exclaiming, "Cayaux is an imbecile !"

"But, my dear Antoinette, why ? He is my lawyer as
well as yours ; he has found an occasion of serving us
both, and I think we may be very well satisfied with him.
It is surely unnecessary for me to add that you may rely
upon my absolute discretion. I am not in the habit of
chattering either about my own private affairs or about
those of my friends."

That was true enough ; and Lady Luttrell, regaining
something of her usual good-humor, remarked, with a
slight shrug of the shoulders:

"After all, we are in the same boat with our neighbors. Everybody is borrowing money in these days—everybody, that is, except a few lucky persons, like you, who can afford to lend it. You are very enviable—and very extraordinary! How in the world do you contrive to be so rich?"

"I have thought it my duty to live within my income," answered Madame de Malglaive, dryly. "For the rest, I do not call myself rich; I shall be contented if, at my death, I can leave my son some moderate addition to his means, which are at present not too large for his needs. I hope also that in due time he will make a satisfactory marriage."

"Let us hope so," Lady Luttrell agreed. "I am not personally a great admirer of the French system of arranging marriages, which leaves the affections out of account; still one naturally wishes that one's children should be well off, and one is naturally glad when—as I know will be the case with dear Madeline—eligible suitors present themselves in such numbers that it is a mere question of picking and choosing."

"Oh, your daughter is very pretty," Madame de Malglaive returned, somewhat tartly. "I trust that you will not be disappointed, and that she will meet with some Englishman wealthy enough to be satisfied with prettiness. In France, as you know, such *partis* are scarcely to be discovered. And when do you expect your son and his charming wife?"

"The date of my son's arrival in England," answered Lady Luttrell, "is uncertain, because it must depend upon the number of times that the troop-ship which is bringing him may break down in the course of the voyage. His charming wife, who is travelling overland, with her little girl, will reach London, I believe, about the same time as we do. In fact, we are hastening our departure by a few days, so that we may be there to welcome her. I wish you were not hastening yours; for we might have been able to provide poor Raoul with something in the shape of entertainment, and I fear that he will not find his sojourn at Saint-Jean-de-Luz of a wild gayety."

The two old friends went on sparring until Madame de Malglaive rose to take her leave. She had rather hoped that Raoul would have appeared before then, and would have been constrained to leave with her; but, upon the whole, she saw no great danger in his presenting himself later. Danger—if indeed there had ever been any—might now be regarded as a thing of the past.

Raoul had saddled his horse, and had started for a solitary ride into the country. He proposed to pay his respects to the Luttrell family at the latest permissible hour, so as to give himself every chance of finding Madeline at home, and, in the meantime, the afternoon had to be killed somehow. But the sun was hot and the roads were dusty, and his self-communings were not of so cheerful a character that he cared to protract them. By four o'clock he was at home again, and shortly afterwards he was walking slowly towards the Boulevard du Midi—with some faint hope, perhaps, of encountering there the only person in Pau whom he desired to see. And, as luck would have it, he did, almost immediately after reaching the terraced garden beneath the old château, descry the approach of a little band of English people, headed by Sir Robert Luttrell and graced by the company of Sir Robert's daughter. They were talking and laughing, they appeared to be very merry together, and Raoul, whose constitutional shyness overtook him at odd times, notwithstanding the self-possession that he had acquired by three years' experience of the Parisian world, dropped his elbows upon the parapet and stared at the distant mountains, instead of stepping forward at once to accost Miss Luttrell. It seemed conceivable that she might not wish to be accosted.

But when she and her friends had advanced within speaking distance, and when Sir Robert had called out, amiably enough, "How are you, De Malglaive?" without stopping, she showed in the plainest and most satisfactory manner that there was no ground for such apprehensions. Unlike her father, she paused beside the young Frenchman, and, holding out her hand with a smile, said:

"What are you doing here all by yourself? Will you not come home with us and have a cup of tea? We have been down to the Plaine de Bilhères to watch the last lawn-tennis tournament of the season, and it is a great relief to meet somebody who neither knows anything about lawn-tennis nor cares whether the season is at an end or not."

That description did not altogether apply to M. de Malglaive, as he presently explained. He accepted the invitation; the company resumed its march; the youth who had been walking with Miss Luttrell, and upon whom it may have dawned that he was in danger of becoming *de trop*, moved on to join those in front of him; the moment seemed opportune for making a sad announcement which had to be made. Raoul's voice, quite as much as his words, testified to the sadness with which the conclusion of his season at Pau affected him; while Madeline, for her part, frankly exclaimed:

"What odious news! And I who have been planning I don't know how many rides and excursions which will have to be abandoned now! I suppose you must go, if your mother wants you to go with her; but—could she not be induced to wait just another little week? Is not this rather a sudden caprice of hers?"

Raoul shook his head gravely. "She will not be induced," he answered. "Yes, it is sudden—I do not know whether it can be called precisely a caprice."

He was not unwilling that Miss Luttrell should divine the name by which it ought to be called, and her quick, inquiring look, followed by a minute of silence, led him to believe that she understood what he could not tell her.

However that may have been, she said no more about the possibility of persuading Madame de Malglaive to reconsider her plans, but began to talk rather rapidly about the luncheon-party to which she had been taken by her father, and which, according to her account, had been excessively long and excessively dull.

"Almost all entertainments are long and dull," she declared. "I see an endless vista of entertainments before me in London, and I would give my ears to be able to escape them! As I was telling you the other day, it is to Pau that we come for our holidays, and now I shall have to begin looking forward to next winter. We shall not find you here then, I suppose?"

"You will assuredly find me here if I am alive," the young man replied, in his grave accents. "But you, mademoiselle—is it so certain that you will return? Is it certain that you will still be Mademoiselle Luttrell next winter?"

She laughed. "Nothing is certain; but I have my own humble convictions. Shall I tell you a secret? I do not think that I shall ever marry an Englishman."

"Why do you say that?" he asked, eagerly.

"Oh, not because I have formed a hopeless attachment for a foreigner," she answered, still laughing; "but I have heard things about English husbands—I have even seen a few things—which do not exactly attract me. Moreover, as I should never be permitted to marry a Protestant, I am not likely to be tempted by a great many offers. I suspect that Pau has far better prospects of seeing me next winter than it has of seeing you."

He reiterated his former assertion with much emphasis. Almost he was inclined to add something to it, fully alive though he was to the danger of precipitation, and convinced though he felt in his heart that, if his fondest hopes were ever to be realized, it would behoove him to be patient as well as resolute. But before he could give utterance to a speech of which he might afterwards have repented, Sir Robert came marching back to say, in an unwontedly sharp tone of voice:

"Do you know what time it is, Madeline? We must put our best foot foremost, or the dinner-bell will have rung before we get our tea."

He only grunted on being informed that M. de Malglaive had kindly consented to form one of the tea-party, and he remained obstinately by his daughter's side during the remainder of the walk.

It would have been plain to Raoul that Sir Robert Luttrell did not covet him as a son-in-law had he reached the point of troubling himself as to Sir Robert's possible wishes in the matter. But he was far from having arrived at that point; he was far from anticipating difficulties at which he would, in any case, have smiled if he had won Madeline's love; for the moment, it was enough for him to have been assured that she did not contemplate marrying an Englishman.

And that assurance, whatever it may have been worth, had to suffice. He spent some twenty minutes at the Château de Grancy in a crowded drawing-room; he took leave of Lady Luttrell and Sir Robert, both of whom appeared to receive the announcement of his impending desertion with fortitude; and when it came to Madeline's turn to speed the parting guest, all she had to say, as she smilingly extended her hand to him, was, " Till next year, then !"

That, however, seemed to him to be a good deal, and he was by no means an unhappy man as he walked away. He ought, no doubt, to have struck while the iron was hot; but how was he, in his ignorance of British customs, to know that? Although he had achieved many conquests— and had achieved them, to tell the truth, as much by audacity as by anything else—he had not for one moment thought of adopting so audacious a course as to ask Madeline Luttrell point-blank to be his wife. Marriage is a very serious matter, and if he had deemed the time to be ripe for a formal proposal, he would have felt it his duty in the first instance to approach Sir Robert, by whom he would assuredly have been sent to the right-about then and there.

CHAPTER XVI

CLARISSA'S RETURN

"Now I really do hope," said Sir Robert Luttrell to his wife, "that we are not going to have trouble with that young fellow; but I am bound to say that it will be no thanks to you if we don't. I took the liberty of watching Madeline's face when she wished him good-bye, and the most unwelcome conclusions forced themselves upon me."

Lady Luttrell raised her shoulders and her eyebrows. "Since he has gone away, and will never be heard of again! Besides, his mother was here this afternoon, and gave herself a great deal of trouble to make it quite clear to me that she was not ambitious of contracting a family alliance. She is rich, and I suppose she wants to be richer. You need not be in the least alarmed."

"What you say is not so very reassuring," rejoined Sir Robert, testily. "Your daughter's future, let me tell you, is not a matter to be trifled with. If Madame de Malglaive is rich, I know who isn't, and there are a few unmarried Catholics in England to whom you ought to be devoting your whole attention. We cannot afford to have the girl refusing a good offer for the sake of some infernal alien whose mother is more prudent than you are."

Sir Robert had become subject to fits of irritability. A general election was at hand, and it was doubtful whether the political party to which he belonged would be granted a fresh lease of power, while it was anything but certain that, even in that event, he would be invited to join the reconstructed ministry. He was conscious of lassitude and failing powers, conscious that younger men were slowly

but surely pushing him up to the peerage which would be
of no earthly use to him, conscious, above all, of the impossibility of making both ends meet without the aid of the
official salary which he had so long enjoyed. Visions of
letting Haccombe Luttrell and retiring to the Château de
Grancy to spend the remainder of his days in seclusion and
economy had often suggested themselves to him of late.
Only he did feel that Madeline ought to be settled in
life first, and that there was no time to be lost. Guy,
whose wife had already £5000 a year and would eventually have a great deal more, might be looked upon as
provided for — supposing, that was, that no danger existed of Guy's being such a very great fool as to quarrel
with his wife.

"Why," he asked presently, in the somewhat querulous
accents with which those about him had but recently grown
familiar, "are not Guy and Clarissa coming home together?
What was the sense of his taking a passage in a troop-ship?"

Lady Luttrell did not know, and therefore could not say.
She had suspicions, but it would have been foolish as well
as useless to impart these to her husband. If there had
been conjugal dissensions—and she had been given to understand by Lady Brook and others that such was the case
—they must be smoothed over. Of course they would admit of being smoothed over; conjugal dissensions always
do when there is a child; and Clarissa, unmanageable
though she appeared to be, would surely recognize her obvious duty after it had been firmly but affectionately pointed out to her. So Sir Robert was begged to go and dress
for dinner and not to worry himself.

Heaven knows that he had never been much given to
worrying himself. In every trouble of a life which had
included what most people would consider a fair proportion of serious troubles he had been sustained by a comfortable conviction that "it would be all right"; and although it had not always been all right, he had lived on
with scarcely diminished equanimity. Now he was getting
old and nervous; yet habit still enabled him to cast away

his cares at a moment's notice, and Raoul de Malglaive, having been removed from his sight, soon ceased to vex his memory. He had not (for his sight was sufficiently acute) misinterpreted the look that he had seen in his daughter's eyes when she bade that young man farewell; but he did not believe that any great harm had been done, because he did not wish to believe it, and for the same reason he dismissed from his mind the unpleasant idea that his son, after espousing an heiress, could so far play the idiot as to live apart from her.

A day or two later he left for London to attend a Cabinet council—Sir Robert generally contrived to have some good excuse for performing his journeys without encumbrances — and at the end of a week he was followed by Lady Luttrell, Madeline, and the remainder of the somewhat unwieldly establishment. Lady Luttrell's ideas of economy fell short of the heroic measure of dispensing with saloon-carriages, and that, no doubt, was why she failed to notice any of her fellow-passengers from Paris until she had stepped on board the Channel boat. But no sooner had she crossed the gangway than she became aware of a tall lady, with a quantity of fair, rather untidy hair, who was scrutinizing her doubtfully through a double eye-glass, and who held by the hand a little pale-faced girl of somewhat similar features and coloring. Lady Luttrell plunged at her with a cry of affectionate recognition.

"Dearest Clarissa!—how extraordinary that we should meet like this! We thought we should be several days in advance of you; but of course you will find everything ready for your reception in Grosvenor Place. And is this my darling little Netta? Dear child! She looks rather white; but English air will soon bring the roses to her ' cheeks. Come and sit down and tell me all about it. Is it going to be rough, do you think? Shall we be sick?"

Clarissa responded to the caresses bestowed upon her with a good grace, but without effusion. She had altered a little in appearance and a good deal in manner. She was attended by two servants, to whom she gave her orders in a quiet, authoritative tone; she was perfectly self-possessed, and had the air of being slightly preoccupied, though anxious to do and say what was polite.

"I am afraid it will be rather rough," she said, in answer to one of her mother-in-law's queries; "but that makes no difference to Netta or me; we are both such good sailors. It is so kind of you to wish us to stay with you; but of course I must go first to my uncle, who is quite alone, now that poor Aunt Susan is dead."

"Yes, indeed!—her death was a great blow to him, and —and to us all," said Lady Luttrell, who had not seen the late Mrs. Dent half-a-dozen times in her life, and had a very indistinct recollection of the deceased lady. "But you must come to us when you end your visit to him."

"Oh, I think not, many thanks," Clarissa answered. "I shall have to begin looking out at once for a furnished house—or perhaps an unfurnished one. One wants to get settled as soon as possible."

Lady Luttrell looked puzzled; it was indispensable that she should look a little more puzzled than she felt. "Does Guy think of leaving the service?" she inquired. "He is such a bad correspondent that one never knows what his plans are; but I understood that he was coming home to join the depot, and the depot is at Kendal, is it not?"

Clarissa was gazing abstractedly through her glasses at the pier-heads, between which the steamer was passing. "I beg your pardon," said she. "The depot?—oh yes, I think it is at Kendal, or some such place."

She either did not see or did not choose to see the notes of interrogation and exclamation addressed to her by Lady Luttrell's eyes; she turned her head to look at the white-caps outside, which were chasing one another merrily before a brisk westerly breeze, and then—

"Have you a private cabin?" she asked. "If not, please make use of mine; I so very much prefer to stay out on deck."

Lady Luttrell had a private cabin, and several profound courtesies on the part of the steamer led her to seek its se-

clusion with ignominious haste. Madeline, who had not
sailed the stormy seas outside Haccombe Bay for nothing,
remained with her sister-in-law, and the latter at once took
her by the hand, exclaiming, in an altogether different tone
of voice, "How good it is to see you again !"

The friendship which had subsisted between these two
young women before one of them had become a young
woman had suffered no diminution through absence. They
had corresponded regularly ; and if Madeline did not know
quite all that there was to know about Clarissa, she knew a
good deal more than other people did. But such information as she possessed was not, it seemed, to be added to on
that occasion ; for Clarissa would answer no questions.

"I am not interesting," she declared ; "my story has
been told—don't all stories end with a marriage ?—whereas
yours is still hidden in the mists of the future. Do you
know, Madeline, that you are perfectly beautiful ? But of
course you know it, and I shall not make you vain by telling you so. How many others have told you so ?—or is
there only one other worth mentioning ? That is what I
want to hear."

Now, Raoul de Malglaive had certainly never addressed
so impertinent a remark to Miss Luttrell, so that there was
no occasion to mention him ; nor indeed had the girl had
so many admirers but that she could emerge without embarrassment from the rather searching cross-examination
to which she was forthwith subjected. Yet, long before
the *Victoria* had ceased executing capers and had been
brought up alongside of the Admiralty Pier at Dover, Clarissa had divined that there was somebody who had succeeded in touching her sister-in-law's heart and that he
was a Frenchman.

"I do not trust foreigners," she remarked, judicially (as
though she had had an exhaustive experience of them and
their habits), "and I am afraid there are very few Englishmen who can be trusted either. If there are any, they
should perhaps be found within the fold of your Church,
which is said to be strict in certain respects. But I hope,

Madeline, you will never marry anybody until you know thoroughly well who and what he is. It is better a thousand times to live and die single than to take the leap in the dark which most girls take."

"Are you speaking of yourself?" Madeline ventured to inquire.

"Oh no; I am only one of a multitude, living and dead. For centuries it has gone on—this abominable injustice of upholding one law for women and another for men; but now at last people's consciences are beginning to be stirred. The whole system must be changed—and will be changed."

She would, no doubt, have been good enough to explain what the system was, and who was going to change it, if her attention had not been drawn off by her little girl, who plucked at her skirts to point to the white cliffs of England, and who wanted to know whether "Father" would be waiting for them on the pier.

"Father" was not, and could not be, there; but Mr. Dent was, and Lady Luttrell, emerging from her cabin, pallid and dishevelled, was grateful for the forethought which had prompted that excellent man to secure a reserved carriage on her behalf. He did not himself enter it, having retained another compartment for Clarissa, whom he had travelled down from London to meet; but he made himself very useful in fetching cups of tea, and he declared that he was only too glad to be permitted to act as a substitute for Sir Robert.

"I was to tell you from the right honorable gentleman," said he, "that he is chained by the leg to the Treasury bench, and that in all probability you will have to eat your dinner without him to-night. As for me, I have obtained leave of absence on the plea of urgent private affairs. It isn't every day, you see, that one's nearest relations arrive from the other side of the world."

"No indeed!—and dear Clarissa is looking so well, isn't she?" murmured Lady Luttrell, settling herself among her cushions. "We quite hoped that she would take up her quarters with us; but she thought you had the first claim, and, as I tell her, she must come to Grosvenor Place as soon as you are tired of her.   At the present moment I don't feel capable of enjoying *anybody's* society.   We have had a perfectly frightful passage, and I have died a hundred deaths since we left Calais !"

Lady Luttrell, who, in the intervals of seasickness, had dwelt with serious uneasiness upon sundry remarks which her daughter-in-law had let fall, was greatly relieved by Mr. Dent's friendly language and attentions.   If there had been anything really amiss he must have known of it, and must have shown that he felt the situation to be an awkward one, she thought.

But in truth he knew no more, or only a very little more, than she did.   Some surmises he had, indeed, formed from the tone of his niece's recent letters and from the circumstance that she had decided to travel home apart from her husband ; but it was, of course, natural enough that, since she could afford to travel comfortably, she should object to such accommodation as is obtainable by ladies on board a troop-ship, and it was possible that Guy had found himself unable to accompany her.   For the rest, he was not much disposed to put questions.   He was thankful that the silence and loneliness of his big, empty house were about to be broken in upon for a season ; he was charmed with the child, who made friends with him at once, and he knew very well that when a woman has anything to relate she needs no pressure or encouragement to induce her to relate it.

The journey to London, therefore, through the pleasant county of Kent—just then bright with the incipient verdure of a fresh year—was accomplished without any allusion to such topics as Clarissa had broached upon the deck of the Channel boat.   Netta, staring out of the window at scenes altogether novel to her, almost monopolized the conversation, and if her remarks were not always intelligible to Mr. Dent, he pretended that they were, while his replies appeared to be found satisfactory.   Some reference also had to be made to Mrs. Dent's last illness and death, as to which Clarissa expressed herself sympathetically. She had scarcely known her aunt; he could not expect her to say more than she did, and was grateful to her for saying as much. But what seemed a trifle ominous was that, although she talked a good deal about Ceylon, her husband's name never once passed her lips.

It was not until the evening, after an affectionate leave had been taken of the Luttrells, and Portland Place had been reached, and the uncle and niece were sitting together over their dessert in the dining-room, that Clarissa cleared her voice and said, with a certain air of determination:

"Now, Uncle Tom, I think I ought to tell you what my plans are."

"I shall be very glad to hear them," answered Mr. Dent.

"Well, that is as may be; but, at any rate, it is necessary for you to hear them, and I am sure that when you have heard all you will admit that they are not unreasonable."

Mr. Dent took his chin between his finger and thumb, and gazed at her fixedly with a slight smile upon his lips. "I trust," said he, "that your confidence will not be misplaced, my dear. However, please go on; I am listening."

CHAPTER XVII

A DISSOLUTION OF PARTNERSHIP

"WHEN a mistake has been made," Clarissa began, in the deliberate, decisive accents of one who is laying down a proposition which may appear novel, but can nevertheless be supported by powerful arguments, "the only wise plan is to acknowledge it frankly, and, so far as may be possible, rectify it."

As she seemed to expect some response, Mr. Dent remarked, blandly, "The audience is with you, my dear. I can only hope that you will always act in accordance with such unexceptionable principles."

"I hope so too—and I have made up my mind to do so," Clarissa declared. "Now, I have known for a long time past that my marriage was a mistake."

"For my own part," said Mr. Dent, "I never thought that it was anything else. Still, it has to be borne in mind that, in the particular instance of matrimony, rectification of a mistake is a somewhat more complicated and difficult process than frank acknowledgment."

"Of course; and I only said that it ought to be rectified as far as might be possible. I am not thinking of a divorce or a legal separation; I merely wish you to understand how matters are, and that I cannot any longer live with Guy. You take the announcement very coolly," she added, with a touch of resentment, on receiving a slight nod for all reply.

"Perhaps I shall warm up when I understand how matters are," said Mr. Dent. "At present I only know that you propose to adopt a course which has obvious drawbacks."

Clarissa sighed. " I am not at all sure," she said, "that I shall be able to make you understand ; still, I can but try. First of all, I must tell you that this is no sudden impulse of mine, and that I am not in the least blind to the drawbacks that you are thinking of. I dare say that there are many good reasons why a wife should submit to anything and everything rather than forsake her husband. Most wives, as you know, do forgive a great deal which husbands would not dream for a moment of forgiving, and, although that is obviously unjust, we are assured that such is the way of the world. The fact is that the way of the world wants altering, and before it can be altered there must be a few martyrs, I suppose. I am ready to be one of them."

"I seem to have heard and read," remarked Mr. Dent, meditatively, " of more cruel forms of martyrdom than unfettered liberty and five thousand pounds a year. But I am interrupting you."

"It is easy to sneer," returned Clarissa, with a somewhat heightened color, " and I am prepared for sneers ; though I hoped that perhaps I should not be sneered at by you, Uncle Tom. You think, I suppose, that I am still a silly, self-willed girl ; but it is not so. I am a woman ; I have grown much older since you saw me last, and I have learned many things which I did not know then. The people who did know might have warned me—"

" Only you wouldn't have listened."

"Well, never mind ; I am better informed now, and, since I can't begin my own life over again, I can at least save others from failing as I have failed."

" By separating yourself from the man whose name you bear, and who is the father of your child ?"

" That will be one step towards the goal. I want women to realize that they are not less entitled than men to the individual freedom which is the birthright of every human being ; I want them to realize that marriage need not, and ought not to, be another name for slavery. And if every woman who is situated as I am would decide to act as I am going to do, we should not have long to wait for a complete reform."

"The difficulty," observed Mr. Dent, "is that only a very few women are blessed with an independent fortune."

"Those who are not can work for their living. It seems to me that that would be infinitely less humiliating than to depend for food and clothing upon men whom they can no longer respect and who have been untrue to them."

"Oh—untrue! Now we seem to be coming to specific charges. May I hear them?"

She said what she had to say, and said it after a fashion which, if not entirely convincing to her uncle, yet extorted from his sense of justice a tacit admission that she had not been too well used. Guy, so far as he could gather, had been guilty of nothing flagrantly scandalous; but the flirtation with Mrs. Durand, which had so nearly brought about an open breach between him and his wife, had been succeeded by other flirtations with Mrs. This and Mrs. That, while his habits, if the account given of them could be trusted, were obviously the reverse of domestic. However, Clarissa did not insist particularly upon that point. She affected to speak with disdain of her husband's philanderings, which she declared were a matter of complete indifference to her, merely mentioning them as affording some additional justification for the measures that she contemplated. What she declaimed against was the iniquity and absurdity of a social compact which chained together two people who had nothing—absolutely nothing!—in common. It was not only that her own tastes were literary, whereas Guy's reading was confined to the sporting-intelligence column in the newspapers; it was not only that he cared for none of the things that she cared for, while she could not bring herself to take an interest in what interested him; but their ideas upon every imaginable subject differed so completely that, when they met at meal-times, they were driven to take refuge in a bored silence.

"And, if you will think of it, is there anything in the world worse than being bored?" Clarissa ejaculated.

Mr. Dent thought that there might be worse things—such as being knocked down and danced upon, for instance, or even nagged at; but he refrained from saying so. He refrained also from the protests upon which his niece had, perhaps, counted; for he was a man whose high reputation for common-sense had been earned quite as much by judicious silence as by speech.

Clarissa wound up by repeating that she had not arrived at her present resolution without having given the subject full consideration, and she added that, to the best of her belief, freedom would be as great a boon to Guy as to herself. She spoke of him somewhat contemptuously, yet with no extreme bitterness. Only once, when she alluded to the death of their infant boy, her composure deserted her and her voice quivered for a moment. Guy, it appeared, had been absent on a shooting expedition at the time, and his reception of the news, when he returned, had been what his wife described as characteristic.

"He said, 'Well, after all, you know, it's only a baby.' I quote that remark of his just by way of showing you how much and how little he is capable of feeling. He did not mean to be unkind; it was his way of offering consolation and pointing out the folly of crying over spilt milk. But I believe it was from that moment that I began to look forward quite definitely to the—the release which was in store for me upon our return to England. For many reasons, it was best to go on as we were while Guy's duties kept him in Ceylon."

"And is he aware," Mr. Dent inquired, "of the release which awaits him?"

"I hardly know. I told him that it would be out of the question for me to live at the depot in the north where he will have to take up his quarters, and he seemed to acquiesce. He said something about getting a house in London. The truth is that he will cheerfully acquiesce in any arrangement which does not threaten his personal comfort; only, after he has seen his people and consulted with them, objections are certain to be raised; so that it will be as well to meet him and them with an accomplished fact."

"Dear me!—what sort of an accomplished fact, I wonder?"

"Well, a house. I shall feel that I stand upon a footing of independence as soon as I have a house of my own—and can lock myself into it, if I choose."

"Ah! And doesn't it strike you that Guy's comfort may be in some degree threatened by the loss of five thousand pounds a year?"

"Of course we shall make a division," answered Clarissa, a little impatiently; "I thought you would take that for granted. As he will be to all intents and purposes a bachelor, he will really be better off with an income of twenty-five hundred pounds than I shall be. But if he thinks he ought to have more than half, he can have more."

"A dissolution of partnership upon the pecuniary terms that you mention," said Mr. Dent, "would, among business men, be considered a highly satisfactory one for the retiring partner. Well, my dear, you are your own mistress, and can dispose of your income as may seem good to you. You will not expect a man of my age and conventional prejudices to approve unreservedly of what you say that you mean to do; but I will, at all events, abstain from offering advice for which I haven't been asked. I will only venture to suggest that you should wait for your husband's return before proclaiming your intentions. Your mother-in-law is a most charming and amiable lady; but I suspect that, if you were to tell her as much as you have told me, there might be—avoidable unpleasantnesses."

"Oh, I shall tell her nothing; I don't feel that I am bound to tell her anything," Clarissa answered, with a gesture of slightly disdainful indifference. "I did feel bound to tell you, Uncle Tom, because, after all, you are the only near relation I have in the world."

She was disappointed, and showed that she was disappointed, at the composure with which she had been listened to by her only near relation; one does not propose

to set the house on fire with the anticipation of being told
that one is free to do as one pleases with one's own.   But
Mr. Dent, even after Clarissa had so far sacrificed her dignity as to ask whether he did not consider her justified
in setting conventionality at defiance, declined to commit
himself.

"I have heard your version of the affair, my dear; I
haven't heard your husband's," he replied.   "How can I
pronounce judgment upon an *ex parte* statement ?   Moreover, I take it that you hold yourself at liberty to snap
your finger and thumb at any judgment of mine."

That was so far true that she certainly had no intention
of yielding to an adverse judgment ; and, after a night of
reflection, she was able to tell herself that she was glad
Uncle Tom had proved so accommodating.   What, indeed,
would have been the use of arguments and expostulations ?
She knew her own mind, and knew well enough all that
there was to be said against, as well as in favor of, amicable separations.   She had not, to be sure, deemed it necessary to mention that she and Guy had parted upon cold
terms, owing to his behavior with a certain actress who
had visited Ceylon in the exercise of her profession.   To
have mentioned that would merely have been to obscure the
real issue—with which actresses had little or nothing to do.

So the first and most important thing to be done was to
seek out house-agents and inspect untenanted houses—an
occupation which, if not precisely exhilarating in itself
(for nothing in the world looks quite so hopelessly unsuitable and undesirable as an empty house), at least kept her
fully engaged for several days and spared her the pertina-
cious visits of Lady Luttrell.   That Lady Luttrell smelled a
rat and was exceedingly anxious to be reassured was evidenced by the cards, scribbled over with affectionate messages, which she left at the door every afternoon ; but
Clarissa was not much afraid of her mother-in-law, whose
measure experience had enabled her to take ; though doubtless Uncle Tom had been right in recommending that revelations should be postponed until Guy's arrival.   As in

duty bound, she called twice in Grosvenor Place, taking care to do so at an hour when nobody was likely to be at home; and when she and her uncle dined there one evening, the presence of other guests rendered confidential intercourse impossible.

"Have you found a house to suit you yet?" Mr. Dent inquired suavely, while they were driving home from this entertainment. "I wouldn't be in too great a hurry about it, if I were you; people always begin by asking a much higher rent than they have any expectation of getting."

He had been curiously, not to say provokingly, impassive upon the subject of his niece's plans ever since they had been intimated to him. It was his habit to breakfast early and be off to the City before she left her room, and when they met at dinner he seldom troubled her with questions as to how she had spent her day. Clarissa had an uncomfortable impression that he did not very much believe her to be in earnest, and that he, too, was awaiting Guy's advent to join in an organized attack upon her impregnable position. Her position was, for many reasons, impregnable; yet it would have been more satisfactory, perhaps, to have been given an opportunity of proving it so.

Opportunity presented itself, about a fortnight later, in the person of Guy himself, who, having disembarked at Portsmouth forty-eight hours previously, had telegraphed at once to his wife, and whose despatch had been forwarded from Sir Robert Luttrell's house to Portland Place. The meeting, which took place in the somewhat stiff and gloomy drawing-room where Aunt Susan had been wont to doze over her knitting in days of yore, partook of the formal character of its surroundings. Guy—smiling, interrogative, obviously embarrassed—made a hesitating forward movement which might have culminated in an embrace if Clarissa had not drawn back. As it was, he contented himself with shaking hands, and saying, cheerfully:

"Well, you got over your journey all right, I hope? Little one all right too?"

Clarissa answered that both she and the little one were
all right ; and then she begged him to sit down.

"I expected to find you in Grosvenor Place," Guy said ;
"but they tell me your uncle won't surrender you yet.
And, after all, I dare say you're more comfortable here,
having this big house practically all to yourself."

"I don't know that I care about a big house," Clarissa
replied ; "but I certainly do feel the necessity of having
one to myself, and I have seen several during the last few
days which I think will do very well for mé.   I want to tell
you, Guy — and I don't think you will be either surprised
or distressed to hear it—that I am going to live by myself
for the future.   We need not quarrel ; we need not even
announce that we have agreed to live apart ; only you must
go your way, which cannot be mine, and I must go mine,
which cannot be yours.   Indeed, that is what we have
been doing for a long time past—under rather less favorable conditions.   Just now your being obliged to join the
depot of your regiment in the North will lend an air of
vraisemblance to the arrangement."

Guy Luttrell, who, since we saw him last, had aged a
little and had put on more flesh, frowned meditatively at
his boots and remained silent for some seconds.   Presently
he looked up, with a smile in his blue eyes, and said :

"Really, you know, Clarissa, I think this is rather a
strong measure to take because I asked little Léonie What's-
her-name — upon my word, I have clean forgotten her
name !—to supper.   I was sorry you were vexed about it,
and I told you so at the time ; but—"

"But I am not taking this measure, which I quite admit
is a rather strong one, on that account, and you know very
well that I am not," interrupted Clarissa.   "I take it because — well, in a word, because it is inevitable.   Why
should we renew disputes which we have had before, and
which never lead to anything except an increased longing
on both our parts to run away ?   It is easy for a man to run
away ; he has barracks and clubs and other places to run
to ; it isn't so easy for a woman."

"You don't seem to be finding it difficult," Guy interpolated.

"I should find it almost impossible but for the happy accident that I have means of my own. It ought not to be so, but of course in the majority of cases it must be so; and that is just one of the injustices which I hope will be set right in the better times that are coming. But I must not trouble you with my notions, which I know you consider fantastic. As we are upon the subject of money, I may as well say now that I should suggest our making an equal division of our income. That would give us about twenty-five hundred pounds a year each, I believe. But I shall be satisfied with less."

Guy rose, and, walking to the window, gazed down for a moment at the broad thoroughfare and the passing vehicles.

"Pleasant to see hansom-cabs again, isn't it?" said he, quite irrelevantly.

His eyelids were, as usual, half-closed; he looked perfectly good-humored, contented, and sleepy; but Clarissa, who knew that her husband, on the rare occasions when he was angry, always looked like that, perceived that she had wounded him, and was not sorry for it. He had so often wounded her, while she had so seldom been able to flatter herself that she had inflicted even a transitory pang upon him!

"Will that arrangement suit you?" she asked, presently.

"Oh, the money arrangement? Well, no—thanks very much—I'm afraid it wouldn't suit me." He turned his back to the window and took two steps towards his wife. "Look here, Clarissa," said he; "I am anything you like to call me, and you are not inclined to call me anything very complimentary, I imagine; but really, strange as it may appear to you, I am not the sort of person who can be bribed to take himself off. I am ready to take myself off free of expense, and you may be sure that I shall never touch a penny of your money."

From this very inconvenient and disconcerting attitude she strove in vain to move him, being a good deal less

touched by his show of unselfishness than annoyed with
him for exhibiting that virtue so tardily and inopportunely.

"But you put me in the wrong!" she exclaimed, at
length.

"I am sorry for that," answered Guy; "but, according
to my view, you were there already, you see. Anyhow, I
can't offer to put you in the right by accepting a retiring
pension. We will say no more about the matter, if you
please—especially as there are one or two other points to
be considered. There is Netta, for instance."

"Of course I shall keep her with me," said Clarissa,
quickly; "you can't expect or wish to deprive me of my
child!"

"No; but I don't expect or wish to be deprived of my
child either. I must be allowed to have free access to her
when I choose."

Clarissa nodded. "I think that is only reasonable," she
said.

"Do you, really? How awfully generous of you! Then
I shall make so bold as to take her out for an occasional
holiday, and perhaps, if I am still alive when she grows
up, she will sometimes come and spend a week with me.
Meanwhile, it will be my endeavor to remind you as seldom
as possible of the painful circumstance that you bear my
name. By-the-way, what do you propose to do about my
people? Are they to be told the whole truth at once, or
allowed to find it out by degrees for themselves?"

"That must be as you think best," Clarissa answered.
"I should have liked to be able to tell them that you
would always have the half of my income, whatever it
might be."

"But as it won't be in your power to tell them that, I
advise you to keep them more or less in the dark. Anything rather than rows! As for me, I shall make haste to
bury myself at Kendal; but you, I understand, mean to
establish yourself in London?"

"Yes, I mean to establish myself in London. I want
you to understand, please, that, although nothing would

induce me to live with you again as your wife, I shall always be glad to see you as—as a friend, and that I would not have separated myself from you now if—if I had felt that it was at all possible to do otherwise."

Guy took several turns up and down the room. More than once he opened his lips, as if upon the point of speaking, but closed them again, and at length he remarked: "Well, I suppose that is about all that there is to be said?"

Clarissa, apparently, had nothing further to add; so he wished her good-bye—without shaking hands this time—and presently the front door was heard to close behind him.

His wife, whose victory was thus complete, was less relieved and less triumphant than she had expected to be. That she had been absolutely within her right in acting as she had done she did not doubt; and if the whole history of her married life were related, many ladies might be found to agree with her. But, then, he had spoiled all by refusing to take her money! She had to console herself by reflecting that he certainly would take it in the long-run.

"He is entitled to it; his father and mother are sure to urge it upon him; and he is so easy-going that he won't be able to hold out against them. Besides which, he will feel the want of it; and he is not a man who can feel the want of anything that is within his reach and refrain from stretching out his hand."

CHAPTER XVIII

PAUL TRIES HIS HAND

"I REALLY don't see what good you are likely to do by reasoning with her or scolding her," said Sir Robert Luttrell. "On the other hand, you may do some harm. It seems to me that for the present, at all events, we had better affect a judicious blindness."

He was sitting in his study, late at night, before a table littered with documents upon which he had been at work ever since dinner, and the state of public affairs was, for the moment, so dubious and dispiriting that he felt little inclination to discuss the unsatisfactory state of private affairs with his wife, who had just returned from an evening entertainment.

"*Mais enfin!—il faudrait prendre un parti!*" exclaimed Lady Luttrell, who sometimes lapsed into her own language when she was perplexed or irritated. "What is one to conclude from Guy's having gone off into banishment, from his refusing to leave the army—as it would be only natural for him to do, now that he has a comfortable fortune—and from Clarissa's having taken this house in Cadogan Gardens, as if her husband's movements were no concern of hers? What," repeated Lady Luttrell, spreading her hands. apart with an eloquent gesture, "is one to conclude?"

"Oh, well, I suppose one must conclude that they are a. pair of fools—or, at any rate, that one of them is a fool,'" answered Sir Robert, impatiently. "Leave him alone and he'll come home. In point of fact, he simply *must*, unless. he wishes to live upon his pay for the future ; for Heaven knows *I* can't afford to keep him. How I am going to keep

12

myself, if our side loses the General Election, as I expect
it will, is more than I can tell you."

"But Parliament isn't dissolved yet, Robert."

"It is going to be ; and as we have scarcely made a single
mistake during all the years that we have been in office, a
grateful country is pretty sure to kick us out.   Perhaps I
ought to be thankful that Haccombe is not entailed ; but
at the present moment I don't feel very much disposed to
be thankful for anything.   Least of all for having a son
who is—saving your presence—such an infernal ass as not
to know when he is well off.   Leave him alone, I tell you,
and let him come to his senses at his leisure."

"As far as I know, Guy has not been in the least to
blame," returned Lady Luttrell.   "The question is what
is to be done about Clarissa ?   Is she to be left alone, to
do exactly as she pleases ?"

"It is always a good plan to let people do as they please
when you have no means of preventing them.   From what
Dent tells me, I gather that the woman is upon her hind-
legs and that she has had some provocation.   You know
what happens when a horse gets upon his hind-legs and his
mouth is touched.   If you will be advised by me, Antoinette, you won't touch Clarissa's mouth just now.   She
means, I take it, to play the idiot, and nobody can stop
her.   After she has had her fling, she will quiet down and
realize that a married woman who has had a split with her
husband occupies an equivocal position in society.   There
is no occasion for us to advertise or acknowledge the circumstance that she has had a split with her husband.
Added to which, we shall make it ten times more difficult
for her to retreat gracefully if we do."

This, it had to be admitted, was sage counsel, and Lady
Luttrell resigned herself to act upon it.   She was extremely
angry with her daughter-in-law; but she contrived, by
putting pressure upon herself, to swallow down her wrath
and simulate ignorance of the obvious.   Clarissa, on her
side, seemed quite willing to be friendly ; though she did
not go out of her way to seek her husband's family, with

the exception of Madeline, who was often with her, and who was assisting her to furnish the house in Cadogan Gardens which she had secured. Madeline probably knew more than her mother did, but was not inclined to be communicative when questioned.

"I am not at all sure that Clarissa is a good companion for you, my dear," sighed Lady Luttrell, who was becoming alive to some of the disadvantages of bringing up a daughter à l'anglaise; but Madeline only professed to wonder what contamination could result from discussions with upholsterers, and indeed it was true that Clarissa and she were chiefly occupied with upholstery at that time.

Mr. Dent had vainly implored his niece to take up her residence with him, pointing out that she would have all the liberty that she could desire under his roof, and that she would do him a great kindness by keeping house for him.

"You wouldn't like my friends, Uncle Tom," was her reply; "and I hope to see a good deal of my friends as soon as I am settled."

Her friends! Where in the world had she picked them up, seeing that she had had absolutely none before her departure for Ceylon, and that Singhalese society cannot be said to be largely represented in London? But it soon appeared that she had for some time past been in active correspondence with certain persons, for whom, so far as he knew anything about them, Mr. Dent had, in truth, no great liking. A few of these, who called upon her in Portland Place, he chanced to encounter—women in strange attire, long-haired, flabby-looking men, whose names he recollected, when reminded of them, to have heard as associated with what seemed to him to be a singularly silly propaganda. Upon the whole, Mr. Dent was quite of one mind with Sir Robert in deeming that Clarissa was bent upon playing the idiot, and had better not be interfered with until she was tired of so doing.

If this good-humored and slightly contemptuous acquiescence in her vagaries was not altogether agreeable to its subject, a different method of treatment was provided for her by Paul Luttrell, who met her at dinner in Grosvenor Place one evening, and who, in expressing the pleasure that it gave him to renew acquaintance with her, told her frankly that the pleasure was not so great as he had hoped that it would be.   Paul, now vicar of a poor parish down Whitechapel way, had acquired a certain notoriety, both as an eloquent preacher and as an occasional writer of articles upon the labor question.   Clarissa, who had read his articles with interest, was unaffectedly glad to meet him again, and not at all sorry to be provided at last with an opportunity of defending herself.   Because, although she had been explicit with Uncle Tom, he had received her statement in such a manner as practically to take the wind out of her sails.

"How do you mean?" she inquired, putting up her glasses to scrutinize her neighbor; though of course she knew well enough what he meant.

"Well, it is never exactly a pleasure," he answered, "to reflect that one has had a hand in bringing about a fiasco, and you may remember that it was I who married you."

"I remember that you performed the ceremony," said Clarissa, smiling; "I remember also that you were by no means enthusiastic about performing it. If anybody ought to have a clear conscience in the matter, you ought. I was only afraid, from the way in which you looked at me just now, that you doubted whether my own conscience was as clear as it actually is."

"Oh, I don't doubt your self-approval—which is what many people mistake for a clear conscience. But perhaps, since you remember so much, you may remember a little conversation that we had before your wedding-day. I told you then that, according to the Christian view, marriage is something more than a mere contract, to be dissolved at any given moment by mutual consent, and you replied, I believe, that you would certainly never wish for an amicable separation from your husband. You have changed your mind, it seems."

"I may as well say at once," returned Clarissa, "that arguments from the Christian point of view don't appeal to me. Christianity has been made to sanction intolerance, persecution, slavery, and I don't know how many other forms of injustice. If you want to be able to blame me, you must find some broader and more human ground for censure."

"I am generally accused of being a little bit too broad in my ideas," remarked the Reverend Paul; "but the line has to be drawn somewhere, and I can't admit that a woman is entitled to break solemn vows which she has taken upon herself with her eyes open."

"But my eyes were not open," protested Clarissa; "that is just the point—or, at least, one of the points. I heard things about Guy after we were married—Mrs. Antrobus and other people told me — which, if I had only known them in time, would certainly have prevented me from taking any such vows. Whose fault was it that I did not know them in time?"

"Ah, there I am partly with you. It is a difficult question—"

"I don't see the slightest difficulty about it," interrupted Clarissa. "In what conceivable case, except in the case of marriage, would you maintain that people ought to be allowed and urged to take a leap in the dark? I, and other women who have suffered, are determined that girls shall not be kept in the dark any longer, if we can help it."

"Nevertheless, there are difficulties and complications. But even admitting that you were not as fully enlightened as you might have been, I still think that, when once the marriage had taken place, you were in duty bound to live with your husband, unless his conduct was such as to practically drive you away from him. And I have heard of no reason as yet for your separating yourself from Guy except that you are not in sympathy with him."

The above colloquy was held after dinner, and as a good many other people were present, Clarissa and her rebuking cleric, who had withdrawn into a recess of the long drawing-room, were in little danger of being overheard or interrupted.

"I don't expect any *man* to sympathize with me," she declared; "not even you, though it does seem to me that the religion which you profess ought to compel you to do so. But there are reasons for my claiming the right to lead my own life which I think you would have to call sufficient if you could afford to be perfectly honest."

"I am, quite sure that I can't afford to be anything else," said Paul.

"Mind, I don't assert that those are the reasons which weigh most with me; only, if it had not been for them, I should perhaps hardly have had the courage of my opinions. If Guy had continued to care for me as he did at first, I might have discovered, and I suppose I should have discovered, that he was a very different sort of person from what I had imagined him to be; but I should not have felt, as I do now, that I was under no obligation whatsoever to spend the rest of my days with him."

After that exordium Paul was prepared to hear the worst; so that what he heard did not scandalize him quite so much as Clarissa had perhaps expected it to do. There had been flirtations, it seemed, and even a good many of them; but to what extent those flirtations had been carried appeared doubtful, although the narrator spoke as if no doubt could be entertained upon the subject. No complaint of ill-usage was put forward.

"He has scarcely spoken an unkind word to me since the day of our marriage," Clarissa said, disdainfully. "That would have been far too much trouble, and would have exposed him to the possible discomfort of a scene, you understand. Courageous as he is supposed to be, there are things which Guy doesn't care to face, and discomfort is the chief of them. If he is going to be a little uncomfortable now, that is no fault of mine. I offered him the half of my income, and I think he ought to have taken it. But he will probably end by taking it."

Paul heard her out without interruption. He thought

he could understand pretty well what was amiss and that this breach was not of necessity an irreparable one; but he took good care to refrain from saying so. The only comment that he permitted himself upon what he had been told was:

"I am not going to undertake my brother's defence; he has evidently not been a pattern husband. Still, I suppose there must be a very large number of worse husbands who are tolerated and forgiven."

"Is there a single wife in the world by whom such conduct as his would be tolerated or forgiven?" asked Clarissa.

"I hardly know; but from all that one sees and hears, I should think so. Besides—"

"Besides, there is a vast difference between a husband and a wife? But that is the very thing that I deny; and I should have imagined that Christianity denied it too. Or do you really maintain that what is an unpardonable sin in the one is only an amiable weakness in the other?"

One is not a parson in Whitechapel without being required to take up an uncompromising stand with reference to such conjugal questions, nor can one occupy that position long without appreciating the beauty and necessity of compromise. Paul adroitly contrived to convey to his sister-in-law the impression that she had had the best of the argument, while reserving to himself full right to disapprove of her action. One result, therefore, of their interview was that they parted very good friends, and another was that the Reverend Paul Luttrell took a third-class return ticket to Kendal the next day.

He was a good fellow—kind-hearted, by no means wanting in intelligence, and conversant, after a somewhat restricted fashion, with the vagaries of human nature. Perhaps, like priests of all denominations, he was apt to rely a little too much upon his own persuasive powers and to assume that, because he rarely failed with those who sought his advice, he was likely to succeed in cases where clerical authority does not count for much. Anyhow, as his means were small and his time fully occupied, he would not have undertaken that long journey unless he had felt tolerably confident of his ability to do two mistaken people a good turn. Accordingly, he was no sooner seated, with a pipe in his mouth, in his elder brother's modest quarters than he deemed it his duty to read that delinquent a sharp lecture.

"You are a great deal more lucky than you deserve to be," Guy was told in conclusion; "for, whatever Clarissa may be pleased to say, I am convinced that if you will only go back to her, beg her forgiveness and resolve to behave better for the future, all that you have done in the past will be condoned. She is under the impression that she is standing up for a principle; but the simple truth is that she is wounded and jealous—as any other woman would be in her place."

"My dear old chap," returned Guy, who, during his brother's harangue had been reclining upon two chairs, with his feet rather higher than his head, and smoking placidly, "I'm awfully glad to see you, and obliged to you for having come all this way to see me; but, as far as your errand goes, a sheet of note-paper and a penny stamp would have answered all the purpose. You won't give me credit for possessing many virtues, I'm sure; but, perhaps you'll allow that I am patient. Well, Clarissa has got to the end of my patience, and I don't propose to beg her pardon any more—that's flat! She may have her grievances and I may have mine; but there wouldn't be the slightest use in discussing them; it's evident, at least, that she can't have much to complain of now, since she has been allowed to have her own way, and since she remains a rich woman, while I'm a deuced poor man."

"She doesn't wish you to be a poor man. On the contrary, she asks nothing better than to make over the half of her income to you."

"So she was kind enough to inform me; but, you see, I don't happen to be built quite that way. I didn't marry her for her money, and I don't want it. Or, to speak with stricter accuracy, I can do without it."

"I am not so sure that you can," said Paul, musingly,

after a pause. "Things are going badly—worse, perhaps, than you suspect. My father doesn't say much, and it is not for me to question him; but I am afraid there can be no doubt that he has been living far beyond his income for many years, and of course his income, like that of all land-owners, has seriously diminished of late."

"That's a funny sort of argument for a parson to use," remarked Guy, laughing.

"Well, such as it is, I am not ashamed of using it," returned his brother. "You say you can do without your wife's money, and I only want to point out to you that it is an open question whether you can or will. I understand your thinking it beneath you to take an allowance from her; but don't you see that there is considerable danger of your consenting—as she expects that you will—to accept that allowance in the long-run?"

"Oh, that is what she expects? Then let me assure you and her, once for all, that there isn't the slightest danger of my accepting it. And, as there is nothing more to be said, I think we'll change the subject now, if you don't mind."

It was not at once that Paul could be induced to change the subject; but he was forced to recognize before he went to bed that his mission had been a complete failure, and he returned to London on the ensuing day, feeling more like a fool than he was at all accustomed to feel. There was no overcoming the imperturbability or gaining the confidence of a man who neither admitted nor denied anything, who neither blamed his wife nor took blame to himself, and who appeared to be satisfied with a condition of things which he must have felt to be thoroughly unsatisfactory.

"The only comfort," reflected Paul, as he journeyed southwards, "is that they would behave in quite a different manner if they weren't still fond of one another. Perhaps the child will bring them together again eventually; one can but hope so. But it is a pity that Clarissa is a rich woman and that Guy is not the man to put up long with the discomforts of poverty. That complicates the situation in more ways than one."

CHAPTER XIX

THE "MOVEMENT"

THE situation was doubtless, as the Reverend Paul Luttrell had discovered, a somewhat complicated one; and so, of necessity, are most of the human situations which arise during a highly civilized epoch. The situation, personal and political, in which Sir Robert Luttrell, for example, found himself, was of so involved a character as to demand his whole attention and to prompt the dismissal, with an impatient shrug of the shoulders, of his daughter-in-law's whims from consideration. With the prospect of compulsory retirement into private life looming upon the near horizon, with estates hopelessly mortgaged, with expenses which seemed to increase rather than diminish, and with premonitory symptoms which could not always be ignored of declining health, how could he be expected to bother himself about matters which, after all, concerned his successor and must be left to his successor to be set right?

"You have done what you could for Guy; hadn't you better begin to try what you can do for Madeline?" he suggested to his wife. "I tell you plainly that, in my opinion, there isn't too much time to be lost; for in all probability there will be no London season for us next year. I must get rid of this house; and I only wish I were half as sure of selling it at a reasonable figure as I am of being out of office before the autumn!"

Lady Luttrell was fain to acquiesce. It was certainly most important to establish Madeline, and, although she took a somewhat less gloomy view than her husband of the political outlook, she knew enough to know that Sir Rob-

ert's chances of being included in a reconstructed ministry were not great. Also she knew that, without the excuse of official duties and the aid of an official salary, it
would be almost essential to give up the house in Grosvenor
Place. Thus Clarissa was suffered for the time being to
pursue her independent career unmolested, Mr. Dent, to
all appearance, aiding and abetting her.

"I shall always think, you know, that you have been
very much to blame," Lady Luttrell could not help telling
that elderly philosopher, when she met him at a dinner-
party one evening. "Surely you ought to have some little
influence over your niece!"

"I should lose what little I have if I were to issue orders
to her," Mr. Dent replied, smiling. "Do you think that
obedience is to be expected of a woman who has £5000 a
year of her own?"

"Obedience is to be expected of all women when they
are managed in the proper way," Lady Luttrell declared,
decisively. "One doesn't issue orders; one has recourse
to other methods—one appeals to their sense of duty, to
their natural affection. Every right-minded woman must
have some natural affection for her parents or—or her
uncle."

"But, my dear lady, I thought you agreed with me that
Clarissa is not in her right mind just now. Besides, I am
so inexperienced, never having had any children of my
own. You must try to forgive me for taking up a de-
tached attitude, and for being powerless to command the
willing submission which I am sure your children render
to you."

Lady Luttrell suppressed a sigh. She herself had rendered unquestioning submission to her parents, in accordance with the French custom, which she felt more and more
convinced, as she grew older, was a salutary one; but Madeline had been brought up as an English girl and had English ideas of independence—in addition to the extravagant
ideas with which it was to be feared that she had been imbued by Clarissa. There could be no absolute certainty

that Madeline would dutifully bestow her hand upon a husband of her mother's choosing. Moreover, universally admired and liked though the girl was, it was by no means easy to choose a husband for her among the very few Catholic bachelors who were to be met with in society. A mother-in-law so beset by pressing cares and anxieties was, as may be imagined, not disinclined to accord at least a temporary respite to Clarissa, who had now taken formal possession of her abode in Cadogan Gardens.

That abode, notwithstanding the extreme rapidity with which it had been rendered inhabitable, was a very luxurious and charmingly furnished one.

"It is one of our fundamental principles," Madeline was informed, "to surround ourselves with beautiful things, or, if beautiful things can't be had, at least with pretty ones. We consider that quite as much a duty as personal cleanliness, and quite as necessary to mental development."

Clarissa had taken to making free use of the first person plural. It seemed (as in the case of writers of leading-articles) to lend a certain dignity and sanction to sentiments which were sometimes startling, often silly, and almost always trite. But who "we" were Madeline did not very distinctly gather. With the names of some of her sister-in-law's new intimates she was dimly familiar, having heard of them as speakers at public meetings and contributors of essays to advanced periodicals; but her acquaintance with their writings was of the slightest, and she did not find them personally attractive. The women, for the most part, affected a style of dress which was neither fashionable nor becoming, while the men—notably a certain fat and rather dirty poetaster named Alfred Loosemore, who was in the habit of dropping in to tea, and whose great reputation for conversational brilliancy appeared to rest rather upon his self-satisfied method of enunciation than upon anything that he actually said—were downright repugnant to her.

"Oh, I don't know that I particularly like him," Clarissa said, in answer to some strongly worded criticisms in which Madeline indulged, after having with difficulty sat him out one afternoon; "I dare say your father does not particularly like all the people who profess Tory principles and support Tory organizations. But Mr. Loosemore is in sympathy with the movement, you see, and for that reason one feels bound to show him some civility."

The "movement," broadly speaking, was the Emancipation of Woman—nothing less ; and with that Madeline also was, or believed herself to be, in sympathy; although, judging by the remarks of the ladies who frequented the house in Cadogan Gardens, it was a little difficult to understand from what species of bondage it could still remain requisite for them to be emancipated. Clarissa, however, did not seem to go quite to the lengths that they did, save with respect to the one subject of marriage, upon which her doctrine was, at all events, intelligible.

"I think that whatever men claim for themselves we have a right to claim for ourselves," she declared. "As matters stand, they claim a great deal too much and we do not claim nearly enough. When that is more generally understood and acknowledged, the first blow will have been struck at a vast deal of vice and misery which is now accepted as inevitable."

She did not always talk nonsense, nor was she always didactic. She was very fond of Madeline, very anxious that the girl's life should prove a happy one, and not without sympathetic intuitions of which age and commerce with the world had wellnigh deprived the kind-hearted Lady Luttrell. It was, therefore, natural enough that Madeline, who could not unbosom herself to her mother, should slip off to Cadogan Gardens upon every available opportunity. If, in the course of her long talks with her sister-in-law, she never mentioned Raoul de Malglaive by name, that was not (as she herself imagined) because that young man was really nothing to her, or because he had given her no sufficient excuse for mentioning him, but because Clarissa did not wish, for the moment, to pronounce any opinion upon a Frenchman of uncertain constancy and morality. What was of primary importance was to dissuade Madeline from hastily

engaging herself to some eligible suitor, brought forward
by Lady Luttrell, and as a means towards that end M. de
Malglaive might be utilized so long as he was not openly
alluded to.

"I have quite made up my mind," was the gratifying
announcement which Clarissa received at length from her
disciple, "that I will never marry a man whom I do not
love, and I am beginning to think, with you, that love
must mean respect. Now I don't see how it could be possible for anybody to respect Lord Stoneyhurst."

"Lord Stoneyhurst!" exclaimed Clarissa, with a start.
"Who is Lord Stoneyhurst? Who asks you to respect
him?"

"Oh, nobody has gone quite so far as to ask that of
me!" answered Madeline, laughing. "But I have been
asked indirectly, and I suppose I shall soon be asked directly, to marry him. He is rich, and a widower, and has
no children; so, although poor Lady Stoneyhurst only died
about a year ago, he is understood to be on the lookout for
her successor, and he has flattered me with a good deal of
attention lately."

"Horrible old profligate!" cried Clarissa, unhesitatingly.

"Well, he isn't exactly that; on the contrary, he is said
to be very devout and charitable. But he is quite old—
forty at least, I should think—and desperately stupid.
One can't feel much respect for a man who never mounts
a horse or fires a gun."

"Well, I don't know about that," said Clarissa, remembering Mr. Alfred Loosemore and others, whose tastes were
not of a sporting character; "but the question of respect
need not arise, since you say that you don't love Lord
Stoneyhurst."

Madeline burst out laughing. "Oh no; I certainly don't
love him," she replied; "but I shall just as certainly be
told that I shall learn to love him. It seems that well-
conducted wives always do learn to love their husbands in
France."

That no such phenomenon could be expected to occur in England was the theme of an eloquent and impressive discourse, to which Madeline listened attentively during the next five minutes. It was hardly necessary to be so emphatic, for she had in reality no intention of espousing the wealthy Romanist nobleman whom both Sir Robert and Lady Luttrell had begun to regard with eyes of fond expectation; still, when battles have to be fought, there is some comfort in being provided with a backer, even though one may place full reliance upon one's own strength, and a few of Clarissa's remarks seemed worthy of recollection and repetition.

It was about ten days later that Lady Luttrell, who had been reasoning tearfully with her daughter, and whom circumstances had given an excellent excuse for shedding tears, was astonished to hear Madeline open the case for the defence with the words " If there be such a thing as sin—"

" *If* there be such a thing !" ejaculated the poor lady, aghast. " My dear child, what can you mean ? Is *this* the sort of doctrine that Clarissa teaches you, in addition to all the other absurdities that she professes ?"

" Well, I suppose it may be uncertain whether some of the things which are called sins ought not to be known by a different name. But I was only going to say that there can't be much uncertainty about the sin of taking vows which one knows that one would never be able to keep. I told Lord Stoneyhurst the truth, and he quite agreed with me that, as that was the truth, he had better look elsewhere for a wife."

" I can't think what you can have told him !" groaned Lady Luttrell. " Something altogether *inconvenable*, I am afraid ; for he said to me afterwards that you seemed to have singularly advanced ideas. One sees where they come from, those advanced ideas, and one sees what they have led to in Clarissa's own case."

" But, mother dear, I think Clarissa is right," returned the girl. " It is a great pity, of course, that she and Guy should not be friends, and perhaps they will make friends again some day; but I think she is right in what she says about marriage. I think it is absolutely essential, in the first place, to love the man whom you marry, and, in the second place, I think there should not be one law for women and another for men. What is considered to make us unworthy of being loved ought to be considered so for them too."

"Oh, dear!" sighed Lady Luttrell, throwing up her hands, "what a very ridiculous way of talking! You have adopted Clarissa's very voice and manner, with your 'I thinks' and your absurd and rather indecent theories. Poor Lord Stoneyhurst, too, of all people! Why, the unfortunate man has been known all his life as a—what shall I say?—as a sort of little saint!"

"Well, he declined to answer some of the questions that I asked him, anyhow," remarked Madeline.

"Wretched child! is it permitted to ask such questions? —for I can easily conjecture what they were. A day will come, I am afraid, when you will bitterly regret having thrown away this chance; but what is still worse is that you will never have a chance of marrying at all—no, not one; *c'est moi qui vous en réponds!*—until you cease to demand the impossible. It is all very fine for Clarissa, who has her own money and can afford to be outrageous; but even she will end by discovering that religion and society, not to speak of common-sense, are not to be defied with impunity."

Any one who sets to work to defy these three powerful forces must, no doubt, be a very courageous or a very foolish person, and it may be that Clarissa was both. Warm approval and encouragement awaited Madeline when the latter came to announce Lord Stoneyhurst's dismissal.

"You have acted quite rightly, and your mother must know in her heart that you have," she was assured. "If only we are true to ourselves, we need not mind hard words."

Nevertheless, certain hard sayings of Lady Luttrell's,

which had been repeated in the course of the interview, had found their way between the joints of Clarissa's armor, while certain soft sayings which assailed her daily from another quarter had a somewhat similar effect. Netta, it might have been hoped — and, indeed, had been hoped — would scarcely notice Guy's absence, seeing how young she was and how frequent his absences had been in Ceylon; but this expectation had not been fulfilled. Perhaps some instinctive suspicion warned the child that there was a screw loose, perhaps the servants had been less reticent than they ought to have been; at any rate, she was perpetually asking for her father, and the explanation that he was obliged to go away to look after his soldiers did not appease her. Why, she wanted to know, could they not go too ? Besides, he had promised to take her to the Zoological Gardens and show her the lions and tigers. She declined, even with tears, to be taken thither by her mother, declaring that unless father were to be of the party she did not want to see the lions and tigers at all. The upshot of all this was that Clarissa, urged thereto by a sense of duty and undeterred by a strong sense of disinclination, wrote a letter to her husband, suggesting that he should, if possible, come up to London for a few days.

"Netta," she wrote, "is fretting about you. She is too young to understand, and it would not be at all desirable to tell her at present, what our relations are. Some day, of course, she must hear the truth; but in the meantime I have no wish to keep her apart from you, and I believe our arrangement was that you should see her every now and then."

Mention was then made of the promised visit to the Zoo, and Clarissa wound up with : "I myself also, if you have no objection, should be glad to have a short conversation with you upon matters of business, which are more easily disposed of by word of mouth than by correspondence."

Guy's reply came in the concise form of a telegram. "All right. Tell little one will call for her Thursday afternoon. See you that evening or next day."

13

And at the appointed time he arrived, looking provokingly good-humored, with a carnation in his button - hole
and a smile upon his lips.

"What a capital house!" said he, on being shown into
his wife's drawing-room. "You know how to make yourself comfortable, I see; but your taste in the way of furniture and knick-knacks was always irreproachable."

Then Netta was brought in by her nurse, and, with a
screech of delight, flung herself into her father's arms.
The fact was that Guy and Netta had been sworn allies
ever since the latter had been capable of articulate speech,
and not the least of Clarissa's grievances against the former was that, although he seemed to recognize no sort of
parental duty or responsibility, he had won and returned
his child's affection. The couple set off almost at once for
the Regent's Park, where, as it subsequently appeared, they
spent a thoroughly enjoyable afternoon.

"Upon my word," said Guy, when they returned at a
rather late hour, "I was awfully sorry you hadn't come
with us. We did a ride on the elephant, and we fed the
bears, and had a high old time with the monkeys—hadn't
we, Netta? Going round the show with a small brat like
that is nearly as good as being a small brat again one's self,
you see," he added explanatorily.

Clarissa smiled—not without some suppressed bitterness.
Her husband was, perhaps, nothing but an elderly brat,
and she could understand how easy it might be for those
who did not happen to have suffered from his peccadilloes
to pardon them; but the excuse carried its own condemnation with it. A man who scuttles his ship and drowns his
crew cannot really be allowed to plead that he only did it
for fun.

However, the wreck which Guy had succeeded in accom-
plishing did not, so far as outward appearance went, look
very much like a wreck; and of this she was painfully sensible after Netta, voluble and excited, had been sent up-
stairs to tea.

"I suppose," she began, "you think I am quite satisfied, now that I have a house of my own, and that, as you put it, I have made myself comfortable."

"Oh, I don't know about that," answered Guy, "because I have never yet had the good luck to find out what will satisfy you; but I should think you ought to be."

"Yet it seems to me that I have not been so very exacting. But we need not revert to bygones. What I wished to say now was that I shall never feel satisfied or comfortable so long as you refuse to take what I consider to be justly yours. Anybody, I think, would tell you that in the case of an amicable separation, such as ours, you are entitled to the half of the income which you would have had to spend if we had remained together, and your refusal has the effect of placing me in a false position."

"Oh, if it comes to that," answered Guy, getting up, "I'm afraid anybody would tell you, and a good many people will tell you, that you *are* in a false position. But that's your own choice, you know; I thought you liked it. Anyhow, I can't offer to make you more comfortable by accepting quarterly checks; so, if that was the business matter that you wanted to talk over with me, I'll wish you good-evening. I have said all I have to say upon the subject already."

Clarissa sat silent for a few moments and brushed her hand once or twice impatiently across her forehead.

"Do you think," she asked, at length, "that it is quite fair to talk as though you, not I, were the victim?"

"I didn't know that I was talking that way," he replied. "I haven't called myself a victim, and you are very welcome to call yourself one, if it makes you any happier to do so."

"You must be well aware that I have a right to do so, and you must also, I should think, be well aware that by sentencing me to riches and yourself to poverty you assume an air of false magnanimity."

"Do I, really?" asked Guy, making rapidly for the door. "I'm very sorry; but I don't see how it is to be helped. Well, good-bye, Clarissa; I'm going to send a doll round

for Netta in the morning, and I shall see her again before
very long, I hope.   But it won't be necessary for you to
stay at home to receive me, you know."

It must be owned that he was a most provoking as well
as a most impenitent sinner, and that his wife was scarcely
to be blamed for the bitter thoughts in which she indulged
after he had left her.

CHAPTER XX

MADELINE MAKES DISCOVERIES

LIFE is so full of worries and bothers that they end by neutralizing one another. It is impossible to think of fifty things at once, and Sir Robert Luttrell, when Parliament was dissolved at the end of June, had so far the advantage over his wife that he really could not spare time to lament the perversity of his heir-apparent or deplore the curtailment of the London season.

" I have no doubt that it is all very unfortunate and very inconvenient," he told her; " but I can't help it; the younger generation must look after itself. My present business is to fight a losing battle to the best of my ability; and as this will assuredly be my last battle, I feel a certain melancholy interest in the job."

Despite the confident utterances of his fellow-ministers and those with which he himself neglected no opportunity of backing them up, he was persuaded that the fight would prove a losing one. His long political experience convinced him that his party had held office for too many years, and, although his own seat was safe enough, he was under no illusion as to his chances of ever again addressing the House from the Treasury bench. *Militavi non sine gloriâ*, he might have said; he had served the Tory party faithfully through thick and thin; a peerage and dignified retirement might have formed no unfitting conclusion to an honorable career, if only he had devoted half as much attention to the management of his private affairs as to those of his country. But, unhappily, his private affairs were in such a terrible mess that he was only too glad to be drawn away from the contemplation of them by public duties; and had Lady Luttrell known how very near an ancient family was to downright ruin, she would probably have been less plaintive over the necessity for quitting Grosvenor Place with Madeline neither engaged nor married, and Clarissa so far from being in a condition of mind to be left to her own devices.

Lady Luttrell, however, had merely a vague, uncomfortable impression that money was no longer so plentiful as it had formerly been, that Guy was in some danger of allowing the handsome income to which he was entitled to slip through his fingers, and that there might be very great trouble with Madeline, unless the girl could somehow be brought to realize that it is the duty of every woman to marry, and, if possible, to marry well. Therefore, on the journey down to Haccombe Luttrell, in which neighborhood her husband had to meet his constituents, she was somewhat fretful and peevish, grieving aloud over the loss of Lord Stoneyhurst, who had always voted with the Liberals, but who might, under the peculiar circumstances of the present election, have been tempted into the opposite camp, and denouncing the avowed Radicalism of Clarissa, who, she had been informed, was making herself quite conspicuous as a champion of the enemy.

"I dare say her eloquence won't affect a very large number of voters," remarked Sir Robert.

But Lady Luttrell said: "One never knows. An incalculable amount of mischief is done by silly women nowadays; and it is very bad taste, to say the least of it, on Clarissa's part to oppose her own family. But of course she only does it in order to annoy us, and really, Madeline dear, I sometimes think—but I am afraid it is useless for me to say what I think."

It was certainly useless; but that did not prevent the poor lady from saying what she thought again and again in terms which were necessarily painful to her daughter. During the period of electioneering and speechifying which followed, and which was not devoid of pleasurable excitement for Lady Luttrell, who enjoyed canvassing and who had plenty of political visitors to entertain, Madeline was by no means in the best of spirits. Neither by her father nor by her mother was she treated with actual unkindness; yet she was made to feel that she was more or less in disgrace. They were clearly of opinion that she had behaved in a very foolish manner, and she herself, now that she was removed from Clarissa's influence, was not certain that she had acted with complete wisdom or prudence. Why had she rejected Lord Stoneyhurst, who, to be sure, was a dull little man, but who would doubtless have proved himself an indulgent husband? Why had she discouraged one or two others, who were less dull and almost as well provided with this world's goods? Why, after all, should any girl refuse a really good offer, seeing that the inconstancy of men is proverbial, and that the love matches of England turn out no better than, if as well as, the *mariages de convenance* of France?

It was on a hot, windless afternoon, when she had been about ten days at home, that Miss Luttrell put these questions to herself, and was so fortunate, or so unfortunate, as to find a conclusive answer to them. She had rowed herself out to the middle of Haccombe Bay in the little open boat which she was permitted to use when the barometer stood at set fair, and now, drifting gently seawards with the ebbing tide upon that still expanse of blue water, she rested on her oars and allowed her thoughts to have free play. This, as good old Father Dormer, who was the keeper of her conscience, had repeatedly warned her, is a very dangerous thing to do; still, one must run occasional risks in a world which is full of hidden perils, and if there was anything specially hazardous in wondering whether she would ever see Raoul de Malglaive again, Madeline was not aware of it. Already, indeed, she had more than once looked back with pleasure and a sort of pensive regret upon her rides and talks with that smart young officer of French cavalry; the only difference was that it had not until now occurred to her to compare him with Lord Stoneyhurst and

other suitors, actual or potential. Of course she knew
very well that Raoul had admired her; but it was altogether improbable—so she told herself, and so all she had
heard from the experienced Clarissa led her to believe—
that absence would make his heart grow fonder. Besides
which, there was no real likelihood of his being at Pau
again during the ensuing winter.

Thus it came to pass that Madeline, preoccupied as she
was with the idea of marriage, and inclined as she had always been to a French rather than an English alliance, began to indulge in dim visions which had the grave, handsome, Southern countenance of her former playmate for
their centre; thus, too, it dawned upon her by degrees that
Pau without Raoul would be a sadly disappointing place of
sojourn. As the boat floated on, and as, regardless of her
complexion, she reclined in the stern, with her hands
clasped behind her head, contemplating the hazy, blue
horizon, the visions grew less dim and the central figure
became more clearly defined. In these closing years of the
nineteenth century young ladies are no longer supposed, as
they used to be, to be impervious to Cupid's darts; nor, it
is said, do they hesitate for a moment to avow to themselves and others that they are "awfully gone on" this or
that member of the other sex whose privilege it has been
to win their maidenly affections; but Madeline Luttrell,
notwithstanding her acceptance of her sister-in-law's modern theories, was in some respects old-fashioned. She was,
at all events, antiquated enough to blush up to the roots of
her hair, for the benefit of the circling sea-gulls and the
sleepy cormorants who were watching her, when she had
exclaimed aloud: "Yes; that is the truth! I do love him
—and I shall never love anybody else!"

Now, after having committed herself to such an assertion
as that—and said it aloud, too—there could be no further
question of British noblemen or gentlemen belonging to
the ancient faith. So far, so good; it is always a comfort
and a relief to know exactly how one stands. But what was
considerably less pleasant was to remember that Raoul had

committed himself to no definite assertion at all, and that he could not be held to blame if he was at that very moment breathing hints of eternal devotion into the ear of some odious countrywoman of his own. Madeline drew out of her pocket a letter which she had recently received from Clarissa, and which contained certain very severe statements respecting the male sex in general.

"They are all the same; I doubt whether one in a thousand is capable of what we call love, or can understand that there is anything to be ashamed of in infidelity. Guy, I am sure, thinks me most unreasonable; it seems to him to be a mere matter of course that his loves should be like dissolving views, and, as I say, nine hundred and ninety-nine men out of a thousand would agree with him. They have been educated to hold these opinions : all that can be done is to educate the next generation differently."

It is, no doubt, at once a duty and a privilege to labor for the welfare of posterity; still, when one has not yet celebrated one's own twentieth birthday, one naturally feels a somewhat keener personal interest in the existing generation, and Madeline could not help hoping that the existing generation might be a shade or two less black than it was painted. She did not know a very great deal about it; she was, oddly enough, under the impression that young fellows are, as a rule, more scrupulous, more unselfish, more religious in France than they are in England; it seemed to her reasonable to suppose that so exemplary a son as Raoul de Malglaive would be a true lover and a good husband. And that he was her lover, or had been a very short time ago, she was, after all, pretty sure.

So Miss Luttrell spent a quiet, enjoyable afternoon, with the sea-birds and the sea-breeze and her dreams to keep her company, until the time came for her to pull back to Haccombe harbor and stroll up to the house, where—as so often happens to poor mortals who have been dreaming of peace —a most disagreeable surprise awaited her. Lady Luttrell took in a large number of French newspapers, and it so chanced that several of these were lying upon the library-table when Madeline entered. The room was empty; everybody, it appeared, was out-of-doors, and the girl carelessly picked up *Le Petit Voyou des Basses-Pyrénées,* which by ill-luck had chanced to catch her eye. Lady Luttrell did not approve of promiscuous reading for young people; but long sojourn in a country where many things of which she did not approve were sanctioned had led to some laxity of discipline on her part, and Madeline broke no rule by perusing the vivacious and not very edifying little print which provided weekly amusement for the inhabitants of Pau.

It provided nothing of that sort for its present reader, who had no sooner curled herself up comfortably in a low easy-chair than her attention was claimed by a paragraph headed *"Charmante Aventure,"* which caused her at once to start back into a more erect attitude. The adventure, to tell the truth, was neither charming nor particularly amusing, since it seemed to have consisted merely of an unforeseen meeting between a husband and wife at a hotel where the latter was accepting the hospitality of a cavalry officer; but much interest was, of course, added to the episode by the description of the lady as *"la belle Marquise de C——,"* while the officer was delicately alluded to as *"le jeune R—— de M——, représentant d'une de nos plus austères familles béarnaises."* The details over which the writer of the paragraph chuckled and its reader writhed may be omitted. The cool demeanor of *"le jeune R—— de M——"* under circumstances of which it was stated that he was not without previous experience; the audacious explanation which he was said to have offered; the ultimate pacification of the irate husband, who, it appeared, had been called upon by his wife to explain his own presence at the hotel, and had been unable to do so without compromising a fourth person—all these things, which took up a great deal of space and were dwelt upon in a highly humorous style, certainly belonged to the category of literature which Lady Luttrell would have deemed unsuitable for young people. But it is needless to say that Madeline read the narrative from start to finish several times over, and when, with a gesture of disgust, she threw the horrible little sheet away from her, she threw all her foolish dreams away with it.

Of course the dreams had been foolish; of course Clarissa was right, and all men were the same, and she wished she was dead! Or rather, no!—on second thoughts she only wished that she was married, and she was very sorry that she had refused Lord Stoneyhurst, and, if he would ask her again, he should have a different answer. Lord Stoneyhurst, at least, would not be found entertaining *belles marquises* at provincial hotels.

Lady Luttrell, who came in presently, accompanied by several ladies who had been assisting her at a Primrose League meeting, would doubtless have pronounced this an extremely sensible conclusion, had it been imparted to her; but no immediate opportunity arose for her admission into her daughter's confidence. Lady Luttrell was very hot, very tired, and, as it presently appeared, deeply discouraged. She held a sheaf of telegrams in her hand, which she had opened in her husband's absence and which brought bad news from many quarters of the United Kingdom.

"The elections are going against us," she announced, as she sank into a chair and begged Madeline to give her a cup of tea at once. "How stupid it is to be beaten like this, when all the decent people are on our side! Those wretched agricultural laborers!—why were we too honest to promise them things which nobody can ever give them? I almost wish now that Robert would lose his seat, so that we might give up meddling with politics altogether."

A chorus of protest arose from Lady Luttrell's friends. Things had not come to such a pass as that, they declared; the Radical majority would be but a small one; the Radical ministry would never be able to retain office; there would be another general election, with another result, ere long, and assuredly it would be impossible to spare so able a man as Sir Robert Luttrell when the next Conservative administration should be formed. But perhaps they did not quite mean what they said; for everybody knew well enough that Sir Robert had had his day.

Nobody, indeed, knew that better than Sir Robert himself. He arrived, just before dinner, from a neighboring town, where he had been addressing a somewhat hostile assemblage; and with him, among others, came Mr. Dent, who had been returned unopposed for his own metropolitan constituency, and who had been doing what he could by means of platform oratory in the West of England to help less fortunate candidates. Mr. Dent, ordinarily so placid, was looking worried and uneasy, Lady Luttrell noticed—far more so than her husband, for whose pallor and obvious fatigue she had been prepared, but who seemed to be in tolerably good spirits, and who laughed, with a shrug of his shoulders, at the inevitable.

"It is such a relief to see Robert taking it so well," she murmured to her husband's friend and confidential adviser; "I was afraid he would be dreadfully upset by those telegrams."

"My dear lady," Mr. Dent answered, drawing her a little farther aside, "he is not taking it well—or rather, it is not taking him well. He is not as young as he was, and nothing but sheer pluck preserved him from fainting in public this afternoon. I came back with him on purpose to tell you so; for I must be off again immediately after dinner to catch the night mail. Don't be alarmed, and don't let him know that I have betrayed him; but do your best to keep him quiet now—and perhaps you might be able to persuade him to see a doctor. Oh no; I don't think there is anything very serious the matter; only at his age and mine slight indispositions ought not to be neglected. I dare say you know," added Mr. Dent, after a momentary hesitation, "that he has troubles on his mind unconnected with politics."

"You mean money troubles?" asked Lady Luttrell, quickly.

"Yes, I mean money troubles. Sooner or later they must be faced, I am afraid; but for the time being he should be induced to forget them, if possible. I have done my best in that direction; will you do the same?"

Lady Luttrell smiled and sighed. "It is never very difficult to induce Robert to forget money matters," she said.

"Ah, I don't know! It used to be easy; it is not so easy now. To tell you the whole truth, he has good reason for being troubled. Well—better days may come; though scarcely for him, I fear."

"If only Guy and Clarissa would be sensible enough to make friends again!" exclaimed Lady Luttrell, with ready comprehension of his meaning.

"Exactly so; but their case, unfortunately, is not one for intervention in its present stage. The present, you see, my dear Lady Luttrell, belongs to sons and daughters, nephews and nieces, and a pretty mess they make of it among them! Our sole consolation must be that they grow older every day."

Not until late that evening, after Mr. Dent had left and the men had retired to the smoking-room, and the ladies, without exception, had gone to bed, was Lady Luttrell's attention drawn to *Le Petit Voyou* by her daughter, who silently pointed out the obnoxious paragraph.

Lady Luttrell put on her glasses, read the anecdote, and was evidently tickled by it; though she felt bound to exclaim:

"But, my child, you should not look at such things; *c'est du dernier mauvais goût!*"

"I dare say it is bad taste to write about such things, and it may be bad taste to subscribe to the newspapers that print them," returned Madeline; "but it is something worse than bad taste to do them."

Lady Luttrell glanced at the girl's disdainful countenance, realized quickly what had occurred, and struck her hands together with a sudden gesture of despairing impatience. She was unhappy about her husband, she was frightened at the impending pecuniary disaster which had been foreshadowed by Mr. Dent, she was beginning to doubt whether the family would ever benefit by her daughter-in-law's fortune, and here, to crown all, was Madeline turning up her nose at another eligible suitor !—a suitor less eligible, to be sure, than Lord Stoneyhurst, yet by no means to be despised, and one, moreover, who, as she now perceived, had had a very good chance of being accepted.

"Decidedly," she cried, "you are losing your senses ! It is ridiculous and improper for a girl to have such thoughts as yours ! You look as if that poor Raoul had committed some horrible crime, instead of—"

"You think that the story is true, then ?" interrupted Madeline.

"True ! And supposing it were true ? As if all young men were not the same !"

"Clarissa says they are all the same," remarked Madeline.

"Oh, Clarissa—Clarissa ! I am sick and weary of hearing of all the silly things that she says. I will admit that sometimes, by accident, she may be right as to her facts ; but the conclusions which she draws from them !—*ça n'a pas le sens commun.* I must take care that you see no more gossiping newspapers, and I do implore you to believe that your mother knows a little more of the world than Clarissa does. As for Raoul de Malglaive, his youthful indiscretions are really no concern of yours."

"None whatever," agreed Madeline, moving towards the door. "So far as I am concerned his indiscretions may know no bounds."

Poor Lady Luttrell might have been more sympathetic, and might certainly have been more judicious ; but she was at the end of her patience, and she let the girl go. Least said the soonest mended, she thought. After all, as Mr. Dent had sagaciously observed, young people do grow older every day.

CHAPTER XXI

CLARISSA GROWS IMPORTANT

DURING the fine summer days which ensued Lady Luttrell declared repeatedly that it made her feel quite ill to read the newspapers, and indeed these had no very cheering information to impart to stanch upholders of the integrity of the empire. However, it was some consolation to find that, if the perversity of the electorate was injuring her health, it had no deleterious effect upon that of her husband, whom the local practitioner pronounced to be sound in wind and limb. "A little overworked, perhaps, and the heart's action not quite so regular as one could wish it to be; but a good long holiday will set that right, let us hope."

Sir Robert was certainly going to have a good long holiday; only, before he could begin to enjoy it, it was necessary that he should return to London for the re-assembling of Parliament and the anticipated vote of want of confidence which would relieve him and his colleagues of the cares of office. Upon this mournful expedition Lady Luttrell was not desirous of accompanying him; but Madeline, for some reason best known to herself, begged to be allowed to do so, alleging that she wanted to hear the debate, and adding that she would be no trouble, as she had received an invitation from Clarissa to spend a week in Cadogan Gardens. Lady Luttrell doubted the prudence of acceding to this request; but Sir Robert said, good-naturedly:

"Oh, let the girl come with me if she likes. Evil communications will hardly corrupt her more than they have done already, and as far as I can understand the matter— which, I confess, isn't very far—our best policy will be to keep upon good terms with Guy's wife. In fact, I shall avail myself of this opportunity to be particularly civil to the lady. One hasn't been a Cabinet Minister for all these years without having learned how to be civil to people whose ears one would prefer to box, for choice."

Sir Robert was, in truth, only too well aware of what important issues depended upon a reconciliation which might be effected by patience and adroitness; he foresaw that Mr. Dent's niece would some day be a very wealthy woman, whereas he neither knew exactly nor wished to know exactly what Guy's probable inheritance would be. Often he said to himself that Guy had been a most infernal ass; but he was conscious that he himself came under much the same condemnation, and if anything was to be accomplished, in the direction of atonement by smoothing down Clarissa's ruffled plumage, the least he could do was to undertake that task.

However, he had hardly taken his seat in a reserved railway compartment, with Madeline beside him, when it was borne in upon him after an unpleasantly convincing fashion that his daughter-in-law might prove a hard person to conciliate. For among the newspapers and periodicals which he had bought to while away the tedium of the long journey was a certain monthly review entitled *Modern England,* which had recently risen into fame; and the first article that caught his eye, as he examined the list of contents, was headed "The Perjury of Marriage," by Mrs. Luttrell. That did not sound promising, and Sir Robert turned over the leaves with a frown, expecting to come upon a narrative of personal experience which would do the writer and everybody connected with her infinite harm. But as he read, he was compelled to acknowledge that Clarissa had not only expressed herself with discretion, but had put her case, such as it was, extremely well. It was not, to be sure, much of a case, since all the world has long ago been convinced that, whatever individual instances of hardship may arise out of the institution of marriage, civilization could not survive the destruction of the family; still, what there was to be urged in favor of a different view was set forth in this article clearly and temperately enough, while the literary style of the composition was, as Sir Robert recognized with surprise, far above the average.

"By Jove!" he muttered, "this is a clever woman, in spite of her being a fool—and a more dangerous breed than that doesn't exist. Once let her make herself famous and there will be the deuce to pay!"

Now, whether a woman can be said to have committed perjury by vowing to love, honor, and obey a man upon whom she subsequently discovers that it is a sheer impossibility for her to bestow such sentiments, and whether, as the gifted authoress contended, the only straightforward course for one who has involuntarily made a vow which cannot be kept is to frankly break that vow, may be questions open to dispute; but there was obviously some abstract justice in the statement that no human being should be held bound by a contract of the nature of which he or she is ignorant. Mrs. Luttrell said at once that she had little hope of winning over sincere believers in the sacraments of the Church, who had firm ground beneath their feet when they took their stand upon an alleged Divine law; but she hastened to add that the number of such persons, even among professing believers, was notoriously small and was daily diminishing. It was for the convenience of society in all classes that the present unjust and unfair system was upheld, and her aim was to show that the convenience of society and the well-being of the community at large would, in the long-run, be better served by its abolition.

"Oh, that's all you want to show, is it?" thought Sir Robert, with some amusement. "I should imagine that it will take you all your time, ma'am."

It must be confessed that she was not entirely successful; yet she did contrive to show that the existing divorce laws are somewhat one-sided, that a vast number of people are chained together like galley-slaves who would be a great deal happier apart, and that received ideas of what constitutes morality or immorality require some clearing up.

14

But, upon the whole, it was not so much what she said as
the way in which she said it that impressed her reader.
With a politician's instinctive knowledge of what, at a
given moment, is likely to tickle the public ear, he perceived that there was no small danger of Clarissa's being
accepted as a prophetess. "In which case," he repeated
under his breath, "there will be the deuce to pay!"

He replaced *Modern England* in his travelling-bag without showing it to his daughter, stroked his chin reflectively for several minutes, and finally said to himself, "I
must have a talk with Dent about this." It was perhaps
a symptom of decaying powers that in all troubles and difficulties Sir Robert now turned at once to Mr. Dent.

And, indeed, it was with Mr. Dent, who met him on the
platform at Paddington, that he proposed to take up his
quarters for a time, the house in Grosvenor Place having
been left in charge of a charwoman. Madeline, for her part,
was driven off to Cadogan Gardens in a smart brougham,
drawn by a pair of fast-trotting cobs. Clarissa, it seemed,
knew how and where to provide herself with the accesso-
ries of affluence.

Quite a little crowd of ladies and gentlemen was assembled round the tea-table from which Clarissa rose to welcome her sister-in-law. They had somehow the air of being
sycophants, Madeline thought, although they were not in
reality precisely that. But they were certainly admirers,
and the eulogistic phrases which they addressed at intervals to their hostess were not easily comprehensible to one
who had but a vague acquaintance with "the Movement."
It appeared, however, that Mrs. Luttrell had accomplished
some feat or other for which she could not be sufficiently
patted on the back; the masculine-looking women with
the short hair and the *pince-nez,* and the feminine-looking men with the long hair and the low collars, emulated
one another in assuring her that she had rendered an
epoch-making service to the cause. If the whole crew of
them had not worn so very much the appearance of being
actors and actresses in a farce, it might have been supposed

that they were in deadly earnest. Of Madeline they took very little notice (a method of treatment to which Sir Robert Luttrell's daughter was not accustomed) and she was sincerely glad when they went away.

"What are they making such a cackling about?" she asked, with a touch of excusable irritation, after the door had closed behind the last of them. "Have you been setting the Thames on fire in the night?"

"Oh no," answered Clarissa; "they are only kind enough to praise a little article of mine in *Modern England*, which I thought you might perhaps have seen. I tried to make clear a part of our programme — the part which relates to marriage—in it, and I own to being rather pleased at the manner in which it has been received. Mr. Loosemore tells me that I have a genuine literary faculty, and Mr. Loosemore is admitted, even by those who differ from him, to be a competent critic. But you shall see the little paper after dinner, if you care to look through it. Come up-stairs to your room now and tell me why you have written such miserable, scrappy apologies for letters of late."

Madeline was not prepared to give the desired information all at once. She had abstained from writing with her customary amplitude because she had not wished to allude to Raoul de Malglaive, and because she had found it so difficult to help alluding to him; but she did not even now intend to confess that she had given her heart away to one who was utterly unworthy of the gift. What she believed herself to be in need of was a little moral support in her determination to think no more of the young man; and if that had been really what she wanted, she certainly could not have applied to a better quarter for it. In the course of the evening she casually mentioned the paragraph in the French newspaper relating to M. de Malglaive, "whom I dare say you may remember as a boy at Pau in the old days," and since—by a mere chance, of course—she had brought *Le Petit Voyou* with her, Clarissa was soon in a position to agree heartily with the girl's remark that it was "a truly disgusting story."

"I mean," added Madeline, after a pause, "that it is disgusting, if it is true. But I suppose it may be a mere invention." Clarissa laughed. "It *may* be; but the chances, you may be sure, are quite a thousand to one the other way. If you had heard half the things that I have heard during the last few months, you would cease to be surprised at any accusation of that kind being brought against any man."

"I don't think I want to hear them," said Madeline.

"One doesn't want to hear them; it is horrible and sickening to hear them. Yet to see things as they are is always better than to remain blind. Things must not and cannot go on as they are: of that I am convinced."

She remained silent for a few moments, and then, meeting with no response from the girl, in whose eyes there was a suspicion of tears, she rose suddenly and, kneeling down beside the latter, threw her arms round her neck.

"Madeline dear," she said, "you haven't told me much, and I won't bother you to tell more than you feel inclined to tell; but I can guess how it is with you. Haven't I been through it all myself? Only in my case knowledge came too late, whereas in yours there is no irreparable harm done yet—"

"I don't know what you call irreparable," interrupted Madeline, who had been made to peruse her sister-in-law's article before this; "you seem to think that unhappy marriages can be set aside at any moment. Not that I have the slightest idea of every marrying M. de Malglaive, who has never asked me."

"Ah, but you must not think that I separated myself from my husband without a struggle, or that my present position doesn't lay me open to daily annoyances. • It is for the sake of others much more than for my own that I am living as I do now. Somebody must begin, you see. But never mind me; it is about you that I want to talk."

And she talked kindly and sympathetically enough for the next quarter of an hour, proving that she at least understood her own sex, if she did not know quite as much as she thought she did about the other, and conveying comfort of a sort to a girl who, being both proud and sore, sadly required a little comfort. That it did not happen to be comfort of the right sort was scarcely her fault. She gave what she had to give, and was in a measure successful.

"But if Frenchmen, as well as Englishmen, are what you say they are," Madeline observed at length, "one had better make up one's mind never to marry at all."

To which Clarissa rejoined: "You might form a much worse resolution. Women don't exist for the sole purpose of marrying somebody and becoming the mothers of somebody's children. That is just what we want to be understood and acknowledged."

It was because she and her friends were of opinion that women are every bit as good as men (when they are not better), and not because contemporary politics possessed any special interest for her, that Clarissa had felt constrained to range herself among the opponents of her uncle's and Sir Robert Luttrell's party. Accordingly, she was quite willing to accompany Madeline to the House of Commons a day or two later and to listen to the debate on the Address, which was certain to terminate in the defeat of the Tory ministry. No orator who is well aware that defeat awaits him can be expected to exhibit himself at his best, nor were the first two days of this somewhat perfunctory discussion productive of any striking displays of eloquence from the occupants of the Treasury bench; but on the third and concluding day Sir Robert Luttrell rose and delivered what has since been pronounced to be the very best speech with which he had ever delighted the House. He was not unaccustomed to delighting an assembly with which he had always been popular; he thoroughly understood his audience and knew exactly how to make his points tell; but on this occasion he fairly surpassed himself. The enemy, as it happened, was unusually open to attack; the methods by which victory had been won at the polls had not been precisely patriotic methods; the programme of the victors was understood to be one which they themselves had until recently condemned in no uncertain tones.

So Sir Robert, whose quiet good-humor and unforced wit proved far more effective than the diatribes of some of his predecessors in the debate, had it in his power to make them look rather foolish and uncomfortable. In his peroration, which was really fine, and which, unlike the rest of his speech, seemed to have been carefully prepared, he foretold the result of tactics which, he said, had never been resorted to before in his long experience, and warned honorable and right honorable gentlemen opposite that they had established a precedent which must inevitably bring about their own eventual discomfiture. Something of the pathos of a last farewell was infused into his concluding sentences, which were measured, dignified, and free from any suspicion of rancor. For indeed he was an old man, and it was not probable that the variable breeze of public favor would ever waft him back to the seat which he resumed amidst loud and prolonged cheering.

Clarissa sighed as she looked down upon the scene from the Ladies' Gallery, remembering the only previous occasion on which she had heard Sir Robert address the House and all that had happened to her and others since then.

"Isn't it almost enough to make one believe that he is right and that the nation is wrong?" she whispered to her companion.

"Why shouldn't the nation be wrong? If right or wrong were a mere question of majorities, I suppose the people who write for *Modern England* would be squashed quite flat," returned Madeline pertinently.

That fate, at all events, could not be prevented by Sir Robert Luttrell or anybody else from overtaking the Tory administration, which resigned office on the following day. The news was conveyed to Clarissa in a note from her uncle, who, rather to her surprise, added : " Will you give me and your father-in-law some dinner if we knock at your door at eight o'clock to-morrow evening? We have been receiving so many condolences from our supporters that we think it would make a pleasant change to be trampled upon by a triumphant adversary."

Mr. Dent not unfrequently claimed the hospitality of his niece, with whom he studiously abstained from discussing controversial subjects, and although he provoked her, she enjoyed his companionship.· As for Sir Robert, she would of course be very glad to see him, and wrote at once to say so ; but she was in some doubt as to whether his intentions in thus inviting himself to her house were of a wholly friendly order.

Whatever Sir Robert's intentions may have been, his manner, when he greeted his daughter-in-law, was friendly in the highest degree, and throughout the evening he took evident pains to make himself agreeable to her. He complimented her upon her article in *Modern England* which he had read, he declared, with sincere pleasure and admiration.

"You won't ask a petrified old Tory to agree with your views," he remarked, smilingly ; "but I am sure you will continue to write as cleverly and charmingly after you have modified them a little."

"I don't think I shall modify them," said Clarissa.

"No ? Yet Tories and Radicals alike are apt to find that some deductions have to be made from the views of youth before middle age has been reached. At all events, by the time that old age has been reached it is possible to enjoy the society of those from whom one differs ; and that is why I hope you will be persuaded to give us a little of yours at Haccombe this summer."

Clarissa had promised to spend the summer at her uncle's country-house in Sussex. She thanked Sir Robert, without committing herself, feeling indeed pretty sure that he could not seriously wish her to revisit Haccombe Luttrell. However, he recurred to the subject when Netta came down to dessert and when, after lifting the child up on his knee, he asked her whether she would not like to stay for a time with her grandparents.

"We can offer you sea-bathing and fishing, and I dare say we might find a pony for you to ride," said he, by way of inducement.

Smiles and dimples appeared upon Netta's round face; but presently she asked, with a sudden accession of gravity and anxiety, "Will father be there?"

"Ah, well, I don't know about that," answered Sir Robert, not at all disconcerted; "your father, I suppose, won't get leave before the autumn. The country hasn't told him yet, as it has been kind enough to tell me, that his services can be dispensed with."

This was the sole reference made to Guy in the course of the evening. At a later hour Sir Robert talked politics, listened with courteous deference to Clarissa's Radical pronouncements, and admitted that there was a great deal to be said in favor of female suffrage. When he rose to take his leave, he declared that he had spent a most delightful evening, while Clarissa replied, with perfect truth, that if the evening had been delightful, it was he who had made it so.

But despite this interchange of amenities, Sir Robert was not a happy man as he left the house. Walking down the broad, deserted street with his old friend—for the night was so hot and airless that they decided to return to Portland Place on foot—he remarked :

"Your system of leaving things to right themselves is all very fine, Dent; but the question is whether they aren't as right already as she wants them to be. I should have liked to see her a good deal more angry and a good deal more triumphant. The pleasure of independence, unfortunately, is just one of those few pleasures which grow rather than pall upon one."

"You speak as a man," answered Mr. Dent; "no woman really likes to be independent, whatever it may suit her to assert. Not that I expect Clarissa to climb down from her perch to-morrow or next day; you will have to give her time."

Sir Robert thought, but did not like to say in so many words, that that was exactly what he could not afford to give. Dent must be well aware that the loss of an actual £5000 a year and a prospective income very much larger would be a serious matter for the Luttrell family; but this aspect of the matter had not been touched upon in previous conversations, and it was rather difficult to take the initiative in alluding to it. So Sir Robert, after a brief period of silence, only said:

"Well, I shall be dead and buried before the curtain falls, most likely. And after me the deluge, eh? Tell me honestly, Dent—can I carry on for another couple of years, do you think?"

"There will be the proceeds of the sale of your house in Grosvenor Place," answered Mr. Dent.

"Yes, I know; but they will be claimed at once, will they not? What I want you to tell me is this—can these people be prevented from foreclosing?"

"Well, yes," answered Mr. Dent, "I may say now that foreclosure can be avoided for the present. I think, considering the pass to which matters have come, you can't do better than leave them to me. Later in the year we must see what can be done."

"Can anything be done?"

"One hardly knows; there are complications, you see. But you may rely upon me to do the best I can for you, Luttrell, and I rely upon you not to worry yourself. At our time of life worry means illness, remember."

"And at our time of life illness is very apt to mean death, I suppose. Between ourselves, Dent, I don't know that my death, now that my political life is at an end, would be a great misfortune for anybody. There would be a certain amount of ready money, I presume, and my wife has her own little property in France. I should leave my family landless and impoverished, but not ruined, I take it."

But to this Mr. Dent, who had stopped to light a cigar, made no reply.

CHAPTER XXII

THE FLOWER-GIRL AND THE POET

RELIEF from public responsibilities did not, of course, enable the ex-Chancellor of the Duchy to quit London forthwith. There were formalities to be gone through; there were the seals of office to be delivered up; there were also sundry matters of private business to be transacted with the family lawyers which Mr. Dent, accommodating as he was, could hardly undertake on his friend's behalf. So it was arranged that Madeline should stay with Clarissa, who was eager to retain her, until such time as her father should be free to escort her home.

"Now I do want you," Clarissa said, "to bring an unprejudiced mind to bear upon the people whom you will meet here at luncheon and dinner. I don't deny that their appearance is rather funny, or that they are quite unlike your mother's friends, or that they sometimes make speeches which it would perhaps be better not to make; but, after all, one must judge one's neighbors by what they do, not by what they say, and these people are really engaged upon a great work."

Nobody would have supposed so, to look at them; they had so little the air of being toilers in any field, and they talked so incessantly that it was difficult to believe they could have time or strength left to do anything else. The men especially did not convey the impression of possessing much physical strength, although they ate and drank more than would have satisfied an average navvy. As for the women, Madeline found them, upon the whole, less repulsive, if not less ridiculous. Stout Lady Kettering, who had the courage to walk about the streets with her nether limbs arrayed in voluminous garments similar to those in use among Eastern ladies; pretty little Mrs. Hamley, the authoress of several startling and realistic works of fiction; Mrs. Knibbs, the loud-voiced champion of free thought and free love, who was said to have driven the late Professor Knibbs to seek peace in self-destruction, and who seemed to have reached an age at which her peculiar opinions were unlikely to involve her in any personal peril—all these were indeed, as Clarissa had said, rather funny in appearance and very unlike Lady Luttrell's friends; yet it was impossible to listen to them long without suspecting that their bark was worse than their bite.

Mr. Alfred Loosemore, on the contrary, who barked in dulcet tones, might be capable of inflicting a nasty, poisonous wound upon the hand that caressed him. Such, at least, was the conviction of Madeline, who abhorred this portly, smooth-shaven poet, with his shock of wiry black hair, his whispered innuendoes, his sententious aphorisms, and his invincible self-satisfaction.

"If you want to know what I think of him," she said to Clarissa; "I think he is a perfect pig—and I only wish I knew how to tell him so!"

"He wouldn't mind," answered Clarissa; "he is accustomed to being called names. Abuse, he always says, is much more to be desired than flattery, because it is quite as complimentary and a good deal less embarrassing."

"He must have queer ideas as to what is meant by a compliment," remarked Madeline; "but if he really likes being called a pig, all he has to do is to apply to me. He will find me ever ready to address him as what he really is."

"Lucky man!" said a voice behind her; "it isn't everybody who gets such a chance of seeing himself as others see him. And who, if one may be permitted to ask, is the gentleman who would enjoy being called a pig by you, Madeline?"

Paul Luttrell had become a frequent visitor of Clarissa's —so frequent, indeed, that he often took the liberty of en-

tering her drawing-room unannounced. Busy and interested almost exclusively in his East End parish, he nevertheless found time to call occasionally upon West End ladies
who likewise were, or professed to be, interested in the work
that he was carrying on, and whose alms were well worth
the sacrifice of an hour or so to secure. As for Clarissa,
she had even gone so far as to give him intermittent personal assistance in that work; for she had recognized from
the outset that the wrongs of women are not confined to
the upper class. So he proceeded to state the errand upon
which he had come to Cadogan Gardens, after bestowing a
fraternal embrace upon Madeline, and cordially agreeing
with her in her appreciation of the talented Loosemore.

"Men like that," he said, in his decisive, parsonical way,
"are a blot upon the face of creation. In healthier times
they would have been knocked on the head, as every human
being deserves to be who preaches a sort of refined unhealth-
iness. It would be a salutary change for you, Clarissa, to
be introduced to some people who are certainly healthy, if
they aren't over-refined. I came to ask whether you would
be disposed to come down to Southend to-morrow and spend
a happy day with me and my flower-girls. I have arranged
a holiday for them, and you said you wanted to see what
they were like. They want very much to see what you are
like, because the dress and manners of fashionable ladies
interest them beyond everything; and as they are sure to be
rather obstreperous, your restraining influence might be a
help to me."

The Reverend Paul, among whose parishioners and friends
were numbered costermongers, professional beggars, and
even professional thieves, had of late been much occupied
with the young women who earn a livelihood by selling
flowers at street corners. He had set up a club for them,
had induced them to attend classes, and had contrived—
not without preliminary difficulty—to win their confidence
and affection. Clarissa, who had been informed that a tendency to rush into hasty and improvident matrimony was
one of their most pronounced characteristics, had often ex-

pressed a wish to be brought into contact with them, and she said at once :

"Of course we will join the party ; there is nothing that I should enjoy more. The only thing is that I am afraid we must be home by eight o'clock, as I have one or two people coming to dinner. Would that be manageable, do you think ?"

"Perfectly manageable," answered Paul. "I don't expect to get home myself until two hours later at earliest ; but as you probably won't so very much enjoy the return in a third-class carriage, with your companions singing street-songs at the top of their voices, it will be just as well for you to retire before our shyness has quite worn off. Madeline, this will give you a glimpse of a section of the community which is altogether ignored by Mr. Alfred Loose-more and his admirers, though it is just as human as they are, and far more numerous."

"The worst of Christians," remarked Clarissa, pensively, "is that they are so uncharitable. Mr. Loosemore's sympathies are really a great deal wider than yours, Paul, though he doesn't profess to be anything but a heathen, and I am sure he would be delighted to come to Southend with us, if you would ask him."

"Ah—well, I don't think I'll ask him," said Paul ; "I shouldn't like to take the responsibility of leading my flower-girls into such doubtful company. With you I know that I am safe. You may expound your theories to them as amply as you please ; such is their indomitable common-sense that they will only roar with laughter at you."

It was rather Paul's habit to be rude to Clarissa, who was seldom affronted by his rudeness ; but after he had gone away she told Madeline what a pity it was that he should be so narrow and so ignorant of what was taking place all around him.

"He looks at everything from the point of view of his own religion and his own sect," she said ; "he doesn't in the least realize the feeling of unrest which exists among

the poor just as much as among the rich nowadays.   Everywhere women are beginning to understand that laws have
hitherto been made by men for men, that these laws are
unfair, and that a great change is near.   You have only to
watch the women's faces to be convinced of that, even
though they still remain mute from force of habit."

Possibly the young women of Whitechapel are a backward
and uninstructed lot.   At all events, the faces of the assemblage which Clarissa and Madeline found marshalled upon
the platform at Fenchurch Street the next day expressed
neither discontent nor anticipation of any change more portentous than a change of air.   That, to be sure, was portentous enough; for most of them had never seen the sea,
and the nature of their vocation was such that they seldom
took advantage even of a bank holiday.   They would not
have given themselves a holiday now, had it not been
"made up to them" by the generosity of certain ladies,
whom they took to be represented by Mrs. and Miss Luttrell; so that a warm and grateful reception awaited the
pair.   They were, to tell the truth, sadly wanting in beauty
of form or feature, while the costumes that they wore would
assuredly have grieved the soul of Mr. Alfred Loosemore.
Those broken, draggled ostrich-feathers, those prodigious
hats, those cheap, frayed ulsters, and, worst of all, those
appalling, misshapen boots formed indeed a spectacle which
could not have been otherwise than painful to a philosophic
hedonist; yet happy faces, even when they are ugly ones,
are, after all, pleasanter objects to contemplate than well-
made clothes, and the two ladies were soon upon excellent
terms with their fellow-excursionists, who were far too excited to display any of the shyness for which Paul had given
them credit.

For the rest, *mauvaise honte* is a malady more common in
Belgravia than in Whitechapel.   Miss Sally Brown, for example, who promptly attached herself to Madeline, and
proved as communicative as she was inquisitive, had probably never suffered from misplaced timidity in the whole
course of her professional career.   Sally, being seventeen

years of age, described herself as "getting on," and had for
some time past been engaged to be married. Acting upon
the advice of the Reverend Paul, of whose sagacity she entertained a high opinion, she proposed to lead her young
man ere long to the altar; for, as she shrewdly observed,
"You've got to tyke 'em when they're in the humor for it,
and I've kep' Sam wytin' just about as long as he'll wyte, I
expect." Sam, it appeared, was a "fruit and vegetable
salesman" by trade; he had a "barrer and a moke" of his
own, and was therefore in a position, with the aid of his
wife's exertions, to support a family. Although he had but
just attained his majority, Madeline gathered that he had
a gay and stormy career behind him, to which the bride-
elect alluded with perfect candor, and even with a certain
pride. The parson had persuaded him to become a total-
abstainer, she herself had weaned him from other temptations to which his temperament rendered him peculiarly
liable, and she evidently thought that he was likely to prove
a better husband from the fact that his bachelor life had
not been altogether exemplary.

These confidences, which were poured out with much
volubility during the railway journey, were partially overheard by Clarissa, who was herself jammed in between two
loquacious maidens, but who could not allow this opportunity of upholding her testimony against the folly of
juvenile marriages to slip. She was not too didactic, she
spoke kindly and sympathetically enough, and her hearers
did not fulfil Paul's prediction by bursting out laughing in
her face; but the doctrine which she preached was obviously
not to their taste, and their answers implied that they suspected her of not knowing much. Sally, indeed, took occasion to whisper to Madeline:

"If the lydy thinks men and women is the same, she's
got a lot to learn!"

"Oh, she doesn't think that," Madeline returned; "she
only thinks they ought to be. And so do I."

Sally shook her head and looked wise, but did not pursue
the topic. One does not go out for a day's pleasuring in

order to discuss the problems of human life, and that glorious August sunshine was a thing to enjoy and be thankful for without thought for the morrow.

The heartiness with which those young women enjoyed themselves upon the beach and upon Southend pier made ample amends for any little embarrassment that might have been caused to their conductors by the noise that they made over it. They could not be restrained from walking six abreast with linked arms and singing aloud, nor did Paul enter any protest when they took to pelting him and one another with wet seaweed; but poor Sally got herself into trouble by taking off her boots and stockings, lifting up her skirts, and wading among the breakers. This, it seemed, was a sad breach of propriety, and her friends felt bound to rebuke it in language so unambiguous that for a moment she was in imminent danger of being reduced to tears. It was, however, a great consolation to her to learn that Madeline herself, when at home, was much given to paddling, and that ladies of the highest station and respectability were wont to exhibit themselves every evening in a far more undressed condition than she had done. Later in the day, when she, together with the rest of the company, had done justice to a substantial meal, she candidly told Madeline that, from all that she had read in the newspapers and had heard by word of mouth, she was disposed to think that the aristocracy might very well take a lesson from its social inferiors.

"Talk about the men, as that lydy did when we was comin' down in the trine!—why, they ain't one 'arf so bad as what the women is! And the women 'd be worse, you may depend, if they wasn't afride to it."

Here Sally, who was a simple, outspoken creature, gave reasons which sounded plausible for the comparatively high standard of morality maintained by her own sex in all classes of the community, adding, however, that in the class to which she belonged distinctions between what she called "honest gals and bad gals" were somewhat more clearly drawn than elsewhere.

"Yes," said Madeline; "but don't you think that if a man would be very foolish—as, of course, he would—to marry a bad girl, a girl is just as foolish when she marries a bad man?"

"Well, you see," answered Sally, "this is the way of it—it don't make 'em bad, not the same as it does us. A man comes to me and he says, 'If I'd ha' met you before, my dear,' he says, 'I'd ha' kep' more stright.' And I says to him, 'You've met me now, Sam,' I says, 'and you've got to keep stright henceforth and forever.' Which, as like as not, he does it."

"And you ask no questions about the life that he has led before he met you?"

"I shouldn't, miss—not if I was you. Men ain't neither hangels nor women. You can't arst them to beyave as if they was married *before* they're married—nor yet they wouldn't do it, if you was to arst them ever so."

With this concise statement of Sally Brown's views, which might not perhaps have obtained the unreserved sanction of the Reverend Paul Luttrell, Madeline had to rest content; for she was now called upon to act as umpire in a foot-race between two Whitechapel Atalantas, and soon afterwards Clarissa and she had to hasten back to London.

"Poor things!" sighed Clarissa, as she settled herself in the railway-carriage; "rough as they are, there is a great deal to like and admire in them. Only they are more backward in some ways than I expected to find them. I am afraid it will be a long time before they realize that their lot in life will never be less hard until they combine in demanding what they are entitled to demand."

Madeline made no rejoinder. She was thinking at the moment that her own lot in life would probably be a hard one if she persisted in demanding what, by all accounts, she was most unlikely to get. It was deplorable that Sam the costermonger should have exercised so little control over himself, deplorable also that Raoul de Malglaive should have been surprised at a provincial hotel in the company of a *belle marquise;* but were they, after all, to be

15

treated as unpardonable sinners because they had behaved
after the manner of their kind? Something in Sally Brown's
philosophy appealed to the common-sense of which Madeline had a rather larger share than her sister-in-law ; yet
she could not but remember that Raoul was without Sam's
excuse, inasmuch as he had already met her before the occurrence of the escapade in question.

At dinner that evening it was Miss Luttrell's misfortune
to be placed next to Mr. Alfred Loosemore, who professed
to be immensely interested in hearing about the Southend
excursion.

"A party of flower-girls—it sounds so pretty !" said he.
"Yet Mrs. Luttrell tells me that they were not pretty.
Things are never what they ought to be, unhappily !"

"Nor people either," returned Madeline. "But I was
quite satisfied with the girls ; I didn't want them to be
pretty."

"Ah, that is so shocking of you ! If you were what you
ought to be, you would want everybody and everything to
be pretty. And what, I wonder," continued the poet, turning round in his chair so as to face his neighbor, and smiling upon her benevolently, "should I be, if I were what I
ought to be ?"

"I'm sure I don't know," answered Madeline, with swift
exasperation, "but I should think you would be dead."

She was rather ashamed of herself after this little outburst ; but she did not appear to have affronted the sublime Alfred, who only chuckled and remarked : "I suppose you think I am too good for this wicked world. I
have often suspected as much myself."

Nevertheless, he may have made a mental note to the
effect that he owed her some return for her civility, and
may even have known a little more about her than she
imagined that he knew ; for not long after this he led
the conversation to the subject of modern society in Paris,
where it seemed that he was as much at home as in London, and among other names he mentioned that of young
De Malglaive, "Who, by-the-way," said he, "hails from

Lady Luttrell's department, I believe. Did you ever come across him at Pau?"

"Yes; I have come across him there," answered Madeline.

"*Ce cher Raoul!*" drawled Mr. Loosemore, who spoke French fluently, and who affected the peculiar, mincing accent which is not displeasing in a Parisian, but is nothing short of maddening when aped by anybody else, "*il n'y a que lui!* His iniquities are always perpetrated with such inimitable seriousness. I am sure there must be scores of ladies who do not believe that he is a monster at all."

"I suppose I must be one of them," said Madeline; "for it certainly did not strike me that there was anything particularly monstrous about M. de Malglaive. He seemed to me to be very like other young men."

"Ah, my dear Miss Luttrell, the sad truth is that we are almost all of us monsters. Ask your sister-in-law, whose mission it is to reform us, and who acquits herself of her mission so exquisitely, whether we are not. At the same time, if I were to tell you all I know about that scandalous Raoul, you would admit that he passes all bounds. But wild horses should not drag such information from me."

Further information was not solicited by Madeline, who turned her shoulder towards the speaker; but, heartily though she despised him, she could not prevent his shaft from reaching its mark. Sally Brown might forgive her mercurial Sam, and might be wise to do so; but it is neither easy nor, perhaps, wise to absolve a sinner whose offences are committed with "inimitable seriousness."

CHAPTER XXIII

"LA BELLE MARQUISE"

IN days not so very long gone by, the pleasant city of Tours used to be held in high favor by French cavalry officers, and thither, under the Second Empire, used to be sent such regiments as, by reason of their aristocratic *cachet*, the authorities deemed it expedient to favor highly. If the aristocrats of Touraine did not openly accept the Second Empire, they at least permitted their sons, nephews, and cousins to wear its uniform, and that these gentlemen should be quartered as far as possible in a province notorious for its Legitimism was perhaps a wise concession to persons whom it might be worth while to conciliate. The Third Republic is understood to have adopted other tactics; aristocratic regiments exist no longer; young men with prefixes to their names are said to have been subjected to many petty annoyances; favor is shown to none (although a touch of disfavor may sometimes be displayed towards a few), and it was doubtless a mere coincidence that the corps to which Raoul de Malglaive belonged, and which still retained the reputation of being a crack corps, formed part of the garrison of Tours during the fine, hot summer which witnessed the defeat of the Conservative party on the other side of the Channel.

To Raoul this was scarcely such a subject for congratulation as it was to his brother-officers; for the many relations and connections whom he had in the neighborhood possessed no special attraction for him, while it was a very great nuisance to be at the beck and call of the Marquise de Castelmoron, whose charmingly situated château over-

looked the broad Loire. It was true that he had once had
a more or less profound admiration for the Marquise de
Castelmoron; it was true that he had been a frequent visitor at her Parisian abode, and that their intimacy had gone
so far that she usually (when they were alone) addressed
him by his Christian-name; but the world can hardly contain persons whom one is more anxious to avoid than those
whom one has profoundly admired once upon a time and
has altogether ceased to admire. Besides, there had been
that stupid affair, which had found its way into the newspapers, had given rise to numerous distasteful jocularities,
and had not yet been forgotten or disbelieved in, notwithstanding the quasi-public *démentis* of M. de Castelmoron
and the circumstance that M. de Malglaive still continued
to be the friend of the house.

The affair in question had been, indeed, stupid enough;
though scarcely, Raoul thought, one which could have been
avoided. What could he do when the woman wrote, begging him to meet her at a certain time and place? It was
idiotic of her to adopt such a method of convincing him
that De Castelmoron was not a pattern husband—especially
as he did not care in the least whether De Castelmoron was
a pattern husband or not—but to decline the rendezvous
would have been practically impossible. Then the absurd
scene which had ensued, the mutual recriminations, his
own impatient offer to fight the irate little man who had
been so easily pacified, the somewhat ignoble understanding which had eventually been patched up between the
husband and wife—all this did not shape itself into a very
agreeable memory or render Raoul particularly eager to be
stationed in the department of the Indre-et-Loire. He
was not, however, aware that an account of the adventure
had found its way into the public press of his own department; still less did he imagine for one moment that any
echo of it could have reached the distant ears of the girl to
whom all his heart and most of his thoughts belonged.

Very often—being so completely without means of ascertaining where she was or what she was about—he had pict-

ured Madeline to himself mixing in that brilliant society
which would naturally be open to the daughter of a Cabinet Minister, surrounded by admirers, oblivious of a certain
fine spring afternoon at Lourdes, and of all that she had
said then and afterwards respecting her disinclination to
marry an Englishman ; so that he had not been sorry to
hear of the general election which, he presumed, would
have the effect of sending her and her people away from
the metropolis to the comparative solitude of the provinces.
But he was quite sorry to learn from the columns of the
Figaro, and other journals which boasted of a foreign correspondent, that Sir Robert Luttrell's party had met with
a hostile reception at the polls.   He even thought that the
occasion might justify the despatch of a few words of condolence from a foreign friend of Sir Robert's family, just as
victory might have been made the pretext for a letter of
congratulation.

And so, after a day or two of hesitation and deliberation,
he sat down and penned a missive to Lady Luttrell which
did credit alike to his head and to his heart.   It was a
composition which no young Englishman would ever have
dreamed of committing to paper ; but, fortunately for him,
he was writing to a Frenchwoman, who, notwithstanding
her long residence abroad, would not be in the least likely
to laugh at him, but would, on the contrary, be sure to appreciate the correctness of his attitude.   The political sentiments with which he contrived to fill three closely written
pages were both unexceptionable in themselves and of a
nature to gratify those who, during a period of transition,
are striving to arrest the too rapid advance of democracy ;
incidental expressions of personal respect for Sir Robert
were well and gracefully put, while nothing could be more
natural or more proper than that Lady Luttrell's correspondent should wind up with a modest request that he
might be recalled to the memory of her daughter.   But
what was so very astute of him was that he managed, before reaching his elaborate concluding phrase, to ask a
question which could hardly in courtesy be left unanswered.

His mother, he said (and this was perfectly true), had written to him lately about her health in terms which caused him some uneasiness. Would Lady Luttrell, who was so old a friend of his mother's, do him the great kindness to tell him whether, in her opinion, he ought to absent himself from France under such circumstances? He asked because he believed that, either in Africa or in Tonquin, there might be a chance of his seeing some active service, and because he had sometimes thought of applying to be transferred to those remote regions. But, of course, his first duty was to his mother, and if Lady Luttrell had noticed any sign of those failing powers to which Madame de Malglaive alluded, a word would suffice to make him renounce such ideas.

Raoul posted his letter with confident hopes of shortly receiving replies to queries which were not stated therein, as well as to the one which was. His mother was a wiry old lady who was likely to live for another twenty years or more, although she sometimes complained of aches and pains. Certainly, however, she would not wish him to fight savages in pestilential climates, nor did he seriously contemplate such a step, save in occasional moments of depression. But would Lady Luttrell care whether he lived or died ?—whether he spent next winter in Sénégal or in the Basses-Pyrénées ? That was what he wanted to know, and that was what he expected to be told ; for he did not doubt her capacity for reading between the lines, and he felt sure that should she deem him beneath notice as a suitor for her daughter's hand, she would find means of intimating as much quite civilly. Moreover, if he had been forestalled, and if the London season had brought about Madeline's betrothal to another man, he would at least have the miserable satisfaction of hearing the truth and being put out of suspense.

He had turned his back upon the post-office, and was pacing meditatively along the broad, sun-baked street, when a shrill voice which he knew only too well called him by name. Madame de Castelmoron's carriage had

been brought to a standstill beside the curb - stone, and
Madame de Castelmoron's beautifully gloved hand was
beckoning to him imperiously. She was a plump, brown-
locked little lady of thirty or thereabouts, who at the distance of a few yards looked fully ten years younger than
she really was ; her round cheeks, her turned-up nose, her
bright eyes, and her very red lips stamped her as belonging to that class of beauties who must needs look young
if they are to be beauties at all, and everything that
art could accomplish towards producing that desirable
result had been employed in her case with skill and
judgment.

"But in what hole have you been burying yourself ?"
she cried ; "*on ne vous voit plus!* And yet you might
have guessed how well I am amusing myself, all alone in
our deplorable château ! Yes, all alone ; for Philippe has
been recalled to Paris on business." With a glance at the
servants, she lowered her voice to add, "That means that
he has returned to his edifying *vie de garçon*. After all, I
prefer that to the insupportable good behavior of which he
has been guilty during the last few weeks. Now at least
he is free, and so am I."

"I congratulate you," said Raoul, gravely.

"You will give me something to congratulate myself
upon if you will come and help to enliven my solitude," returned the lady, graciously. "Next Thursday, at *déjeûner*
—oh, there is no need to raise your eyebrows—I shall have
a little party to meet you, including my aunt De Richemont, who is a model of all the virtues. In the afternoon
we shall perhaps go out sailing on the river—always under
the strictest surveillance, you understand."

Raoul accepted the invitation without enthusiasm, but
not without a certain sense of relief. He did not want to
breakfast with Madame de Castelmoron or to go out sailing
with her ; but it was something to be assured that she had
no intention of placing him in any more compromising
situations. He forgot all about her as soon as she was out
of his sight, and reverted to the musings which she had

interrupted. In a week's time, he calculated — or, allowing for all possible delays, in ten days' time — he would
know how far he would be able to count upon the support
of the Luttrell family in his suit. After that there would
be his mother's certain opposition to be overcome and
·Madeline's own consent to be gained. The third achievement was doubtless the most important, and might prove
the most difficult of accomplishment; but he placed it last
because he did not see how it could be undertaken at all
until the other two had been disposed of. In France respect for parents has survived loss of respect for everybody
and everything else.

It was, at all events, scarcely possible for Raoul, nor apparently was it expected of him, to entertain much respect
for Madame de Castelmoron, at whose château he duly presented himself on the day appointed by her. The Castel-
morons were well known to be half-ruined (indeed, Raoul,
whose privilege it had been to accommodate M. le Marquis
with more than one loan, sometimes wondered how many
people it took to pay Madame la Marquise's dressmaker),
and their provincial establishment was regulated upon
principles of the strictest economy. The house was crum-
bling for want of repairs, the furniture had not been renewed for many years, the servants were few, and the
cooking far from first-rate. On the other hand, one was
always sure of being amused at the informal entertainments
which Madame de Castelmoron organized from time to
time. So, at least, Raoul's brother-officers, three or four
of whom he found already seated in her *salon* when he
made his entrance, were wont to affirm, and certainly their
subsequent conduct seemed to show that they had grounds
for making the assertion. Several young and frisky ma-
trons had been asked to meet them; the conversation
which took place at the round breakfast-table was more
highly seasoned than the dishes; there was a great deal of
loud laughter, and probably the only two guests who failed
to enjoy themselves were Raoul de Malglaive and Madame
de Richemont, a quiet old lady who was afraid of her niece,

and who also (for her own good fortune and that of others) was stone-deaf.

Madame de Richemont raised no objection when an aquatic excursion was proposed later in the afternoon, only pleading that she might not be required to take part in it. "For," she said, plaintively, "I have always looked forward to dying in my bed, like a good Christian." But she would perhaps have felt it her duty to enter a mild protest, had she accompanied those ladies and gentlemen to the river-side and witnessed their embarkation. It was scarcely *convenable,* she might have urged, that her niece and M. de Malglaive should occupy a tiny sailing-boat all to themselves; but as her remarks would assuredly not have been listened to if she had been present, her absence was of the less consequence.

Raoul, for his part, did not particularly mind this enforced *tête-à-tête;* he had foreseen what awaited him, and he bore it with philosophy. It was the old story which was poured into his ears—the story to which he had listened so many times, and in which, if the truth must be confessed, he had once believed. Philippe's cruelties and infidelities, Madame de Castelmoron's lamentations over a marriage into which she had been coerced when a mere child, the excuses which she put forward in defence of certain undeniable irregularities of her own—all this had to be heard, sympathized with, and responded to after the only appropriate fashion that Raoul knew of. It took a long time, and Madame de Castelmoron, who held the tiller, would have capsized the boat a dozen times in the course of the interview if there had been any wind; but the weather, though close, dull, and threatening thunder, was still, and the sail flapped loosely as Raoul and his fair companion drifted down the broad, glassy stream. One of them was far away in the spirit, while the other, who was accustomed to his taciturn, absent ways, flattered herself that he was dreaming about her.

He was dreaming about a very different person—about one whose ideas respecting the subject upon which Madame de Castelmoron wás descanting with so much fervor had always seemed to him to be painfully just, albeit opposed to those of the rest of the world. He would not have liked Madeline Luttrell to know what his life had been, he would not have liked her to see him where he was now—and yet he could have sworn to her with a clear conscience that she was the only woman in the world whom he had ever loved. Would she believe him, he wondered, if the time should ever come for him to take that oath? In the face of facts with which she might easily be made acquainted, it really did not seem certain that she would.

He was startled out of his rather despondent reverie by a warning shout from one of the rowing-boats astern which contained Madame de Castelmoron's friends. He glanced over his shoulder, saw what was coming, and made an instinctive clutch at the tiller, which he failed to secure. But in any case, he would probably have been too late. The sudden gust which came sweeping across the water caught the diminutive craft before he knew where he was, and in another moment he was performing an involuntary act of descent towards the bottom of the Loire. At the best of times he was no great swimmer, nor is a tight cavalry uniform quite the most suitable costume that could be designed for feats of natation; still, he did not lose his presence of mind, and his first thought, on rising to the surface, was naturally for the lady whose heedlessness had brought about this catastrophe. Not a little to his relief, he heard her calling him by name in accents which proved that she was in no danger of being drowned.

"Scramble up on the boat, Raoul! As for me, I shall stay where I am until somebody can give me a hand."

The boat was floating on her beam-ends; Madame de Castelmoron, who, by better luck than she deserved, had been thrown into the sail, was seated there, with one arm flung round the mast; prompt assistance was forthcoming, and a few moments later the shipwrecked pair were on land, drenched, but safe.

"*Coup de théâtre manqué,*" remarked Madame de Castelmoron, looking down ruefully at her dripping garments. "If, at least, you had saved my life after an exciting struggle, that would have been some compensation for the ruin of a new gown; as it is, you will have to buy me another one, and we will say no more about it. Come, let us walk home as fast as we can before the thunder-storm begins. It is true that we need not be afraid of rain now; but I am afraid of lightning, and these ladies, I am sure, would be very much afraid of admitting us into their boat in our present condition."

It is certainly wiser for people who are wet to the skin to trust to their own legs rather than to any other means of locomotion; but Madame de Castelmoron, who never exerted herself if she could help it, yielded to the solicitations of her friends, submitted to be enveloped in shawls, and sat down in the stern of the rowing-boat, whither Raoul reluctantly followed her. He was not allowed to return straight to his own quarters, as he wished to do; he was assured that somebody should be despatched at once from the château to fetch a change of clothing for him, and he did not like to mention that an attack of fever and ague, which had placed his life in jeopardy some two years before, had compelled him to be rather careful about contracting chills.

The unfortunate consequence of this was that, whereas Madame de Castelmoron was not a penny the worse for her ducking, M. de Malglaive perforce remained her guest that night. He made a valiant effort to leave the house with the rest of the party, who lingered, chatting and sipping sweet Malaga wine until the expected thunder-storm had spent itself, but found that he was physically incapable of doing so. His teeth were chattering, his head was swimming; he was in no state to disobey the commands of Madame de Richemont, who insisted upon his being put to bed at once, and upon sending for the doctor.

Before many hours were past he was in a high fever; and on the following day two of the most competent medical men of Tours were shaking their heads over him. It was impossible, they declared, to say as yet what his malady might turn to; but what admitted of no doubt at all was that he would have to remain where he was for an indefinite length of time.   That being so, it clearly behooved Madame de Richemont, who dwelt hard by, to take up her temporary residence under her niece's roof; and this she did willingly, being a kind-hearted old lady as well as an excellent nurse.   Madame de Castelmoron, too, rose to the level of the occasion, and, during the days and nights of anxiety which followed, proved that a woman may be vain, silly, unscrupulous, yet retain some of those qualities which in all ages have been the property and the glory of her sex.

As for the patient himself, he was happily unconscious of a condition of things which, had he had his wits about him, would probably have worried him to death.   To be so indebted to Madame de Castelmoron, of all women in the world!—to be nursed by her through a dangerous illness! —what more cruel trick could Fortune have played upon him ?   However, he was raving and tossing in delirium the whole time; so that his chances of recovery were not impeded by any suspicion of where he was.

CHAPTER XXIV

A LITTLE DOSE OF POISON

IT can hardly have been in consequence of skilful and assiduous nursing that Raoul de Malglaive escaped the rheumatic fever with which he was threatened by the doctors; but his illness, no doubt, might have proved a much more serious affair than it did had he been less carefully tended, and it was only natural and right that when he was restored to consciousness and convalescence he should feel exceedingly grateful to the kind ladies who waited upon him. One does not, in such times of weakness and pleasant drowsiness, vex one's brains greatly with connected thought. Raoul was but dimly aware of the circumstances which had landed him in that cool, spacious room; for several days he was content to lie there passively, to listen to the sounds of life which floated to him through the open windows, to watch Madame de Castelmoron moving softly hither and thither in her becoming airy draperies, and to murmur a few words of thanks to good old Madame de Richemont when she arranged his pillows for him or made him swallow his medicine.

This enjoyable semi-trance was brought to a somewhat abrupt termination one morning by Madame de Castelmoron, who, after bringing him his breakfast, asked, with a smile, "And, pray, who is Madeline?"

"Madeline?" repeated the invalid, glancing uneasily at his questioner, and falling forthwith out of dreamland into the domain of actualities.

"Yes; the Madeline whom you invoked without ceasing in your delirium. It is a droll name. Madeleine—Madelon—*à la bonne heure!* But whoever heard of a Madeline before ? For the rest, in the world to which she probably belongs an original label is a *trouvaille,* I suppose."

The world to which Madeline Luttrell probably belonged !—he was upon the point of giving utterance to the horror with which such an insinuation filled him, but checked himself. Was it not, after all, better to leave ill alone ?

"Is one responsible," he asked, reproachfully, "for what one may say or do in delirium ?"

Madame de Castelmoron laughed. "It is for what you did when you were in full possession of your senses that you ought to be held responsible," she replied. "But do not be alarmed ; you are in the house of a discreet friend, who may have one or two little sins upon her own conscience, and who is not so easily shocked by the sound of feminine names as I am sure your mother would be. *À propos,* are you not very much obliged to me for having omitted to telegraph or write to your mother ?"

He could not but own that he was ; although he now reflected, with a pang of remorse, that a good many of Madame de Malglaive's constant missives must have remained unanswered.

"Are there any letters for me ?" he asked.

"A mass," answered Madame de Castelmoron. "We thought it best not to trouble you with your correspondence before ; but if you feel that you are in a state to grapple with it, it shall be handed over to you."

It was handed over to him shortly afterwards, and, naturally enough, he selected from the pile for first perusal a letter which bore an English stamp and an English postmark. Not without some acceleration of the heart's action and some trembling of the fingers (for he was still far from having recovered his ordinary strength) did he tear open Lady Luttrell's envelope and read the very friendly and gracious reply with which it had pleased her to acknowledge his condolences. Lady Luttrell, as we know, had never been inclined to look with an unfavorable eye upon Raoul de Malglaive as a possible son-in-law. She knew that he would be, if he was not already, very comfortably off; she suspected that her daughter was not ill-disposed towards him, and she had had melancholy and provoking proofs of her daughter's reluctance to espouse a suitable person merely because that person happened to be suitable. Clearly, therefore, it would be a sad mistake to let Raoul ship himself off for Tonquin, and she wrote that, since he had done her the honor of consulting her upon the subject, she must earnestly dissuade him from giving his mother so much pain.

"One understands," said she, "your weariness of garrison life and your desire for something a little more exciting; but I think that if you were to banish yourself from France you might afterwards deeply regret having done so, and I am persuaded that, upon consideration, you will abandon this idea. Frankly, I shall be very much disappointed if we do not see you at Pau next winter. My husband and my daughter, who thank you for your amiable remembrance of them, beg me to say that they share entirely the opinion which I have permitted myself to express."

This last statement was purely apocryphal, neither Sir Robert nor Madeline having been so much as informed that a letter had been received from young De Malglaive; but Lady Luttrell considered herself at liberty to round off her phrase in that way, just as most people consider themselves entitled to send "love" or "kind remembrances" to their correspondents from members of the family who do not chance to be in the room at that moment. Lady Luttrell, in fact, did not mean a great deal by her letter; she merely thought that it would be a tempting of Providence to snatch away the bait from a nibbling fish, and was not altogether averse to landing him, in the event of other lines failing to secure a heavier one.

But Raoul, with his imperfect comprehension of English ways, took her to mean far more, and attributed a significance which it did not deserve to her mention of her daughter. To say in so many words that a young lady will be disappointed if she does not see you at a certain time and place—is not that to say everything ? He would have been capable of despatching a formal offer of marriage to the young lady's parents then and there, if he had not reflected that it would be scarcely respectful to his mother to take so portentous a step without consulting her, and if he had not felt only too sure that his mother would be against him in the matter.

Consequently, he refrained from committing that foolish action ; but he proceeded forthwith to commit another at least equally foolish ; for, in his joy and exultation, what must he needs do but admit Madame de Castelmoron into his confidence ! It is quite impossible to explain or account for the amazing things that men of ordinary, or even extraordinary, common-sense will do when they are in love. The wondering student of human nature can but take note of such phenomena and humbly pray that he himself may be preserved from ever requesting a woman at whose feet he has once knelt to sympathize with him in the transfer of his allegiance to one younger, more beautiful, more innocent, in every way more desirable than she. Raoul may have thought — most likely he did think — that the fair recipient of his confidences was fonder of admiration than of admirers ; his modesty may have forbidden him to suppose that the loss of one admirer out of so many could be a source of any vexation to her ; he may also have considered that there is a certain incongruity between nursing the sick and flirtation. But perhaps the truth was only that, being so happy, he could not for the life of him help telling somebody how happy he was.

Madame de Castelmoron's face while he was narrating his love-tale might have furnished him with an instructive study if he had had eyes to see it ; but all he saw was that she was smiling pleasantly upon him, and that she appeared to take a deep and sympathetic interest in what she was being told.

"Sincere felicitations !" said she, when he had finished.

16

"For myself, I abhor Englishwomen ; I find them stupid, ungainly in their movements, and spoiled for all social purposes by their unfortunate habit of having such enormous families. But your Madeline, we will hope, is an exception to the general rule. At any rate, I presume you think so; and that is the essential point, is it not ?"

He certainly thought so. To speak of Madeline Luttrell as "stupid" or "ungainly in her movements" was to display so absurd an ignorance of the person alluded to that it seemed quite necessary to describe her in detail; after which it was difficult to help indulging in rhapsodies, which were listened to without interruption.

"And yet," observed Madame de Castelmoron, gently, at length, "it is not such a very long time, Raoul, since you were ready to swear that your whole heart belonged to some one who is rather nearer to you now than Mademoiselle Luttrell."

He had the sublime fatuity to reply, "You must forgive me. One imagines one's self in love a hundred times ; but I believe that no human being is ever really in love more than once. Besides, you only amused yourself with me for a time ; you will forget my existence, I am sure, long before I forget your kindness—and Madame de Richemont's."

"I do not, I confess, propose to hang myself in consequence of your infidelity," she returned, dryly; "since you are a man, you could scarcely, without a frank paradox, be faithful to any one woman. But those hundred imaginary loves of which you speak !—it is rather a large number. Do you not think that the enchanting Madeline may have a question or two to ask you about them ?"

Ah! that was just the trouble. Raoul quoted sundry strange and disquieting speeches which had fallen from the lips of his beloved, and which made him apprehensive that she might demand from him more than he had it in his power to bestow upon her. He was very anxious to have Madame de Castelmoron's opinion upon this singular aspect of his case. Assuredly, he had not lived the life of a saint, and no one could regret more than he did the follies of which he had been guilty; but he did not think that he had been much worse than his fellows, nor could he see that the past had a great deal to say to the future.

"*À tout péché miséricorde,*" he concluded, with an appealing glance at the little lady beside him, who had much ado to keep her countenance.

She shrugged her shoulders. "This comes of losing your heart to an Englishwoman," she remarked; "they are unheard - of, with their ideas and their theories! Nevertheless—I do not say it to discourage you; but it seems to me that, without being an Englishwoman, this young lady might find some little things to object to in what you have done and are doing. Your presence here at this moment, for example—what would she think of that, I wonder?"

Raoul was rather afraid that she would not like it, and hoped that she would not hear of it—although, to be sure, it admitted of an explanation which must be acknowledged by everybody to be entirely satisfactory. For the rest, there was no great danger that she would hear of it. The dangers and difficulties which he foresaw were of another kind, and would, he thought, demand a good deal of circumspection on his part. He told his amiable adviser all about it; he did not disguise from her that there would be trouble with his mother; he pointed out—and she quite agreed with him—that he had as yet received no more than an implied permission to pay his addresses to Miss Luttrell; he was inclined, upon the whole, to think that he had better possess his soul in patience until he should meet her once more at Pau during the coming winter.

Madame de Castelmoron replied that, by her way of thinking, that would be a good plan. She added that she was infinitely obliged to him for having done her the honor to seek counsel of her, that she had never in her life heard anything more charming or touching than the romance with which she had been regaled, and that, as it was quite time for him to take his *bouillon,* she would go and inquire why it had not been sent up-stairs.

Outside the door she paused, clinched her teeth and her

hands, and hissed out a few words which would have taken Raoul completely by surprise had he overheard them. He had been perfectly correct in his conjecture that she cared very little about him as an individual; but she cared a great deal about her vanity, which he had contrived, during their long colloquy, to lacerate and trample under foot in a style that would have been resented by the meekest of women. Since she lived in the nineteenth century, and since she had no ambition to be guillotined or even sent to prison, Madame de Castelmoron abstained from putting poison into his broth; but that he should be made to smart for his atrocious conduct seemed to her to be as indispensable as that she herself should preserve a placid and friendly exterior.

Consequently, Raoul was entertained with the greatest care and kindliness for another ten days at the château on the banks of the Loire, which he quitted at last with many heartfelt expressions of gratitude to its mistress. Consequently, also, an anonymous missive, written in a disguised hand and disfigured by numerous intentional blunders in grammar and spelling, was despatched to Miss Luttrell, whose address it had been no hard matter to obtain. A careless invalid who leaves his correspondence lying about can scarcely expect to have secrets from his nurse.

At Haccombe Luttrell that year the early autumn was, as it not unfrequently is in the far west, a season of calms and hot weather. The equinoctials were coming, but the winds seemed to be taking a rest in preparation for that annual outburst of fury; the skies were clear and serene, the harvest had been gathered in without a drop of rain, and Guy, who had come down to shoot his father's partridges, groaned over the labor of toiling up hill and down dale under so scorching a sun. Sir Robert, who was not feeling very well, declined to share his fatigues; economy being so imperatively necessary, no other sportsmen had been invited to stay in the house; so that Guy was fain to fall back upon the companionship of his sister, who often walked beside him, and with whom on those occasions he had several serious talks. Of his own disastrous matrimonial affairs, which she was anxious to discuss, he had little to say, giving her to understand that he had spoken his last word upon that subject; but he warned her with much earnestness against allowing herself to be led away by Clarissa's morbid notions.

"I don't suppose you want to be an old maid," said he; "I never met a woman who did. And if you begin by thinking that no man is good enough for you, you'll be apt to end by thinking any man good enough. One has seen that happen before now. Besides, the whole thing is such utter nonsense! Take my advice, and when you meet a man whom you care for, be satisfied if he's a gentleman and a good chap. Don't you get making inquiries about whether he has been what you call 'dissipated' or not. If you mean to go in for that sort of thing you'll have to confine your attention to curates—and Heaven knows whether even curates are as good as they look! I shouldn't think they were. The average man, you may depend upon it, will be all right, so long as his wife doesn't play the fool, and the average man is bound to have had experiences which he doesn't care to talk about to his wife."

Such speeches as this were not wholly unwelcome to Madeline, although, as a matter of principle, she believed Clarissa to be in the right and her brother to be in the wrong. The truth was that she was secretly eager to pardon one whom she had pronounced to be unpardonable; and if—as seemed to be the case—the male standard of morality was so different from, and so very inferior to, the female, perhaps he ought not to be blamed for having been what others are. Possibly, too, that odious newspaper story had been exaggerated or even false. Her heart was further softened when her mother made casual mention, one day, of Raoul de Malglaive's letter, saying that it had really been very pretty of the young fellow to write, and that she hoped they would meet him at Pau when they returned thither.

"He threatens to betake himself to Tonquin or Sénégal,"

added Lady Luttrell, laughing; "but I don't think he was very serious about that, and I have told him that he owes it to his poor old mother to abandon such fantastic ideas."

Now, it was impossible to suppose that M. de Malglaive would ever have entertained such ideas unless he had been in low spirits, and it did not seem altogether probable that he had written to Lady Luttrell for the sole purpose of telling her how sorry he was that Sir Robert's political party had been left in a minority. Madeline, therefore, sometimes permitted herself to wonder whether, after all, she was going to be as lonely and miserable for the rest of her days as she had made up her mind to be; and the arrival, one morning, of a foreign letter bearing the Tours postmark caused her to catch her breath and pause irresolutely for some seconds before tearing it open.

Alas! the contents were not what she had expected, nor was the signature, at which she at once glanced, that of Raoul de Malglaive. His name, indeed, occurred frequently in the four clumsily written pages which Madeline hastened to read through, but the writer, who signed herself "Une Malheureuse," had nothing good to say of him. Not without reluctance, she averred, had she decided to place herself in communication with Mademoiselle Luttrell; but, as she had reason to believe that a heartless libertine had designs upon the happiness of that young lady, her conscience would not permit her to remain silent. Statements—some of which were true, but most of them false — followed; Madame de Castelmoron, "of whose house he has now-been an inmate for three weeks, under the pretext of having been taken ill there," was not spared; in conclusion, Madeline's anonymous correspondent remarked, "He will tell you, no doubt, that he loves you, and I do not say that he will be insincere; he has so many loves! But, humble as I am, it does not suit me to go shares in such favors, and I think, mademoiselle, that you will feel as I do."

We are all agreed, as a matter of theory, that people who are afraid to sign their names are unworthy of a moment's attention ; but theory, unfortunately, is one thing and practice is another. Had Madame de Castelmoron been present in the flesh (as she was in the spirit) when her little dose of poison reached its destination, she would doubtless have felt herself fully and satisfactorily avenged.

CHAPTER XXV

"An enemy hath done this thing"—such was the perfectly sensible conclusion to which Madeline came, after she had torn Madame de Castelmoron's composition into very small fragments and was staring at them with a dull heartache which was to be assuaged by no conclusion of that nature. Raoul might have been painted in rather darker colors than he deserved, his nameless accuser might have had other motives than had appeared for attacking him; but what then? Was not the mere fact that he had made so bitter an enemy of a woman proof sufficient of his guilt? At all events, plain statements of facts, such as his prolonged sojourn in the house of the *belle Marquise de C.*, are susceptible of easy proof or disproof, and are scarcely likely to be made unless they can be substantiated.

Now, there are certain offences which may be pardoned with more or less of an effort, and it is often asserted that we must needs forgive anything and everything to those whom we really love; but there is one thing which never can be and never ought to be forgiven, and that is treachery. In her heart Madeline knew well enough that Raoul de Malglaive had loved her; in her heart she had always expected that he would end by telling her so; and now it seemed that such was actually his intention. Yet this did not prevent him from amusing himself in the meantime with philanderings of which he naturally assumed that she would never hear. That might be a man's notion of honor and fair play: it was not hers, nor could she avoid the conviction that she had bestowed the best that she had to

give upon one who had already received many such gifts
and placed no exaggerated value upon them. She could
no more recall what she had given than she could have
caused one of her limbs to grow again, if it had been cut
off. Had he been the greatest scoundrel upon earth, she
must still have continued to love him; but what was a
matter of absolute certitude was that she would never
marry him. Indeed, she derived a certain half-conscious
solace from the prospect of scornfully rejecting him in a
few months' time. Madame de Castelmoron, it must be
owned, knew what she was about when she credited Miss
Luttrell with a disinclination to "go shares" in any man's
affections.

From that day forth Guy noticed that his homilies upon
the subject of matrimony were listened to by his sister
with a decided falling off of patience and interest. She
was ready to go out shooting with him; she was ready to
applaud him when he shot well—as, in truth, he almost
always did—and she liked to hear anecdotes about sport in
Ceylon and elsewhere; but she told him frankly that she
had made up her mind with regard to questions upon
which he differed from her, and added that she was rather
tired of being exhorted to do what she had no intention of
doing. Once she horrified him by calmly announcing that
she had thoughts of entering "the religious life."

"Good Lord!" he exclaimed, aghast; "go into a con-
vent, do you mean? My dear child, you must be insane!
Nuns don't have faces like yours."

"Yes, it would be a sad waste, wouldn't it?" returned
Madeline; "all your sex would have a right to feel that
they had been defrauded. But I only said I had had
thoughts of it; I don't suppose I shall do it. They tell
me I have no vocation."

"Whoever 'they' may be, I trust they will continue to
impress that undoubted truth upon you," said Guy.
"One thing is that you will hardly excite their cupidity;
for I'm afraid you will never have much money to give
them. It's partly on that account—"

"Oh yes, I know," interrupted the girl; "it's partly, if not chiefly, on that account that you want me to marry. Yet, if the worst comes to the worst, we shall not starve, I presume, and there are greater miseries than poverty. Surely you must acknowledge that, considering that you might be a good deal better off than you are, if you chose."

This home-thrust had the desired effect of causing Guy to change the subject. If there was one thing of which he was thoroughly determined, it was that he would never touch another sixpence of his wife's money, and from sundry hints which had been conveyed to him since his arrival at Haccombe Luttrell he was well aware that the maintenance of his determination would entail the risk of something like a quarrel with his parents. He had, in fact, been at no small pains to avoid being left for five minutes with his father, and had rushed round to the stables immediately after dinner every night, upon the plea that he was required to attend to a sick horse. At length, however, an evening came when he was not permitted thus to make his escape.

"Sit down again, my dear fellow," said Sir Robert; "there are several things that I must tell you, and if you don't want to hear them, I am sure I don't want to say them. But sooner or later one finds that one has to do what one doesn't want to do. One doesn't particularly want to die, for instance; yet I am going to die."

"So are we all," remarked Guy.

"Yes; but I mean that I am going to die very soon. You needn't say anything about it to your mother—it would only distress her and do no manner of good—but I have had symptoms lately—I remember my father's death and how things went with him towards the last—well, the long and the short of it is that it behooves me to set my house in order, as far as I can."

Sir Robert and his eldest son had always been pretty good friends, although it had never been their custom to interchange affectionate phrases. Guy got up quickly now, walked round the table, and, laying his hand upon

the elder man's shoulder, looked earnestly into his face
for a moment.   That was quite enough ; they understood
each other ; and if Sir Robert's laugh was a little tremu-
lous, his weak state of health was a sufficient excuse.

"I may hang on for another year or so," he resumed ;
"there's no telling.   But then, again, I may go out at any
moment ; and perhaps I ought to ask your pardon before
it is too late.   When I succeeded my father, I came into
an unencumbered estate and a fairly large income ; what
you will succeed to, I am sorry to say, is a property so
heavily mortgaged that, unless you have a great deal more
money at your disposal than I shall be able to leave you,
it will hardly be in your power to prevent foreclosure."

"Don't you bother about that," answered Guy, replying
rather to the pathetic, pleading look in his father's eyes
than to anything that had been said ; "it's no fault of
yours that land isn't what it used to be, and I don't forget
that you have had to pay my debts more than once.   Of
course one is rather sorry that the old place should pass
into the hands of strangers ; but, after all, what's the use
of trying to live in a style that one can't afford ?   *I* shall
be all right ; I've known for a long time past that it wasn't
my destiny to become a landed proprietor."

"But it may yet be your destiny," said Sir Robert, with
a certain subdued eagerness ; "it may be—well, I should
call it your duty.   I can't tell you who the mortgagees are ;
the whole thing is in such a muddle, and I have never had
any head for figures.   Dent has managed these matters
for me, and I have a strong impression—I should not be in
the least surprised to hear that he held the mortgages himself.   If so—"

"Yes ?" said Guy, his face hardening a little.

Sir Robert did not finish his sentence.   He shifted his
position slightly, poured out a glass of wine, which he
drank, drummed with his fingers upon the table-cloth for a
minute, and then continued :

"I must get your mother to ask Dent down here for a
few days ; I want to talk to him about business matters.

But if we ask him, I think we ought to—indeed, it seems to me that we must—ask your wife too."

"By all means," answered Guy, composedly. "Of course you will mention that I am here, and then she can choose for herself whether she will accept the invitation or not. Only I had better say at once that there isn't going to be a reconciliation."

"But why not?" demanded Sir Robert, irritably; "in the name of common-sense, why not? I know nothing of what your married life has been; but it is easy to guess the origin of this foolish split, and surely—considering how much depends upon it—surely, if you have done wrong, you ought not to be above admitting as much."

"Oh, if I have done wrong, I'll admit as much," said Guy; "but it is exactly because so much depends upon it that I can't do more. However, I may tell you for your comfort that I don't believe Clarissa would consent to live with me again even if I crawled on my hands and knees to implore her to rescue me from poverty. She would make me a very handsome allowance, I am sure; but unfortunately I am so wrong-headed that I should prefer poverty to the allowance."

Sir Robert groaned. He could have dealt with two wrong-headed people, he thought, if his own head had felt a little more clear, and if he had had the prospect of a little more time in which to deal with them; but now loss of time might mean loss of everything!

"At least," he said, finally, "you will be civil to her, if she comes, I hope."

"Of course I will," answered Guy, laughing. "Shall we go into the drawing-room now?"

But he was not given the chance of keeping or breaking his word in that respect; for, a few days later, Mr. Dent wrote to say that he himself would come to Haccombe Luttrell at once, but that his niece had engagements which would prevent her from accompanying him. The old gentleman arrived just before dinner one evening, and was at once taken to task by Lady Luttrell, who, without having all her husband's reasons for disquietude, still thought it high time that an estrangement which had already lasted far too long should be brought to an end.

"Why haven't you brought Clarissa with you? It is really too bad of you! You must have known how we are longing to see her and our darling little Netta. And now that Guy is here too!"

"The chief reason why I have not brought her, my dear lady," answered Mr. Dent, smiling, "is that she wouldn't come. If you are acquainted with any way of making independent persons do what they decline to do, I should be glad to hear of it. We have all heard, to be sure, that the most obstinate of donkeys may be persuaded to advance by the ingenious expedient of dangling a carrot before his nose; but, candidly now—do you think that, under all the circumstances, Guy could be made to play the part of a carrot?"

"Really I don't know," answered Lady Luttrell despondently; "but I am quite sure that Clarissa is playing the part of a donkey."

Mr. Dent did not contradict her. It is to be feared that, if he had given utterance to the thought that was in his mind, he would have said something about Clarissa's and Lady Luttrell's sex altogether out of keeping with the urbane manners for which he was deservedly renowned. But in truth there are only too many donkeys of both sexes in the world; and when one is a shrewd old banker and man of business, one must perforce admit that many of one's best friends merit that uncomplimentary description.

As for poor Sir Robert Luttrell, whom no member of the House of Commons would have thought for one moment of calling a fool, his folly in the management of his private affairs had been very great indeed, and it was now much too late in the day to tell him so. Mr. Dent had told him so on previous occasions emphatically enough, but without any good result: the only thing to be done at present was to remind him that the sale of his London house had placed a considerable sum of ready money to his credit.

"Your father," said Mr. Dent to Guy on the following morning, "must not be worried about money. I will take it upon myself to say that, so long as he lives, there shall be no occasion for him to be worried. After his death, of course, the inevitable will have to be faced."

"Do you think he is really so ill, then?" asked Guy.

Mr. Dent sighed. "I think it would take very little to kill him; and that is a sad thing for me to have to say; because I am an old man myself, and I have seen most of my friends start already on the journey which leads to swift oblivion. I know very well that I shall sign my own death-warrant on the day when I retire from business: that is the way with us all. And your father, you see, has practically retired. He has been talking a good deal to me about you and Clarissa. If his mind could be set at ease upon that subject, I have very little doubt that his health would benefit."

"I'm afraid that's impossible," said Guy.

"I am afraid it is."

Mr. Dent resumed, after a short pause. "May I ask whether you are very angry with your wife?—angry, that is, to the extent of refusing to take her back or be taken back by her?"

"My dear sir," answered Guy, "it is my wife who, rightly or wrongly, is angry with me and has chosen to separate herself from me. When she comes and tells me that she regrets having done so, it will be time enough for me to consider what I ought to do. But neither to please her nor you nor myself, nor even to prolong my father's life, am I going to take one single step to meet her. Please, understand that, once for all."

Mr. Dent nodded. "I see," said he. "Well, I have observed no symptoms of regret on her part as yet, and I can't pretend to think that any step you could take would bring you nearer to her. I suspect that you have not behaved as well to her as you ought to have done; but perhaps you will allow me to say that, in my opinion, you are behaving very like a gentleman now. You are aware, no

doubt, that by being just a shade less punctilious you would
make yourself secure of being tolerably well-to-do for the
rest of your days."

"You mean," said Guy, "that Clarissa is rich now, that
she will be very much richer when you die, and that she
would make me rich as soon as look at me—a good deal
sooner than look at me, in fact. Yes, I am aware of that;
and I still say that I have no conditions to propose to her,
except the one which I have insisted upon all along—that
I am to see Netta as often as I like."

"Then," said Mr. Dent, "let us hold our tongues. Your
brother, I hear, is coming down to-day. Will you, if you
get the chance, warn him that he will do no good by boasting of his influence with my niece? His influence, at the
present stage, amounts to zero; but, being a parson—and
a most excellent and hard-working parson too, I am sure—
it is difficult for him to realize that, and your father is
sure to consult him. Try to make him see that your father must not be agitated, and that the subject of your
marriage is one of several subjects which had better be regarded as forbidden for the present."

Paul, who, in obedience to the solicitations of his
parents, was about to spend his well-earned annual holiday in his old home, had determined, it must be confessed, to take that opportunity of saying once more what
he felt it to be incumbent upon him to say; but, after
a short interview with Guy and another with Mr. Dent,
he rather reluctantly consented to comply with their
wishes.

"Of course," he told the former, "I would not for the
world say or do anything to upset my father; but you
seem to admit that it would do him a great deal of good
to hear that there was a prospect of your making friends
with Clarissa, and that prospect certainly ought to exist. I
don't altogether stand up for her; I don't say that I consider her justified in having left you; yet you will admit,
I suppose, that there have been faults on both sides. And
the help that she has given me in my work among the

poor does seem to me to show, after all, that her heart is in the right place."

"I dare say it does," answered Guy, "and I trust that the poor are properly grateful. But I'm afraid her heart won't find its way to this place, poor as we are down here. Moreover, you won't persuade me to invite it, charm you never so wisely. So, if the governor says anything to you, please tell him that it will be all right one of these fine days (which, I am sure, is what you think), and begin to talk about something else."

In this way Sir Robert's uneasiness was to some extent allayed, and, although he had become curiously listless, silent, and apathetic, none of those about him, with the exception of Mr. Dent, could see that his condition was such as to warrant alarm. Paul, recognizing that Guy was in no humor to be preached to, sensibly refrained from preaching to him; but he assured Lady Luttrell and Madeline that he did not at all despair of ultimate success.

"I think," he told the latter, "I may say that I have some little influence over Clarissa, and I shall try to use it at the right moment. While neither she nor Guy will condescend to take the first step, one can only hold one's peace and have patience ; but it is very evident to me that they are too angry with one another to remain apart forever."

His influence over Clarissa, which, according to Mr. Dent, amounted to zero, amounted in reality to rather more than that; though it certainly was not powerful enough to bring about a change in her convictions. She admired him for his life of cheerful self-sacrifice ; she was interested in the work upon which he was engaged, and flattered when he allowed her to take an amateurish share therein ; she knew, too, that he had not been in the least impressed by achievements of hers which had won her adulation in other quarters, and perhaps that inclined her to think more highly of him. She had, it appeared, been present at the nuptials of Sally Brown, and had profited by the occasion to deliver a lecture upon matrimony so op-

posed to the precepts of the law and the teaching of the
Church as quite to shock the newly married couple.

"However," said Paul, "she provided the wedding-gown
and paid for the subsequent feast, besides presenting Sam
with a substantial sum towards the enlargement of his
stock in trade; so I suppose they thought it would be uncivil and ungrateful to argue with her. Afterwards Sam
confided to me that, although she was a nice lady, he
feared she was 'a bit off her chump.'"

Madeline was not altogether disposed to concur in Sam's
verdict. "Clarissa may be wrong about married people,"
she remarked; "when once they are married, they are
married, and I dare say they ought to bear whatever may
happen; but it seems to me that almost all marriages are
a mistake. Why shouldn't one keep one's liberty?"

Paul and she had been out sailing together, and were
running swiftly back towards Haccombe harbor before the
wind, when she put this query. Her companion sapiently
replied:

"The general opinion is that married women have more
liberty than spinsters, and no women, married or single,
really care a straw about liberty. That is the unquestionable truth—though I confess that it isn't unquestioned."

"Well, I am as free as I want to be, anyhow," Madeline
declared, "and I am satisfied to remain as I am. I should
like just to stand still, or sit still, for the rest of my
days."

"I doubt very much whether you would," returned
Paul, laughing, "and it is certain that you can't. You
have appeared once already in the first column of the
Times; you must appear there once again, and in all probability you will appear more than once. Do you imagine
that Clarissa or anybody else is going to alter the inexorable monotony of human existence? As for your remaining
where you are in a literal sense, that is clearly impossible;
for what you and I still call 'home' is only a house which
belongs for the present to our father and will soon belong
to somebody else. I don't urge you to marry against your

17

inclination; but I can't shut my eyes to the fact that the best thing you can do is to marry."

"You too!" exclaimed Madeline, impatiently. "If you only knew how sick I am of having that advice thrust upon me, and what a relief it is to meet a single human being, like Clarissa, who is less inexorably monotonous!"

"But I was not offering advice," said Paul; "I was only venturing to make an assertion."

That his assertion was justified by impending and inevitable events was proved to them after a melancholy fashion when they reached the house, in front of which the doctor's dog-cart was waiting. The doctor himself came out, as they were entering, drew Paul aside and whispered a few words to him.

"A seizure?" repeated the latter, in startled accents. "What sort of seizure?"

"Oh, well; a stroke of paralysis, to call things by their names. He will get over it this time, I think; he has already recovered consciousness; but—" The doctor broke off and shook his head ominously.

"Of course," he added, "I have sent a telegram to London for further advice, since Lady Luttrell desired me to do so. I shall be back myself in a few hours."

Then he assumed a cheerful countenance for Madeline's benefit. "Don't distress yourself, my dear young lady. Your father has had a rather alarming little attack; but he will be much better to-morrow, we hope. Meanwhile, he is to be kept quite quiet, please; so you must not go up to his room."

CHAPTER XXVI

CLARISSA STRAINS HER CONSCIENCE

THE first column of the *Times,* in which, as Paul Luttrell had told his sister, the names of us all are bound to appear at least twice, was soon to announce that the Right Honorable Sir Robert Luttrell had ceased to form one of the community which he had long and faithfully served. The same newspaper would contain a full obituary notice of the deceased statesman, and possibly even a leading article, recapitulating the incidents of his public career; for in the autumn there is always a little difficulty about finding matter for leading articles, and although Sir Robert had never been among the very foremost of his contemporaries, he had rubbed shoulders with them.

All this Mr. Dent foresaw, not having been deceived by the partial rally which had enabled the doctor to speak comforting words to Lady Luttrell; all this was foreseen also by Lady Luttrell herself, whose grief was the more pitiable to witness because, through long practice, she had learned to keep her emotions under control and affected to believe that there was no reason for serious alarm. Her drawn, gray face and despairing eyes gave the lie to her speech. It was all over, then, at last!—and she knew it. She had been a most devoted wife, gladly sacrificing herself, her wishes, her inclinations, her fortune even, for the man who now lay dying; presently she would be a widow, and would have to plod along the remainder of her life's journey without that kindly, careless, selfish companion, whose will had been her will, whose successes had been her successes, and whose ruin, alas! must be the ruin of those

who survived him in a somewhat greater degree than his
own.   The rich of this world, who are so often said to be
no happier than the poor, have at least this one great advantage that, when the sorrows which are common to
humanity fall upon them, they are not compelled to put to
themselves that painful, humiliating question, "How shall
we be able to afford it?"   Lady Luttrell, who had once
been rich and was rich no longer, could not help wondering what terrible change of fortune awaited the family,
though she tried not to think about it, and hated herself
for doing so at such a time.

Meanwhile, the patient was pronounced to be almost out
of immediate danger.   Almost, but not quite, was the verdict of the eminent London physician, whose fee might
have been saved, for any good that he had it in his power
to do.   He stayed a night in the house, approved of the
measures taken by his provincial colleague, was extremely
guarded in what he said to Lady Luttrell, and told Guy
candidly that it was a question of months at the best, days
at the worst.

"I need scarcely tell you," he added, "that it is of the
utmost importance to avoid mental disturbance or anxiety.
If there is anything that your father wishes for, he should
have it; and, so far as I was able to understand him, there
seems to be something."

No doubt this fashionable physician, who heard all that
was said and rumored in high society, knew well enough
what it was that poor Sir Robert's stammering tongue had
striven to articulate; and how could Guy respond otherwise than as he did to the plea which soon afterwards was
addressed to his own ears?   He bent over the pathetic,
prostrate figure on the bed, met the entreating eyes with a
reassuring look and answered:

"It's all right; don't worry.   We'll send for Clarissa,
and she ought to be here by the day after to-morrow.
You'll be ever so much better by that time, I expect; only
you aren't to talk now, you know."

Sir Robert's eyes closed, he smiled feebly and his features

relaxed. His daughter-in-law must, in common humanity, come to him; in common humanity, too, she would, it might be hoped, seem to assent to his wishes; but her husband did not much relish the thought of conveying the summons which would have to be conveyed.

"Will you write to her?" he asked Mr. Dent. "I think you are the proper person to do it."

"Oh, I have telegraphed already," answered Mr. Dent; "she will arrive to-morrow evening. I am very sorry for you; but I know you will behave as a gentleman should in a difficult situation. There are many other things that might be said; but it is probably better not to say them. For the time being, all we have to think about is to make your father's last hours as easy as we can."

Lady Luttrell, poor woman, was less considerate and less reticent. She chose to assume that her son had promised a great deal more than he had done; she thanked him, with tears in her eyes, for having made the concession which he could not, she said, have refused without cruelty and ingratitude to his dying father; she tried hard to make him say in so many words that his wife (and her fortune) were about to be restored to his keeping; and when at last he was forced to remind her that there must be two consenting parties to that bargain, she declared such a statement to be in defiance of all laws, human and divine.

"It stands to reason, Guy, that everything rests with you. Dear Clarissa, I know, must feel that; though she has been allowed to go her own way all this time, and though perhaps she may have had a few little things to complain of. But you will ask her pardon, my dear boy! —you will not be too proud to do that, when I am not too proud to implore it of you on my knees!"

Lady Luttrell did not literally go down upon her knees; but she abashed herself quite enough to make her son feel extremely uncomfortable. He avoided promising what it would have been out of the question for him to perform by saying vaguely that of course he would do what he could, and by undertaking to meet Clarissa at the station on her arrival.

The next day, therefore, he was standing on the platform to receive his wife, and he was not at all sorry to see that she was accompanied by Netta, who, for her part, was overjoyed to see him. The presence of the child was a ' protection to them both; possibly, thought he, it might have been to serve that very purpose that the child had been brought. Nevertheless, after they had taken their seats in the carriage and he had reported, in answer to Clarissa's sympathetic inquiries, that his father was a shade better, it was necessary to say something, by way of clearing the ground. So he began, in his usual good-humored, leisurely accents:

"I don't know whether you will have guessed why you were summoned by telegram in such a hurry; but most likely you have. The old people, naturally enough, have been appealing to me and are going to appeal to you. I am sorry that you should be bothered in this way; but really it is no fault of mine. The doctors, in fact, make a special point of it that my father is not to be thwarted or contradicted; so you see—" He shrugged his shoulders expressively.

Clarissa straightened herself up, drew in her breath and looked out of the window. "I am afraid I do not quite see," she answered presently, in a hard voice. "What is it that I am expected to do?"

"Something that you have not the slightest intention of doing and will never be compelled to do," replied Guy, laughing a little; "please don't suppose that you are expected by me to depart from your very clearly expressed intentions. But my mother will attack you, and so will the poor old man, and so will Paul; I am not even sure that your uncle won't have a word or two to say. Now, don't you think it would be for their happiness and our own comfort if we were to tell a few harmless little fibs?—or at least to leave them under a false impression?"

Clarissa turned round and looked at him with an irritated, disdainful air which he knew only too well. "I am not much accustomed to telling fibs or conveying false impressions," said she, shortly.

"Upon my word, if it comes to that, nor am I; but I feel that I am in a rather tight place this time. It's almost a case of life or death : anyhow, it's a case of making death hard or easy. There are pecuniary considerations, you see ; in fact, those *are* the considerations. He counted upon the family fortunes being retrieved by—"

"If that is all," interrupted Clarissa, quickly, "it should be easy to set his mind at rest. You know perfectly well that I am ready at any moment to give up the half, or three-quarters, of all that I possess, or ever shall possess."

"Yes, and I hope you know perfectly well that that kind offer will never be accepted. The governor, you may be sure, knows it, too. There wouldn't be the slightest use in talking such nonsense to him, and—"

He broke off to clutch Netta, who was craning her head out of the carriage-window to stare at the fallow deer in the park and who had almost overbalanced herself. For the next few minutes he was occupied with the child, promising to show her all the animals, laughing at her ecstatic ejaculations and talking to her in the childish language which she was wont to use and which he understood. It had always been a source of secret wonder and provocation to Clarissa that Netta should be so devoted to her father. What had he ever done to earn the child's love, beyond amusing himself with her at times, as he might have amused himself with a favorite dog? When the carriage was within sight of the house she touched him on the arm to attract his attention, and said, hurriedly :

"Very well, then ; your father shall be deceived, if it is really so important to deceive him. But I will not tell lies to the others."

"Just as you like," answered Guy, smiling in his placid, aggravating way. "You would save us both a lot of botheration if you could strain your conscience a point or

two further; but the main thing, no doubt, is to deceive
the dear old man."

Clarissa was not called upon to practise deception upon
anybody that evening; for the news which met her and
her husband, when they entered the hall, was that the
patient was not so well. The patient, in truth, had had a
second seizure, the doctor had been sent for in hot haste,
and throughout that night Sir Robert hovered between
life and death. In the morning he rallied once more and
recovered consciousness; but his power of speech was
gone. It was unlikely, the doctor thought, that he would
ever be able to articulate again, though he might linger on
in the same condition for weeks.

Under these sad circumstances the advent of Clarissa
had less importance and was productive of less immediate
annoyance to herself than might otherwise have been the
case. She did not even see her mother-in-law until she
had been twenty-four hours in the house, and when at
length Lady Luttrell, with haggard cheeks and reddened
eyelids, came downstairs to enfold her in a clinging embrace, her compassion and emotion rendered her willing
to consent to anything that might be demanded of her.
All that she was asked to do was to come into the dying
man's room for a few minutes.

"I am sure he wants you," poor Lady Luttrell said,
"though he cannot tell us so; and—and I dare say Guy
would not mind coming at the same time."

Perhaps it was scarcely fair—even at the moment Clarissa felt that it was scarcely fair—to turn so pathetic a
juncture to such practical account; but she comforted
herself with the thought that her action could not be misunderstood by her husband, and also that she was prepared, in the matter of money, to do all that Sir Robert
probably wished. Only for a few minutes were she and
Guy admitted into the darkened sick-room; only for a
few minutes did they stand looking down upon that
mournful, speechless wreck which still bore a famous
name, but in which it was impossible to recognize the

brilliant statesman of former days. Somebody—it may have been Lady Luttrell—joined their hands; a faint gleam of satisfaction came into Sir Robert's eager, restless eyes, and then the nurse hurried them away.

As soon as they were in the corridor outside, Clarissa ·suddenly burst into tears.

"It is so dreadful!" she faltered. "It seems almost like perjury!—I wish I had not done it!"

Guy, who was not less moved than she was, answered her, for that very reason, in colder and more measured accents than usual.

"I am sorry," said he, "to have inflicted this ordeal upon you; but there are ordeals which can't very well be shirked. I don't think there is any need for you to reproach yourself; you can explain as soon as you like to everybody whom it concerns, except my father, that you didn't in the least mean what you may have appeared to mean."

She threw a glance of concentrated anger and scorn at the unimpassioned speaker, dashed the tears from her eyes and hastened to leave him. How, she wondered, as she sped along the vacant, echoing galleries of the old house, could she ever have loved, or ever imagined that she loved, a man so callous and so shameless? Clarissa's chief grievance against her husband (although she was not aware of that) was that he had never at any time seemed to be ashamed, while he had more than once contrived to give himself a false air of being the injured party.

Anyhow, his conduct had the one satisfactory effect of enabling her to act, without compunction, as he had suggested, and to inform her uncle and Paul and Madeline that her compliance with Lady Luttrell's request must not be misconstrued. Mr. Dent merely shrugged his shoulders, and Madeline, who for the time being could think of ·nothing but that her father was upon the point of death, said little more than that she was sorry; but Paul expressed himself with some severity.

"You are foolish and you are wrong," he told her; "a

day will come when you will repent of having allowed this opportunity to slip through your fingers. However much Guy may have been to blame in the past, it is you who are to blame now. One or the other of you must needs take the first step, and you ought to understand why it is more difficult for him than for you to do so."

"You talk as if I *wanted* to live with him again!" exclaimed Clarissa; "you either don't understand or you pretend not to understand that I would a great deal rather die than submit to such humiliation. The truth is that I ought not to have come here at all, and I am very sorry that I came."

However, as her husband had assured her, she had no reason to be sorry; for nobody was the worse off in consequence of what she had done, while Sir Robert, it may be hoped, was the better. His breathing ceased quite suddenly, two days later, when he was supposed to be asleep, and, in the solemn hush of death which ensued, all sounds of discord and controversy ceased.

A man who has played so conspicuous a part in public affairs as Sir Robert Luttrell cannot disappear from this world's little stage without a certain amount of stir and bustle, without messages of condolence from exalted personages, avalanches of letters and telegrams, deputations even, and floral tributes innumerable. During the days which elapsed before his father's body was borne to the family vault upon the shoulders of a dozen stalwart tenants Guy was fully occupied in making the acknowledgments that were expected of him, and his privacy was not invaded by his wife. Nor, to tell the truth, did he think much about her, having so many other things to think about, and being, besides, honestly grieved by the loss which he had sustained. Sir Robert had been a good and kind father to him—or, at all events, such was his conviction; although the conviction of some sons and heirs, situated as he was, would, it may be, have been different. But when all was over, when the blinds were drawn up once more, when the past was quite past and the present and future had to be faced, the fact that he had a wife with whom his relations were not all that could be desired was brought home to him.

"I have nothing pleasant to tell you," said Mr. Dent, who was one of his deceased friend's executors; "so the sooner we get through our necessary talk the better. But I am afraid it will take rather a long time to make everything clear to you."

It did take rather a long time — so long, indeed, that Guy's attention frequently wandered from the precise, methodical narration to which he was ostensibly listening. Mr. Dent and he were sitting in what had been Sir Robert's study; faint shafts of autumn sunlight fell upon them through the high, narrow windows, beyond which could be discerned a prospect of pale-blue sea and fields and hills and yellowing woods. A thousand vague and incongruous memories jostled one another in the mind of the man who should have been, but was not, the heir to that far-stretching property, while the man to whom it actually belonged plodded doggedly on with his cut-and-dried statement of facts and figures. When at last he ceased, Guy remarked:

"The upshot of all this appears to be that I haven't an acre or a shilling to my name, and that I am really your guest at the present moment."

"No," answered Mr. Dent, "it is not quite so bad as that. When everything has been put straight and all claims have been met, you will have, as nearly as I can calculate, about £30,000 to live upon. Your mother, of course, has her own property, in addition to the sum settled upon her on her marriage. I don't know whether I have convinced you, but I trust I have, that in making myself your father's creditor and getting this estate into my own hands, I did what seemed to me to be the best that I could do for him."

"Oh, I'm quite sure of that," replied Guy, who, as a matter of fact, had not very well understood the details of the historical sketch which had just been laid before him. "I never expected to save as much as £30,000 out of the wreck, and I knew I shouldn't be able to live here. As the place had to go to somebody else, I am very glad that it goes to you."

"I am a man of business," said Mr. Dent; "I have always been very careful about the investment of my money, and I am, in a certain sense, a rich man. But of course, as I have pointed out to you, a considerable portion of what I possess is represented by this estate, and the investment is scarcely one which I should have made for choice. Well, now, you know what I am—an old fellow with one niece, who will naturally inherit all he has to leave, and whose husband you happen to be. Is it too much to hope that there will still be Luttrells at Haccombe Luttrell when there are no more Dents anywhere?"

An impulse which he did not try to resist prompted Guy to take the old man's hand. "I see," said he; "I understand—and I'm really as grateful to you as if—as if the thing could come off. But it can't possibly come off. If it was out of the question a week ago—which it was—it's doubly out of the question now. Luttrells there may be at Haccombe after you and I are wiped out; for you can tie the property up for Netta, if you choose, and her husband can take her name. But I assure you that you are now in the presence of one Luttrell who will spend the rest of his days elsewhere."

"I was prepared," remarked Mr. Dent, after a short pause, "to hear you speak like this. I don't know that, for the moment, I can profitably say or do anything more. I have told you what my hopes are, and what, in spite of all, they will continue to be. One thing only I should like to beg of you: don't make the realization of them quite impossible."

"It couldn't be more impossible than it is."

"Oh, it could. There is the President of the Divorce Court, you see, to whom you might be tempted to give an excellent opportunity of setting you and others free."

"When I give Clarissa an excuse for applying to the President of the Divorce Court," answered Guy, "I'll give you and her leave to call me what neither of you has the right to call me at present."

Mr. Dent glanced keenly at him for an instant, smiled and folded up his papers. "Well," said he, "I think that is about all. The family lawyers will inflict a good many more wearisome hours upon you; but I dare say you have had as much business talk now as you can stand in one day."

CHAPTER XXVII

A DRAMATIC PERFORMANCE

MR. ALFRED LOOSEMORE, who, besides being a minor poet and an essayist, was a close student of contemporary manners, never allowed an opportunity of augmenting his somewhat slender income to escape him, if he could possibly help it. In the year with which we are concerned, therefore, he judged that the time had come for him to write a play, and that this play, in order to secure the certainty of a run, must deal with the relations between the sexes, a subject which just then was engaging a large measure of public attention. The result of an effort which gave him remarkably little trouble was such as to exceed his most sanguine anticipations. "Equality," which was produced early in November at the Whitehall Theatre, was received with qualified approval by the critics and unbounded favor by audiences which, night after night, crowded the building from roof to basement. The plot of the piece, to be sure, was no great things; but the dialogue was smart and occasionally witty, the author had caught cleverly enough the tone of a certain section of society, and his theme—the claim on the part of a young wife to start on even terms with her husband and do everything that he did—happened at the moment to be a popular one. What showed that Mr. Loosemore thoroughly understood his public was that nobody could feel quite sure, when the curtain fell, whether he had meant to support or to ridicule the "movement" with which his name was to some extent identified. The friends and the foes of that movement were alike puzzled; but the great majority of both were pleased, while the minority, who held Madeline Luttrell's opinion respecting the playwright, felt at least bound to go and see the fellow's latest bid for notoriety. Accordingly they went, and helped to replenish the overflowing coffers of the management.

Now, as soon as ever Mr. Loosemore heard that his friend Mrs. Luttrell, who had now become Lady Luttrell, had returned to Cadogan Gardens for the winter, he hastened to send her a charming little note, enclosing a ticket for a box and begging her to patronize his "poor dramatic trifle." He did not expect so gifted a writer to think much of it from a literary point of view, he said; but possibly it might divert her, and possibly she might detect in it some feeble attempt to familiarize "the great stupid mob of our fellow-creatures" with ideas which she was so far better able than he to expound.

Clarissa, to tell the whole truth about her, rather liked being called a gifted writer by one who had long ago earned that appellation for himself; moreover, she wanted to see a play of which she had already heard and read a great deal. So, on the appointed evening, she went to the Whitehall Theatre all alone, having failed to find any one to accompany her; and when the first act was over, she was forced to the conclusion that if this was really meant as an attempt to back her up, it was indeed a feeble one. The play might be clever, and, after a fashion, she thought that it was; but there were situations in it which bordered upon downright farce, and there were others which, by her way of thinking, passed the borders of decency. This young married woman who (quite properly and reasonably) proclaimed her intention of facing married life upon a basis of equality, and who met the remonstrances of her bewildered husband by reminding him that she merely asked for the liberty which he himself demanded, was not at all the type which Clarissa and her friends desired to set up. It was hinted, if not actually stated, that she imitated her husband's vices, instead of insisting upon his abandonment of them; and if he was made to look foolish more than once, so was she.

When, immediately after the fall of the curtain, the click of the opening door behind her caused Clarissa to turn her head and Mr. Alfred Loosemore stepped delicately out of the dark background, she put up her glasses to look at him and said, with some asperity:

"I wonder you are not ashamed of yourself! I have always suspected that you were not serious, and now I am sure of it. This is much worse than I thought it would be."

"How cruel of you to condemn a humble scribbler unheard!" murmured Mr. Loosemore, holding Clarissa's hand in a soft, protracted grasp—he had a way of shaking hands which aroused murderous inclinations in the hearts of some persons whom he honored in that way. "You have only seen the beginning of the little business as yet, and I hoped you would understand that the lady's plan is simply to give her spouse a salutary object-lesson. In the second act we become quite pathetic, and in the third—"

"Well, what about the third?" inquired Clarissa. "How does your play, which strikes me as being nothing but a caricature so far, end?"

"Oh, it's inconclusive; that's just the beauty of it. You wouldn't have me wind up with a commonplace, *bourgeois* reconciliation, would you? The highest art, you know, is never didactic, never precise—only suggestive."

"But what are you going to suggest?" Clarissa wanted to know.

"Ah, that's just it! I suggest all manner of things, and the audience takes its choice. *Il y en a pour tous les goûts.*"

Mr. Loosemore loved to talk about all manner of things; but most of all he loved to talk about himself, and he proceeded to gratify that not uncommon taste, while his neighbor's ear was turned towards him and her eyes wandered over the crowded house. Presently she flushed a little and drew a quick breath; for in the stalls directly beneath her she had recognized somebody whom she had scarcely expected to see. Guy, she had been given to understand, was at Kendal, and likely to remain there throughout the winter; he had not spoken of coming up to London when they had parted at Haccombe Luttrell, after a scene which she could not recall without deep vexation and a sense of having been rather unfairly treated, nor was it agreeable to her to become aware of his vicinity, Yet, after a fashion, she was sorry for him; after a fashion, too, she was almost remorseful. It had been a shock to her to hear that Haccombe belonged to her uncle and would probably, in the long-run, belong to herself. She had understood how much more difficult her position was rendered for her by that unforeseen state of affairs; and if the scene alluded to had been painful and unpleasant, it was not, to do him justice, Guy who had made it so. She thought of Lady Luttrell's bitter reproaches, of Paul's stern disapproval, and of the silent entreaty in Madeline's eyes, and she felt, as she had often felt before, that these good people were hardly to be blamed for regarding her as the cause of all their misfortunes. But at the time she had not felt like that. 'She had felt that she was being driven into a corner, that they were taking advantage of circumstances which she had had no hand in bringing about, and that they asked her to make a sacrifice which they had no right to demand. Was it her fault that her husband refused to take what she freely and willingly offered him? Was it her fault that it had become impossible for her ever to live with him again as his wife? Guy, in his good-humored, imperturbable way, had taken her part, had stood between her and his mother, and had contrived to avert an actual breach of friendly relations; but she had left the place, sore and angry, carrying with her the recollection of certain sayings on her mother-in-law's part which it was not easy to pardon. The dowager was still at Haccombe, packing up her belongings and making preparations for the final flitting which must soon be undertaken; but she was only there on sufferance, whereas, if things had fallen out differently, she might of course have remained on in her old home for an indefinite length of time.

18

These were not satisfactory reflections, nor were they of
a nature to increase the interest of an innocent and mis-
judged woman in Mr. Alfred Loosemore's play, the second
act of which was now in full progress. The author remained at Clarissa's elbow, and was kind enough to point
out to her the special merits and beauties of the action as
each presented itself; but even he (though he was as dense
in some respects as he was quick in others) could not help
perceiving that her attention was engaged elsewhere.

This second act was doubtless intended to be touching,
and indeed it contained situations which caused the pit and
gallery to blow its collective nose; but the whole drift of
the piece—so far as her preoccupation enabled her to
follow it—struck Clarissa as insincere and irritating, and
she was very much disposed to agree with her husband,
who, shortly after the curtain had fallen once more, exclaimed : "Did you ever listen to such sickening, mawk-
ish rot in your life before ?"

For Guy, having caught sight of her, had entered her
box, as if that had been quite the natural thing to do, and
it was with the ejaculation just quoted that he greeted
her. By way of reply, she hastened to introduce him to
Mr. Alfred Loosemore, who remarked, sweetly :

"So sorry you don't like my play ! Still, it is original
of you to dislike what everybody else admires, and one is
always rejoiced to encounter originality."

"Oh, are you the author ?" said Guy, in anything but
conciliatory accents. "I shouldn't have said what I did
if I had known that ; but I can't very well eat my words
now. As everybody else admires you and your produc-
tion, I dare say it doesn't much matter what I think about
them."

He was so rude, and continued to be so rude, notwithstanding the bland politeness of Mr. Loosemore, that the
latter was not long in executing a graceful movement of
retreat. Guy Luttrell was a big, powerful man, and the
mere idea of a possible resort to physical violence is repugnant to all refined, highly-strung natures.

As soon as he had departed, Guy took the chair which he had vacated and said: "What a very offensive brute! I have always heard that he was a chap whom one couldn't sit in the room with, and he doesn't seem to have been maligned. Is it permitted to ask whether you are one of his admirers?"

"I think he is clever," answered Clarissa, coldly. "I don't know in what way he is inferior to other men, and in some ways he strikes me as being superior to them. But the subject is not one upon which you and I are likely to agree. I did not know that you were in London. Are you going to stay any time?"

"The inside of a week, I expect. I have come up to meet my people, who are on their way to Pau, where they mean to live in the future, I believe. Shall I find Netta at home to-morrow afternoon? I thought of taking her to Madame Tussaud's or to see Corney Grain, whichever she likes best."

Clarissa would have liked to say that Netta, for whom a governess had now been engaged, could not be allowed to take a half-holiday upon such short notice; but, not choosing to depart by a hair's breadth from the understanding to which she had committed herself, she replied: "Of course it can be arranged, if you wish it. Perhaps you will come and lunch with us first, at two o'clock."

"Well, no, thanks; I don't think I will: that would make us rather late, you see. I'll call for Netta about half-past twelve, and we'll feed together at a pastry-cook's. At her time of life it's grand sport to feed at a pastry-cook's, you know."

He had recovered his good-humor, which the sight of Mr. Alfred Loosemore had temporarily disturbed, and he laughed heartily at Clarissa's earnest entreaties that he would refrain from stuffing the child with sweets. Gregory's powder, he declared, might be relied upon to counteract the effect of over-indulgence.

"Besides," he added, "it will do Netta no harm to be spoiled, for once in a way, now. When she is twelve or fourteen years older, she will be apt to find her father as strict a disciplinarian as she will want to meet."

Clarissa remained silent and pensive. Did he think, then, that he was going to have a voice in the training and education of his daughter? So far as she could remember, nothing of that sort had been stipulated for, and she foresaw that there might be trouble ahead. But Guy at once changed the subject, and began to talk cheerfully about his mother and Madeline, of whom he gave a reassuring account. They had written in better spirits of late, he said, and the change to the South of France would do them all the good in the world. He was very glad that they were leaving Haccombe, where everything, naturally, must remind them of their loss. Upon the whole, he showed so much tact and good taste in touching upon a delicate topic that Clarissa could not but be grateful to him, and, if only he had not been what he was, she would have met him in a more friendly spirit than she felt able to command. Presently the final act of the drama began, and then he jumped up, saying:

"Well, I'll be off now; I can't stand any more of this stuff. Tell Netta to prepare herself for wild excitement to-morrow."

Wild excitement was in store, a little sooner than that, for people who were altogether unprepared to meet with any such experience. Hardly had Guy left her before Clarissa became conscious that something had happened. A subdued murmur was audible in all parts of the house; some of the people in the stalls stood up; the actors paused in their parts, glanced irresolutely at one another and appeared to be frightened. Then arose a sudden, hoarse cry of "Fire!" which was taken up and spread through the building with infinitely greater rapidity than any flames could have done, and instantly there ensued a frantic, senseless stampede, which the manager, who rushed upon the stage and implored the audience to keep their seats, was quite powerless to check. Clarissa, startled and bewildered, would doubtless have joined in the general flight if her husband had not burst into the box in time to stop her.

"Stay where you are !" he called out, peremptorily. "For God's sake, don't attempt to stir till I come back. I'll see whether it's possible for you to get out ; but I don't believe it is. These lunatics are trampling one another to death in the passages."

Clarissa obeyed instinctively and without a word. She was not conscious of being particularly frightened, although her heart was beating fast ; but she was quite conscious that in a moment of such emergency Guy was entitled to take the command, and she was content to let him do so. He was absent for some three or four minutes, which represented a full quarter of an hour to her imagination. Then he returned, panting a little—for indeed he had had to fight his way back to her side—and said, quietly :

"It's no good ; you're as safe here as you would be anywhere, and I think they are getting the fire under. But I couldn't really find out anything, except that all the exits are hopelessly blocked."

Clarissa turned and looked at him, something of her old admiration for his physical courage returning to her as she noticed that he was unaffectedly calm.

"You think we are going to be burned to death, don't you ?" she asked, with an irrepressible shudder. "It is a horrible way of dying !"

"Oh, I dare say it will be all right," he answered, composedly. "With ordinary luck we ought to have a very fair chance of escape. Only we should risk losing what chance we have if we tried to bolt."

Almost as he spoke the lights were suddenly extinguished, and they were left in total darkness. It was natural that his hand should seek hers, and natural that she should find comfort and encouragement in that firm grasp. For a period of time, which was not to be measured by ordinary methods of computation, they stood silently thus, listening to the confused hubbub of shouts and shrieks which arose from all sides and half-choked by the clouds of smoke and the pungent, acrid odor with which the theatre was becoming filled.

"Guy!" gasped Clarissa at length.

"Well, my dear?"

"I want to ask you—I want to ask you something. If this is to be the end of our lives, you can't mind telling me. You did care for me once—what did I ever do to lose your love? Why were you so cruel to me?"

His answer, if he made any, did not reach her ears. She was vaguely aware of being clasped in his strong arms; then a deadly sickness and faintness overpowered her, and when she came to herself—lo and behold, she was out in the open air! Somebody had drenched her with cold water; a few stalwart policemen were keeping back the gaping crowd which had collected in the street, and Guy's voice was saying: "She'll do now. Just clear the road for me, will you, while I lift her into the carriage."

Presently she was in her own carriage and was being driven at a round pace down the Strand, with her husband by her side.

"What has happened?" she murmured, as he wrapped a shawl round her head and a rug over her shoulders. "Did I faint?"

"Oh yes, you fainted," he replied, briskly; "best thing you could do, under the circumstances. Sorry that fool chucked a bucket of water over you, though it had the desired effect. Only you must mind you don't get a chill now. It would be rather hard luck," he added, with a laugh, "to catch one's death of cold after being so nearly roasted alive."

The conflagration, it appeared, had been speedily subdued. Nobody, so far as Guy knew, had been burned, although a good many people had been hurt, and some perhaps killed, in the crush. "It served them jolly well right," he said, rather unfeelingly. Clarissa listened to, but scarcely took in, his unimpassioned account of what had occurred and of the commonplace sequel to a scene with the memory of which her nerves were still vibrating.

When the carriage drew up at the door of her house in Cadogan Gardens, he accompanied her as far as the hall and delivered her into the care of her servants, to whom he explained matters in a few words.

"I'll retire now," said he. "If you'll be advised by me, you'll go straight to bed and have something hot to drink."

"But, Guy," she exclaimed, stretching out a detaining hand, "you—you will come again to-morrow, won't you?"

"Of course I will," he answered; "I shall want to hear how you are after all these emotions. Besides, I have to keep my appointment with Netta, you know. Good-night!"

CHAPTER XXVIII

GUY GIVES NO TROUBLE

WHO does not know the miseries, the bewildered, disgusted, unavailing self-reproaches of "the next morning"? It never is, and never can be, pleasant to awake to the memory of having made a perfect fool of one's self overnight; yet for such pangs a certain alleviation may be found, if only one can feel quite sure that other people have been just as bad. This consolatory reflection was lacking to Clarissa when she opened her eyes in broad daylight and strove to recall the details of an episode which had promised to be tragic, but had ended in a distressing anticlimax. "What did I do?—what did I do?" she asked herself, as she sat up in bed, frowning and pushing back her disordered flaxen hair. Alas! the answer was only too clear and distinct—no whit less distinct than her recollection of what Guy had refrained from doing and saying.

"Oh, why," she ejaculated aloud, with a short laugh of vexation, "am I not the heap of cinders that I expected to become when I behaved in that ridiculous way!"

Pulvis et umbra sumus; we shall all be a mere heap of dust soon; and perhaps, in view of that comforting certainty, it is hardly necessary for us to advance matters by scattering metaphorical ashes over our persons, as we are apt to do when conscious of having been a little more ridiculous than usual. But the last offence with which poor Clarissa was inclined to upbraid herself was that of being habitually ridiculous, and her consequent humiliation was the more profound. To have cast herself, faint-

ing, into the arms of the man whom she so heartily despised; to have given him to understand that she still
loved him and coveted his love; to have even parted from
him, after the tame termination of an uncalled-for scene,
with a flattering request that he would call at her house
on the morrow—was it possible that she—*she*, of all people
in the world !—could have lost her head to that extent ?

And the worst of it was that Guy had not lost his head
for a moment. Most likely he had known all along that
the danger was rather apparent than real; most likely he
was even now chuckling in amusement over reminiscences
which caused her to writhe. Well, she would have to eat
dirt, she supposed; she would have to explain to him,
when he came, that cowards must not be held responsible
for words uttered under stress of panic; and then, if he
were disposed to be magnanimous— But she did not
believe that he would be magnanimous. He had never
really shown himself so ; although circumstances had
enabled him from time to time to affect an air of magnanimity. While her maid was helping her to dress, she tried
hard to recover a little of her self-respect by depreciating
her husband, and she was in some measure successful. At
all events, she thought it highly probable that, before the
morning was over, he would have justified the poor opinion that she entertained of him.

Now, as that opinion was scarcely to be shaken or altered by any line of conduct that Guy could have taken
up, it is difficult to say whether the line which he actually
did adopt was judicious or the reverse, but possibly it
might have rendered Clarissa less angry had it been more
open to exception. He arrived shortly after mid-day to
make inquiries and claim his daughter, and he was so ur-
banely determined to ignore everything beyond the bare
fact that a lady whom he had had the privilege of escorting home had sustained a shock to her nerves that explanations for which he did not ask could not very well be
forced upon him.

Clarissa, who had been reading the newspaper on his

entrance, remarked, presently: "I am glad to see that
they don't mention my name in the account that they give
of the fire. I was afraid that I might have been noticed,
and that there would be some idiotic paragraph or other
about me."

She had, in truth, been horribly afraid that her name
would be mentioned — and Guy's too. What "copy"
might not have been constructed by an intelligent and
descriptive reporter out of the incident of Lady Luttrell's
rescue from death by the husband from whose protection
she had withdrawn herself! But Guy only laughed and
said :

" A fire seems an important event when you happen to
be in it; but I suppose fires occur in some part of London
pretty nearly every night, and there were no lives lost on
this occasion, it seems. I dare say the papers think they
have done enough in the way of personal particulars by
recording the fortunate escape of your friend Loosemore.
I should think he was the sort of chap who might be trusted to run no foolhardy risks."

Perhaps Guy did not quite realize that Lady Luttrell
had won a position of almost equal public notoriety with
Mr. Alfred Loosemore : there were, indeed, several things
which Guy did not seem quite to realize. However,
whether his slightly irritating nonchalance were genuine
or assumed, it was doubtless a matter for congratulation
that he should make light of the whole affair and cut
short such expressions of gratitude as Clarissa felt bound
to offer him.

" Oh, there's no occasion to thank me," said he ; "any
of the attendants at the theatre would have done as much
for you, and I suppose I should have done as much for any
of the attendants. One can't leave a swooning fellow-
creature inside a burning house, you know."

Well, that observation had at least the merit of candor,
if it did not err on the side of fulsome flattery. Clarissa
felt that she had said as much as she was expected or desired to say, and she did not attempt to detain her husband

after it had been intimated that Miss Netta was ready and
waiting for him down-stairs. But it was with flushed
cheeks and tightly compressed lips that she presently
watched the pair drive off together in a hansom; and although she was aware that Guy had, in a certain sense,
dealt leniently with her, that did not prevent her from being bitterly incensed against him. Incensed, and perhaps
also a trifle jealous; for she could not endure the thought
that their child's affections were divided between them.
What had he ever done to deserve Netta's affection, beyond amusing himself with her sometimes when he felt an
inclination that way? To be sure, the task of rewarding
Guy and men like him according to their deserts seemed
to be one almost too hard for the powers of even enlightened and reforming ladies.

Clarissa, not being best pleased with herself or with anybody else that day, naturally took revenge upon the numerous friends who had heard reports of her adventure,
and who came to ply her with condolences, congratulations, and inquiries. Even Mr. Alfred Loosemore, when
he called in the course of the afternoon, met with scant
courtesy at her hands, and was told in so many words that
the anxiety with which he professed to have been torment-
ed on her behalf would have been easier to believe in, had
it led him to attempt her rescue, instead of making a dash
—as he owned he had done—for the stage door.

"My dear lady," he replied, with smiling imperturbability, "I am constitutionally timid, and I don't pretend to be
anything else. The beauty of me is that I never do pretend to be anything but what I am, and the odd thing is
that I am commonly considered to be made up of pretence
and affectation. I should have enjoyed nothing more than
bearing you heroically in my arms through the flames and
smoke; but at the time it seemed to me of such paramount
importance that I myself should escape being singed!
What would you have? Poets are thin-skinned folks,
while it is a law of nature that heroes should be provided
with hides. Who, I wonder, was the pachydermatous gen-

tleman who is said to have played the hero for your
sake ?"

Since he did not know, she felt under no obligation to inform him. She contented herself with remarking, dryly,
that it is useful, in case of emergencies, to have among
one's friends a few dull-witted persons who do not mind
running the risk of being scorched; and soon afterwards
her visitor, perceiving that she was out of temper, took his
departure. Nothing, Mr. Loosemore thought, is more unbecoming a woman than to be out of temper, and he had so
sincere an admiration for Lady Luttrell that it pained him
to see her exhibit herself under an unbecoming aspect.

The return of Netta at a late hour, and in a state of gar-
rulous, incoherent excitement, did not, unfortunately, tend
to restore her mother's impaired amiability. Netta had
been having a grand and memorable time of it. She had
been treated to all the unwholesome delicacies that her
soul loved; she had been taken to the German Reed entertainment, of which she expressed unqualified approval;
finally, she had been partaking of tea and muffins at a hotel with her grandmother, who had just arrived, and who,
it seemed, had charged the child with a message to the effect that a visit from "granny and Aunt Madeline" might
be expected on the ensuing afternoon. That being so,
Netta wanted to know whether the duty that she owed to
her family did not demand the concession of another half-
holiday.

Clarissa replied somewhat sternly in the negative. She
was all the more determined not to spoil her child because
it would have been a great deal easier and pleasanter to do
so than to maintain discipline. Guy, being irresponsible,
could of course afford to be indulgent, and she mentally
accused him of taking a rather unfair advantage of his ir-
responsibility.

He was, however, at least considerate enough to abstain
from accompanying his mother and his sister when they
called in Cadogan Gardens the next day. Possibly he had
foreseen that the meeting would not be marked by any

excess of cordiality on either side, and had thought that he would best consult his own comfort by evading it. In truth, the dowager had neither caresses nor affectionate speeches at the service of her daughter-in-law, with whom she would now have been ready to quarrel upon very slight provocation. She had called because both Guy and Madeline had urged her to call; but she wished it to be understood that she altogether disapproved of Clarissa, and she certainly managed to make that much clear to the dullest comprehension.

"Pray, do not trouble to return our visit," she said, when she rose, after conversation had been carried on in a polite, distant style for ten minutes; "we have only two days in which to get all our shopping done, and you would be sure not to find us at home. Perhaps you will allow me just to say good-bye to dear little Netta now; it will be a long time, I am afraid, before I see her again, poor child!"

Lady Luttrell, in her widow's weeds and with her worn, anxious face, was a sufficiently pathetic figure, and was, perhaps, to be excused for being irreconcilable. Some tears fell from her eyes upon the curly head of her grand-child, for whom she had brought various presents, wrapped up in silver paper. While she was bending over Netta, Clarissa whispered to Madeline: "Must we part like this? Could you not dine with me to-morrow evening?"

"Oh yes," answered the girl, "I should like to come. I am sorry," she added, with a significant glance at her mother; "but—can you wonder?"

Clarissa could not and did not wonder. She, too, was sorry; only it was quite out of her power to make Lady Luttrell glad. Some day, perhaps, justice would be done to her, and it would be acknowledged that a chain of circumstances which had resulted in the impoverishment of her husband's family had been none of her creating. Meanwhile it was something to be thankful for that Madeline remained faithful: besides which, she was under the impression that Madeline stood in need of counsel and assistance. Was there not only too much reason to fear that this return to Pau might imply a return to temptations which ought to be strenuously resisted ? The girl must be encouraged and implored to stand firm.

It was assuredly not with any view to securing an ally in this benevolent design that Clarissa asked Alfred Loosemore to partake of her hospitality at the same time; for she did not so much as know that he was acquainted with Raoul de Malglaive. In point of fact, the man invited himself, as he had a cool habit of doing; and when, as before, he was placed next to Miss Luttrell at the dinner-table, he at once remembered that he was still a little in her debt. For debts of that particular kind Mr. Loosemore had a singularly tenacious memory.

"So you are going back to Pau," said he, between the soup and the fish; "and no doubt you will meet that young miscreant De Malglaive there. I would ask you to give him a message from me if I could word it so as to be fitted for transmission through such a medium. But you might mention that if he thinks the banks of the Loire are out of sight of Paris, he makes a very great mistake. Then he will ask you what you mean, and you will be able to tell him quite honestly that you don't know, but that I do. Ah, why haven't I a face and manner like his ! It would be so delightful to be sure of never being found out—or of escaping condemnation even when one was !"

"There are people," returned Madeline, "whose faces and manners ought to prevent any fair - minded person from condemning them for doing anything."

Having thus relieved her feelings, she resolutely refused to be drawn into further conversation by the poet, and devoted her attention to the other guests, of whom some half-dozen were present—for it was very seldom that Lady Luttrell sat down to a solitary dinner. But the other guests were only interesting in so far as that they were all talking about their hostess's adventure at the theatre, of which Madeline now heard for the first time. Later in the evening, when they had gone away, and when Clarissa had begged her to stay a little longer, she asked :

"Is it really true that Guy saved your life the other night? He never said a word to us upon the subject."

"He certainly would not have told you that he saved my life," answered Clarissa, with an annoyed look, "because that would have been nonsense. He was at the theatre, and he came into my box, and I was stupid enough to faint, and then he helped me out to my carriage—that was all. It was a provoking thing to have happened, and embarrassing for both of us; I am glad he had the good taste to say nothing about it."

She proceeded, without drawing breath, to deliver the earnest exhortation which she fancied that her sister-in-law might require, and to repeat, with increased emphasis, all that she had urged before against licentious Frenchmen.

"You need not be in the least alarmed," was the calm and satisfactory answer which she received; "I happen to have heard quite enough about M. de Malglaive to convince me that he is as black as you or any one else could wish to paint him. Why you should imagine that I am in any especial danger from him I don't know; but I can assure you that I am a great deal more unlikely to marry him than you are to forgive Guy. And that is putting things rather strongly, isn't it?"

"Yes," answered Clarissa, after a pause, "that is putting things strongly, if by forgiveness you mean what I suppose you mean. So long as you are determined never to marry a man whom you neither love nor really know, I am satisfied. As for Guy, I suspect that he is tolerably well satisfied too, and that he would think Haccombe Luttrell a dear bargain at the price of having to live there with me. He and I are good friends—as good friends as it is possible for us to be. But I hope I shall not have to see him again before he leaves London."

"Oh, he has gone. Paul has undertaken to see us off from Charing Cross, and he wanted to get back to Kendal as soon as he could. You know that he thinks of giving up the service?"

"I did not know," answered Clarissa. There was a certain relief in hearing that she would not be called upon to meet her husband again for the present; yet she was unreasonably mortified by this prompt confirmation on his part of the indifference which she had ascribed to him.

"Yes," Madeline resumed; "he says he can live more cheaply out of the army than in it, and as he will have about £1000 a year now, he will be able to get on as a bachelor."

"But not in London, I hope?" asked Clarissa, apprehensively.

"Ah, that I can't tell you. Wherever he may be, I am sure he will interfere with you as little as possible. Of course he will want to have Netta with him sometimes."

"Yes, he will want that," agreed Clarissa, frowning, and as years go on— However, there is no use in meeting trouble half-way."

"There must always be troubles when married people who have children decide to live apart," observed Madeline.

"Quite so; only there would be far worse troubles if they decided to go on living together. That is the whole gist of our argument."

But readers shall not be wearied with a recapitulation of the arguments used by Clarissa Luttrell and those who agreed with her. These ladies have stated their case so amply with the aid of tongue and pen that everybody must know all about it by this time.

CHAPTER XXIX

WHETHER HIS MOTHER WOULD LET HIM OR NO

THERE are many ways, easy and difficult, of acquiring popularity; but perhaps the surest of all is to be constantly cheerful. Smiling faces, like sunshine, are always welcome in a world which, taking it altogether, is not too provocative of smiles, and it may have been Raoul de Malglaive's persistent gravity that had prevented him from being ever really liked by his brother officers. Their respectful admiration he had, indeed, earned by the success with which he was understood to have laid siege to the affections of innumerable ladies; but as a comrade they found him rather a dull dog, and after he recovered from his illness and returned to duty he chose to dwell in a seclusion which they did not trouble themselves to invade. By his refusal to join in the *"rallie-papiers"* and other diversions organized by these light-hearted youths, and by his evident disinclination to mix with the society of Tours, he made for himself a few enemies; but their enmity did not take an active form, nor was he even conscious of it. In Madame de Castelmoron he might, to be sure, have recognized a possible foe, had he reflected upon the severe blow which he had dealt at that lady's self-esteem; but Madame de Castelmoron, who speedily quitted her country residence, was as speedily forgotten by him, and he asked for nothing better than neglect on the part of his neighbors.

When the news of Sir Robert Luttrell's death reached him he despatched, as was only fitting, a letter of sympathy to the widow, and this, after a considerable lapse of time, was suitably acknowledged. Lady Luttrell wrote some-

19

what hurriedly, but the language that she used was of a nature to give him encouragement. She had decided, she mentioned, to make her home for the future at Pau ; she hoped to be established with her daughter at the Château de Grancy before the end of the year, and she looked forward to seeing a great deal in a quiet way of old friends. "Among whom your dear mother is one of the most valued. I like to think that you have given up all idea of deserting her in her solitude."

Thus reassured, Raoul patiently watched the fall of the leaf, the daily darkening of the skies, and the approach of winter. Time never moves very slowly when there is a total lack of incident to mark its progress, nor can those whose thoughts are wholly occupied with the future be altogether unhappy in the present. December came upon him almost as a surprise, and it was with something akin to elation that he took his seat in the Southern express. He knew, of course, that his difficulties were only about to begin, and that failure might very well be in store for him, yet, at the worst, he was going to see Madeline once more, and at the best—well, nothing forbade him to dream blissfully of the best, while the train rocked and swayed at full speed on its course towards Poitiers and Bordeaux.

Stern old Madame de Malglaive, who for weeks past had been ticking off every day and hour that brought her nearer to her son, received him, on his arrival, without any extravagant demonstrations of affection.

"You have become thinner," she remarked, after he had enfolded her in a filial embrace, "and your eyes look heavy. That feverish attack of which you only told me after you had recovered from it was more serious than you pretended, perhaps ?"

"It was not in the least serious, and, such as it was, it left me a very long time ago," answered Raoul, laughing. "If my eyes are heavy, it is because I have been travelling all night. But you, *ma mère*—you do not seem to me to be as strong as you were when I left you."

The truth was that Madame de Malglaive's face was perceptibly yellower and more wrinkled, while the withered hands which still rested on Raoul's shoulders trembled after a fashion which was quite new to him.

"I am nearly a year older," she answered, shortly; "at my time of life strength does not increase. For the rest, I do not complain of my health, and I am still able to attend to my affairs and yours—which require attention. Nevertheless, I shall be ready to take my retreat as soon as you are ready to leave the army and manage your property yourself."

It was not impossible, he thought, that he might ere long be ready and willing to do that; but he kept his own counsel, not wishing to disclose his hopes prematurely, and being well aware that they would not command his mother's immediate sympathy. He preferred to ask, with a smile:

"What retreat? Not one that will take you away from your home and mine, at least? Do you think I know enough about agriculture to dispense with your help?"

Madame de Malglaive was evidently gratified; but she jerked up her bony shoulders and made a grimace. "*Mon Dieu!*" said she, "it is true that you may count upon being robbed on all sides when I am gone; but there will be a little money for you in the bank, and possibly—who knows? —your wife, when you make up your mind to take one, may bring you a little more. Possibly, too, your wife will wish to get rid of a sour old woman."

She added, after a short pause, "You remember the De Villars? They have come to end their days in their own province, now that he has definitely abandoned his diplomatic career, and they have promised to breakfast with us to-morrow."

Raoul smothered a sigh. The Marquis de Villars, a wealthy and capable personage, who had subjected the loyalty of some of his friends to a rather severe strain by taking office under the Empire and representing the Republic as ambassador at one of the principal European courts, had an only daughter. It was not difficult to guess why he had been invited to breakfast. At the same time, Mademoiselle de Villars was no more to be dreaded than any other young woman, and Raoul was fully prepared to learn that some young woman, or even several young women, had found provisional favor with his mother.

Indeed, very soon after he had had the privilege of being presented to the fair Blanche de Villars on the following day he felt that Fate had been unexpectedly kind to him, and was quite grateful to the girl for being so palpably impossible. It was not that she was deficient in good looks or in accomplishments, for she was rather pretty, in a florid style, and she had plenty to say for herself; but she belonged to a type which is of comparatively recent development in France—a type equally abhorrent to Raoul and to his mother, and scarcely understood by either of them. Mademoiselle de Villars, being no longer in the very first bloom of her youth, had seen a great deal of the world, and had not neglected her opportunities. Her conversation was not precisely that of an *ingénue*, nor did she scruple to let M. de Malglaive know that reports of some of his escapades had reached her, and to rally him upon them. In England she might have been called rather fast and noisy; in the provincial society of her native land a far less lenient judgment was likely to be pronounced upon her.

So Raoul, with a mind at ease, answered her in her own coin, while the brisk, gray-headed marquis did his best to entertain a hostess with whom he had nothing in common, and Madame la Marquise allowed her eyes to roam round the scantily furnished dining-room. Her daughter's future abode, she may have been thinking, was not luxurious, and the match would scarcely be a brilliant one; still, sundry previous attempts at arranging a brilliant alliance for Blanche had fallen through, and the De Malglaives were said to be a great deal richer than they looked. Upon the conclusion of the repast, Madame de Villars, who had hitherto only troubled herself to speak in monosyllables, graciously allowed it to be inferred that she was a consenting party. She signified as much by requesting M. de Malglaive to exhibit his garden to her daughter.

"As for me," she said, "I am going to take my husband to pay a few visits of obligation which Blanche will be glad to escape. We will call for her on our return."

They were absent a full hour—an hour which seemed very long to Madame de Malglaive, who spent it in unwonted inaction in her *salon,* while the young people were exploring the ill-kept pleasure-grounds.

"*Ça y est!*" she was saying to herself; "I was sure he would be attracted to her—though she is scarcely attractive to me. After all, it is a good marriage, and there should be a good *dot.* Provided that she does not ruin him!—for one can see that she is extravagant. As for me, I shall have to pack up my bundle and go; I shall never be able to endure it! When all is said, one place is as good as another to die in. I should have preferred to die where I have lived; but it is not to be thought of. There would assuredly be a quarrel, and I must not quarrel with Raoul's wife."

Notwithstanding these and other melancholy reflections, the old lady was, or pretended to be, dismayed when her son, after escorting Mademoiselle de Villars to her carriage, entered the room and threw up his hands with a gesture of horrified deprecation.

"My dear mother," he exclaimed, "of what can you have been thinking? But she is atrocious — that Blanche whom you are so obliging as to offer me!"

"She makes the effect upon me of being a little emancipated," Madame de Malglaive replied; "but I am old and behind the times. I thought that a young girl of that description would appeal to your tastes."

"God forbid! According to what she tells me, she has appealed to the tastes of too many men to have any power left for gratifying mine—which, besides, are quite simple. I have not the right to pose as an absolute innocent; but I assure you that your Mademoiselle de Villars has been making my hair stand on end."

Madame de Malglaive smiled grimly. She liked to hear her son describe his tastes as simple; there would be a certain satisfaction in snubbing the De Villars, who had been a shade too patronizing; and Blanche, apart from the substantial dowry which she might be expected to bring, was not the most desirable of daughters-in-law. Moreover, the old lady had more than one string to her bow.

"Enough!" she said; "we will think no more about it. All I wish for now is that you should abandon your bachelor life and relieve me of cares to which I begin to feel that I am no longer as equal as I was. Only choose for yourself; you will not find me hard to please."

The assertion, without being false, was most unfortunately misleading. Raoul naturally thought that he saw his opportunity, and upon the impulse of the moment he took advantage of it.

"Would you like me to tell you all the truth?" he asked. "I have already chosen: it remains to be seen whether the only woman in the world whom I can ever marry will consent to take me for her husband. I have a little hope; but I cannot call it more than a very little. However, I shall soon know; for Lady Luttrell wrote to me not long ago to say that she would be here about this time. They may even have arrived, perhaps?"

Heavy clouds gathered upon Madame de Malglaive's brow. "What!" she exclaimed; "you are still thinking of Antoinette Luttrell's daughter, a foreigner who will not have a *liard*—it is I who answer to you for that! I hoped you had overcome that foolish fancy, of which I saw the beginning last spring. No; they have not arrived yet; but they will be here in a few days. I understand now why Antoinette wrote to me with such affection—she who, during the long years when she thought herself rich and took me for a poor woman, could scarcely find time to call upon me! You have been in correspondence with her, then?"

Raoul defended himself and Lady Luttrell. Certainly he had written to her to convey his condolences on her husband's death ; but he had not breathed a word of his intentions with regard to her daughter, nor had he any good reason for believing that such overtures would have been favorably received.

"I know," he added, "that you are prejudiced against Miss Luttrell; but surely that cannot be on the ground of her being a foreigner. She is, after all, so little of a foreigner! And as for money, am I not well enough off to disregard that consideration ?"

"I do not admit that you are rich," his mother returned ; "and if, by care and economy, your property has been made to yield more than it did in your father's time, you have the better right to demand an equivalent. *Donnant, donnant!* — these Luttrells, who have squandered their patrimony, and are now reduced to poverty, would not object to profit by what others have saved; that is easily understood ! But the De Malglaives were not created to supply their wants."

All the subdued rancour and jealousy of a lifetime found expression in her hard words and her harder countenance. Her old schoolfellow Antoinette de Grancy, who had become a *grande dame* and had seen the highest society of France and England, while she herself had been buried in penurious, provincial obscurity, had, consciously or unconsciously, inflicted many a humiliation upon her. Now the tables were turned ; and if the money which she had so painfully and laboriously heaped up for her son's benefit was to go into the pockets of upholsterers and dressmakers, at least Antoinette's daughter should not have the spending of it. She had not a great deal to say against Madeline personally ; although, in the course of the discussion which followed, she did contrive to say something. Her strength, as she very well knew, was to sit still.

"I oppose myself formally to the project," was her final and dogged reply to Raoul's entreaties and remonstrances.

He sighed. "And yet," he said, gently, "I cannot renounce the project. Listen, *ma mère:* I love this Englishwoman, since you persist in calling her an Englishwoman ; and because I love her—"

"Ah, bah !" interrupted Madame de Malglaive, roughly, "you talk at your ease about your love ! How many other women have you loved ? How long will it be before this one follows the rest ? Have I reproached you ?—have I spoken to you about these things ? Have I ever grudged the money which has been lavished upon persons whose names are well known to me, though I do not care to sully my lips with them ? No ; I have said to myself that there would be an end to such follies—that you would weary of them in due season, as your forefathers wearied of them. Love !—that may be an excuse for follies, but Heaven knows that it is no excuse for marriage !"

Raoul hung his head. "It is true," he said, "that I have been guilty of many follies, of which I repent, now that it is too late. It is true that you have been very good to me and very forbearing. Believe me, I am not ungrateful."

"It must be confessed," returned his mother, with a harsh laugh, "that you adopt a droll fashion of proving your gratitude. *Allons!* you are the master ; it is for you to choose between me and a penniless girl whose pretty face has fascinated you for the moment, and I perceive that you will not hesitate. Let me tell you, however, that on the day when you marry Miss Luttrell you will see the last of your mother."

She started up and left the room with a quick, firm step ; though he noticed that she paused and staggered for an instant on the threshold.

He did not follow her—what would have been the use, seeing that he could not say what she wished him to say ? —but his heart sank within him. He had been, he felt, inexcusably maladroit. He should have waited, before speaking, to ascertain whether his love was returned or not : then he might have presented himself to his mother with a case so strong that she would scarcely have been able to resist it. As matters stood, he had made sure of her determined resistance, and he knew that what she had threatened to do she would do ; for it was no habit of hers to utter unmeaning menaces. Now, it was very nearly as impossible a thing for Raoul de Malglaive to let his mother leave his house in anger as it would have been to stab her through the heart.

But when the dinner-hour brought them together again a change had come over her demeanor. She was silent, subdued, no longer combative, and almost humble in her anxiety that her son should partake of the dishes which she herself left untouched. She looked old and ill ; and in truth she was both. As soon as the servants had re-tired, and it was possible to talk about subjects more inter-esting than the instability of the existing government and the steady degeneration of Pau society, Raoul moved his chair round the table, so as to place himself at his mother's elbow, and said :

"You are making yourself unhappy too soon. It is not certain that I shall ever offer myself to Miss Luttrell, and it is still less certain that she will accept me if I do. I can-not obey you ; I cannot give her up ; but I want you to believe that I would make any sacrifice, short of that, to please you—and the time has not yet come for either of us to make a sacrifice."

The truce at which he hinted was agreed to at once. Madame de Malglaive laid her trembling hand—the hand which all her efforts could not keep from trembling—upon her son's, and answered :

"Raoul, you must pardon me ; I have said things to you which I ought not to have said, although they were true. Yet—you are all that I have in the world, and, as you say, this marriage is not yet arranged. You will not be in a hurry ; you will see and judge for yourself—perhaps you will change your mind ; and why should I be deprived of the only joy that remains to me ? Let us say no more about the matter, and try to forget—to forget—"

Her voice broke ; her eyes suddenly filled with tears, which brimmed over and rolled down her withered cheeks ;

undoubtedly she was no longer the woman that she had been. Nevertheless, while the mother and son embraced, each recognized that the other was incapable of yielding, and that the course of events alone, which both were well-nigh powerless to direct, must decide between them. Meanwhile, they were genuinely, if a little absurdly, sorry for one another.

CHAPTER XXX

"LA BELLE DAME SANS MERCI"

LADY LUTTRELL and Madeline, attended by a retinue somewhat more numerous than they required or could afford to maintain, reached the Château de Grancy to find two bouquets awaiting them. One of these, which was composed of hot-house blooms, put together with some degree of skill by a local florist, bore the card of the Vicomte de Malglaive, whose *"hommages respectueux"* it purported to represent; the other, which was much larger, was a mere bundle of flowers, obviously culled from the donor's own garden, who had scribbled upon a half-sheet of paper a few words of welcome to the friend of her youth. Madame de Malglaive had as yet no quarrel with the friend of her youth, and perhaps wished it to be understood that she had none : what Raoul may have wished to be understood by a gift which was at once handed over to Madeline the recipient did not know; but she allowed his orchids and gardenias to wither upon their wired stems, whereas his mother's floral tribute was duly utilized for the decoration of the drawing-room and dining-room.

"Very amiable of them to have thought of us," Lady Luttrell remarked, complacently; "no doubt we shall have a visit from them to-morrow."

Her prescience was not at fault; for they both called on the following day, although they did not come together, and only one of them was admitted. Raoul, who presented himself early in the afternoon, was informed that the ladies were a little fatigued after their journey and were resting; Madame de Malglaive, arriving some two hours later, was more fortunate.

"Ah, dear friend," she exclaimed, as she advanced into the rather desolate-looking room where Lady Luttrell was sitting alone, "what pain it gives me to see you all in black! How this reminds us that our own lives are very near an end!"

She was not insincere. compassion costs nothing, and her compassion was quite at the service of one for whose designs she could make allowance, while firmly bent upon frustrating them. Lady Luttrell, on her side, was touched, grateful, sorry for herself and willing to believe that others must be sorry for her; so that for some little time the interview between the two ladies was of an affectionate and cordial character. But of course they did not part without the exchange of a few veiled thrusts and parries.

"And so you have not yet married your daughter? Poor child! I regret it for her sake, as well as for yours. Naturally, occasions will have presented themselves in London which cannot be expected to recur, since you do not contemplate a return to England; and here—eh! one does not, as you know, marry one's children here without a *dot*."

"I assure you that I am not in such a hurry. Madeline, fortunately or unfortunately, is difficult to please : otherwise she might have made more than one excellent match by this time. Personally, I do not covet for her a husband who covets money ; but my ideas upon such subjects are probably very different from yours. And your son? Have you succeeded in finding a partner for him among these good provincials, who cling so naïvely to the old-fashioned *bourgeois* notion that marriage is a mere question of barter ?"

"I have never before heard that notion described as belonging peculiarly to the *bourgeoisie*. No ; like you, I am not in a hurry, and Raoul, like your daughter, is a little difficult to please. I hope, nevertheless, that he

will soon decide to settle down, and we have many neighbors and friends who can scarcely be called provincial,
although they happen to possess properties in Béarn. For
my part, I am not more ambitious than another; I shall
only require my daughter-in-law to be of good family and
to be sufficiently well provided for."

"And you think he will make a point of dutifully com-
plying with your requirements ?"

"I do not doubt it; Raoul has always been the best of
sons. With your English habits of looking at things, my
dear Antoinette, you have forgotten what the family
means to us. Not for the world would I say anything to
distress you; but your eldest son, who married a rich
woman only to get himself divorced by her—can you conceive that such a scandal would ever have been permitted
here ?"

"Yet divorces are more frequent in France than in
England, I believe. Not that Guy is divorced from his
wife. But, when all is said, I have no cause to complain
of my son, and I trust that you will find yours as submissive as you expect. Tell him to come and see us when he
has a spare half-hour. We shall be enchanted to renew
acquaintance with him, and you will not, I am sure, accuse
me of meditating an alliance between him and my portionless daughter."

It was a bold stroke on the part of Lady Luttrell, who
was meditating that very thing, to use such direct language, and her antagonist, visibly disconcerted, could only
reply :

"He will not fail to pay his respects to you. I need
hardly tell you that I have no fear of the occurrence of im-
possibilities."

Thus, like a couple of duly accredited plenipotentiaries,
the two ladies concluded their conference with mutual
expressions of regard, neither deceived nor deceiving, yet
fairly well satisfied with a drawn battle. The fact was—
and possibly they were aware of it—that they were quite
powerless. Raoul had only to insist and Madeline to con-

sent. Pressure might be brought to bear upon the former in one direction and upon the latter in another; but the case was hardly one for prohibition or coercion.

Now, during the next week or ten days the puzzle to Lady Luttrell (Madame de Malglaive, being better informed, was less bewildered, if not less anxious) was to discover what the intentions and wishes of the young people really were. They met every day; they apparently took pleasure in one another's society; the riding expeditions of the previous winter were resumed, and Madeline, who had now no horse of her own, willingly accepted M. de Malglaive's offer of a mount: yet their demeanor, somehow, was not quite that of lovers, nor did they seem to be altogether at their ease together.

One of them, in truth, was by no means at his ease, and Lady Luttrell could not have been more puzzled than he was. What was he to conclude from the frank, but undefinably cold, friendliness with which the girl whom he loved received him? What was the meaning of her mother's marked amiability and encouragement and her own readiness to welcome him, tempered by occasional caustic allusions, the drift of which he could not always perceive? Something was wrong; something had happened to alter and harden her; but as she was neither rude nor disagreeable to him, he had no excuse for asking what it was, and was fain to try and persuade himself that she was only a year older. After all, she had passed through many experiences, including a complete change of circumstances and a London season, since they had parted in the spring, and no one knew better than he did how evanescent is the first freshness of youth.

"Do you remember, mademoiselle," he ventured to say one day, "telling me that you looked upon your time at Pau as a holiday? You should be contented now that your holiday is to be permanent."

"Have I the air of being discontented?" she asked. "On the contrary, I am charmed to think that I shall probably end my days here; although I can well understand

that other people might find the place insupportable out
of the season. You yourself, for example — you would
soon begin to pine for Paris or even for Tours, would you
not ?"

"I have done with Paris, and I hope I shall soon have
done with Tours," he replied. "For the rest, every place
is what its inhabitants make it. If you knew how I have
longed for Pau, and—and for the meeting with you which
Pau has meant to me all this time !"

"So much as that ? Well, you have gained what you
longed for, and I hope the result comes up to your expectations."

It was on the tip of his tongue to answer that it did not,
that he had misgivings which she alone could confirm or
dispel, that he suspected her of being displeased with him,
although he was unconscious of having done anything to
merit her displeasure ; but she was looking him so straight
in the face, and the smile upon her lips was so much more
suggestive of mockery than sympathy, that his courage
failed him. Their conversation ended, as several preceding
ones had ended, with a change of subject and an interchange of commonplaces which left them no nearer to an
understanding than they had been at the outset.

Meanwhile, Madame de Malglaive, assuming an attitude
of expectant non-intervention, did not attempt to prevent
her son from visiting the Château de Grancy as often as it
might please him to do so. She withdrew nothing and
reiterated nothing ; perhaps she divined that by thus remaining silent and quiescent she made him a good deal
more uncomfortable than she would have done by the
adoption of active tactics. She did, it is true, in the exercise of a somewhat unwonted hospitality, invite sundry
neighbors, with their marriageable daughters, to breakfast
and dinner ; but she refrained from asking Raoul's opinion
of the young ladies. She merely exhibited them to him,
as it were, so as to let him see that the Department of the
Basses-Pyrénées could, if called upon, produce in sufficient
numbers what he ought to require. Also she looked ill

and sad. Doubtless she only did that because she happened to be both, and because she could not help it ; but
the effect was, nevertheless, considerable. There were
moments when Raoul almost doubted whether he had the
right to break his mother's heart. But he reflected, with
a rueful smile, that the course of events was much more
likely to break his own ; so for a time he allowed events to
take their course, becoming a little less hopeful every day,
yet deriving some measure of comfort from the fact that,
while Lady Luttrell was openly on his side, Madeline did
not seem to be openly against him.

Colonel Curtis, looking scarcely older than when we last
saw him at his accustomed post, was gazing out of the club
window one evening when a lady and gentleman on horse-
back passed at a walking pace beneath him.

"I expect," he remarked to the companion who was stationed at his elbow, "that we shall hear before long of *that*
little affair being settled."

"Daughter of Sir Robert Luttrell's, isn't she ?" said the
other. "Man's a foreigner, I presume, or he wouldn't
ride with such a long stirrup. Sorry to hear that poor old
Luttrell was pretty nearly smashed up when he died."

Colonel Curtis wagged his head solemnly. "I am afraid,"
he replied, "that there is a sad change there, and I can't
wonder that my old friend Lady Luttrell should be so anxious to establish her daughter anyhow and anywhere. She
would have preferred an English marriage, no doubt ; but
this young De Malglaive—whom you probably don't know,
as the best French families hold so much aloof from winter
visitors nowadays—is worth securing. Well born, you see,
and extremely well off ; it is an open question whether she
could do better."

Colonel Curtis conveyed, and wished to convey, the impression that he had been consulted upon the point. His
neighbor, who was acquainted with his harmless little peculiarities, smiled slightly and said, "You have signified
your approval, then ?"

"My dear fellow, how could one disapprove ? It is so

essential that the girl should marry; and although Raoul has been a rather gay youth, there is no reason why he should not become a pattern husband. Besides, he is, or will be, very rich. His mother has been saving for years and years—you have no idea how thrifty these French people are, or of the small sums upon which they contrive to keep up appearances—and when she dies, I should say there will be a good lump of money for him. A good lump of money," the Colonel repeated, emphatically.

"Consequently, if he is smitten with the young lady—who, from the few glimpses that I have had of her, strikes me as being one of the prettiest young ladies I have ever seen in my life—all he has to do is to go in and win, eh?"

"Exactly so. And an uncommonly lucky beggar he is, in my opinion!"

Raoul, who was very far from coming under that denomination in his own opinion, might have been faintly amused if he could have overheard what lookers-on thought of his chances. He himself knew not what to think of his chances; certainly it had not occurred to him that they could be improved in any way by his comparative wealth and Madeline's comparative poverty. This ride from which he was now returning, and during which he had been practically left alone with Miss Luttrell by the considerate friends who had accompanied them, had not been satisfactory to him, nor, in spite of her apparent willingness to accept his society, could he flatter himself that his suit had made the smallest progress.

"Will you not come in and have tea with us?" she asked him, when he had helped her to dismount at the door of the Château de Grancy and the horses had been sent away in charge of a groom. "It is so warm this evening that I don't see why we shouldn't have tea out in the garden."

Of course he accepted the invitation, and when it presently transpired that Lady Luttrell had not yet returned home, his pulse, for a moment, beat more quickly. But Madeline's, he could see, did not. The situation, evidently, had nothing thrilling or suggestive for her, and he

20

sighed as he seated himself by her side on the terrace, in full view of the rosy mountains. As he did not speak for a minute or two, she turned her eyes upon him with that air of ironical scrutiny which she had often affected of late, and which never failed to make him wince.

"You look unhappy," she remarked; "is it permitted to inquire whether there is anything particular the matter with you?"

"I *am* unhappy," he answered, with a sudden, half-despairing resolution to be kept in suspense no longer; "and I think, mademoiselle, that you know well enough what is the matter with me. Yet I must tell you—it is necessary to tell you! And it will be useless, no doubt."

"You have something to tell me?" she said, interrogatively. The smile into which her lips were curved was not a friendly one; her eyes, which he had once thought so sympathetic, had a mocking glitter; for an instant he was reminded of a cat playing with a mouse, and he resented her cruelty, though he could neither account for it nor say precisely in what it consisted.

"Yes," he answered, rather doggedly; "something which will be no news to you and will give you neither pleasure nor pain, I imagine. As for me, the pain of hearing that you do not love me will be no greater now than it would be a week or a fortnight hence, and I had better take it at once. In a week or a fortnight you would say just what you are going to say to me now, would you not?"

"Probably," she replied, without any diminution of composure. "Am I to take this as a formal declaration, then?"

He jumped up and stretched out both his hands towards her with an imploring gesture. "Don't speak to me like that!" he exclaimed. "You do not love me—very well; that is my great misfortune, for which you might pity me, and for which I cannot help thinking that you would have pitied me a year ago. But to love you as madly, as devotedly as I do—surely that is not an offence!"

"To speak honestly," answered Madeline, calmly, "I do

not consider it a very high compliment. It may be perfectly true, and I should think it is, that you honor me for the present with what you choose to call your love; but as I am neither the first nor the second person whom you have honored in that way—"

"Ah," he interrupted despondently, "I have sometimes been afraid of this! You have sometimes said things to me which — which— And yet, if you only understood! It is out of the question for me to discuss such matters with you, and I wish with all my heart that my life had not been what it has been. But how could I know—how can any one know—what real love is until he has experienced it?"

"How indeed? But what I was going to say was that, since you have so frequently experienced what you have mistaken for love, I do not despair of your recovery in the present instance. After such uninterrupted successes, it is mortifying, perhaps, to meet with a solitary failure; but never mind! *Ça vous passera.*"

"Can I not convince you!" he cried. "Will nothing that I can say make you believe that you are all the world to me?"

"Oh, you convince me. I believe that you care a good deal for me, and that you are quite wretched because I do not return your affection. But you hardly expect me to marry you, I suppose, in order to relieve your wretchedness!"

Raoul looked down in silence. Of course he did not expect that—nor had he expected her to reject him after a fashion which betrayed positive repugnance. She had, at least, not detested him that afternoon at Lourdes when he had picked up the wild-flower which she had allowed to drop within his reach; she had liked him, if she had not loved him, before her departure for England. Yet she must have been as well aware then as she was now that his career had not been precisely that of a candidate for the priesthood.

"Is this your last word?" he asked, at length. "Will you never relent?"

"Never," she replied. And then, after a short pause: "I might have prevented you from asking me to marry you; but I did not wish to prevent it. I wanted to have this opportunity of assuring you that there are some girls in the world who would die rather than marry a man of your character. I do not say that there are many; still, there are some, and I hope there will be more. You do not attempt to defend yourself; you know in your heart that you have no defence to offer, and that you would shrink away from me in horror and disgust if I had done a single one of the things which you look upon as mere trifles in your own case. There!—we will say no more about it; but please believe that between you and me there is a chasm across which we cannot by any possibility join hands."

Had Clarissa been privileged to listen to the above speech, she would have felt proud of her disciple and pleased with herself; but, in the absence of Clarissa, there was neither pride nor pleasure for anybody. Madeline, after the man whom she still loved, notwithstanding his iniquities, had meekly accepted his dismissal and had gone his way, felt that she had been sententious, puritanical— not even explicit. For, after all, his chief crime was his recent treachery, not the laxity of his conduct in days gone by, and she had given no hint to that effect. Meanwhile, she had slammed the door of possible compassion and re- pentance in her own face: such as he was, she had lost him forever. Raoul, for his part, walked away, thinking once more of Sénégal and Tonquin. He had been judged with extreme severity, and, if it had been worth while, he might have made out a case for himself to which an im- partial and merciful judge would have allowed some weight. But since Madeline cared nothing for him, what would have been the use of appealing to her mercy or impartiality?

"It is all over," he said to himself; "I have nothing left to live for now; and if I had no mother, I would put a pis- tol to my head at once."

CHAPTER XXXI

MADAME DE MALGLAIVE RESIGNS THE REINS

ASSUMING—as nine out of every ten of us do assume—that life, even under adverse conditions, is preferable to death, it was fortunate for Raoul de Malglaive that he had a mother, and also that he was neither cruel enough nor cowardly enough to inflict upon her so terrible a blow as the suicide of her son would have been. But for her, he would willingly have terminated an existence which had ceased to offer any attraction to him, and which, moreover, was rendered somewhat additionally bitter to him at that moment by the thought that maternal sympathy was the last thing which he could expect. Walking up the straight avenue that led to his abode and hers, he debated with himself whether he should immediately tell her of his defeat and have done with it, or whether he should allow her to find out for herself that she had now no more to fear from the Luttrells than he had to hope. He had not yet made up his mind one way or the other when he was met by a *coupé* which had just left the house and which was brought to a standstill as soon as it had passed him.

A little, rotund man, with a short iron-gray beard, jumped out and hailed him by name. "Hé! Monsieur Raoul; I must say two words to you."

Raoul, with some surprise, recognized Dr. Leroy, a rather rare visitant in a household where no one had ever been permitted to indulge in imaginary ailments. "Is one of the servants ill?" he inquired. "I do not ask you whether you have been called in to see my mother, who,

I believe, has never consulted a medical man since my birth."

The doctor dropped his bullet head beneath his round shoulders and spread out his hands. "*Parbleu!*" he returned, "it is more than a year that she has been consulting me—and with reason! Oh, at my house, not here, and with a hundred precautions against discovery. She has a courage and an obstinacy— *Enfin!* that could not continue forever, and she has been forced to take to her bed, where she will remain, if you please, for the present."

"Do you mean that she is dangerously ill?" asked Raoul, aghast.

"I hope it may be long before you are as ill as she is, *mon garçon;* but we must all come to it sooner or later. I speak to you frankly; the time has come for frank speaking, in spite of her prohibitions. She has a disease of the heart which is absolutely incurable, and which has caused her atrocious sufferings, poor woman! I do not say that the end will come next week or next month or even next year; but this is the worst attack that she has had, and her power of resistance is not what it was. You need not mention, when you see her, that I have betrayed her secret; she holds to keeping you and everybody about her in the dark, and there is no harm in indulging her fancies. But, for your sake, as well as hers, I could no longer venture to remain silent."

Raoul, half-stunned by this intelligence, which was imparted to him with a crudity perhaps neither unintentional nor unkindly, could only murmur: "I thought her looking aged and ill : but not so ill as that! And she said that she did not complain of her health."

"I believe you!—it is not one of her habits to complain. For the rest, she will have less pain now, I hope, and I shall not scruple to use remedies which we prefer not to employ in the earlier stages of these maladies. As for you, your presence is one of the best medicines that can be given to her, and I forbid you to deprive her of it! You must obtain leave; you must abandon your profession, if necessary—"

"That is of course," interrupted Raoul; "I should not dream of deserting her."

"So much the better! She has not been too tender with you, perhaps, and I assure you that she is not too polite to me; but you would be the most ungrateful of sons if you did not adore her, and, for my part, I admire courage and fortitude whenever I come across them. *Une maîtresse femme!*"

About ten minutes later Raoul, in compliance with his request, was admitted into his mother's bedroom. He did not rush up thither without having given any warning of his approach, such impulsive methods of procedure being altogether opposed to the traditions and regulations of the household; but he was unable to conceal his agitation, as he entered, and this was at once detected and disapproved of by the stern old woman who was half sitting, half reclining in bed, with a faded knitted shawl wrapped round her shoulders.

"It seems," said she, "that Leroy has been telling you some of his fantastic histories. They are incorrigible, these doctors! Once let them gain a footing in your house and you may be sure that they will hasten to exaggerate everything, lest you should discover how well you can get on without them. It is true that I found myself a little indisposed to-day, and since he ordered me to go to bed, here I am—one has the air of being an imbecile if one calls in the doctor and then refuses to obey him. But I am already much better, and by to-morrow, or perhaps the next day, I shall be about again as usual. There is no need for you to assume a tragic countenance."

Her own countenance was tragic enough, with its ghastly pallor, its bluish tinge about the lips, and the deeply traced lines of age and suffering which it exhibited; but her son answered her as he knew that she wished to be answered. The doctor, he confessed, had frightened him for a moment; it was so unprecedented an event for her to be confined to her room. But he did not doubt that she would soon be herself again; all he begged of her was not

to be in too great a hurry, and to remember that her
strength could not be what it had been twenty years back.
Then he seated himself by the bedside, noting, with a
pang of self-reproach, as he did so, the meagre and inexpensive surroundings which accorded with her ideas of
luxury, and added:

"I was going to ask whether you could see me before I
heard of your being unwell. I have some news to give
you, and I think you will consider it good news."

Madame de Malglaive's breathing became short, and the
pupils of her sunken eyes grew large. What was he going
to say? He understood that agonized, unspoken query
and hastened to relieve the questioner.

"It is not very good news from my point of view," he
said, steadily, forcing himself to smile while he spoke;
"after what I told you a short time ago, you will know
that it cannot be that. But to you it will be a comfort
and consolation to hear that Miss Luttrell has refused absolutely and finally to marry me."

"She has refused!" ejaculated Madame de Malglaive,
incredulously; "you tell me that that girl refuses to marry
my son?"

He nodded. "Why not?" he asked. "It is quite simple; she does not love me, and, like many other Englishwomen, she will not marry a man whom she does not love.
Since she will never be my wife or your daughter-in-law,
we may do her the justice to respect her motives, may we
not?"

The sick woman's fingers plucked nervously at the quilt
which covered her knees. Comforted and consoled she
certainly was; yet she had not expected this; she would
have preferred rejecting the Luttrells to being rejected by
them, and she could not bring herself to thank Madeline
for having had the audacity to spurn a De Malglaive.

"Then," said she, after a pause, "you will think no
more about the girl?"

"I cannot promise that," answered Raoul, smiling
again; "but I shall think no more about the possibility of

her becoming my wife, for she has convinced me that
there is no such possibility.   I am sorry that she has come
between us, *ma mère*," he went on, stretching out his hand,
which the old woman took; "it has not been her fault,
and I do not think that it has been mine; there was no
help for it.   Anyhow, the trouble is at an end now; and
we are friends once more, are we not ?"

Madame de Malglaive made a slight gesture of assent.
It was not in her nature to express what she felt, and she
may have been more moved with compassion for her son
and more sensible of his affection for her than she thought
it wise to reveal.   All she said was, " It is best so; believe me, it is best so."

He sat with her until the room grew dark, and as the
light failed her manner gradually softened.   She seemed
to have forgotten the fiction upon which she had at first
insisted that there was nothing grave the matter with her;
she spoke of the abandonment of his military career as
though that had been an understood and inevitable step;
she mentioned certain particulars connected with the
management of his property to which she would assuredly
not have alluded, had she anticipated ever resuming control over it; and more than once she exclaimed, wistfully,
" If only you had the wife who will be so indispensable !"

The pathos of it all was not lost upon Raoul.   He said
what he could and as much as he dared, keeping with
some difficulty the sound of tears out of his voice.   Earlier in the afternoon he had thought himself in despair;
but most people know how pain in one part of the body
may be deadened by sudden twinges in another, and this
fresh sorrow served as a partial anodyne to him.   At all
events, it diverted his thoughts from himself and swept
away the last vestige of resentment that he had felt
against the mother who, during so many years, had lived
only for him.   In spite of Dr. Leroy, in spite of the
conviction which she herself unwittingly betrayed every
minute, he clung to the hope that he was not yet to be
deprived of her.   She did not seem to be dying; with her

marvellous energy and vitality, she was surely capable of overcoming an attack which might be regarded merely in the light of a first warning; the main thing was to take the burden of daily work off her shoulders, and this he was fully determined to do.

But Madame de Malglaive belonged to that class of human beings who either die in harness or turn their faces to the wall when harness cannot be resumed. She did not leave her bed on the morrow, nor on the following day; she had not, in fact, the strength to get up, and Dr. Leroy shook his head over her when she was not looking.

"I give her a month," he told Raoul, in his brusque way; "all we can do for her now is to spare her unnecessary suffering, and I have told the nurse what to do if I should not be within reach."

That the dying woman had consented to be placed under care of a professional nurse was in itself an event of ominous significance. She had evidently no illusions; although she did not yet choose to admit the truth to her son, and assured him, as day succeeded to day, that she was getting better. He, on his side, had been too well drilled to disobey her unspoken commands. They understood one another; but the pretence which she considered desirable was kept up, and in the long conversations that they held together there was no lessening of the formality which had ever marked their intercourse.

A great many people, of whom Raoul personally received a few, called to make inquiries. Perhaps he would not have cared to include Lady Luttrell among that select few if she had not made such a point of it; but since she did, he descended to the cold, bare *salon* where she was waiting for him, and was touched by the genuine feeling which she displayed.

"Oh no, madame," he said, quietly, in answer to her, "there is not the smallest hope now. At first there appeared to be a possibility; but that has vanished. I am sorry that she is not equal to seeing you; besides myself, she sees only the doctor and the priest."

Lady Luttrell made use of her pocket‑handkerchief, which was really required ; for she was a tender-hearted woman.   Moreover, she had more reasons than one for earnestly desiring to say a few words to her old friend. These, she was gently and firmly given to understand, could not be said ; nor, unfortunately, was it possible to transmit all of them in the form of a message.   So she was fain to be satisfied with sending such a message of grief and affection as all the world might hear ; after which—as Raoul's bearing remained somewhat distantly polite, and he seemed to be ready to open the door for her—she suddenly and impulsively seized him by both hands.

"I wish," she exclaimed, "I could tell you how sorry I am for you !   It is not your dear mother's illness alone ; I know—I have heard from my daughter—of your—your disappointment.   It is a disappointment to me too, and a very great one !"

Raoul bowed gravely.

"But I want you to believe," Lady Luttrell went on, with much earnestness, "that all is not over yet.   I can see that Madeline is unhappy ; though she is perverse and will not listen to reason.   She has imbibed notions which have no common-sense from my daughter-in-law, who, as I dare say you are aware, has been a sad trial to all of us. In a word, I shall be distressed, and I think you will be mistaken, if you accept Madeline's answer as final."

Encouragement of that nature, however well meant, was scarcely convincing.   Raoul said what seemed to be requisite in acknowledgment of his visitor's kindness ; but he did not see how Madeline could be made to love him by the rehabilitation of his character (supposing that to be possible), or even by the relinquishment on her part of notions which had no common-sense.   As for Lady Luttrell, the causes of her anxiety to bring about an alliance which she was powerless to command were not so very far to seek.

Indeed, if these had not already been tolerably apparent to him they would have been rendered so that same evening by an announcement which his mother decided to make, on being informed of Lady Luttrell's visit.

"That poor Antoinette !" sighed Madame de Malglaive; "I am sorry for her and I am at peace with her. They tell me that I ought to be at peace with all the world now, lest this illness of mine should terminate as all illnesses are liable to terminate. Nevertheless, it is right that you should know why she was so eager to see me, and that you should be put upon your guard against her manœuvres. The truth is that she is in my power, and that, in case of anything happening to me, she will be in yours. Her house and her land, upon which I have advanced money, might be claimed by us; for she has paid no interest, and, from what I have been able to learn of her affairs, she is hardly in a position to pay any. Her husband, who was a careless spendthrift, forgot, I suppose, that he had eaten up her fortune during his lifetime, and made his will under the impression that there was no need to provide for her. She is to be pitied—oh yes, she is to be pitied, no doubt — but we, at least, have done her no wrong and have nothing to atone for. In the days of her prosperity she would have laughed at the idea of marrying her daughter to a De Malglaive: it must be admitted that we are entitled to respectfully decline her advances now."

"There is no question of advances," returned Raoul, in a pained, irritated voice—for he could not endure to think of Madeline as liable to be influenced by considerations of merely worldly expediency. "I have had my answer, and I shall not ask for it to be repeated. But if we have it in our power to injure people who have done us no injury, we shall never exercise that power, shall we? I am sure you would not do that, or wish me to do it, *ma mère.*"

Madame de Malglaive, propped up in bed and breathing with occasional difficulty, responded by a gesture which was not precisely one of assent. She was, as she had said, at peace with her old friend; she did not want or intend to injure anybody; yet—to make a free gift of a large sum of money, which represented the hard savings of years, went against the grain with her.

"'Never,'" she remarked at length, "is a big word. What is ours is ours, and we have to consider those who may come after us. I do not suggest that you should turn Antoinette and her daughter into the street; but to buy their property in order to make a present of it to them— *mon Dieu!* that would be going rather far, and I do not see how their self-respect could permit them to agree to such a transaction."

" Of course it would not," said Raoul; "nor would my respect for them permit me to make such an offer. All we have to do, it seems to me, is to refrain from claiming the interest."

" Perfectly. Only formal claims have been made, and must be made, from time to time. And it was my duty to warn you of the reasons which these people will have for trying to—how shall I say it without giving you offence? —to ensnare you."

Raoul nodded. " It is understood," he answered. Presently he added : " You need have no fear of my being ensnared. Miss Luttrell is incapable of acting in that way, and her mother—well, her mother, who may be pardoned for desiring to do so, is in reality not less incapable. That chapter is closed."

Madame de Malglaive sighed. Perhaps the chapter was closed : she could but hope that it was. What she knew for certain was that there would be no more chapters in the story of her own life, and that she would be unable to dictate those which were still wanting to complete the story of her son's. She had done her best during her tenure of power; now she had to resign the reins of government and to realize, what none of us can realize without some little difficulty, that she was not indispensable.

It was not from her son that she was likely to get any help towards the realization of that rather saddening truth. To him she was, if not indispensable, at least so essential a factor of existence as he had hitherto known it that his own life seemed to him to be ebbing away with hers. There would, of course, be an after-life; but he could not imagine what it would be like, nor did the prospect of it smile upon him. From his childhood, when *"Maman,"* less 'stern and unbending in those far-away days, had been the recipient of all his confidences, there had always been one person upon whose spoken or unspoken sympathy he could implicitly rely; even the cloud which had latterly arisen between them had not, as he well knew, diminished her love for him. Soon there would be nobody—absolutely nobody in the wide world—to whom it would signify one jot whether he blew his brains out or retained them, such as they were, in their normal position. Thinking of all this, and the poor return that he had made for so many years of maternal devotion, he had much ado to restrain himself from making one of those scenes which he had been educated to hold uncalled-for and unbecoming.

However, he did restrain himself, and up to the end the word "death" was pronounced neither by mother nor son. Certain words of information and advice were bestowed by the former upon the latter—in case he might need them—and Raoul was given opportunities, of which he availed himself, to gladden the poor old woman's heart by proving that he was not ungrateful nor insensible; but there was a tacit understanding between them that tears and un-availing lamentations were to be dispensed with, and that restoration to health was to be treated as a probable, not an impossible, event.

The end, when it came, was not, unhappily, one of those which are dwelt upon afterwards in the memory with melancholy pleasure and consolation. Some people die easily and some die hard: poor Madame de Malglaive's constitution was such that she was bound to fight for her life, and all that can be said is that she bore her necessary sufferings with heroic fortitude. What could be done to mitigate those sufferings was done; and thus, for four-and-twenty hours before she passed away she had ceased to recognize those about her.

"To think," exclaimed Raoul, after he had closed his mother's eyes and was standing with Dr. Leroy alone in the death chamber, "to think it should have come to this—that I am thankful she is gone!"

"Several thousands besides you, *mon garçon,* say that every day," returned the doctor, who could not afford to let his feelings get the better of him. "What would you have? Death is a necessity and pain is a necessity. But the world goes round just the same, and it is our good fortune that we very soon forget both when they are out of sight."

CHAPTER XXXII

PERFECT CONDUCT

"I AM at the orders of Monsieur le Vicomte," said M. Cayaux, who for many years had been Madame de Malglaive's trusted man of business; "I do not permit myself to make representations which—which, in short, it would not become me to make."

He had, however, already taken the liberty of pointing out that when one possesses a handsome fortune, in addition to a very considerable amount of real estate, one does not, as a rule, turn one's back upon the place where one ought to be residing and solicit military employment in the neighborhood of the equator. M. Cayaux had been shocked and distressed by the instructions which Raoul had given him, and by the young man's incidentally expressed intention of pursuing a career of adventure among turbulent West African tribes. For what conceivable reason could one who was apparently in his sober senses, and who was from every point of view enviable, desire to court an obscure and inglorious death?

No reply was vouchsafed to this very natural question, and M. Cayaux, a little affronted, yet alive to the duty of retaining a wealthy client, could but profess himself ready to do whatever he was told to do. For the matter of that, his instructions were quite simple, and left him with a perfectly free hand, save in one particular. Under no circumstances was he to take legal proceedings against tenants or others who might be in arrear with their payments. For the rest, he was to collect rents, adopt such measures as might seem to him advisable in the interest of his employ-

er, and assume that he had *carte blanche* in the probable
event of his employer's exact address being undiscoverable.

The bare, gloomy room in which this unbusinesslike conference was held had been the scene of many previous con-
ferences between M. Cayaux and Madame de Malglaive,
whereby the latter's capacity for transacting matters of
business had often extorted a reluctant tribute of admiration from the former. But Madame de Malglaive lay, silent forever, in the cemetery, where her remains had been
deposited with due pomp and ceremony two days before,
and it looked very much as if the work of her keen, active
life were in danger of being wantonly thrown away. Did
this foolish, yet peremptory, young man imagine that an ab-
sentee, however conscientiously served, can escape loss ?—
or that money, however plentiful at the outset, will stay in
the pockets of those who treat it with contemptuous indifference ? It is annoying, no doubt, to have every item of
one's honest accounts scrutinized and questioned ; but it is
almost worse to be ignored and left to one's own devices,
with the prospect of neither praise nor blame as the result
of one's exertions.

But Raoul had no sympathy to bestow upon a clever lawyer who took some legitimate pride in his work ; nor would
he have been closeted with M. Cayaux at all if that worthy
man had not insisted upon an interview.

"It seems that I am rich," he said. "So much the better ; for riches mean liberty, and liberty is the one and
only thing that I covet. That being so, you will understand that I decline absolutely to be chained up anywhere,
and you will appreciate my dislike to being worried with
petty details."

He had quite made up his mind to return to his regiment and to transfer himself from it at the earliest opportunity to some distant part of the world, where soldiering
would not be a mere affair of parades and manœuvres. As
for remaining in the Basses-Pyrénées and in due course
espousing the daughter of some neighboring proprietor—
well, that was perhaps what his mother would have wished

21

him to do, and if she had lived he might have made an
effort to gratify her; but now that she was gone, and that
his proceedings could no longer affect her happiness one
way or the other, what did it signify? He longed to escape from that mournful, empty house; he longed—not
indeed to forget, but to begin the new life which lay before him and to shake off the trammels which still bound
him to the old and dead one. Thus nature asserts herself,
and thus all living creatures are compelled to obey the law
of incessant decay and renewal which keeps the outer crust
of this planet fresh.

Not within two days of his mother's funeral, however,
was it possible for Raoul to desert the home which could
never again seem like home to him. There were fifty
things to be done which could not well be intrusted to
others; there were conventional observances to be attended to; there were friends to whom he was bound, in decency and gratitude, to bid farewell. And if Lady Luttrell
(whose notes and messages had been frequent and who had
laid an exquisite wreath upon his mother's coffin) had to
be included among these, perhaps the duty of calling at
the Château de Grancy was not altogether distasteful to
him. Nothing would be altered—he was very sure of that
—by the exchange of a few parting words with Madeline
and a last look at her face; but he hungered and thirsted
after both, and there was no valid reason why he should
deny himself either.

He placed the Château de Grancy at the end of the list
of houses at which it behooved him to present himself, arrayed in that garb of profound woe which has fallen out
of use in England, but remains indispensable on the other
side of the Channel. He naturally wished to wind up with
the only people whom he was at all anxious to find at home,
and, not being a vain man, it did not occur to him to think
how much better he looked in a smart cavalry uniform than
in the sable suit hastily provided for him by a local tailor,
and the tall hat, swathed nearly to its summit in a black
band, held together by little glass-headed pins. He was

aware of being handsome—he had been so often and so
fervently assured of that fact that he could scarcely be in
ignorance of it—but since his good looks had not enabled
him to find favor in the eyes of Madeline Luttrell, he set
no store by them.

The ladies were at home, he was glad to hear from the
servant who answered his ring at their door, and presently
the elder of them was holding him affectionately by both
hands, while she murmured the sympathetic phrases appropriate to the occasion. As for the younger, who, when her
turn came, gave him only one hand and said nothing at all,
he saw that she, too, was sorry for him, despite her silence.
More than that he could not, and did not, expect.

"And is what I hear true?" was Lady Luttrell's first
inquiry. "Is it the case, as M. Cayaux affirms, that you
mean to shut up your house and go away for an uncertain
length of time? I hope not!"

"It is very amiable on your part, madame, to wish that
I should stay here," answered Raoul, with his grave smile,
"but I hardly know how I should occupy my time if I
were to do that. It is essential for a solitary man to have
occupation of some sort, and that of a soldier is the only
one of which I have any knowledge. So I have come to
take leave of you and to thank you very sincerely for all
the kindness that you have shown me."

To the interior of Africa it was not necessary to allude;
nor did Lady Luttrell imagine that anything more than a
temporary change of scene was in the young man's mind.
She could quite understand, she remarked, after he had sat
down, his wish to escape for a time from surroundings
which must of necessity be painful to him; but with a
property so large as his had become, it would of course be
impossible for him to absent himself indefinitely, and the
management of it would doubtless, in the long-run, provide him with all the occupation that he could require.
She had a good deal to say in that sense—and scarcely a
word of it did he hear, his whole attention being engrossed
by a furtive contemplation of Madeline, who, with her

back to the light and her hands loosely clasped upon her knees, sat facing him.

At the expiration of ten minutes or so Lady Luttrell abruptly rose.

"I must beg you to excuse me for a moment," she said; "I am obliged to run away and scribble a few letters before the post leaves. But please do not go away until I return; I must say a word to you about a small matter of business, if this is really to be our last sight of you for the present."

Such behavior was a little strange, and would assuredly have been pronounced the reverse of *convenable* by the late Madame de Malglaive; but Raoul was aware that strange customs prevail in English society: added to which, he was too rejoiced at being left alone with Madeline to criticise the propriety of her mother's conduct.

He was rejoiced; but he was not in the least sanguine. The fact of his having lost his mother since their last meeting could not have changed the feeling of dislike and disdain with which he was regarded by her; still, it might prompt her to speak kindly to him, and he wanted to carry away the memory of some kinder speech than that in which she had so emphatically signified to him that he must look elsewhere for his future wife.

"I ought to apologize, mademoiselle," he began, "for inflicting my company upon you; but, as Lady Luttrell appears to wish—"

"Oh, her wishes—" interrupted Madeline, and then suddenly stopped. "Her wishes," she resumed, presently, "are not always the same as mine; but in this instance they are partly the same, I suppose; for I should have been sorry if you had left the place without my having told you that I do feel for you in your trouble. I believe," she added, with much generosity, "that you were really fond of your mother."

"Yes," answered Raoul, "I was really fond of my mother. You mean, perhaps, that you do not believe in my being really fond of anybody else, except myself."

"I have no means of knowing—what does it signify?"

"It does not signify to you, mademoiselle; but it signifies a great deal to me. Imagine that there is one person in the world whom you not only love, but worship, and that that person not only does not love you, but despises you. Would you not wish him to think a little better of you, if he could? That would do him no harm and would make some difference to your happiness, would it not?"

"I think you use rather exaggerated language," answered Madeline. "I do not want to say anything unpleasant; I would much rather say something pleasant and friendly, now that you are going away. But I cannot say what is untrue, and I am afraid I cannot pretend to believe what is incredible."

"What do you call incredible?" asked Raoul, eagerly. "You cannot mean my love for you!"

"Yes; that is what I mean, since you force me to say so. It is not the sort of love that I care to have. It has been given, as you know, to so many other women before you ever saw me—and since."

"Ah, no!" he exclaimed. "You wrong me there, and you would not speak in that way if you understood!"

He tried to make her understand; he related to her, as honestly as his respect for her presumed innocence and ignorance would permit, the story of his past life; he did his best to persuade her that, although his senses had been reached by other women, his heart had never belonged, and never could belong, to any one but her. And, to tell the truth, he very nearly succeeded; for she loved the man and had already half forgiven him. However, she had to steel her heart against his eloquence by the memory of his intrigues with Madame de Castelmoron and her anonymous correspondent, as well as by the more recent memory of a rather stormy conversation with her mother that very morning. Even if she could have conquered her pride so far as to condone the past, she could not have consented to marry Raoul de Malglaive in order that the fallen fortunes of her family might be retrieved. For the rest, he did not ask her to marry him : that he appeared to take it for granted that she would never do. All he begged was that she would judge him a little less harshly in her thoughts for the future ; and she had just made the re-quired concession when Lady Luttrell re-entered the room.

The eager questions discernible in Lady Luttrell's eyes met with no decisive response. Those worn-out eyes of hers, which had to be supplemented by glasses now before they would do the work demanded of them, saw only a young man and a young woman who were apparently upon terms of amity, but whose respective chairs were separated by a wider space than could have been wished. Nor were her ears gladdened by any such announcement as she had fondly anticipated. It was impossible to tell whether what ought to have taken place during her absence had taken place or not ; yet when Raoul got up, nothing could be more distressingly evident than that his plans remained unaltered. For, as he took the hand extended to him by Madeline and bent over it, with his heels together, in an attitude which we in our country only assume on being honored by the recognition of some member of the reign-ing dynasty, all he said was :

"Adieu, mademoiselle, and a thousand thanks !"

For what imaginary boon did he owe a thousand thanks to a girl who had but too obviously thrown away chances at which every consideration of duty and expediency should have prompted her to grasp ? Lady Luttrell, with rage in her heart and a smile upon her lips, postponed putting that query to a more convenient season, and said, pleasantly :

"About that little matter of business that I mentioned just now ? Can you spare me five minutes ?"

M. de Malglaive was courteously willing to spare as many minutes as her ladyship might require, and he had no dif-ficulty in divining the nature of the business matter which was about to be unfolded to him.

However, she did not immediately embark upon it after she had led him into an adjoining room, where Sir Robert, in days gone by, had been wont to attend to correspondence and about which a faint odor of cigar-smoke still clung. She had to begin by eliciting from him statements which confirmed her fears, and by futile assurances that it would be a great mistake on his part to let initial failure discourage him. Girls so seldom know their own mind; Madeline, in particular, was a little wilful by nature, and had been rendered more so through the baneful influence which her eccentric sister-in-law had obtained over her; she really must not be taken as literally meaning all the absurd things that she said!

He cut these assurances short and demonstrated their futility by replying: "Madame, I am infinitely obliged to you; but I have not the pretensions which you ascribe to me. From the moment that your daughter has no love for me—and she has convinced me that she has none—it only remains for me to withdraw. As to the question upon which you wished to speak to me, may I assume that it has reference to the mortgage held by my mother upon this house?"

Poor Lady Luttrell, mortified and humiliated, was fain to confess that it had.

"Cayaux has been here, and has been almost insolent —he who used to crawl to my feet and declare that it was an honor and a privilege to serve me! What can I do? I have never been accustomed to poverty; I hardly understand yet what it means. All I know is that I cannot pay away what I have not got. And it seems that I have already overdrawn my account; the bankers write—"

"Madame," interrupted Raoul, to whose cheeks a dark flush had slowly risen, "if M. Cayaux has permitted himself to be insolent to you, you may rely upon it that he has acted without my knowledge or sanction, and that he will have no opportunity of repeating the offence. I shall take my affairs out of his hands at once."

"No, no; you must not do that! If you can afford to quarrel with the man, I, unhappily, cannot; he has raised money for me in various quarters, and I do not wish to make him my enemy. Only you might, perhaps—remembering that your mother and I were old friends and that I am hard pressed for the moment—you might, perhaps, give him instructions—"

Alas! why is it impossible to offer money, or the equivalent of money, to those for whom one would gladly shed one's heart's blood? Lady Luttrell was Madeline's mother, and to Raoul de Malglaive Madeline represented much more than the value of his not very valuable life. Yet all he could do was to promise that the annoyance to which his petitioner had been subjected should not recur, and to apologize for the over-zealous conduct of his representative in endeavoring to collect unimportant arrears.

"Probably M. Cayaux misunderstood me, and imagined that I wanted everything to be set in order before I left. I will take care that you shall not be troubled by him again, and I trust you will think no more about it."

Lady Luttrell could not repress a sigh of relief. "If you knew how terribly I have been worried, and how everything seems to be going wrong with me! I had hoped—but if that is not to be, I will say no more. And, since it is not to be, I must make other arrangements, I suppose. When I have only myself to think of, questions of expense will be more manageable, and I shall be able to pay what I owe you."

He winced ever so slightly; for Madeline's marriage to another man, though he knew it to be inevitable, was not a prospect upon which he could allow his mind to dwell without wincing. But he kept up appearances, and, having little more to say, said little more. Lady Luttrell was sorry for him, though of course not quite so sorry as she was for herself; his conduct, she admitted, after he had taken his leave, had been perfect.

The conduct of her daughter, however, had been very far from that; and it seemed nothing short of a duty to let the girl know at once, in trenchant language, how selfishly, wantonly, and irretrievably she had played the idiot.

The little scene which ensued shall, with the reader's

kind permission, be omitted from this unpretending record of the fortunes and misfortunes of the Luttrell family. Do we not all—we, that is, of the so-called sterner sex—hasten to beat an ignominious retreat when we see that there is going to be a row among the women - folk ?   It is not pleasant to assist at such rows, which will occur from time to time in the best-regulated families, and which are more painful, perhaps, to lookers - on than to the actual combatants.   Undignified and discreditable things are apt to be said in the course of them which it is well not to hear, or, having heard, to forget.   Lady Luttrell, taking her altogether, was a good woman and a good mother : why should anybody wish to see her behaving as if she were neither ? Moreover, a dispassionate and disinterested critic may be willing to admit that she had been sorely tried.   To be within grasp of the solution of all one's difficulties and anxieties, and to be defeated by the obstinate perversity of a girl who refuses to recognize on which side her bread is buttered—it must be confessed that this is enough to upset the sweetest of tempers.

So tears were shed that evening at the Château de Grancy, and inmates of that heavily mortgaged residence, who really did not deserve so very much blame, were severely condemned.   Never shall we be able to do justice to one another here below, try as we may ; but it is always a comfort to feel that we individually are in the right, and both Lady Luttrell and Madeline took that consolatory conviction to bed with then.

CHAPTER XXXIII

"THE GIRL OF THE FUTURE"

WHITHER is an ex-military man who has not an acre of land to call his own, but who is in the enjoyment of a modest competence, to betake himself if not to London? Sir Guy Luttrell, while admitting to himself that there were reasons against his settling down in the capital of his native land, could not, on severing his connection with the Cumberland Rangers, see what alternative course was open to him. One wants to be within reach of one's friends, if one does not always want to be within reach of one's nearest relations, and London, after all, is surely a large enough place to hold two people whose anxiety to avoid one another is mutual. So in the middle of the winter, when hunting-men were anathematizing the frost, and warm sunshine was flooding the hills of distant Pau, Sir Guy took up his quarters in certain rooms that he knew of near one of his clubs, resolved (as indeed it was his nature to be) to make the best of what could not be helped. He did not make his advent known to his wife, preferring that she should become aware of it — as she certainly must ere long — through her uncle, upon whom he found it necessary to call.

Mr. Dent gave him a very friendly reception, answered with businesslike lucidity various questions respecting money matters, and was equally unhesitating in his response to a further query which Guy addressed to him towards the conclusion of their inteview.

" Well, yes; since you ask me, I should say that you had better keep in the background for the present. Clarissa, as I dare say you know, is somewhat conspicuously in the foreground just now, and the moment is hardly propitious for plucking her by the sleeve."

"I don't want to pluck her by the sleeve," said Guy; "I dont't want to interfere with her in any way. Only it might be as well for her to be told that I am here. I shouldn't like her to imagine things—such as that I had come up to London to spy upon her, for instance. She has a rather vivid imagination, you see, where I am concerned."

Mr. Dent contemplated the speaker with a suspicion of a twinkle in his eye. "Yes," he agreed, "Clarissa is the victim of imagination for the time being. One foresees a day when she will become the victim of stern realities; but that day has not yet dawned. Meanwhile, the last thing that she is likely to imagine is that she is being spied upon. There is nothing secret about her proceedings : on the contrary, she appears to court the fullest publicity."

"I can't for the life of me understand why," said Guy, in a dissatisfied tone of voice.

"Nor can I; but the female sex is often a little difficult to understand. However, as I say, I should keep out of sight, if I were you. One of the few assertions that can be made quite positively about women is that nothing reawakens their interest and affection like neglect."

Guy emphatically disclaimed any designs upon Clarissa's reawakened interest or affection. His sole wish was to do the straight thing—that, and also to see his daughter when he should think fit to do so. He was, therefore, of opinion that the circumstance of his being in London should be mentioned casually to his wife.

"Very well; I'll casually mention it," Mr. Dent promised, smiling, "and if you prefer to steer clear of Cadogan Gardens, I dare say I can arrange occasional meetings between you and Netta here. She generally honors me with a visit on Saturday afternoon, that being my weekly half-holiday as well as hers."

"Perhaps I'll look you up some Saturday afternoon, then," said Guy. "All the same, if I want to have a look at Netta, I shall take the liberty of calling in Cadogan Gardens and asking for her. That's in the compact."

The compact, as he was beginning to feel, was not an altogether satisfactory one, and might stand in need of revision, or at least of more exact definition, at some future date. Clarissa was free to go her own way, but her freedom must not extend to the right of bringing up his only child to follow in her footsteps. Yet, as matters stood, the child's education was left in her hands, and could hardly be taken out of them. Guy Luttrell was not a man who had ever troubled himself much about the practice of the Christian religion; still, he did not account himself a heathen, and was quite decidedly of opinion that all boys and girls—especially all girls—ought to be taught what he had been taught in his youth. A nice sort of young woman Netta might be expected to develop into if her notions of right and wrong were to be drawn from no other authority than that of a misty philosophy!

His brother Paul, who did him the favor to dine with him one evening at his club, was able to allay these paternal misgivings.

"The child is receiving regular religious instruction," Paul told him. "She is being duly educated to believe what her mother disbelieves—or professes to disbelieve."

"H'm! that sounds a bit inconsistent."

"It is comically inconsistent, of course; but Clarissa thinks she gets out of the difficulty by applying the old saying of *populus vult decipi* to the case. She says everybody ought to be given the chance of accepting doctrines which everybody would like to accept."

"She does, eh? Do you see much of her?"

"Not very much in these days. For one thing, I am too busy, and for another thing, I can't quite stand her associates. She is hand and glove with people some of whom, according to my humble judgment, ought to be on the treadmill or working at Portland breakwater, with their hair cut; so, as there is no particular use in telling her so, it is best for me to keep my distance and thank her by post for the checks that she sends me as often as I ask for them."

Clarissa's associates may not have been criminals, and assuredly did not regard themselves in that light; but they were notorious for holding and promulgating views which were described as "advanced," and although they were pretty generally laughed at, they were so far successful that they had made themselves universally talked about. Now, the average, every-day English gentleman does not like his wife to be mixed up with persons of that class, even though he be amicably separated from her; and when Guy found that he could seldom glance at a newspaper without reading how Lady Luttrell, supported by Lady Kettering, Mrs. Hamley, Mrs. Knibbs, and others, had been delivering spirited addresses upon social subjects from a public platform, he felt that his name was being trailed in the dust. What was the good of going on in that way? What did she mean by it?—she, who in former days had been almost too modest and retiring to please him. Nor was it by newspaper reports alone that he was vexed. He had a large acquaintance; he met friends every day, and not all of these were so discreet as they might have been. Their jocularities, to be sure, could be promptly checked and their innuendoes serenely ignored; still there were moments when Sir Guy Luttrell was a sore and angry man.

"By Jove, I will!" he ejaculated one day, on learning from an evening journal that "that very fluent speaker Lady Luttrell" proposed to lecture on "The Girl of the Future" at the High Street Hall, Kensington, on the morrow; "I'll go and hear what she has to say. Lord knows where the High Street Hall is; but I dare say a cabby can find out, and admission to the entertainment appears to be free. It will be interesting to be told what one's daughter, who happens to be one of the girls of the future, will be like if she follows her mother's instructions."

Hostile criticism, as represented by Guy, was admitted without question at the appointed hour into a building which was already three parts full and showed signs of becoming inconveniently crowded. It was the boast of Clarissa and her friends that they never attempted to pack their meetings; and if—as sometimes happened—dissentient voices were raised, they rather enjoyed the interruption, feeling comfortably assured of the support of the majority. The overwhelming majority of the audience, Guy noticed, was composed of ladies. Here and there a masculine head, bald or exuberantly hirsute, could be descried amidst the vast congregation of hats and bonnets; but there were certainly not enough men present to raise the standard of revolt, even had they felt disposed to do so, and, judging by their appearance, those few did not belong to the fighting variety. He himself was placed next to an amazing woman who, for reasons best known to herself, had donned a hunting-stock and a covert-coat, and who presently exchanged vociferous greetings with his other neighbor, a rather pretty girl, arrayed in a loose stuff gown of yellowish-green hue, which was cut very low in the neck and displayed a double string of amber beads. This young person, it presently appeared, was an artist, and Guy was vainly wondering why colorists by profession should so often seem to be ignorant of the effect of adjacent color upon the human complexion when his attention was diverted into another channel by the remarks of the loud-voiced lady in the covert-coat.

"Oh yes, she is sure to speak well; she always does. I only hope what she says will be fully reported this time. The nuisance is that newspapers are apt to cut out just the most important passages of one's speech. The British public hasn't been cured of its absurd squeamishness yet, I'm afraid."

"So Clarissa is in the habit of saying things which are unfit for publication, is she?" thought Guy to himself. "This is indeed an exhilarating prospect!"

But the girl on his left, as if to reassure him said: "Well, the subject doesn't *sound* a very shocking one, does it?"

"That entirely depends upon the method of treatment,"

returned she of the covert-coat, oracularly. "There is the ideal of the future, you see, and there is the actual—or, rather, the probable. If she tackles the probable, as I hope she will, she will have to make some people's ears tingle before she sits down."

Further conversation was arrested by the appearance upon the platform of a little posse of ladies and a single gentleman, in whom Guy at once recognized the self-satisfied Mr. Alfred Loosemore. Lady Kettering, who took the chair, was also known to him by sight; the others, whom he now for the first time had the privilege of beholding, he mentally characterized as "an uncommon plain-headed lot."

Well, Clarissa, at all events, had not seen fit to make herself additionally ridiculous by adopting any eccentricities of costume. She was quietly and becomingly dressed; she bowed slightly, but gracefully, in acknowledgment of the plaudits which greeted her, and, after a few introductory words from the chairwoman, she advanced to the front of the platform and began her address without the smallest appearance of embarrassment or any aid in the shape of notes or manuscript.

Her exordium was of a nature to engage the sympathies of her audience—even of that member of it to whom the sight of a lady spouting from a platform to several hundreds of her fellow-citizens was altogether abhorrent. She modestly confessed that her knowledge of the girl of the present was somewhat restricted; she said she had heard a good deal about girls of her own small class which might or might not be true, and upon which she did not propose to dwell; she was also willing to admit that in the future, as in the past, large allowances would always have to be made for variety of individual character. But her excuse for working in the direction in which she was working and for speaking as she was about to speak lay in her firm conviction that the influence of women was practically unbounded. "Are we not the majority?" she asked; "is it not acknowledged nowadays that majorities have the right to control minorities ? And ought we not to be ashamed of ourselves if we neglect to use for good the power which we undoubtedly possess ? As for me, I do not pretend to exceptional experience, still less to exceptional wisdom ; I only claim to have realized what many of us seem content to ignore, that our actual position is an absurdity and an anachronism, and that it depends upon ourselves whether that position shall be amended or not."

That, so far as it went, was all very well, and a fair-minded listener could but own that ladies who stand up for the equality of the sexes have a right to make what they can out of the unquestionable fact that there are more women than men in England. Moreover, it was possible to smile good-naturedly at Clarissa's confident statement that the extension of the parliamentary franchise to women was inevitable and imminent, while Guy was not concerned to deny that their influence, even in their unenfranchised condition, was enormous. But when he was told that the exercise of that influence, as well as of any subsequent power which might accrue to them, for good would imply the abolition of every species of restraint which has hitherto been placed upon their actions, he began to feel a little irritated. That sort of talk, he said to himself, was downright bosh ; and if it had been permissible or worth while to disturb the harmony of the meeting, he could quite easily have given grounds for holding it to be bosh. He shifted about impatiently in his chair, while the lady in the covert-coat, divining him to be an ignorant outsider, favored him with a glance of scornful challenge. But Clarissa, whose short-sighted eyes had not revealed to her the presence of her husband, went on, warming with her theme.

" Can any one imagine that when the government of this country falls—as it will fall—into our hands, the existing law relating to marriage and divorce will be maintained? Can any one imagine that when we become—as we must become—the guardians of public and social morality, men will be permitted to yield to every temptation and passion of their nature, while women are ostracized for a single

false step ? I think not. I think you will agree with me
that the time has very nearly come for the injustice of
centuries to be repaired, and for supreme authority to be
taken away from those who have so shamefully and selfishly misused it."

The audience, with a very few mute dissentients, signified that it was in complete agreement with the speaker,
who proceeded to say that women did not, of course, claim
or desire to imitate the vices of their whilom masters.
What they did claim, and what they were going to obtain,
was recognition of the fact that mastery was the inherent
attribute of neither sex. Their superiority in point of numbers would, to be sure, enable them to outvote their opponents and get their own way ; but as theirs happened to
be the right way, that should be a matter of general satisfaction.

Then, after those who were responsible for the actual,
and very evil, condition of things had come in for a good
deal of eloquent denunciation, the Girl of the Future was
described after a fashion which must have disappointed
the lady in the covert-coat ; since that marvellous prod-
uct of years to come appeared to be the realization of the
ideal far more than of the probable. She was not, it is
true, the realization of Guy's ideal—this majestic, self-con-
fident young woman, who knew all that there was to know
about everything ; who stood upon precisely the same level
as her brothers, having been educated precisely as they had
been ; who saw no reason why she should not select a husband, instead of being selected by him, and who was prepared to send her husband about his business if, after marriage, he should prove unworthy of her regard. But Guy
was only a man ; and, as he began to suspect, a somewhat
old-fashioned one into the bargain. The whole business
would have been less provoking if it had not, from Clarissa's point of view, been so completely logical and ational.
Once grant her the premise that one human being, whether
of the masculine or the feminine gender, is the same as
another, and you were bound to admit that women may do

22

all that men may do. But the premise was demonstrably preposterous, and he was unable to conceive how anybody out of a lunatic asylum could think otherwise of it.

It may be that Clarissa's hearers were a pack of lunatics: perfect sanity, after all, is the exception, not the rule. At all events, they clapped her loudly when she resumed her seat, and Guy's artistic neighbor remarked: " Well, that was all very true—and very encouraging. Only I don't think I should quite like to propose to a man and be refused by him."

Covert-coat snorted rather disdainfully ; perhaps she was so far sane as to be free from any intention of courting that particular form of humiliation. "I call that a very tame sort of lecture," said she. "I doubt whether Lady Luttrell knows as much as I do about the girls of the present and what they are likely to develop into. Blame the men as much as you please—I'm sure I don't want to stand up for them—but it is impossible to treat a subject of that kind adequately without at least *some* reference to the prevailing low standard of morality."

This lady evidently felt that she had been beguiled into wasting her time, and she stumped off without waiting to hear the concluding observations of Lady Kettering, which related chiefly to costume. From these Guy gathered that his daughter, if she fulfilled her destiny and acted in accordance with the spirit of the age, would walk about the streets in knickerbocker breeches and gaiters, and ride to hounds in a cross-saddle.

"I'm damned if she shall !" was the audible ejaculation which was forced from him, and which caused the lady-artist to survey him for a moment with languid wonderment.

Then, conscious of having made a fool of himself, he jumped up and shouldered his way towards the exit, thus missing a neat little speech from Mr. Loosemore, who rose to propose a vote of thanks to the chairwoman, and who took that opportunity of mentioning how entirely he was in sympathy with the objects for which the meeting had been called. Youth, he said, was so charming, so wonderful, so beautiful, that men—diffident by nature—often hesitated to approach it. In the future—that future which, he trusted, might not be remote—it would be permissible for girls and women, however young and beautiful, to take the initiative with their mute adorers; and who could doubt that this would prove conducive to the greatest happiness of the greatest number? Perhaps, after all, it was just as well that Guy did not hear Mr. Alfred Loosemore's comments upon Clarissa's lecture.

His own comments, which were of a stringent and plain-spoken order, were expressed shortly afterwards to Mr. Dent, who seemed to be a good deal diverted by them.

"My dear fellow," the old gentleman said, "what did you go out into that wilderness for to hear? By your account, Clarissa must have been quite moderate, and, having taken up the crusade which she has taken up, I hardly see what other prophecy she could have offered to you. For my own part, I find it easy and simple to abstain from attending her lectures, and I should have thought that a similar course would commend itself to you."

"That's not the question," returned Guy. "So far as I am concerned, she is perfectly welcome to go on playing the—the—well, whatever you like to call it, in public; though I confess I should be rather better pleased if she would see fit to drop my name. But what I have quite made up my mind about is that Netta shall not be a Girl of the Future."

"Strictly between ourselves," remarked Mr. Dent, smiling, "I suspect that her mother's mind is at one with yours as to that: there are always such wide distinctions to be drawn between the adoption of theories and the application of them. Anyhow, no difficulties will be placed in the way of your restraining influence and mine. I have told Clarissa that you are in London, and, if you will do me the favor of lunching with me on Saturday, you will meet your daughter, who, I believe, is anxious to see you. Luckily, she is not yet of an age to comprehend theories or be instructed in them."

Luckily, she was not; and Guy, in the course of a very pleasant afternoon spent with Netta at Hengler's Circus, had no instructions to give, though he had a few rather awkward queries to evade. But time slips away with horrible rapidity, and he perceived that the day was almost at hand when it would be necessary for him to define his position. And on that fateful day would it not also be necessary that Netta should, once for all, take either his side or her mother's?

CHAPTER XXXIV

IT became an understood thing that Guy should lunch every Saturday in Portland Place with Mr. Dent, and that Netta should be conducted thither in time to welcome him obstreperously on his arrival. Those were pleasant meetings, followed by pleasant afternoons; although each renewal of them rendered their inherently temporary character more manifest.

"Things can't go on like this," was what Guy always said to himself, as he walked or drove away in the dark, leaving Netta to be conducted back to Cadogan Gardens under the care of her great-uncle's butler; and in truth the arrangement was an unmanageable one, notwithstanding Clarissa's apparent acquiescence in it.

He himself had not yet called in Cadogan Gardens, nor had he received the slightest intimation that a visit from him was expected or desired. It was evident enough to him that his wife, knowing how powerless be really was to interfere with her plans for the child's education, had resolved to allow him no excuse for complaining of her, and was the more willing to comply with his wishes because they could not seriously conflict with her own. To Netta, who was persistent in her inquiries as to why he never came home with her, he had to tell fibs — and he hated telling fibs. Upon the whole, he could not help seeing that he had made a mistake by coming to London; that he was doing, and could do, no sort of good by domiciling himself there, and that sooner or later he would be constrained to "have it out" with his wife once more.

Of course it was only with reference to Netta and her future that he contemplated a resumption of negotiations; yet, as the days and weeks went on, and as gossip of one kind and another reached his unwilling ears, it began to dawn upon him that a word or two might be obligatory concerning Clarissa's own conduct. She was her own mistress, no doubt, and if it amused her to make herself conspicuous in a style which few ladies would care to affect, that was her affair; still, she bore (and even flaunted, as he sometimes thought) a name which had not hitherto figured on posters or on the backs of sandwichmen, while she was the mother of the sole coming representative of that ancient name. Perhaps she did not quite realize the sort of remarks that are sure to be made about a lady who is separated from her husband, who lectures publicly upon risky subjects, and whose public appearances are invariably countenanced by a beastly cad, like that fellow Loosemore. Now, whether Mr. Alfred Loosemore was a "beastly cad" or a gifted poet or a quick-witted charlatan —and there were people who classed him under one or the other of these designations, while a few declared him to be entitled to all three—there was not much difference of opinion respecting his moral character, nor was he the kind of person with whom any man in his sober senses would permit his wife to become too intimate. That much Guy gathered, and was assured, at the club and elsewhere; so that it grew to be a question with him whether he did not owe it to himself and his family, as well as to Clarissa, to enter a humble remonstrance.

However, he put off the evil day, foreseeing that, when it came, it would be a very evil day indeed, and possibly it would have been postponed a good deal longer but for a trivial incident which chanced to arouse his ire. Rather late in the winter a hard frost set in, which lasted until every sheet of ornamental water in London was frozen to the depth of several inches, and Netta loudly demanded that her half-holiday should be devoted to watching the skaters. She herself had been forbidden for the present to put on skates, much as she longed to do so, and, being a good, obedient little soul, she did not hint at any evasion of her mother's orders ; but she said she would dearly love to look on, and she had probably discovered by that time that her father was not the man to deny her anything that he had it in his power to grant. So they went first to the Regent's Park, and admired the dexterity of adepts ; after which they drove across to Hyde Park, and surveyed from the banks of the Serpentine the more amusing, if less graceful, performances of the general public. It had just been agreed between them that it would be permissible for Netta to step upon the ice and slide, and precautions were being adopted for enabling her to make the attempt without appreciable risk, when a victoria, the occupants of which were but dimly visible through the haze of the declining day, was pulled up hard by. Its occupants were but dimly visible, but Guy, whose eyes were good, recognized his wife, and recognized also in the lolling, fur-enveloped figure by her side the gentleman whom he had once taken the liberty of describing in her presence as a "very offensive brute." Clarissa, whose eyes, as we know, were not good, failed to recognize either her husband or her child. She stared at the scene for a moment through her double-glasses, said something to her companion, who shrugged his shoulders, and told the coachman to drive on.

The incident, as has been said, was trivial in itself; and although there was something indescribably provocative in Mr. Loosemore's attitude and the manner in which he smoked his cigarette (why is it that some men cannot smoke a cigarette in the company of a lady without having the air of deliberately insulting her ?), Guy might have allowed it to pass but for the audible remarks of a couple of bystanders.

"Oh, Lady Luttrell, is it ?—the Woman's Rights champion. I suppose the man isn't Lord Luttrell, or Sir Somebody Luttrell, or whatever he is ? Those aren't the sort of rights that she stands up for, eh ?"

"Rather not ! That's the great Alfred Loosemore ; and

I should say that before he drops her she'll **have gained**
some additional practical knowledge of **woman's wrongs.**"

The two boobies moved off, chuckling **and cackling,**
while Guy felt the blood mounting to his head. It **was** not
his habit to show temper, nor did he hurry Netta away
from her sliding, which was continued with much success
for another quarter of an hour; but when the light failed
and the skaters began to depart, he said he would take her
home.

"No, not to Uncle Tom's this afternoon; we are so far
on the way that I may as well deliver you in Cadogan Gardens myself. Besides, I rather want to see your mother."

This was good news for Netta, who may have guessed,
or have been informed by the servants, that all **was** not
quite as it should be between her parents, and who, after
she had been lifted into the hansom which was presently
called, expressed a hope that, since he was coming with
her, she would be allowed to have tea in the drawing-room.
But when they reached their destination she submitted
without a murmur to the decision of her father, who
said :

"I think I'll wish you good-night now, little **woman.**
Toddle off to your own quarters, and some other day, perhaps, we'll all have tea together."

She was a docile child; moreover, she was tired and
sleepy, as she always was after the exertions and excite-
ments of her half-holiday. Guy, after committing her to
the care of the nurse who had been summoned, followed the
butler up the thickly carpeted staircase. He had noticed
a man's sable-lined coat, flung down upon one of the chairs
in the hall, and was therefore not unprepared to find Mr.
Alfred Loosemore reclining upon a low sofa near the fire,
over which Clarissa was stooping to warm her hands.

Clarissa, for her part, had been altogether unprepared to
hear her husband announced, and was obviously taken
aback by his entrance. But Guy, who was never disconcerted, or at all events never showed that he was so, advanced, holding out his hand, while he explained, calmly,

"I have brought Netta home, and as they told me that you were in, I said I would come up and pay my respects."

"I told Uncle Tom that I should be glad to see you at any time," answered Clarissa, with a not very successful effort to imitate his composure.

"Yes; the message was duly delivered, thanks."

"I think you have met Mr. Loosemore already," Clarissa resumed, after a momentary silence.

"How do you do?" said Guy, with a slight motion of his head towards the recumbent figure.

Then he drew a chair up to the fireside, seated himself and proceeded to talk about the severity of the weather, pointedly ignoring the observations interjected from time to time by the poet. The latter, who, to do him justice, was no fool, speedily perceived that retreat would be judicious and appropriate; so he rose slowly and gracefully, retained Clarissa's hand while arranging a meeting with her for the morrow, and was ushered out by Guy, who held the door open for him with ceremonious politeness, and only betrayed through some subtle and undefinable method a heartfelt inclination to kick him out of it. When the door had been closed, Clarissa stood upon the hearth-rug and looked interrogative.

"Yes," said her husband, in reply to all the questions which were visible in her eyes, "I *have* one or two things to talk to you about, and there are one or two things about which I am not altogether satisfied, and that is why I have intruded upon you. To begin with, what are you going to make of Netta? Not a Girl of the Future, I trust. I may tell you that I listened to your lecture the other day; and I wasn't edified by it—not a bit! If you propose to educate my daughter into the belief that there is no difference between women and men, I shall have to object."

"Netta is my daughter as well as yours," observed Clarissa, her voice trembling a little. "For the present she is being educated just as all other children of her class are educated; but when she grows older, I must of course tell her what I believe to be the truth and what I do not believe."

"Quite so; and I must do the same. Which will be rather awkward, won't it?"

"Yes, I suppose so; but I see no possible way out of the difficulty. I don't deny your rights, and I presume you will hardly dispute mine. Paul will tell you that Netta has been taught to say her prayers and to accept the Bible as the inspired word of God. What more can I do? Considering what a failure I have made of my own life, I cannot be expected to encourage her to imitate me."

"At the risk of appearing uncivil, I must say that I sincerely hope she will not be tempted to do that. It is a question of taste, no doubt, and you are welcome to yours. But you will not be welcome to push my daughter on to a platform, and teach her to declaim to a mixed audience upon the relations of the sexes. In point of fact, I can't and won't allow anything of the sort."

These were brave words; but they were scarcely well chosen, nor was the threat which they implied of a nature to disarm opposition. Clarissa, whose cheeks had become pink, instantly turned at bay.

"What do you mean? That you will take my child away from me? Then you will have to get authority from a court of law, and I do not think that, when I have told what I shall be forced to tell, a decision will be given in your favor. It is cowardly and unmanly of you to strike at me in this way! I have offered to share all I possess with you; I ask nothing better than to hand over the half of my fortune to you now; I have agreed to your conditions; I have not prevented you from seeing Netta; I don't want to prevent you from taking a part—such a part as may be possible—in her training. As for her ever lecturing in public, you must know perfectly well that I could not wish her to do that. I myself *hate* doing it!—I only do it because I am convinced that it is my duty. Is it because your own life has been so blameless and so un- selfish that you can't give other people credit for an honest desire to do what they think is right?"

This outburst had a sobering effect upon Guy, who indeed had no thought of appealing to the aid of the law, and who was to some extent reassured by his wife's promise that he should have a voice in the training of her child.

"I dare say you think it right to go on as you are doing," said he, "and I dare say it doesn't become me to condemn anybody. I only venture to say that I don't want your particular principles to be instilled into Netta. At least, there is one more thing which perhaps you will think that I haven't a right to say; but I can't go away without saying it. I don't half like your intimacy with that fellow who has just left the house. He's a nasty, unwholesome sort of rascal, and he doesn't bear the best of reputations, and you may depend upon it that, in your position, you can't afford to be seen driving about with him."

Women, as most of us should be willing to acknowledge, possess more than one noble quality which is denied to us; but magnanimity cannot be included in the list, and Clarissa, from whose mind a great weight of fear had been removed by the opening words of her husband's speech, was not in the mood to submit tamely to its conclusion.

"You are really most kind and thoughtful," she returned, disdainfully; "but, in spite of your warning or your command—which do you intend it to be?—and in spite of the position in which I find myself, I shall continue to choose my own friends. I think I remember that, when you were in a position of rather less independence, you used to choose your own friends, and that the reputation of some of them was not quite above reproach. As for Mr. Loosemore, whom I like and admire, I certainly shall not drop his acquaintance at your bidding."

She neither liked nor admired the man; but some latitude of statement must be allowed to an indignant lady. She really did admire a few of his literary productions, and a few of them were really, in a certain sense, deserving of admiration.

"Very well," said Guy, who was also rather indignant; "you must go your own way, then, I suppose, and I must go mine. I am sorry that they cannot be made to run alongside of one another; but it is very evident to me that they can't."

"That," agreed Clarissa, "would, I should think, have been evident to most people some time ago. I shall always be ready to listen to any complaints that you may have to make and any suggestions that you may have to offer about Netta's education; but as regards my own manner of life, I don't feel that I owe obedience to your orders."

Guy shrugged his shoulders and raised the siege. What else could he do? He had intended to present an ultimatum; but in order to adopt such a course with any prospect of success it is necessary to be backed up by the means of enforcing one's demands, and these were scarcely at his disposal. He had been beaten, and he knew that he had been beaten; for, after all, nothing short of removing his child altogether from her mother's guardianship could prevent Clarissa from carrying out what he presumed to be her designs. Meanwhile, he could not but deplore, though he might be powerless to lessen, his wife's avowed liking and admiration for that effeminate writer of erotic verses.

After that day Guy fell into a condition of chronic low spirits, which was scarcely to be wondered at, considering that he had no work to do, that his invitations to join shooting-parties were less numerous than of yore, and that he could hardly—even if the weather had permitted of it— have afforded to hunt regularly from London. Some intermittent comfort he might have derived from talking things over with Mr. Dent; but poor Mr. Dent was laid up with a sharp attack of bronchitis, and when the old gentleman was able to leave his bed he went off to the south coast to recruit, taking his niece and daughter with him; so that Saturday half-holidays could no longer, for the time being, enliven the monotony of a purposeless existence. That Satan finds some mischief still for idle hands to do is a discovery which was probably made rather earlier than in the day of the late Dr. Watts, who, indeed, does not seem to have been quite the person to hit upon startling discoveries; yet the frequency with which that eminent divine's

words are quoted proves, at least, that he managed to earn
the gratitude of his fellow-countrymen by clothing a truism
in precise and easily remembered language. Guy Luttrell's
hands were idle, and his temperament rendered him prone
to yield to temptations whereby we are all liable to be assailed. It has to be owned that, during the remainder of
that winter, old and long-discarded habits got the upper
hand of him. Why not? he may have asked himself. He
was of no good, and never would be of any good, to a single
living being; his wife was only his wife in name and would
be a good deal more comfortable without him; his child,
though some ostensible control over her was conceded to
him, could not in reality be influenced one way or the
other by anything that he was likely to say or do; and if he
drank himself to death—what then? He might do so, if
he liked, with the agreeable conviction that he would not
be acutely missed. Only he sometimes thought that before
he quitted these mundane scenes he would enjoy administering just one good sound thrashing to Mr. Alfred Loosemore.

CHAPTER XXXV

REPENTANCE

ON one of those hopelessly rainy days to which the climate of Pau is somewhat subject, and which so sorely try the temper and patience of its patrons, Madeline Luttrell shut herself into her bedroom and sat down to write a long letter to the only person in the world who could be expected to feel the slightest interest in such news as she had to impart. This, at least, was what—being in a very dismal mental condition—she said to herself. Of course, as a matter of strict accuracy, there were just a very few other people who cared a little for her; there was Paul, for example; there was Guy; there was even a third person, whose affection for her, now that he had departed forever, might be admitted to be sincere, so far as it went. But her brothers were poor correspondents, while the third person, for obvious reasons, did not count. The sympathy of her sister-in-law, however, might surely be relied upon: and indeed it was high time for her to acknowledge two missives, composed largely of anxious questions, which had reached her from Clarissa, and which she had not until now felt in the mood to answer.

"I ought to have written before this," she confessed; "but you put me off by repeating homilies for which I have told you again and again that there was no sort of necessity. Of course, M. de Malglaive honored me with the offer which you seem to have been so much afraid of my accepting, and of course I made the only reply that it was possible for me to make. I dare say you may have heard of his mother's death. She was not a very nice old woman ; but I think he must have been really fond of her, and since he has gone away and I shall never see him again, there can be no harm in my saying that I believe he was very fond of me too. Perhaps men are not like us ; perhaps they do all sorts of things that they have no business to do, and yet— However, I know you think that if they are not like us, they ought to be ; so I won't make excuses for him. He had none, worth mentioning, to make for himself. Mamma was very angry with me for refusing him : he is extremely well off, it appears, whereas we are most uncomfortably poor. But I could not have married him on account of his being well off, and I am glad that he has left the place. Nobody seems to know where he has gone ; but mamma is sure that he will not come back while we are here, and the chances are that we shall remain here until we die. How unfortunate it is that one should be compelled to put another person, and perhaps several other people, to so much inconvenience !

"Not that the inconvenience, according to mamma's ideas, is at all likely to be permanent. She has forgiven me ; she is bent upon finding somebody else for me, since M. de Malglaive won't do. I don't know whether she would laugh or cry if I were to tell her that I am determined to live and die an old maid. Probably she would do both ; and that is why I take very good care to tell her nothing of the sort. Poor mamma !—she has many worries and anxieties which you and I might have spared her if we had been able to look at life as she does ; and sometimes I wonder whether we are so much wiser than she as we think we are. At all events, she does what she is convinced is her duty ; and although nothing but disappointment can be in store for her, I don't make her miserable by saying so. I am as gracious as possible to the young men and the old men (some of them are as old as the hills) whom she asks to the house, and to whom she has the air of offering me in much the same manner as a horse-dealer who, without any question of buying or selling, exhibits what he has in his stable. 'Slightly blemished, but well bred on

both sides, perfectly sound and, as you see, very taking to
the eye. I don't care to part with her; still, I am willing
to listen to reasonable proposals.' The reasonable proposals haven't been made yet; they will be made soon, and
then there will be trouble—endless trouble! I don't want
to catch the small-pox, because it is said to be such a particularly unpleasant disease while it lasts; but if only I
could have had it and could wear the trace of it, I should
be able to look forward to the future with comparative
ease of mind!"

Madeline's letter, which was a lengthy one, was continued
in much the same strain, and was productive of genuine
distress to its recipient, who hastened to despatch epistolary consolation and encouragement.

"I can *fully* understand," Madeline was assured by return of post, "how you feel—haven't I been through it all
myself? One tries to make allowances; one tries to believe
that a man who has led an abominable life can change his
nature all of a sudden and keep the vows that he is ready
to take. But it is not so; and in the case of M. de Malglaive, at any rate, I am *sure* that it has not been so. Mr.
Loosemore, who is a great deal in Paris and who knows him
well, smiles at the idea of his becoming a domestic character. I need not say that neither to Mr. Loosemore nor
to any one else should I dream of mentioning your name in
connection with his; but I have found opportunities of
making inquiries about him, and what I have heard con-
vinces me that you are to be warmly congratulated on
having dismissed the man."

Such congratulations were about as welcome as were the
writer's bitter allusions to her own matrimonial experiences
and to Guy's recent unwarrantable interference in matters
which did not concern him. It was difficult to avoid the
impression that Clarissa, however right she might be in
theory, was something of a firebrand in practice. However, she and Mr. Loosemore had doubtless formed a correct estimate of Raoul de Malglaive; although their opinion of him had been neither required nor desired.

Readers of wide sympathies—and, after all, we human beings are not such a poor lot but that some such must fall to the share of the humblest narrator—may find that they have a crumb of compassion to spare for Lady Luttrell, who at this time was using every effort to marry her daughter. Her desire to do so was surely pardonable, seeing that she knew not how to make income square with expenditure, that she had never in her life been accustomed to economize, and that she owed more money than she could by any possibility pay. The daily humiliations to which she was subjected, the thinly disguised insolence of M. Cayaux which she had to ignore (for was not Cayaux's own long bill still unadorned by a receipt stamp?), the misery of knowing that an end must soon come to all this—it was but natural that she should long to remove Madeline from participation in such sordid cares, and if the poor lady was a somewhat worldly mother, she cannot fairly be called a selfish one. So, in spite of the deep mourning which prevented her and her daughter from attending social entertainments, she contrived to attract many bachelors to her house, and of these a sufficient number seemed to find the bait which she pathetically dangled over their noses worth rising at.

Madeline, as she had boasted with truth in her letter to her sister-in-law, was gracious to them all. She might have added that she displayed remarkable ingenuity in bestowing special marks of favor upon none. Her object was to stave off the evil day, and it seemed not unlikely that she might be able to do this until the winter season should be at an end and winter visitants should have given her up in despair. Meanwhile, she rode the horses of some of them; for she had now no horse of her own, and her mother did not object to her accepting an occasional mount, and following the hounds was the one pleasure in life that remained to her. Miserable we may be, and condemned to lifelong misery; yet while we still inhabit our bodies, and while those bodies continue to be healthy, there will be good moments for us every now and then.

23

What no hunting man or woman can be expected to count as a good moment is one of those when considerations of humanity render it imperative to pull up while hounds are running; and such an experience fell to Madeline's lot one nice cloudy afternoon. The yellow-haired Frenchwoman whom she had noticed for the first time that day, and whose notion of riding appeared to be to rush like an express train at every discoverable fence and ditch, had certainly earned the rather nasty cropper which she had got; still it was impossible to leave her in a huddled-up heap upon the ground, and not another soul was in sight. Madeline first tried to stop her fellow-sportswoman's runaway steed; then, having failed to do so, she turned round, dismounted with a sigh, and approached the victim, who had struggled into a sitting posture and was moaning dismally.

"Have you hurt yourself, madame?" she inquired.

"I have not a whole bone in my body," replied the unknown, "unless it is my neck. If I recover—which is scarcely probable—I promise you that I will never get upon the back of a horse again! It is my husband who will rub his hands when he sees me carried back to the Hôtel de France upon a stretcher!—he, who had warned me that this galloping across the fields had no commonsense. One must do Philippe the justice to admit that his common-sense never deserts him when there is a question of risking his skin."

The lady's loquacity seemed to be a reassuring symptom; yet she was really hurt. She nearly fainted after she had been persuaded to rise to her feet, and was with difficulty revived by a draught from Madeline's flask. Also she complained of excruciating pain in her right arm, which hung helplessly by her side and was probably broken. What was to be done with her? Madeline was nominally under efficient chaperonage, and the elderly widower whose horse she was riding had willingly promised Lady Luttrell not to let her daughter out of his sight; but man proposes and the vicissitudes of the chase dispose. Neither chaperon nor widower could be descried by one who, to tell the truth, had been doing her best to give them the slip; the district was a sparsely inhabited one, and as for returning the whole way to Pau on foot, that was not to be thought of.

"Do you think, if I gave you my arm, you could manage to walk as far as the road?" asked Madeline. "Then you might sit down while I canter on to the nearest house and get assistance."

The stranger nodded assent, and a couple of hundred yards or so of rough ground were eventually traversed; though not without a good deal of trouble and many halts. She did not lack courage—this pearl-powdered, golden-haired lady—and Madeline, while not particularly liking the look of her, paid her the tribute of admiration which her fortitude deserved.

"What would you have?" she asked, when she had been gently lowered on to the bank by the wayside and had been duly complimented. "One does things which must be done because they must be done. Once let me get hold of a good doctor, and I will deafen him with my screams!"

As luck would have it, a *coupé* which Madeline recognized hove in sight at that very minute, and presently Dr. Leroy, intercepted on his way from visiting a country patient, was bending over the unknown lady, who did not carry out her threat while he passed his blunt fingers lightly and deftly over her person.

"*Allons!*" said he, "this is not a formidable affair."

Then he kicked off his shoe, placed his foot under her arm-pit, and with one strong tug, which drew a sharp, involuntary cry from her, restored the dislocated shoulder to its position.

"*Vous voilà tout à fait remise, madame,*" he remarked. "As for the bruises and the shaking, you will have news of them to-morrow; but you will be none the worse for them. Now, if you will permit me to offer you a seat in my carriage, I will conduct you back to Pau. Mademoi-

selle Luttrell, I know, is capable of mounting her horse
without assistance and finding her own way home."

The yellow-haired lady started slightly on hearing the
name of the Good Samaritan to whom she had been addressing voluble expressions of gratitude.

"What!" she exclaimed.   "Mademoiselle is English?
It is true that she rides like an Englishwoman; but to
speak French like a Parisian—that is what does not explain itself!"

"My mother is French," said Madeline.

"*Au fait!*—that is, I think I recollect having been informed of the circumstance."

Then, while she was being helped into the doctor's
brougham, she added: "It would be very amiable on your
part, mademoiselle, to come and see me to-morrow.   Without you, I might have remained lying here until I perished;
it follows that I have a claim upon you, does it not?   You
will come, then?   A thousand thanks!   Madame de Castelmoron, Hôtel de France—*à bientôt!*"

So this was the "*belle marquise*" whose relations with
Raoul de Malglaive had provided journalists with matter
for the delectation of their readers, and at whose house the
young man had pretended, for purposes of his own, to be
taken ill!

"If she had only told me her name a little sooner!"
ejaculated Madeline.   "But it would have been necessary
to do what one could for her in any case, and I am rather
glad that I did not know who she was.   Naturally she has
come to Pau in order to meet him—that shows, at least,
that they do not correspond.   Not that it makes the smallest difference to me, or that I am concerned to quarrel with
his rather odd taste.   I will ask mamma to leave cards and
inquire for her to-morrow.   That will be as much as politeness demands, and I really don't want to see her again."

Nevertheless, Miss Luttrell was shown, on the following
afternoon, into the sunny *salon* at the Hôtel de France
where Madame de Castelmoron, extended upon a sofa, was
reposing her aching limbs.   It was perhaps true that Made-

line did not want to see her again; but we are strongly tempted at times to do things which we do not want to do, and feminine curiosity is notoriously a powerful incentive. Moreover, there is no reason why she should not be allowed credit, among other motives, for a little genuine kindness of heart.

Such credit was, at all events, accorded to her by the bruised lady on the sofa, whose own heart was not, after all, a particularly unkind one, and who had long ago found consolation for the treacherous conduct of "*ce pauvre De Malglaive.*" Madame de Castelmoron had, as a matter of fact, actually forgotten that her former admirer's property was situated in Béarn when she decided upon spending a part of the winter at Pau; but she had been reminded of the circumstance by what she had heard from M. de Larrouy and others, and the story of Raoul's hapless love-affair —which was the common talk of the place—had made her feel almost ashamed of having despatched a certain letter that we know of. She was quite ashamed, now that she was under such obligations to Madeline; she was determined to undo the mischief that she had done; and that was why, after she had made her visitor sit down beside her, she lost no time in beginning:

"It is curious that we should have met like this. I have heard so much of you from our friend M. de Malglaive, who was very ill at our house near Tours last summer, and who—to speak the whole truth—raved about you from morning to night in his delirium. Oh, you need not blush; there is nothing to blush for in having made a conquest of M. de Malglaive, who, I assure you, is not too easy to please. *Apropos*, what has become of him? I thought he told me he had a mother in these latitudes whom he was in the habit of visiting."

Madeline gave explanations which were entirely superfluous, seeing that her questioner had already been informed of Madame de Malglaive's death. What she did not think it necessary to explain was Raoul's abandonment of his home and return to his regiment. It was left for

Madame de Castelmoron to account for the young man's singular conduct, and this was done without hesitation or ambiguity.

"One has only to look in your face to understand how you have treated that unfortunate!—one has even the temerity to think that one can detect some signs of remorse. Frankly, mademoiselle, a little remorse would not be out of place. *Bon Dieu!* what would you have? A young man who adores you, who is, to say the least of him, not precisely ugly, and who possesses all the virtues which are wanting to most young men! Believe me, it is not every day, nor every year, that you will meet with his equal."

"But when one does not care enough for a person to marry him—"

"Ah, bah!—did I not tell you that your face is an open book? You will not make me believe that M. de Malglaive is nothing to you—*allez!*"

Madeline was furious with herself for having betrayed what she was powerless to conceal; yet she could not help longing to embrace Madame de Castelmoron, nor could she repress an intense eagerness for further particulars respecting Raoul's sojourn at Tours.

"Is it so certain that M. de Malglaive possesses the virtues that you speak of, madame?" she asked, with a fine assumption of sceptical indifference. "His vices and his virtues are no affair of mine; but common report gives him more of the first than of the last."

"I was waiting for you there! I was sure that he had been calumniated—the more so because he himself told me that he was afraid of what you might hear, and because he is far too handsome and too rich to be secured against the attacks of jealous and unscrupulous women. Come! —what is it that they have told you about him? I may be able to convince you that they had nothing but lies to tell —I, who know at least what his life has been since you caused him to make a complete alteration in it."

These two ladies were precluded by obvious difficulties

from being perfectly candid with one another. The elder, with every wish to serve an interesting and deserving couple, was not prepared to go quite the length of confessing that she had written an anonymous letter, while the younger could hardly be expected to admit in so many words that she had only refused M. de Malglaive because accusations had been brought anonymously against him. But enough could be said, and was said, to satisfy Madame de Castelmoron's conscience and to gladden Madeline's heart.

"As for years gone by," the former wound up by saying, "I do not undertake to answer for them; one may suppose that a young officer of cavalry, with every opportunity in the world for amusing himself, has not altogether neglected his opportunities. But what I should be willing to stake my existence upon is that since he met you he has abandoned all follies. Those who have represented the contrary to you deserve nothing but your contempt, and—if I may be permitted to say so, mademoiselle—I think that he deserves an apology."

Madeline smiled and replied that he should have one, if he wished for it, the next time she saw him, but that it was impossible for her to make immediate amends, seeing that she had not the slightest idea of where he was. She deemed it incumbent upon her, as a disciple of Clarissa's, to add that, in her opinion, the offences of previous years ought not to be lightly dismissed, as though they had never been. Were men to be allowed· to do exactly what they liked, while women, for one solitary offence of the nature alluded to, were to suffer the extreme penalty of the social law?

Madame de Castelmoron's shoulders were too stiff to be shrugged; but her hands and her eyebrows acted as deputies.

"Neither you nor I," she returned, "are responsible for social laws. We must take the world as we find it; and nothing can be more positive than that you will never find a husband in it if you demand that his history should bear comparison with that of a young girl fresh from the *Sacré Cœur*. It is for you to decide what you will do ; but if I were in your place, I should write two words to that poor De Malglaive, whose regiment is still at Tours, and who can scarcely be elsewhere than with his regiment."

The advice was kindly meant, but it was manifestly out of the question to act upon it, Madeline thought. Yet before she went to bed that night she had acted upon it, and, what was more, she had posted her letter. When one has been guilty of an injustice, ought one not—even at the cost of some personal humiliation and the risk of being misunderstood—to acknowledge as much ? Madeline, in the composition of a missive which had given her no little trouble, had acknowledged that much and no more. She wished M. de Malglaive to know, she wrote, that she had heard reports about him which she had since discovered to be untrue, and she was sorry that, in consequence of her belief in those reports, she had said things to him which she would not have otherwise said. She hoped that he would be so kind as to accept this expression of regret on her part, which she had felt that it was only fair to send, but which of course required no reply.

Whether it required a reply or not (and one does sometimes take the liberty of hoping for what one cannot request), it received none, and at the end of a week Madeline ceased to watch for the arrival of the postman. Evidently she had been taken at her word, and there was nothing to complain of in that. Only she wished that she had been a little less precipitate in adopting a course which, after all, had been perhaps uncalled-for.

CHAPTER XXXVI

RAOUL S'EN VA-T-EN GUERRE

THE habitués of the principal restaurant in Tours were begged, one evening, by the proprietor to pardon any slight shortcomings that might be noticeable in the attendance, his entire staff having been requisitioned for a *grand dîner d'adieu*, offered to M. le Vicomte de Malglaive by his brother-officers. M. le Vicomte was about to proceed, at his own wish and by his own request, to West Africa, in order to take part in an expedition which was being organized for the chastisement of certain turbulent tribes. "*En voilà un qui ne craint ni les boulets ni la fièvre, hein? Avec ça qu'il est riche à millions et qu'il appartient à la vraie noblesse. Sont-ils heureux de trouver des gaillards de sa trempe pour servir leur République du diable!*"

At Tours it is still permissible, sometimes even desirable, to display royalist leanings. For the rest, nobody can help admiring courage ; and although, as has been mentioned before, Raoul de Malglaive was not exactly popular among his comrades, they felt bound to applaud his spirited conduct, now that he was upon the point of leaving them. They themselves were as brave as there was any need for them to be, and would have disgraced neither their regiment nor their country had they been called upon to show what they were made of ; still, one does not, unless one is weary of life, volunteer for service in an obscure little campaign and a pestilential climate. Now, De Malglaive, who was young, rich, well born, and in excellent health, could not possibly be weary of life ; so that his action in soliciting a staff-appointment out there in Senegambia commanded their respectful admiration. It was "*très crâne*," they said, and the least they could do was to give him a dinner and drink to his safe return.

He would gladly have dispensed with that banquet, which he felt that he was accepting upon false pretences; the speeches, the toasts, the somewhat boisterous gayety of his entertainers, were not much to his taste, and he had more than half a mind to tell them candidly that what he thirsted for was not glory, but oblivion. Such an avowal, however, would have been incomplete without further explanations, which obviously could not be given; so he held his peace and tried to look like the ardent warrior whom he represented. At the Ministère de la Guerre, where he was made to dance attendance for many days before his request was granted, he had been regarded as a very ardent warrior indeed. The post for which he asked was not, to be sure, a highly coveted one, and a less conspicuous personage might have had it without much ado; but there were the newspapers to be considered, and a republican Minister who confers an appointment, however undesirable, upon a viscount of the old nobility is apt to lay himself open to vexatious criticisms. Also, why the devil should M. de Malglaive desire to get himself massacred *là-bas?* If to belong to one of the best regiments in the service and to be quartered in one of the favorite garrisons did not satisfy him, he must be singularly hard to please! But by dint of steady persistency, and by the exertion of such influence as he could command, Raoul had finally got his own way. He was now under orders to report himself at Sénégal forthwith, and was to embark at Toulon within twenty-four hours of the moment at which his health was being proposed in felicitous terms by his colonel.

He responded briefly, expressing his deep sense of the honor conferred upon him, together with a modest hope that he might not prove unworthy of the uniform which he wore. In discarding it for that of a staff-officer, he should not forget, he said, the traditions of the famous corps in which it had been his privilege to acquire the rudiments of military knowledge ; and he trusted that, in the not very probable event of his return from the wars, he would be received with the same kindness which had softened for him the regret of departure.

His remarks were, of course, loudly applauded ; but his language was thought to be a little stilted and pedantic, while that allusion of his to the improbability of his escaping with his life was not approved of. No doubt the chances were that he would leave his bones in the desert ; but one does not say such things. They are scarcely in accordance with usage, and they tend to throw gloom upon festive gatherings.

With the best will in the world, poor Raoul could hardly have avoided being a wet blanket. Assuredly it was not the thought of what he had to expect at his journey's end that saddened him ; but he had always been of a somewhat melancholy temperament, and the irony of his fate in possessing everything, except the one thing which he cared to possess, was just then very present to his mind. Moreover, he was unable to find the stale old anecdotes and the broad *gauloiseries* with which the evening terminated in the least amusing or enlivening. It was with sincere relief that he saw the approach of the hour at which he had to catch the night mail to the South.

His hosts escorted him to the railway-station in a compact band ; they were, after all, good fellows, and he was not ungrateful to them. There was much shaking of hands before he took his seat ; then, while caps were waved and a parting cheer was raised, the train began to move.

"Messieurs," said the colonel, oratorically, as he turned to leave the platform, I recommend to you the example of our comrade and friend. It is with such officers that the glories of France have been gained."

Officers who set little store upon their lives are no doubt useful and valuable subordinates to seekers after glory; but it was perhaps open to question whether much glory was to be reaped out of a miniature expedition into the interior of Senegambia either by France or by the leader of that expedition or by Raoul de Malglaive. The latter, at all events, anticipated none. He stretched himself out in the corner of the railway-carriage, and, finding that sleep was not within his capabilities, fell to musing over the situation into which he had drifted. That situation, from the common-sense point of view, was sufficiently absurd. Succinctly stated, it amounted to this—that he was going to Africa to throw his life away, simply and solely because a girl of whom he had chanced to become enamoured had declined to have anything to say to him. Yet it is a well-known and universally recognized fact that the emotion of love is transient. In two years—three years, at the outside—he would be himself again ; Madeline Luttrell would be merely a sentimental and rather pleasant memory ; while he would be still young and his material prosperity would in all probability have increased rather than diminished. Who but a consummate fool would resign, in what had all the appearance of a fit of childish ill-temper, the prospect of a long period of earthly felicity ? Raoul de Malglaive, who was not a fool, who looked forward to no conscious existence beyond the grave, and who saw no reason for flattering himself that he was more constant or consistent than the average human being, did not attempt to support his decision by argument. Very likely, if he lived long enough, he would recover from this malady, as he had recovered from physical maladies ; very likely he would become as other men were, and would learn to value life for the material pleasures it had to offer him; very likely he would conquer his present disgust for those material pleasures. But we belong perforce to the present, not to the future, and although he acknowledged that it might eventually become possible for him to return to what he had left behind him, he really could not find that possibility an alluring one.

" *C'est égal, j'en ai assez!*" he said to himself.

The train rushed on through the night while this luckless spoiled child of fortune passed in mental review the incidents of his brief but somewhat exciting career. They had not excited him, those incidents; he had derived neither happiness nor profit from them—nothing, save an increased and very depressing acquaintance with the seamy side of human nature. On the other hand, they had robbed him of his only chance of true happiness. For, when all was said, Madeline was perhaps right: he was unworthy of her, and could never again make himself worthy of her. There was a chasm between them, she had told him, across which they could never join hands. Well, that was an unusual thing for a young lady to say; but there might be truth in it, for all that. Anyhow, her refusal of him was irrevocable, even if his past could have been atoned for.

From Bordeaux, which was reached early in the morning, the traveller's course lay straight across France; so that, although he did not actually pass Pau, he was not very far from that place at the moment when Madeline was learning from Madame de Castelmoron that he had been calumniated. It would have surprised, but scarcely encouraged, him to see those two ladies in conference together. He had never suspected the one of having penned an anonymous letter about him; still less could he anticipate receiving an apologetic letter from the other. And since that apologetic letter did not each Tours until after he had embarked on board the transport which was to convey him to the neighborhood of the equator, he was spared the misery of doubting—as he might otherwise have doubted—whether he had not been in rather too great a hurry to cut himself off from the land of the living.

France, which we are so often assured (by Frenchmen) leads the advanced guard in the march of civilization, must be acknowledged to have fallen back among the stragglers in the rear so far as railway travelling is concerned, and it was not until twenty-four hours later that Raoul was enabled to pace the deck of the hired vessel which was getting up steam in Toulon harbor. A small draft of reinforcements was to take passage with him, and he watched these poor fellows coming on board—shouting, singing, three parts drunk, most of them — with sincere commiseration. He had read and heard enough to know a great deal better than they did what they were going to and what only a very few of them could hope to escape; it seemed a little hard that all that youth and exuberant health should be sacrified, while hundreds and thousands to whom youth and health were valueless were left at home to grow dismally middle-aged and old at their leisure.

Well, at all events, the ship took away one young and healthy man who was not in the least enamoured of existence on the surface of this planet: more than one out of five hundred would doubtless have exceeded the average, even in these days of secular education, when death has naturally lost the greater part of the terrors ascribed to it by those who for a matter of two thousand years have been wont to assert that to die is gain.

One voyage is very like another, and all voyages are apt to be ineffably tedious. To Raoul, who was impatient to arrive at his destination, the slow progress of that ancient tub, which accomplished her nine knots with a fair wind and was not asked to do more than hold her own against a foul one, was so exasperating that at length he took the liberty of addressing some courteous remonstrances to the captain.

"You are in a great hurry to reach the most accursed country in the world," remarked the latter, laughing; "believe me, you will be in a still greater hurry to turn your back upon it. For the rest, you need not fear that the expedition will start without you; they have lost too many men already to be able to dispense with those whom I am taking to them, and in those regions one chooses one's own time for fighting. *Par exemple,* one cannot always choose the place. That remains at the choice of the enemy; and if you ask me whether a battalion and a half and a squadron or so of cavalry suffice to meet hordes of savages who are not badly armed—*ma foi!* I should hesitate to make the reply which was given to the Chamber a few days ago by a couple of responsible Ministers."

The captain's somewhat pessimistic views were not shared, it appeared, by the handful of officers who were Raoul's fellow-passengers. These gentlemen, though not altogether pleased at having been ordered to a climate which is so commonly fatal to white men, expected to give a speedy and decisive account of their opponents. According to them, it was to be an affair of a month, or two months at most ; after which the customary rewards in the shape of promotions and decorations would follow. After all, it was worth while to take the chance of fever and make sure of honorable distinction. They were not bad specimens of their class ; and if they found M. de Malglaive, who belonged to a different class, cold and distant in his manner, that was not because he looked down upon them, but because it was out of his power to share in their uproarious gayety.

However, nobody could feel very gay or continue to be very uproarious when at length the voyage came to an end at the mouth of the Sénégal River. That mournful, desolate land, sweltering in overpowering heat by day and shrouded in chilly white vapors by night, had a sinister aspect of which the significance impressed itself even upon the most thoughtless of these new-comers. One stops laughing instinctively at the sight of a funeral procession or the sound of a tolling bell ; for indeed death, when we are brought face to face with it, is not precisely a laughing matter.

Raoul, who proceeded up the river to the town of Saint-Louis in advance of the troops, said to himself more than once, with a rather dismal smile, that there was not much doubt about his finding what he had come to Africa to seek. Supposing that he escaped the bullets and spears of the enemy (and persons who are ready to welcome bullet and spear wounds generally do escape them), the climate might be relied upon to undertake his affair. He remembered the attack of fever and ague through which Madame de Castelmoron had been so good as to nurse him, and thought that he was a tolerably promising subject for future and less easily vanquished attacks.

On reaching Saint-Louis de Sénégal, a dreary, silent town, the population of which is rendered piebald by only a slight sprinkling of white people, who spend the greater part of their monotonous, weary days in wishing themselves anywhere else, he hastened to report his arrival to Colonel Davillier, the officer who had been placed in command of the projected expedition. He was not too well received by the brusque, sunburnt little personage, with bloodshot eyes and a fiercely turned-up mustache, upon whose staff he had been appointed to serve.

"What the devil," Colonel Davillier wanted to know, "do they expect me to do with a reinforcement of five hundred men who are not acclimatized and a young dandy —saving your presence—from Paris? It is not with such a pitiable force as that that we shall make our way to Timbuctoo: you and the Minister for War may take my word for it! *Enfin!*—since there is no help for it, let us go into the desert to be massacred. Plan of campaign?— there is no plan possible! *À la rigueur* I will grant you a first successful engagement; but after that, we shall have to count with the Touaregs, who, I assure you, are not to be despised, and who, moreover, have been well furnished with arms by our good friends the English. Ah, those English!"—

Colonel Davillier, who was an honest man and a brave soldier, entertained opinions of us as a nation which are unfortunately shared by many of his compatriots who are both honest and brave. Raoul, having reasons of his own for believing that we are not quite so black as we are painted, undertook our defence in the course of subsequent conversations; but he could not overcome the prejudices of his chief, nor was the Governor of Senegambia, to whom he had brought a letter of introduction, disposed to back him up. That discontented, yellow-faced official (a residence of two years at Saint-Louis de Sénégal is enough to sour any official's temper and ruin his complexion) evidently felt that somebody must be blamed for the futile military operations which had been conducted, and were going to be conducted, under his auspices; and, since he was precluded by his position from cursing the home authorities, he found a little relief in denouncing British perfidy. "A vile commercial race, who would sell rifles to their own enemies rather than miss the chance of doing a good stroke of business," he said.

But whatever might be the outcome of this little war, and whoever ought to be held responsible for the catastrophe which both the governor and the commandant appeared to anticipate, a start had to be made, and as soon as the new drafts had been disembarked, Raoul found himself provided with plenty of work. His spirits rose—as the spirits of every man who is worth a brass farthing are sure to do—with enforced activity; he began to look forward to the fight which was at hand; he almost forgot that he had come to Africa to die, not to gain victories, and at the end of a week he had won the friendship and esteem of his chief.

"*Sapristi!*" Colonel Davillier exclaimed, "if all Parisian dandies resemble you, *mon garçon,* I ask nothing better than to have half a dozen of them sent out to me. What I have difficulty in explaining to myself is why a dandy who can afford to amuse himself in Paris should ever have requested to be sent here. Glory?—fame?—*allons donc!* How many out of the thirty-eight millions who inhabit France will hear our names, do you think, or say masses for the repose of our souls after our bones have been picked clean by the jackals and the vultures?"

Well, in his case, there might possibly be one, Raoul thought—domiciled at that moment in the Department of the Basses-Pyrénées. Not being ambitious, he wished only to dwell for a short time in the memory of that one, and it did not seem extravagant to hope that, if he was to die, she would divine for whose sake he had laid down his life.

24

RAOUL, who had brought no servant to Africa with him, engaged a private of the native *tirailleurs* to serve him in that capacity. This gigantic negro, Salem by name, was a Mahommedan from the Soudan. He was without credentials; but then, as Colonel Davillier remarked, there was not a man under his command who was likely to possess any credentials worth speaking of, and Salem, if not precisely an accomplished valet, seemed to be a good-natured creature. Raoul took a fancy to him because he grinned from ear to ear upon the smallest provocation, because he was said to have fought like a demon upon previous occasions, and because he kept his person scrupulously clean. Salem, on his side, conceived a prompt and profound affection for his new master, who, instead of hitting him over the head for negligence or stupidity, merely pointed out to him with grave kindliness what his duties were, and whom he loudly proclaimed to be "*bon comme un gâteau.*"

Like all negroes, Salem was loquacious, and at odd times Raoul learned a good deal from him about the nature of the fighting which awaited them both. He did not take a very rosy view of their prospects. If it was to be only a question of chastising certain black tribes and then returning as quickly as possible to Saint-Louis, well and good: that might be done; although there were more rifles and ammunition in the interior than ought to have been allowed to penetrate so far. But if they were to proceed northwards into the desert, without adequate transport and without means of communication with their base, that would be quite another affair. The Touaregs, those terrible veiled horsemen of the Sahara, who seldom risked a pitched battle and whose whereabouts it was impossible to ascertain at any given moment, were capable of giving unpleasant surprises to the most skilful European commander.

"*Bien méchants ces gens-là, et bons guerriers, va! Tu n'as pas besoin de les chercher, les Touareg — mieux vaut rester chez toi!*"

Raoul did not quite gather whether this advice was addressed to him personally or to the French nation in general; nor did he feel altogether sure of Salem, who seemed to view the possible discomfiture of the whites with a touch of exultation. However, he remarked that, so far as he was concerned, all he had to do was to obey orders, and his retainer agreed with him that such was the whole duty of a soldier.

"*Moi, j'aurai soin de toi,*" he added, encouragingly; "*si tu ramasses la mort, c'est que moi n'y serai plus.*"

The man himself was obviously not afraid of death; that is one advantage of having an easily comprehended creed and being absolutely convinced of its truth. .He had seen a good deal of service and had been badly wounded more than once; he chattered about his feats of arms—not indeed without some admixture of bombast, yet with a childlike simplicity which rendered it easy to guess when he was lying and when he was not. It took a good deal to kill him, he observed, complacently, and in truth his magnificent physique lent confirmation to the boast.

But it would not take a great deal—it would not even take a Touareg, perhaps—to kill a young European whose health had never been of the best and who had no sufficient motive for struggling against the maladies of a feverstricken region. Raoul, fully realizing this, and impressed not only by the discouraging hints of Salem, but by the despondent shakes of the head in which Colonel Davillier frequently indulged, ended by regarding his death as a foregone conclusion and asking himself whether he had made all the arrangements which a man ought to make under such circumstances. As a matter of fact, he had not made them; but he thought that he had. What would be the use of his leaving a will? There was nobody in the world who would care to possess his few personal belongings, and as for the property, that must of course go, in any case, to a cousin of his whom he had never seen. Oddly enough, it did not occur to him to despoil that unknown person, or those unknown persons— for probably there were several among whom a division would have to be made—in favor of those who were no blood-relations of the De Malglaives. He had been brought up to look upon the claims of the family as sacred, and he did not even remember how great a boon he had it in his power to confer upon poor Lady Luttrell by bequeathing the Château de Grancy to her. Had he thought of this, he would have executed a testament forthwith; but he himself had never been poor, and he had clean forgotten the incidents of his last interview with Madeline's mother.

What, of course, he did not forget was his last interview with Madeline, and what he, naturally enough, desired was that he should not be too speedily forgotten by her. She did not love him—that, no doubt, must be regarded as conclusive, and he had proved that he so regarded it by coming out to Sénégal to die. Still, she had promised that she would try to think less harshly of him for the future, and there could be no great harm in his writing a few pages to her which she would never read until he should have passed beyond reach of pardon or condemnation.

So, one hot, airless night, when sleep was out of the question, notwithstanding all the fatigues of the day, he sat down and penned a missive which was destined to cause more suffering than he contemplated or wished. He did not, indeed, imagine that it would cause any suffering at all: he only wanted Madeline to know the whole truth; and, somehow or other, there was less difficulty about making the truth apparent to her by a letter, written practically upon his death-bed, than there had been by word of mouth.

"Now that it is all over," he wrote, "and that no fancies of mine can offend you or help me, I please myself by imagining that you might have cared for me, if I had not led the sort of life which you so often gave me to understand that you could not forgive. You were, perhaps, right, and it is certainly true that I have a past behind me of which I have no reason to be proud. Yet I think you make a mistake in supposing that a man's future must resemble his past, and I can swear that you made a very great mistake when you said that my love had been given to other women as well as to you. These few lines will not reach you until I am dead; so you will believe that I could have no motive for telling you a lie. I have never loved any woman but you, and since that day at Lourdes— do you remember, I wonder, that we sat for a time on the bank of the Gave and that you dropped a flower, which I ventured to pick up?—since that day I have never made the faintest pretence of doing so. It seems to me that a man ought not to be judged too severely for having done as other men do, provided that he repents and amends his conduct. Is not that, after all, the teaching of the religion which you profess?

"But this, you will say, is not very much to the point, seeing that you would not have loved me even if I had had nothing to repent of. I acknowledge it; yet you will not grudge a dying man the fancies which I mentioned just now, and you will understand my longing to be—I will not say respected, but at least pitied and absolved by you. If I were a good Catholic, I should send for a priest when I felt my last hour approaching, should I not? Well, not being a good Catholic, it is to you, mademoiselle, that I turn with my plea for absolution. If there is a life beyond the grave—but although there may be such a life for some people, I feel almost sure that there can be none for me— my love for you will remain hereafter what it has been here. Otherwise I should assuredly cease to be myself.

I do not wish to think about the remainder of your life in this world—I know what must happen, and I cannot pretend to be entirely resigned. But what I can say with sincerity and truth is that my last thought will be of you, mademoiselle, and that my last wish will be for your happiness."

On the following evening Raoul dined with the governor, who invited him, Colonel Davillier, and one or two others to partake of the last meal which they were likely to eat under civilized conditions for some time to come. The governor was, or affected to be, sanguine of the success and the speedy return of the expedition: perhaps he thought that the least he could do for his guests was to assume a cheerful countenance.

"Your fashion of serving our country is a more enviable one than mine, *messieurs*," said he. "You are going to make your little war at the best season of the year; you have some hope of excitement before you and some hope of being back in France before the summer; whereas I must sit still in this terrible place, with nothing to do but to write despatches which nobody will read and receive instructions which nobody could carry out. All I beg of you is not to ruin my chances of promotion by failing to discover the enemy!"

"Oh, we shall discover the enemy—or he will discover us," answered Colonel Davillier, rather grimly; "there is no need to be disquieted on that score."

"*Allons!* you ask for nothing better, I imagine. As for M. de Malglaive, who has already been performing prodigies, I am told, I shall look forward to making honorable mention of him in my report of your victory."

The governor was extremely kind and friendly to Raoul, who, after dinner was over, took an opportunity of confiding to his care an envelope addressed to M. Cayaux at Pau. This contained the letter which M. Cayaux was requested to be so good as to deliver to Miss Luttrell; it might have given rise to gossip which would have caused annoyance to Miss Luttrell had her name been submitted to the scrutiny and curiosity of a colonial official.

"One is not precisely certain, M. le Gouverneur," Raoul explained, "that one will have the honor of seeing you again. Might I beg you, in the event of anything happening to me, to forward this letter to my man of business? It is rather important that in that event—but not otherwise—it should reach his hands."

"Count upon me," the governor replied. "But I hope and believe that it will soon be my duty to give this document back to you, instead of despatching it to its destination."

Raoul, for his part, felt that it would be almost ridiculous of him to escape from the perils which he had courted, and which, by all accounts, were quite ready to give him a welcome. To come safe and sound out of an affair to which hardened old soldiers like Colonel Davillier could not allude without significant grimaces would have something of the effect of an anticlimax. Yet so strong is the animal clinging to life which infects us all that there were moments when he could not help shuddering at the thought of what awaited him. When once the bustle and confusion of embarkation were at an end (for the troops were to proceed up the Sénégal River as far as boats could take them) he had nothing to do but to lie on deck beneath an awning and listen to the unending chatter of Salem, who regaled him with grewsome descriptions of the tortures inflicted by his fellow-countrymen upon those who were so unlucky as to fall into their hands alive. As for the pagan tribes whom it was the ostensible object of the mission to chastise, they would make no very formidable stand, Salem thought; it was only on the northward march across the desert that trouble might be anticipated, and Raoul perceived that his servant was anxious to discover what had not yet been revealed—namely, how far towards the north the force under Colonel Davillier's command had been ordered to make its way.

He was less in danger of committing himself to indiscreet revelations because his chief had not been particularly communicative with him. There was, he knew, some idea of joining hands with another body of the French troops, which was believed to be advancing up the Niger; it was possible that, if all went well, Timbuctoo might be reached and occupied; but it was much more probable that a hasty and inglorious retreat would be the result of operations which, as Colonel Davillier often grumbled, were not being undertaken seriously.

" *Allons nous faire casser les reins !*" he was wont to say, quoting a valiant and unfortunate commander, who, as all the world knows, had been ordered nearly a quarter of a century before to achieve the impracticable upon a less obscure stage.

In any case, the advance towards the scene of hostilities seemed likely to be protracted to an extent which was trying alike to the patience of the officers and to the health of their men. The boats progressed very slowly up the sluggish, yellow river; the heat was scarcely to be endured; already sickness had broken out, and everybody, except Salem and his native comrades, was languid and a little discouraged. Melancholy, desolate plains stretched away to meet the horizon on the right hand and on the left; from time to time a group of stunted palms and a glimpse of thatched huts showed where a native village was situated; but, with these rare exceptions, not a sign of life, vegetable or animal, was to be discerned in that terrible, burnt-up land, which is apt to resent the intrusion of man by sullenly refusing him the means of maintaining his existence. To Raoul the whole thing had the effect of a huge funeral procession—differing only from other funeral processions in that those who formed it were deliberately attending their own obsequies. What an absurd tragi-comedy it was! —this dream of ultimately uniting Algeria with West Africa; this insane rivalry among the European nations to secure what never could be worth securing; this wanton, useless waste of human life. "If all these poor devils were like me," he thought to himself "*à la bonne heure!* But it would be difficult to get together a battalion, or even half a battalion, of men who have lived as long as they wish to live. Even I, in spite of everything — even I dislike the idea of having a dozen blunt spears thrust through my body. Heaven grant that these savages may be armed with the rifles that we have heard so much of!"

But perhaps the perfidious English had been maligned, or perhaps the first hostile body which Colonel Davillier's troops encountered had omitted to profit by British perfidy; for this combat was productive of a signal victory for civilization. It took place on the day following that of the disembarkation of the force at a point where the river ceased to be navigable, and when the enemy had been put to flight, the victors had but few casualties to deplore. It was an affair of no importance, Colonel Davillier said; still, it had the effect of putting him and everybody else into a good humor, and the news, which was sure to spread rapidly into the interior, would, it was hoped, facilitate further operations.

Further operations entailed a slow, cautious forward movement across burning sands, in search of foes who remained persistently invisible. Every day the number of men who had to be sent back, invalided with fever or sunstroke, increased; every evening the native spies and scouts returned to camp, reporting that they had nothing to report; the suspense and the silence ended by telling upon the nerves of those who would assuredly be held responsible for a surprise or a disaster.

And yet, after all, they allowed themselves to be surprised. They had encamped, as usual, after taking all the ordinary precautions against a night attack; Raoul, who had spent some time in his chief's tent, pouring over a boldly speculative map, had gone to lie down and had at last fallen into a light, uneasy slumber. Then on a sudden arose a clamor which caused him to start up, with every sense on the alert. There was a wild discharge of firearms, a thunder of galloping hoofs; shouts and shrieks resounded on every side; Salem dashed excitedly into the tent, holding out a sword and a revolver. "*Viens, viens vite! Les Touareg!—les Touareg!*"

The engagement which ensued beneath the stars and in the dim light of the coming dawn was rather a massacre than a fight. Colonel Davillier lay dead upon the sand in a pool of blood, his skull battered and his arms outstretched; in a very brief space of time scarcely an officer remained who had not shared his fate; there was nobody to take command, and even if there had been anybody, nothing could have been done with the men, many of whom had not even contrived to reach their arms, and who were flying, panic-stricken, in every direction—only to be cut down by their mounted assailants. The native *tirailleurs* alone made a stand, but were speedily overpowered. As for Raoul, he did what he could, but soon recognized the impossibility of doing more than selling his own life dearly. At such moments a man does not ask himself whether his life is worth much or little, and Raoul, hard pressed on all sides by an indistinct crowd of horsemen in floating burnouses, fought with the fury of a wild-cat. Salem, staggering and smothered in blood, but still erect, was at his elbow, and kept supplying him with fresh cartridges for his revolver; for several minutes — which of course seemed like half-an-hour—he managed to stand at bay and beat off those who charged down upon him. But he was completely surrounded, and he could no more have escaped than a spent fox can escape the overtaking hounds in the open. Presently a tremendous blow at the back of the shoulder—it was only a bullet, but it felt like the stroke of a sledge-hammer—brought him to his hands and knees; he rose for a moment, but instantly fell again, pierced and hacked by a rain of wounds, of which the pain cannot have been very great. The horsemen swept over his body and that of his faithful black attendant, in pursuit of fugitives. All was over; Colonel Davillier's force was absolutely annihilated, and doubtless it was as well both for him and for those who had served upon his staff that they were beyond reach of courts-martial. When catastrophes occur, somebody must needs be blamed, and it may be that the unfortunate officers who thus perished in the desert were to blame for doing so. It will be agreed, however, that Raoul de Malglaive, whether he merited blame or not, could not fairly be called unfortunate, seeing that he had found in the desert exactly what he had gone thither to seek.

A mere handful of men effected their escape, joined the rear guard and were eventually brought back down the river to Saint-Louis; but long before their arrival the bad news, travelling with the proverbial rapidity of bad news, had reached the Governor of Senegambia, whom it reduced wellnigh to despair.

"It is only to me that such things happen!" the poor man exclaimed; "I may say good-bye now to all hope of promotion. Nothing can be more certain than that I shall be severely censured for this—especially since not a single officer survives. And yet God knows that every order I gave was given in obedience to instructions! That unhappy Davillier!—what could he have been thinking of to get himself cut to pieces *à propos* of nothing at all! Oh, I pity him; certainly I pity him—and the rest of them. I deplore their fate. But, when all is said, it is a soldier's trade to die in battle. The injustice of it is that a civilian should be condemned to die by slow degrees of fever in banishment, by way of atonement for a military mishap."

It was hardly to be expected that a man so full of sorrow for himself and so preoccupied with drawing up regretful despatches should recollect the request of one unfortunate member of the late Colonel Davillier's staff; but there is no great trouble involved in dropping a letter into the mail-bag, and Raoul's last wish was duly complied with.

"One must suppose," remarked the governor pensively, "that that young man was not in full possession of his senses. Naturally, he cannot have expected to die; yet he should have known that people who come out to this part of the world have no very sure prospect of living. And to come here voluntarily into the bargain! I am not, I hope, more of a coward than another; but I assure you it is not in Sénégal that I should be found if I had one half of the fortune which he is said to have left behind him!"

CHAPTER XXXVIII

A RECEPTION IN CADOGAN GARDENS

MR. DENT, who had been ordered to Hastings by his doctor to recover from bronchitis, did not get well quite as soon as he expected and wished, and was consequently disposed to be a little querulous in his comments upon the advice of that distinguished physician.

"Nobody but an ass," he remarked, "would send one down to a deserted watering-place in the middle of the winter by way of raising one's spirits. When a man reaches my time of life he is bound to have something or other the matter with him, and whatever he may have is pretty sure to be best adapted for home consumption. Besides, I have really no business to keep you in this deadly-lively hole when you must be sighing for the delightful and intellectual society that you have left behind you in London."

Clarissa laughed, as she turned her head towards the old man who was seated beside her in an open carriage. "How cross you are, Uncle Tom!" said she; "that is a sure sign of convalescence. I am sorry you find it so dull here; but Hastings has done us all good, and you must admit that we get more sunshine here than we should in London. As for the intellectual society for which you accuse me of pining, you know very well that I don't really like those people."

"This is the first intimation to that effect that I have had from your lips, my dear. I was under the impression that you adored them."

Clarissa laughed again. Hastings had certainly done

her good, if it had not accomplished all that it might have done for Mr. Dent. During that quiet, unmolested time with her uncle and her child she had been happier than for many months past ; she had given her mind a rest, she had had somebody to take care of (which is what all women love), and she was quite willing to excuse an occasional outbreak of petulance on the part of her patient.

"Well," she answered, "of course I like them in a way. That is, I like them for holding the opinions that they hold, and for having the courage of their opinions. I never said that I was particularly devoted to them as individuals."

"I am glad to hear that," observed Mr. Dent, pensively, "because some of them seemed to me to be so dirty in their persons and nearly all of them are so ugly. I can't pretend to any accurate acquaintance with their opinions— of which they entertain a vast variety, do they not ?"

"At all events," said Clarissa, "they are agreed upon what I consider the main point. And that is a question of such simple, elementary justice that I can't understand how any one can honestly differ from them. Why on earth shouldn't a woman's position be the same in all respects as that of a man ?"

"If you come to that," returned Mr. Dent, rather tartly, "why shouldn't pigs have wings ?"

Perhaps, as Clarissa had suggested, he was entering upon that stage of convalescence which is generally associated with irritability. Anyhow, he was determined not to be drawn into an argument upon a subject which he had hitherto persistently declined to argue, and he cut short his niece's eager rejoinder with :

"It's no use, my dear ; in me you see the embodiment of obstinate, convinced conservatism, and you would only waste your breath by reasoning with such an antiquated fossil. What makes me so disagreeable at the present moment," he added, with a smile, "is that I can't get on without any work to do, and that I doubt whether I am quite fit to return to work yet."

"You are never disagreeable, Uncle Tom," said Clarissa,

laying her hand affectionately upon the old man's shoulder; "but I am sure you ought not to go back to your work until you are a little stronger." She paused for a moment, and then resumed hesitatingly, "Why should you not go down to Haccombe Luttrell for a time? It is a mild climate, and—"

"God forbid!" interrupted Mr. Dent.

"But, as the place is yours, and as it will have to be kept up, I suppose—"

"The place is mine, and it is being properly kept up. I am quite aware of my duties and responsibilities, which are both troublesome and expensive; but I don't include among them any obligation to visit personally a place upon which I shall in all probability never set eyes again. I am no more capable of filling poor Luttrell's shoes than he would have been of filling mine."

Clarissa sighed. "That seems a very unsatisfactory state of things," she ventured to remark.

"Very unsatisfactory indeed," agreed her uncle, dryly. "Perhaps I am not altogether to blame for it, though."

She understood what he meant. Had matters fallen out as he might reasonably have expected them to fall out at the time of her marriage, it would have been so natural for him to hand over the estate to her and her husband; and with his wealth the sacrifice could doubtless have been very well afforded.

"I wish—" she began, and then checked herself.

"May one be permitted to hear what you wish?" Mr. Dent inquired.

"I was only going to say that this Luttrell estate, which neither you nor I want, is wanted very badly by the man to whom, in a certain sense, it ought to belong, and—"

"Yes?"

"One hates talking to anybody about his will; it sounds as if one wanted him to die! But you know what a dreadful misfortune your death would be for me, and I want you to know—I have wanted to say this ever so many times—that I should think it a great misfortune to inherit Haccombe Luttrell."

"I will bear your wishes in mind," answered Mr. Dent; "but I am bound to say, as a business man, that the course at which you hint does not commend itself to me. You would like, I gather, to see Sir Guy Luttrell in the enjoyment of the property which was held by his fore-fathers. So should I; but it is evident that, setting all other difficulties aside, this can only be accomplished in in one of two ways. Either I must die—and really I see no reason why I should not live for another ten or fifteen years, provided that I am not sent to Hastings again—or else— But we are to regard the alternative as out of the question, are we not?"

"Quite out of the question, I am afraid," replied Clarissa, decisively.

It was quite out of the question, and she was quite sure that it was not she who had rendered it so. Nevertheless, she was conscious that the two people for whom she cared most in the world, Netta and Uncle Tom, would have been considerably happier and better off if she could have brought herself to submit to or ignore what women have submitted to or ignored for generations. To avoid the conclusion (which was, of course, a false though a plausi-ble one) that she must be an exceptionally selfish woman, she had to fall back upon the old plea that she was fighting the battle of her sex, and no omelet can be made without breaking of eggs.

At the end of another week she was set free to renew this noble conflict; for Mr. Dent, who had now recovered both his health and his temper, was eager to return to business and to the House of Commons. Netta, on the other hand, quitted the seaside with deep regret, London having no attractions for her, save one—and that one she did not mention. Notwithstanding all the scrupulous precautions which Clarissa fancied that she had taken, the child had discovered that it was best not to mention her father's name. She was a good little thing—rather sub-

dued and old for her age, as only children are apt to be—
and she was already becoming a companion to her mother,
who would fain have prolonged their sojourn in a spot
where companionship was less liable to interruptions than
in London. But duty before everything! When one has
identified one's self with a great work one has no longer
the right to neglect it.

Doubtless it was from a sense of duty that Clarissa,
shortly after her return to Cadogan Gardens, sent out invitations for one of those receptions of hers which were
always largely attended, and which were generally marked
by certain features that distinguished them from ordinary
receptions. Among those whom she had invited chanced
to be Mrs. Antrobus, whose card she had found on the
hall-table one day and to whom it seemed right to show
this civility. Not that she was very anxious to see Mrs.
Antrobus again or to be reminded of days which had painful associations for her; but she presumed that, if her old
friend should see fit to respond to the invitation, she would
be discreet enough to avoid allusions to those days.

But discretion had never been a prominent characteristic of the excellent Mrs. Antrobus, who marched up the
staircase with her accustomed military stride and greeted
her hostess in loud, ringing accents, as of yore.

"Well, how are you? Better in health than your husband, I should say, by the look of you. I met your husband in the street the other day, and had a long talk with
him."

"Indeed?" said Clarissa, chillingly; for she was painfully aware that at least a dozen persons who had grouped
themselves round her were pricking up their ears.

"Yes, indeed—and, to tell the truth, that's my chief
reason for being here now. This sort of thing," continued
Mrs. Antrobus, with a circular wave of her arm, "isn't
much in my line, and, having no daughters to take out, I
don't feel bound to go to parties when I'm in London;
but I thought it would be an opportunity—"

"Yes, exactly," interrupted Clarissa, hurriedly. "So

good of you to come, and I shall enjoy so much having a
chat with you about Mrs. Harvey and all the others! Only
I think we must wait until a little later in the evening;
just now I can't very well desert my post."

"All right; I don't mind waiting," answered Mrs. Antrobus, good-naturedly, as she passed on into the prettily
furnished and lighted rooms where a heterogeneous assemblage was collected.

Clarissa's receptions, as has been said, were of a nature
to attract all sorts and conditions of men and women;
since something unusual, in the shape of a speech or a
recitation, was pretty sure to take place during the course
of them, for the edification of the initiated and the amusement of the unregenerate. On the present occasion Mrs.
Hamley, the popular authoress, had very kindly consented
to read aloud a few passages from her latest, and as yet un-
published, novel. She had established herself in a picturesque attitude in Clarissa's boudoir and was turning over
the leaves of a type-written manuscript when Mrs. Antrobus,
following the set of the general current, came within sight
and hearing of her. Mrs. Hamley was a pretty woman,
who wore extremely pretty clothes. It was, indeed, chiefly
in order to defray the cost of those clothes (so she was
wont to confess, in moments of expansion, to her intimates) that she had taken to writing novels which could
not be described as exactly pretty. For the rest, she honestly believed that she was a highly talented writer, and if
anything stood in the way of her doing full justice to her
gifts, assuredly it was not a misplaced bashfulness.

When the room was as full as it could hold, and when
silence had been obtained, she began, in a clear, pleasantly
modulated voice, to read the description of an impassioned
love-scene, which, though dissociated from its context,
could leave no doubt in the minds of the audience as to
the mutual relations of the personages concerned therein.
To do Mrs. Hamley justice, she had a certain command of
powerful and striking language, while her singular lack of
reticence caused everybody to wonder what on earth she

25

could be going to say next. That, perhaps, **was the** secret
of her success. Having left her lovers at a point where it
really seemed to be quite necessary to leave them, she
hastily skipped a number of pages, and proceeded to draw
a realistic picture of the death of one of them, under peculiarly unpleasant conditions. Not an incident of this unfortunate gentleman's last illness was omitted, not a detail of his malady was left to the imagination; and when
at length he expired, Mrs. Hamley's hearers were too deeply impressed to applaud, save by a low, awe-struck murmur.

One of the audience — a tall, gaunt lady with a hook
nose—did not even join in that respectful tribute. She
snorted aloud, turned on her heel, and, descrying Clarissa,
who was standing near her, plucked her by the sleeve.

" Come out of this," said she ; " I want to talk to you,
and I don't want to distinguish myself by being sick in
public."

" I must confess," said Clarissa, while she was being
hurried towards the unoccupied corner of the drawing-
room upon which Mrs. Antrobus had her eye, "that that
last scene was rather disgusting."

" Oh, it was simply filthy !—though I don't know that it
was quite as bad as the first one. That woman ought to
be dragged through a horse-pond or made to stand in the
pillory !"

" I don't like Mrs. Hamley's books," said Clarissa, "and
I am not even sure that some of her terrible descriptions
are true ; but—"

" There's no ' but ' in the question ; you ought to be
ashamed of having such a shameless creature in your
house. I'm no prude ; one doesn't command a regiment
—at least, I mean one isn't a commanding officer's wife—
for so many years without knowing what scamps some men
can be. But, upon my word and honor, I believe the
worst of them would blush to behave like your innocent-
looking little friend in there ! What does she mean ?
What is she driving at with all that nastiness ? I suppose
the revolting death of the man was intended to be a sort

of retribution for his sins; but, by her own showing, the woman was every bit as bad. I have no patience with such indecent and immoral nonsense."

Clarissa smiled—not being much affronted by this indignant outburst, so characteristic of the typical British matron.

"You take the good, old-fashioned view," she remarked; "you stick to the theories which, I quite admit, have been found to work out extremely comfortably—for men. But really the other view—the modern view—is not quite such tremendous nonsense as you think. There is a good deal to be said for it."

There is indeed a great deal to be said in support of it, as most of us know, to our sorrow, and Clarissa started glibly with her too familiar thesis. However, she was not suffered to proceed very far.

"My good woman," broke in Mrs. Antrobus, "what is the use of talking like that? You may talk until you are black in the face, but you won't alter the laws of Nature. Suppose men *do* have the best of it; suppose it *is* better fun to be a man than to be a woman—what then? You can no more make yourself into a man than the frog in the fable could turn himself into an ox; and the result of these ridiculous claims on the part of women is only that they deprive themselves of the happiness which Providence meant them to enjoy. Take your own case, for instance—"

"I would rather not take my own case, please," interrupted Clarissa.

"Very likely; but I would rather take it. In fact, I am here to take it. Why are you going in for all this rubbish, which you don't really like and in which you don't really believe? Why are you making yourself notorious, as well as ridiculous, by writing articles in magazines which nobody with a grain of common-sense thinks of taking seriously? Why are you thoroughly unhappy, in spite of your money and your cheap celebrity? Simply because you have chosen to quarrel with a very good fellow, who might have been a much better fellow if you had given him half a

chance.   Don't interrupt!—I'm going to have my say out,
and then you can have yours.   I don't deny that you had
grievances; I don't deny that your husband gave you some
reason to be displeased with him out in Ceylon ; but what
I do make so bold as to assert is that you were very nearly
as much to blame as he was at the time, and that you are
punishing yourself and your little girl quite as much as you
are punishing him now.   When Guy Luttrell joined us, I
suppose everybody but you knew he had been rather wild
in his youth, and some of us may have wondered what sort
of a husband he was likely to make; but he was devoted to
you—as indeed he is still, for the matter of that—and it
only rested with you to domesticate him completely.   Instead of doing that, you must needs put on airs of superiority and make home so dull for him that he was
driven to seek amusement elsewhere."

Mrs. Antrobus paused, not because she had finished, but
to take breath, and Clarissa struck in with :

" I am sure you mean to be kind ; but you only half understand.   I could, and did, forgive my husband for many
things which he did not seem to think required forgiveness ; but there were others which made me feel that it
was impossible for us to go on living together.   Why you
should say that he is devoted to me I cannot imagine ; he
is fond of Netta, after a fashion, I know.   But if he had
cared in the least for me, he never would have behaved as
he did when—when—I dare say you have forgotten all about
it—when my little boy died."

" My dear," answered Mrs. Antrobus, her hard face soft-
ening, "you must not expect men to feel as we do about
babies ; it isn't in them.   They think it a far greater misfortune to lose a good, faithful horse or dog, whom they
knew and who knew them, than a squalling infant who is
no more to be distinguished from other infants by their
eyes than one thoroughbred is to be distinguished from
another by mine.   Besides, you won't make me believe that
you have deliberately condemned your husband to go to the
deuce for no worse offence than that."

"I don't know what you mean by 'going to the deuce,'" said Clarissa.

"You would if you saw him. That is, unless you are an even greater fool than I take you for. The long and the short of it is that the poor fellow is in despair. He *is* fond of you, whatever you may be pleased to say, and you yourself admit that he is fond of the child. Well, he sees plainly enough that he is to be banished from you both for the rest of his days, and he has nothing to do, nor anything particular to live for. Consequently, as I say, he is going to the deuce—and I'm sure I, for one, don't wonder at it!"

"It is quite impossible"—began Clarissa.

"It is no such thing!" interrupted the other. "For *him* to make advances would, I grant you, be almost impossible; it was not by his wish that this split took place, and he could hardly sue for a reconciliation which would make him a rich man as well as a happy one. But it wouldn't cost *you* very much to put your twopenny-halfpenny pride in your pocket and send for him. What's the sense of being miserable all round, when a few words would set everything right?"

Mrs. Antrobus was by no means at the end of her arguments; but at this moment Clarissa was called away, and the two ladies did not meet again that evening.

"However, I'm glad I came," thought the elder, as she descended the stairs. "I flatter myself that I have done some little good; and if that Hamley woman hasn't made her see that the sooner she shakes herself free of this gang the better, why—nobody could!"

CHAPTER XXXIX

MR. LOOSEMORE SUSTAINS A REBUFF

IT was Paul Luttrell who, in a rather peremptory manner, cut short his sister-in-law's conversation with Mrs. Antrobus.

"If you can spare me five or ten minutes before I go away, I shall be much obliged," he said ; and Clarissa acceded to his request without demur, partly because she had fallen into the habit of obeying him and partly because she was glad of an excuse for leaving Mrs. Antrobus's questions and representations unanswered.

However, she began to think that she had fallen out of the frying-pan into the fire when the Reverend Paul, after leading her into the now deserted boudoir, attacked her sternly with — "Really, Clarissa, you are exceeding all bounds ! It just comes to this, that if you want decent people to come to your house at all, you will have to revise your visiting-list."

"You mean Mrs. Hamley, I suppose," said Clarissa ; "I am sorry she shocked you; but even if some of her writing isn't in quite the best taste, she is sincere, I think, and nobody denies, I believe, that her own life is perfectly respectable."

"I know nothing about Mrs. Hamley," answered Paul, who was looking very cross ; "I did not arrive until after she had concluded her reading—which, by all accounts, I am to be congratulated upon having missed. What I was not so fortunate as to miss was the recital of one of his own poems by your friend Mr. Loosemore. You were not in the room at the time, I noticed, and perhaps it is just as well that you were not. All that I can tell you is that, if he were to come down into my parish, where, as you know, we are not exactly mealy-mouthed, and if he were to dare to read such abominations aloud to a mixed audience of men and women, the men would chuck him neck and crop into the river before he reached the middle of his performance."

Now, the truth was that some of Mr. Alfred Loosemore's poems were quite unfit for the ears of a mixed audience, and Clarissa detested them with all her heart; but she was tired of being scolded, besides being deeply dissatisfied with herself for having courted scoldings; so she only said :

"Dear me! Well, I hope for his sake, then, that he will refrain from visiting the East End. But I am afraid I can't promise to strike out the name of a great poet from those of my acquaintances because, according to you, he would not be appreciated by costermongers."

"A great fiddlestick!" returned Paul, contemptuously. "If you don't know the difference between a poet and a man who has acquired a certain facility for melodious verse-writing, you have still a great deal to learn. And indeed, Clarissa, it is a melancholy fact that you still *have* a great deal to learn—little though you may be disposed to acknowledge it."

"You have at least," observed Clarissa, with pink cheeks, "the comfort of reflecting that you never miss an opportunity of correcting my ignorance by telling me all that you know. But perhaps even that doesn't comprise the whole sum of human knowledge."

"Perhaps not; but you must allow me to give you credit for being a little less well informed than I am respecting Mr. Alfred Loosemore. Otherwise, I am convinced that you would never have permitted people to couple your name with his, as I am sorry to say they are doing."

"Oh, is that it?" said Clarissa, who was now thoroughly angry; "I thought it was only his poem that you objected to. Well, the next time you hear my name coupled with Mr. Loosemore's, you can say that I consider it a great

honor to be one of his friends.   As we have been out of
town, I haven't met him for a long time ; but I hope to see
much more of him, now that we have returned."

"You must excuse me telling you that you are a very
silly woman," said the Reverend Paul, severely.

"Must I ? I confess I don't quite see why. I should be
sorry to have to remove your name from the visiting-list in
which you take such a kindly interest ; but, really, if you
claim the privilege of insulting me as often as you please, I
shall begin to doubt whether I had not better begin the
work of revision with you."

Paul was given to being dictatorial, and he had been
considerably ruffled ; but he was not so foolish as to lose
his temper.

"Come, Clarissa," said he, "we mustn't quarrel, whatever happens. I apologize for calling you silly, though I
can't say that I have changed my opinion yet. I shall
change it, and admit as much very gladly, when you drop
that fellow; and I am sure you would drop him if you
really understood what he is. That poem of his was
atrocious, and his having the face to recite it in your house
was more atrocious still, in my opinion ; but I ought to
have remembered that you didn't hear it. Please forgive
me if I spoke more rudely than I had any right to do."

Clarissa accepted the olive-branch. After all, she was
fond of her brother-in-law, and had no wish to fall out with
him. Moreover, she was not, in the depths of her heart,
very far from concurring in his estimate of the poet. But
friendly relations became endangered once more when Paul
proceeded to deliver what he meant to be a very consider-
ately worded little lecture upon the perils inseparable from
her position. Some ladies might, he said, if their tastes inclined them that way, run the risk of receiving persons of
evil reputation ; but not a lady so young and so unfortunately deprived of any natural protector as she. To despise
scandal and gossip was all very well ; but it was neither
wise nor right to give the scandalmongers an excuse, and
what could any woman expect who showed herself in the

Park with Mr. Alfred Loosemore lolling beside her in her carriage ?

"Ah," said Clarissa, drawing her brows together, "you have been talking with Guy, I see."

"Well, yes, I have been talking with him once or twice lately; although it must be several weeks, I think, since he last mentioned—oh, here the man comes! I had better be off, or I shall be telling him what I think of him before I can stop myself. I was going to say a word or two to you about Guy; but that will keep. Shall I find you at home if I call, some day soon, between five and six o'clock ?"

"Yes, I dare say you will," answered Clarissa, looking more resigned than delighted. Was he, too, going to preach to her that her duty was to set aside all her own plans and inclinations, in order that Guy might be saved from himself ?

Mr. Alfred Loosemore advanced with a slow step and an unctuous smile, to say what a charming evening he had spent and to take leave of his hostess. Clarissa always hated shaking hands with him, and was always glad if she happened to have a glove on when that form of salutation was gone through. At that particular moment she was, perhaps, less disposed than usual to pardon his little peculiarities ; for she pulled her hand away from him, after he had held it for some seconds, and turned to say good-bye to somebody else before he had half finished what he had to say.

Presently she saw his broad back and his wiry head of hair disappearing through the doorway, while a few words of the bland gallantries which he was addressing to the lady at his elbow were wafted to her ears. "I think," she remembered Madeline saying to her once, "that he is a perfect pig !" Well, one could understand that some people might view him in that unflattering light, and certainly there were times when he almost looked as if he deserved to be so viewed. At any rate, it was permissible to be angry with him for having displayed such a conspicuous lack of good taste as he appeared to have done that evening. In other words, Clarissa was angry with him as well as with several other people, including herself, and under such circumstances it is always a comfort to be provided with a specific cause for complaint against somebody.

Consequently, she was not altogether displeased when, late on the ensuing afternoon, Mr. Alfred Loosemore was ushered into her presence. She did not want to see him; she wanted to go and sit in the nursery with Netta, who had been rather ailing and fretful since their return to London, and whom she had only just left, in order to write a few necessary letters. Still, since he had come, she would take that opportunity, she thought, of administering the rebuke which he had earned. So he had no sooner made himself quite comfortable in a very low easy-chair than she began:

"I was not in the room when you were so kind as to read one of your poems aloud last night, Mr. Loosemore; but I am afraid, from what I heard afterwards, that you did not make a very happy choice. I hope, if you ever honor me in that way again, you will be a little bit more careful."

"Were they shocked?" asked the poet, with languid amusement. "How nice of them! One so seldom gets the chance of shocking anybody nowadays—which is a distinct loss, you know."

"Is it?" said Clarissa, curtly. "Well, I suppose there will be no great difficulty about shocking people of average refinement so long as the highways and byways of every large town remain what they are now. I should have thought that you aimed at something a little higher and a little less easy of accomplishment than that."

"My dear Lady Luttrell, what have I done that you should accuse me of cherishing lofty ideals? Have I ever pretended to be anything but 'the idle singer of an empty day'?—or should it be the empty singer of an idle day? I am ready to accept either adjective, because both are so entirely applicable to me; all I do deprecate is an unmerited charge of seriousness."

"If you really do not believe in what you affect to be-

lieve, I am sorry for it," said Clarissa, coldly. "I, at all
events, am quite serious."

"Of course you are; and nothing could be more becoming to you. I often wish," continued Mr. Loosemore,
throwing back his head meditatively—"might I light a
cigarette? Thanks so much!—I often wish that I could
get some capable artist to paint you, as you stand upon the
platform, with those wonderful, short-sighted eyes of yours
gazing far away above the heads of the nonentities who are
listening to you, and as you declaim your delicious paradoxes with all the air of an inspired prophetess. I used to
dabble in that form of art myself once upon a time—there
are so few forms of art in which I have not dabbled! But
I fear that my neglected capacities would be hardly equal
to doing you justice. They considered me quite a promising pupil in Paris, I remember; still—"

"Did they?" interrupted Clarissa, who was less anxious
to be entertained with Mr. Loosemore's reminiscences than
to elicit from him an explanation of his remarks respecting
herself. "But what do you mean when you say that I declaim paradoxes?"

"Ah, now I have got myself into trouble! It is so terrible to be asked what one means!—and one never is asked
unless one is so incautious as to stray from the safe path of
obscurity. But, when you come to think of it, are we not
all paradoxes? Is not life itself paradoxical?—and would
it be half as delightful as it is if it were not?"

"I don't think that life for the majority of the people is
at all delightful, and I think that you are talking very
great nonsense," returned Clarissa, with some asperity.

"How charming you look when you are angry!" exclaimed the poet, lazily. "It is inexcusable of me to say
things that make you angry; yet"—he waved his plump
hand towards her, as she sat upright in her chair, frowning at
him—"who could deny that there is my sufficient excuse!"

Now, all this was extremely impertinent, and Clarissa
was determined to let him see that she thought so. The
personal compliments with which he had been so good as to

favor her she preferred to ignore—for, after all, poets are not quite like other men, and it might appear rather silly and prudish to object to his putting his admiration into words ; but she desired to be informed—yes or no—whether he was or was not in sympathy with the "movement" which she and others had so much at heart. If not, she was sure that she might speak for her friends as well as herself in saying that they would rather dispense with his presence at future meetings.

"And indeed," she was provoked into adding (for the broad smile with which this announcement was received was enough to provoke anybody), "I do not quite understand what, in that case, can be the object or meaning of your visits to me."

It was a positive fact that she did not understand ; but to expect Mr. Alfred Loosemore to believe that would have been much the same thing as expecting him to believe that he himself did not understand women—which would have been palpably absurd. He at once made the reply for which he considered that he had been virtually asked ; and made it in terms so unambiguous, accompanied by gestures so alarming, that for one moment he was in imminent danger of having his face slapped.

Happily, Clarissa regained control over her scattered senses in time to avoid so undignified a method of retaliation as that ; but in the matter of verbal castigation she did her best to give this impertinent offender his due. Impenitent he was, and remained, after she had said all that she had to say. Worse than that, he remained incredulous. Very likely it was not in the man's nature to conceive that he had been welcomed and made much of in Cadogan Gardens merely because the mistress of that establishment was the victim of a fixed idea, and because— much more in joke than in earnest—he had ranged himself among the supporters of that idea. Very likely, also, experience had taught him that feminine rebukes should not be accepted too literally. So he rushed light-heartedly upon his own destruction.

"You make me feel like a very naughty boy indeed," he declared; "but do I really deserve to be whipped or put in a corner? Can I help loving you? And, since I do love you, isn't it my duty, as well as my right, to say so? If that is not the meaning of the doctrine that you preach, then I have been sitting humbly and admiringly at your feet all this long time under a total misapprehension."

"You most certainly have," returned Clarissa, "if you imagine that I have ever preached the doctrine that it can be any man's right or duty to speak of love to a married woman."

"A married woman? — *allons donc!* Surely, if you meant to tell us anything at all, you meant us to understand that you were not that! I have always thought that your strongest argument against the institution of marriage—an argument in which I entirely agree—was that it prohibits, or professes to prohibit, subsequent *affaires de cœur.* We are seekers after truth, are we not?—and the truth quite evidently is that the heart of neither man nor woman can be restrained from obeying the voice of nature by a legal or a religious ceremony. Even if you and I had met some years ago, and if we had been man and wife at the present moment—"

"That will do," exclaimed Clarissa, exasperated beyond endurance; "what I have said about marriage may have been misunderstood by some people; I have expressed myself badly and have conveyed false impressions, no doubt. But I really cannot plead guilty to having ever said or done anything to justify the extraordinary conclusion at which you appear to have arrived. I assure you that never—never by any possibility!—could we have been man and wife. The bare idea of my falling in love with *you*—or indeed of any woman's falling in love with you—strikes me as being almost too ludicrous to be revolting!"

This very unequivocal statement had the effect of bringing conviction home to the soul of the poet. He rose, with such grace and dignity as he could command under rather trying circumstances, and prepared to take his departure.

"You are—pardon me!—a little bit inconsistent and just a little bit absurd, dear Lady Luttrell," said he. "You want, I gather, to run with the hare and hunt with the hounds—which is always a rather difficult performance to carry through successfully. Of course I apologize for having, as it seems, so completely mistaken the nature of your sentiments ; but I really do not think that I owe any apology to Sir Guy Luttrell, or to you, Sir Guy Luttrell's nominal wife. And I am sure you will agree with me that this interview had better be regarded as confidential."

"I certainly do not feel inclined to talk about it," answered Clarissa. And then, enlightened by a look of suppressed anxiety which she detected in Mr. Loosemore's eyes, "Oh, I shall not request my husband to break your bones, if that is what you mean," she added, with a scornful laugh.

But when her visitor had left her, Clarissa could not help thinking how Guy would have enjoyed lifting the poor creature up with one of his strong arms while he laid a hunting-crop across his back with the other. If Guy were only different in some respects from what he, unhappily, was! If it were only true, as Mrs. Antrobus had ridiculously asserted, that he was still devoted to her ! At certain moments—when one is quite alone and when it cannot signify—one is apt to indulge in misgivings as to the wisdom of a course to which one is absolutely committed, and even to think of those by whom one has been injured with a leniency and an affection which it would be both foolish and dangerous to display before witnesses. Clarissa, for the time being, was feeling a little out of conceit, if not with the "movement," at least with the movers; while the unpleasant experience through which she had just passed made her feel, not unnaturally, that, as matters now stand, it is a hard thing for a solitary woman to fight her own battles. And everybody was against her !—

Uncle Tom, Paul, Mrs. Antrobus—was it, after all, worth while to contend against these for the sake of Mrs. Hamleys and Alfred Loosemores? If Guy had chanced to walk into the room at that critical juncture, there is no saying what might not have happened.

But it was not Guy who startled Clarissa out of a despondent brown-study; it was Netta's nurse; and the woman's face, as well as her voice, displayed a good deal of uneasiness.

"If you please, my lady," said she, "would you come and see Miss Netta. She do complain so of her head and her throat, and she's that feverish I'm almost afraid she must be sickening for something."

CHAPTER XL

PALLID FEAR

IT is all very well to hold advanced theories respecting the equality or inequality of the sexes, and to assert that if there be any difference between the two, it is only such as has been produced by the age-long tyranny of the one over the other; but Nature always claims the last word, and a woman whose child is sick or in danger seldom fails to prove that Nature had her reasons for adopting a system which may not be wholly exempt from drawbacks.

Clarissa, forgetting all about the subjects with which she had been so preoccupied, rushed up to the nursery, three steps at a time, and was met, when she opened the door, by one of the saddest sounds in the world—the sound of a child's low, irrepressible sobbing. Netta was not much given to tears; she had always been taught that such displays of emotion were unworthy and disgraceful; but the pain in her head and her throat was so great that she had been unable to restrain herself, and now, on her mother's appearance, she hastened to offer a feeble little apology.

"I can't stop them, mother; they *will* come!" she said, pointing ruefully to the heavy drops which trembled upon her eyelashes.

"What is it, my darling?" asked Clarissa, taking the child upon her knee.

But that was just what neither Netta nor anybody else present could tell. "Oh, I'm so bad!—I'm so bad!" was all that the small sufferer could moan, as she nestled down, with her head upon her mother's shoulder.

The nursery governess stood looking on sympathetically.

She was a well-meaning young woman ; but she happened to be a fool, and that was why she said, with the bland precision of utterance which she affected :

"To *me* this looks very like the beginning of enteric fever or diphtheria. I have been thinking so all day, and only just now I was saying to myself, 'How Netta reminds me of poor dear Archie just before his last illness !' I had a poor little brother who died of diphtheria two years ago, and my dear mother succumbed to typhoid. So, you see, I am not altogether without experience of these things, Lady Luttrell."

"If there is any danger of an infectious disease, you had better go away at once, Miss Stevens," answered Clarissa, subduing a strong inclination to box the woman's ears. "Nurse and I can do all that is necessary until the doctor comes."

But of course Netta wanted to know what diphtheria was and whether people always died of it ; so that while she was being put to bed, her nurse had some little trouble in reassuring her.

"Bless your 'eart, no, my dear ! 'Tis nothing but a feverish cold, I expect, and whatever 'tis, we'll soon get you well again. Now, don't you fret, but lay down, like a good girl, and see if you can't get off to sleep, while me and your ma sends William to fetch the doctor."

Netta laid her aching head down upon the pillow, as she was bid : probably she understood quite well why the nurse and her mother left the room for a moment. But nurse had no answer to give to the eager questions addressed to her by her mistress's eyes.

"I really couldn't say, my lady—not if you was to offer me a thousand pounds ! It might be measles or chicken-pox or one of a number of things—which all children has to go through them. But I don't see no call to be uneasy yet; and as for that there Miss Stevens, she don't set foot in Miss Netta's room again, not while *I'm* there to drive her back—that she may depend !"

The nurse and the nursery governess had that love for

26

one another which commonly subsists between such func-
tionaries.

Clarissa was partially comforted for the time; yet the
doctor, when he arrived, could not or would not allay her
apprehensions. It was quite impossible, he declared, on
being begged at least to say that there was no risk of
typhoid or diphtheria, to pronounce an opinion upon the
case in its present stage. In all probability decisive symptoms would show themselves by the following morning,
when he would return. For the moment, there really was
not much to be done; though he would write a prescrip-
tion which, he hoped, might relieve the child's head a little.
Then he asked several questions as to where his patient
had been lately, nodded rather gravely when he was informed that she had been away from home, and so left
Clarissa to face as best she might some twelve or fourteen
hours of agonized suspense.

She sat up in the nursery all through that long night,
refusing to be relieved in her watch, and when she was not
reading fairy tales or talking to the child, who dozed fit-
fully but did not obtain much rest, she suffered in advance every horror that could be in store for her. Typhoid,
contracted at Hastings—that, she was sure, would prove
to be Netta's malady, and that it would terminate fatally
seemed to her, in those dark hours, to be a foregone conclusion. Clarissa had emancipated herself from the trammels of
outworn creeds; but this did not preserve her from a shuddering dread lest the impending calamity should fall upon
her as a punishment for having left her child to the care of
servants, while she herself was devoting her time and attention to the improvement of humanity at large. What with
fear and what with self-reproach, she had made a sorry
spectacle of herself by the time that the doctor reappeared
in the morning, and he looked at her with surprise and
disapprobation when he heard that she had not been to
bed at all.

"This won't do, Lady Luttrell," said he, drawing her
aside, after he had made an examination of his patient;

"you must take ordinary precautions, unless you wish to be the next victim; and if you have never had scarlet-fever—"

"Oh, is it only scarlet-fever? How thankful I am!" exclaimed Clarissa. "I felt certain that it must be something worse!"

"Well, scarlet-fever is bad enough to satisfy most people," observed the doctor, smiling; "but, so far as one can judge at present, your little girl has everything in her favor. Only, if you insist upon helping to nurse her, as I suppose you will, you must obey orders, please; and the first order I have to give you is to keep yourself in as healthy a state as you possibly can."

Two days later, when the fever was running its course without complications, but had not reached its height, a card was brought to Clarissa, who had secluded herself from the rest of the household behind a barrier of sheets impregnated with disinfectants, and she was informed that the gentleman who had sent it up wished particularly to speak to her, if only for a few minutes. She was off duty just then, the trained nurse who had been engaged having taken her place; so she advanced to the top of the staircase and called down to Paul Luttrell, who was standing in the hall:

"Netta is going on quite well; but she can't turn the corner for another three or four days, I believe. I mustn't come any nearer to you, for I am full of the germs of scarlet-fever."

"Oh no, you aren't," returned Paul, who had come half-way up the stairs to meet her; "you won't have any germs about you yet awhile. And if you had, I shouldn't be alarmed; I am constantly visiting scarlet-fever patients."

With a little persuasion, she was induced to descend and to accompany him into the drawing-room, where he sat down, remarking that he had had a rather long walk.

"And you promised to grant me an interview some day soon, if you remember," he added, smiling.

"Oh yes," answered Clarissa; "but that was before

this trouble came upon me. Nothing else seems to be of
the slightest consequence now. If you were going to
repeat the warnings that you gave me about Mr. Loosemore, you needn't. I have found out that he is not a
gentleman, and I shall not receive him any more. I hope
you consider that satisfactory."

"Quite satisfactory, so far as it goes," answered Paul.
"I wish, for your sake, that you had made the discovery
a little sooner; but that is a detail. The real object of my
visit—"

"Oh, your real object wasn't to inquire for Netta,
then?" she interjected, sharply.

"Of course I wanted to hear how Netta was; and, no
doubt, I could have heard from the servants, without disturbing you. But there is just one thing, perhaps, which
ought to take precedence even of a mother's duty to her
child, and that is—"

"Oh, a wife's duty to her husband, I suppose," interrupted Clarissa, impatiently. "But must I really be
worried with all this now? It is so useless, and I am so
very tired of it! Haven't I listened meekly again and
again to everybody who has thought fit to lecture me?—
and hasn't everything that could be said upon the subject
been said?"

"I don't know," answered Paul: "but I should think
not. At all events, I have something to say to you now
which I haven't said before. I am going, for the first
time, to appeal to your pity and to—what shall I say?—
your better feeling. You have discarded, I believe—or
you pretend to have discarded—the religion which seems
to me essential and indispensable; but you must have
filled its vacant place with some other more or less vague
form of religion, and you will probably agree with me that
no form of religion can be worth much which does not
involve self-abnegation."

"I know so well what is coming!" sighed Clarissa.
"Guy is falling into bad habits—as if idle men didn't always fall into bad habits!—and it is my business to save

him from himself; isn't that it? But why am I to be singled out for this praiseworthy work? Was I so brilliantly successful at a time when I might have been supposed to have some little influence over him? Were his habits so exemplary in those days? I really cannot see why my pity or my better feeling should be invoked on such grounds. What I am perfectly conscious of is that he has been a heavy loser in point of money by our separation; but that is through his choice, not mine. I have always been, and I always shall be, ready and willing to surrender the half of what I possess to him."

"And you must be aware that he will never be ready or willing to accept a sixpence from you. So far, his pride is absolutely right and justifiable, I think. As regards other matters, I don't say—his conduct may not have been exemplary, and he may owe it to you to ask your pardon. But, for obvious reasons, it would be a harder trial to his pride to make the first advance than it could be to yours. The truth, I firmly believe, is that pride, and nothing else, is keeping you two apart. You aren't happy, and by this time you have both found out that you can't be happy, apart; and just see the results of your pleasing experiment! You, for the lack of something better to do, are making your house the meeting-place of a set of grotesque libertines, while he—"

"Well," said Clarissa, as the orator paused; "what is he doing?"

"He is taking to drink, if you wish to have the fact plainly stated. What I have seen on more than one occasion lately makes it impossible for me to doubt that that is what he is doing—and indeed he scarcely denies it."

"I am afraid," said Clarissa, coldly, "that I have neither the skill nor the experience which is required for the reform of confirmed inebriates."

"Now, Clarissa, don't take up that tone with me, whose trade it is to go to and fro from week's end to week's end among men and women who have brought trouble upon themselves through their sins and their follies. I am neither to be snubbed nor deceived by such a very indifferent actress as you are. Guy is not a confirmed inebriate; but he will end by drinking himself to death, all the same; and if he does, you—and you alone—will be to blame for it. He is thoroughly miserable, and I suspect that he is thoroughly penitent into the bargain; but he is much too proud to come to you and say so, and I think you ought to understand how difficult it would be for him to do that. That is why I appealed to your pity. Now I have obeyed my conscience, and you must act as you please. Only one thing I am sure you will admit: if he wishes it, he has a right to see Netta."

"But not now!" exclaimed Clarissa; "you forget the risk of infection. Why, I should not dream of allowing him to enter her room, even if he were living in the house."

Paul laughed: Clarissa's words, as well as something which he saw in her face, had told him as much as he wanted to know.

"Whatever shortcomings may be laid to Guy's charge," he remarked, "cowardice, I believe, has never been numbered among them. It is not fear of infection that is likely to keep him out of his daughter's room when he hears that she is ill. He hasn't heard yet, I believe."

"Then I do hope," said Clarissa, earnestly, "that he will not be told. Why should he be told? Of course, if there should be any"—she paused, and then brought out the word with an effort—"any danger, I would let him know. Yes, if that comes—but I pray and believe that it won't—I promise you that I will send for him at once."

And that, upon subsequent reflection, seemed to her to be as much as any reasonable being could expect her to promise. She had been moved both by what Paul and by what Mrs. Antrobus had said; she was sorry for Guy, and half, though only half, inclined to believe their assertions respecting him; moreover, several things had worked together of late to shake her confidence in herself. But for that very reason she hastened to don a triple armor of obstinacy. She was resolved not to be vanquished by her emotions—those terrible emotions, against which she had so often made a point of cautioning others of her sex, and to which, in her opinion, the subordination of women was so largely due !

Nevertheless, it was not so easy to keep her emotions under proper control during the trying days which followed. Netta's was a somewhat sharp attack of the fever; the child's mind often wandered, and at such moments she would keep calling for her father in piteous, forlorn accents to which nobody could listen quite unmoved. To be sure, she never asked for him when she was in full possession of her senses; but that was almost worse; because there were occasional mute interrogations in her eyes, and because she had evidently realized that mention of him would not be welcome. Meanwhile, Clarissa was informed that Sir Guy called twice every day to inquire how his daughter was, although he sent no message and made no attempt to enter the house. It became necessary to sit down very calmly and dispassionately and call to mind indisputable facts, such as Guy's conduct in Ceylon, his ostentatious indifference respecting his wife's proceedings in London, his total lack of sympathy with the crusade to which she had committed herself. What could be more foolish or more futile than to consent to a patched-up reconciliation which, in the nature of things, must result in a second and probably more serious breach ? Besides, he had not asked to be allowed to see Netta, and certainly it would not be safe for him to do so. Perhaps, in her heart of hearts, she was a little displeased with him for omitting to make a request which she had resolved not to grant, while she was decidedly displeased with Paul for having told him of the child's illness. Under the circumstances, it would have been more sensible, as well as more considerate, she thought, to say nothing.

Possibly it would; but any censure that may have been due to want of sense and consideration should have fallen upon Mr. Dent, who had been Guy's actual informant, and who insisted very strongly upon the propriety of pushing investigations no further than the doorstep.

"You could not be of the slightest use," the old gentleman urged, "and I am afraid you might be a good deal in the way. I suppose I am at least as nervous and as anxious as you are; but, since it isn't in our power to help Clarissa, the next best thing for us to do is to refrain from bothering her."

The truth was that Mr. Dent did not wish Guy to brave the danger of infection. Netta, he trusted, would shake off the malady, as children, when they are taken every care of, generally do, and would be none the worse for it; Clarissa, too, must take her chance: there was no help for that. But there would be only a poor chance, he suspected, for a man of Guy's age and in Guy's state of health. Mr. Dent, who saw many people every day and belonged to several clubs, knew very well what was wrong with Sir Guy Luttrell's health, and was not a little distressed by the knowledge; yet he wisely abstained from remonstrances. He knew other things besides; he knew, for instance (who relates such things? and through what devious channels do they end by reaching the ears of all whom they concern?) that Mrs. Antrobus had given Clarissa a well-deserved scolding, and that Clarissa had inflicted an equally well-deserved sentence of dismissal upon Mr. Alfred Loosemore. Consequently, he saw land, and held silently on his course, as he had done from the first, like the prudent old person that he was.

"When Netta gets well," he told Guy, "she will have to be taken away somewhere for change of air; but I should think they would be back in London by the beginning of the summer, and then you will be able to see her again. I can arrange meetings between you at my house, you know, as I did before; for you naturally won't care to call at her mother's house."

"How do I know that I shall ever see her again?" the younger man asked, rather hoarsely. "How do I know that she is going to get well? It is all very fine for you,

Mr. Dent; you talk at your ease; you have never had children of your own, and you don't understand. But this is trying me rather too highly, I can tell you; I don't promise that I shall be able to stand it much longer."

"My dear fellow, what would you have? You don't, of course, propose to force your way into Clarissa's house now; and afterwards—well, it is unfortunate that her house doesn't happen to be your house; still, such is the fact: and if she chooses to shut her door in your face, I don't quite see what you can do, except make occasional arrangements to meet your daughter elsewhere."

This was a little cruel of Mr. Dent; but his motives have been mentioned, and he was just as well aware as Paul was that his apparently easy-going companion was an intensely proud man. In any case, Guy's forbearance was not to be put to the test much longer; for one evening, when he presented himself as usual in Cadogan Gardens, the butler, instead of answering his question, said:

"Would you please to step in, sir; her ladyship would like to speak to you."

"Is anything the matter?" asked Guy, apprehensively. "Is Miss Netta worse?"

The man looked down. "I believe the doctor don't speak quite so hopefully to-day, sir," he replied.

So Guy, with blanched cheeks and a tremor of the limbs which he could not subdue, crossed the threshold, prepared for the very worst.

CHAPTER XLI

CLARISSA LOWERS HER COLORS

THE room on the ground-floor into which Guy was shown was untenanted; so that he had time to take himself in hand and recover at least some outward show of composure. But the anxiety which was gnawing at his heart made every moment that he was kept waiting seem like an eternity to him, and he paced impatiently to and fro, muttering that if somebody did not come presently, he would ring the bell. Upon a table which he passed and repassed during his restless march lay a heap of newspapers, pamphlets, and magazines. He picked up one of the latter and glanced at the list of contents on its cover. "The Political Disabilities of Women, by Lady Luttrell," he read. He threw it down, thus exposing to view a second bill of fare—"The Law of Divorce: What it is, and what it ought to be. By Lady Luttrell." He was, of course, perfectly unreasonable and absurd; but he felt as if Clarissa had been leaving her child to die while she shouted out to the world her crude notions as to subjects which nothing compelled her to touch. Good heavens! what had mothers to do with politics, or wives who conducted themselves decently with divorce? For the matter of that, by what right was he, Netta's father, detained there as a humble suppliant until such time as it should please his wife to grant him an audience?

Guy was so constituted that pain of any kind always made him angry; and it was an angry, threatening face that he turned towards his wife's drawn and haggard one when she appeared in the doorway. But he did not speak, because, to tell the truth, he was so much afraid of what she might be going to say that his question stuck in his throat. What she did say was:

"I promised Paul that I would send for you if—if there was any change for the worse, and—"

"I don't know anything about your promises to Paul," interrupted Guy, roughly, "and I don't care what they were. What about the child? Do you mean that she is not going to get over this?"

"We can't tell," Clarissa answered. "The crisis is over; but she does not seem to have rallied as we hoped that she would, and yesterday I could see that the doctor was not satisfied. So this morning I asked him whether there was any danger, and he said there was. And he thought it would be better for you to be within reach. That is all I know," Clarissa concluded, raising her heavy-lidded eyes for a moment.

She looked so crushed and so despairing that his heart went out to her; but it was against his nature to sympathize with despair, and besides, as has been said, he was, for the time being, a wrathful man.

"Danger?" he repeated, sharply; "what sort of danger? Are you doing anything?—have you taken any steps to obtain a second opinion? You don't propose to sit still with your hands before you, I presume, and wait idly for the end to come."

Clarissa glanced at him with a sort of dull wonder. She was standing by the window and twisting the blind-cord between her long, slim fingers.

"We can easily have a consultation, if you wish," she said; "but it will do no good. There is nothing the matter, except that Netta's strength is exhausted: her heart is weak, they say. The doctor does not think it at all likely that there will be an immediate change, one way or the other; only—"

"Only she might sink at any moment. Is that it?"

Clarissa made a sign of assent, and gazed out with lustreless eyes at the white road, where a high wind was rais-

ing swirling clouds of dust. It was evident that she had
abandoned all hope; evident also that neither her husband's presence nor any other external circumstance had
power to rouse her from her lethargy. After a minute of
silence, Guy said :

"I suppose I can go up to her room ?"

"Yes; I will take you up there. She sleeps a great
deal now—it is not a refreshing sleep, though, the nurse
says—but when she is awake she always asks for you. She
is really anxious to see you now, I think ; when she was
delirious, one did not pay so much attention to what she
said, of course."

"She *has* been asking for me all this time, then ?" exclaimed Guy, an expression coming over his face which
might have reminded certain dead-and-gone politicians of
what his father had looked like when, about a quarter of a
century back, the Tories had had reason to suspect their
leader of having betrayed them. "I might have known
it ! And you did not consider it your duty to say a word
to me ?"

Clarissa turned away from the window and sighed wearily. She was in no condition to quarrel or to defend herself against attack ; but she answered, "There was the risk
of infection to be thought of, and the risk still remains.
However, as Paul said, that will scarcely deter you."

Guy responded only by a grunt, and moved towards the
door, which he held open for her. Thus, without ex-
changing another word, they mounted the staircase, Clarissa leading the way, and passed through the swing-door
which separated the schoolroom and the nurseries from
the rest of the house. Then Clarissa pushed aside a sheet
saturated with carbolic acid, looked over her shoulder to
beckon to Guy, and the next instant he was standing beside Netta's bed.

The child was only half awake, and blinked at him,
knitting her brows, without recognizing him. Her cheeks
had fallen in, and there was no vestige of color in them ;
yet she looked so much less ill than he had expected that

he could not help ejaculating, "Come! this isn't such a shocking bad job, after all. We'll beat the doctors yet!"

At the sound of his voice Netta broke into a glad little cry. "Oh, father, I did want you so! Why didn't you come before?"

She held out her small, wasted hands, and Guy was stooping over to kiss her when a black arm, adorned with a broad linen cuff, was thrust before his face, while at the same time his coat-tails were violently jerked from behind.

"No, if you please, sir," said the sick-nurse, who was the owner of the arm, decidedly; "by the doctor's orders, there must be nothing of that sort. I'll put a chair for you on the other side of the bed, where you can sit; but we would rather you didn't bend over it more than you can help."

Well, if there was to be no kissing, it was at least permitted to the father and daughter to remain hand in hand while they embarked upon a prolonged, desultory conversation, during which both Clarissa and the nurse withdrew. They had a hundred things to say to one another; but it was Guy who did most of the talking. After the first excitement of seeing him passed off, and she had given him a description of her holiday at Hastings ("But that was ever so long ago, before I was ill," she said), Netta fell back upon her pillows and her eyelids closed involuntarily. She was not asleep, and she squeezed his fingers every now and then to let him know that she was listening; but the effort of articulation was evidently too much for her. So he remained there, chatting cheerily about any subject that came into his head and planning all manner of expeditions for the good time coming, when she should be strong enough to get about again, until at length her grasp relaxed and her breathing became more slow and regular. Then he rose and stole on tiptoe into the adjoining room, where he found the nurse alone.

"I have persuaded her ladyship to go and lie down until the doctor comes," the woman said. "She really ought to take more rest."

"I dare say she ought," answered Guy. "Now, tell me honestly, please—because I'd rather ask a nurse than a doctor for an honest opinion any day—what do you think of this case?"

"Well, sir," answered the nurse, who was a stout, pleasant-looking woman, approaching middle age, "I can't say I think any too well of it; though I've seen many a worse one recover. So long as she can go on taking nourishment we needn't feel much alarm; but there's great weakness you see—very great weakness."

"People don't die of weakness, unless they're allowed to die, "Guy declared, resolutely. "Look here—on the day that my little girl is pronounced out of danger you shall have a check for £100."

The nurse smiled. "I shouldn't be allowed to take that, sir," she replied; "but you may depend upon me to do all that can be done, without any bribe. Oh, there's no offence; I know how you feel, and it's true enough that money has saved life before now. But you're wrong in thinking that people don't die of weakness; that's just what they do die of, a great many of them."

"Well, at all events Netta shall not die of it," was Guy's confident rejoinder.

He did not mean to leave the house without having seen the doctor; so, while Netta slept, he chatted to the nurse, with whom he soon established friendly relations, and who took the liberty of giving him some plain-spoken advice as to the management of his health, with which her experienced eyes told her that he had been trifling. Guy Luttrell was one of those grown-up naughty boys to whom sick-nurses take instinctively, recognizing in them predestined as well as submissive patients.

After a time Clarissa reappeared, accompanied by the doctor, and, as soon as the visit of inspection was at an end, Guy followed the latter down-stairs.

"Better; certainly a little better since the morning," was the satisfactory verdict returned; "perhaps seeing you has done her good. But I must warn you, Sir Guy, that for a long time after she recovers, you and Lady Luttrell will have to be very careful of her."

"You may be sure that she shall be taken care of, if only you undertake that she shall recover."

"My dear sir, I should as soon think of undertaking to produce rain or fine weather. There is, and there must be for some time to come, cause for grave anxiety; but hope never did anybody any harm, and it is better to be oversanguine, as you evidently are, than to be needlessly despondent, as I fear that Lady Luttrell is."

From that day forth Guy presented himself every morning in Cadogan Gardens and, without let or hinderance, took what it pleased him to regard as his turn of duty in the sick-room. The nurse had solemnly promised to despatch a messenger for him instantly, in the event of any emergency arising, Netta always greeted him with joy, and by Clarissa his presence was tolerated, if not precisely welcomed. His relations with his wife, indeed, were but little affected, one way or the other, by these daily visits of his to her house. As soon as Guy put his nose in at the door Clarissa walked out of it; they seldom exchanged so much as a word; nor was the intruder, for his part, at all dissatisfied with an arrangement which conceded to him all that he demanded. One day, however, just as he was about to leave the house, he was informed by the butler that her ladyship wished to speak to him for a moment, and, on obeying the summons, he found her seated at her writing-table.

"Well," he said cheerfully—for he was in much better temper by this time than on the occasion of their last interview—"I believe it is going to be a case of *quittes pour la peur*, after all. I think, and so does the nurse, that Netta is beginning to put on flesh, and I am sure she is less apathetic than she was."

Clarissa sighed heavily. "You may be right," she answered; "but I dare not hope. I see no real improvement, and even if there were an apparent improvement one would not feel safe."

" Come, Clarissa," said her husband, not unkindly, "you mustn't make up your mind to look at the dark side of things. Supposing that the worst happens—but it isn't going to happen!—we shall have time enough to grieve after we are beaten : for the present, what we have to do is to put our heart into our work and show a brave face. That will be best for our patient as well as for our-selves."

" Yes, I know," answered Clarissa, with a wan smile, " and I do try to look as if I believed what I can't believe; but I see little things which I suppose you don't notice, and I am certain that the doctor—"

She had to break off and press her fingers firmly upon her quivering lips. Only a very hard-hearted man—and Guy's heart was as soft as need be—could have held out against the wish to comfort her, as she sat there, looking so utterly miserable and forlorn, with dark circles under her eyes and horizontal lines of distress upon her forehead.

"My dear girl," he said, gently, "you are worn out and ill; that is why you are determined to meet trouble half-way. As for the doctor, if you don't trust him, we'll call in another, or two others. I think myself that it would be more satisfactory to have a consultation."

She shook her head. "Oh no ; it isn't that. All the doctors in London could tell us no more than we know; and I am not a bit ill—only I feel somehow as if a decree had been pronounced against which it is useless to rebel. But I didn't send for you to talk in a way which you must think very silly. What I wanted to tell you—I thought perhaps I ought to tell you—was that I am sorry I was so rude when you came here, one afternoon in the winter, and objected to my being so much with Mr. Loosemore. At the time it seemed to me impertinent of you to interfere, and I said I liked and admired the man—which was not quite true. Anyhow, I neither like nor admire him now, and our acquaintance, I hope, is at an end."

"I was sure you would find the fellow out sooner or later," observed Guy, composedly. "If you would like me to dust his jacket for him, I'll find an opportunity of doing it without creating any public disturbance."

For one moment Clarissa's countenance cleared; she broke out into an irrepressible laugh; and domestic differences might have been composed there and then had Guy known how to profit by the occasion. But he was quite serious; he saw nothing to laugh at, and presently Clarissa, too, became once more serious and sad.

"Of course I don't want you to assault Mr. Loosemore," she said; "he wouldn't be in the least worth assaulting, even if he deserved it. That is all: don't let me keep you any longer. I only thought that, as I had been in the wrong, it was my duty to apologize."

She had a queer motive for apologizing, the nature of which he could scarcely be expected to guess at the time, but which was to be revealed to him later. He went away a little puzzled and a little amused, wondering whether she imagined that he was jealous of the discomfited Loosemore, and why she should care if he were. If he was not jealous, it must be owned that Clarissa was; and that was one of her reasons for always quitting Netta's room the moment that he entered it. The child was happier alone with her father, she thought—and what mother could make such an admission to herself without a pang? But Clarissa behaved very well about it. It may be that she was too unhappy to behave badly, and that the approval of Paul, who took it for granted that she had made friends with her legitimate lord and master, had no more power to vex her than the uneasy protests of Mr. Dent, who was haunted by a presentiment that Guy would catch the fever and succumb.

Upon the principle that what is worth nothing never comes to harm, Guy considered himself pretty safe from that risk; still, for the sake of his friends, he took precautions, and was seen no more at his club or in places of public resort. He did not find that the time hung heavily upon his hands; he spent nearly the whole of it in Cadogan Gardens; the joy of seeing Netta slowly picking up

27

strength was sufficient for him, and he refused to be discouraged by the very guarded utterances of the doctor.

But at length there came a dark day when he was met, on the way to his wife's house, by a messenger who had been despatched to summon him; and the first person whom he saw in the hall, when he hurriedly entered, was Clarissa. She was deadly pale and trembling from head to foot; she caught him by the arm, drew him into the room where he had been kept waiting for her once before, and stammered out:

"It has come at last—what I have been dreading all along! She has had one fainting-fit after another, and they say—they say—"

Guy made at once for the door; but Clarissa held him back, saying, "No; not yet! For the moment it is over, and she is better; but she must not be startled or excited. Only the doctor thought you ought to be at hand, in case —in case of this happening again." She added, after a break, "He expects it to happen again; he is up-stairs, and he says he will not go away until—"

"Until the end?" exclaimed Guy, finishing in horror-struck accents the sentence which she had been unable to force from her lips. "Good God! is it so bad as that? Can nothing be done?"

"Oh, I don't know!—I don't know!" wailed Clarissa, wringing her hands distractedly. "Nothing human can be done, I believe—it is her heart that is affected, and each fresh attack leaves her with less power to resist the next— nothing human can be done; but perhaps something super-human might. How can one tell? I have prayed day and night; but I don't think there is much use in praying: one must deserve to be heard, perhaps, before one's prayers can be listened to." She swallowed down, not without difficulty, an obstruction in her throat and went on: "Guy, I want you to say, if you can, that you forgive me, and I want to assure you that, if you have ever done me any wrong, it is freely and absolutely forgiven. 'Forgive us our trespasses, as we forgive them that trespass against us'—those are the words, you know, and they *must* be sincerely spoken, or they are only a mockery."

"My dear," answered Guy, laying his hand upon her quivering shoulder, "they can be spoken quite sincerely by me, I promise you."

"Yes; but I don't know whether you fully understand what I mean. I mean that I am willing—or rather that I implore—to be taken back and to live with you again as your wife. You won't refuse me, will you? I feel as if nothing short of that would be of any use! I will give up everything that you dislike; I will never speak at meetings or write for magazines again; I will try to atone for all the trouble that I have given you. If you care at all for me—or for Netta—you won't turn away from us because I have made myself talked about, or because I am rich, or for any reason like that!"

Guy did not smile at this pathetic attempt to drive a bargain with the Lord of life and death—an attempt which Clarissa, in her character of an *esprit fort*, would have been the first to compassionately deride, had the case been that of another woman. A slight mist clouded his blue eyes as he took his wife's hand and answered, gently, "Say no more, my dear; we'll let bygones be bygones."

If he spoke with a mental reservation, it was on her account that he made it; for what honorable man could hold a woman in Clarissa's agitated condition to the strict letter of her word? For his own part, he had never wished to be separated from her, and wished it less than ever now that a common calamity had brought them close together once more.

She gave a great sigh of relief. "You are very good," she said; "I must try to thank you some other time. Will you come up-stairs now?"

It was not into Netta's room that they went, but into that adjoining it, where Mr. Dent and Paul Luttrell were seated. Presently the doctor stepped in quietly and joined them.

"She has dropped off to sleep," said he; "I think we

may safely assume that there will be no immediate recurrence of the alarming symptoms. I am obliged to leave you now; but the nurse knows exactly what to do in case of an emergency, and I shall be back in the course of the afternoon. There has been a marked improvement during the last ten minutes."

Clarissa looked almost triumphant; but Guy, who could not share her faith in the efficacy of the remedy to which she had had recourse, followed the doctor out and asked point-blank whether there was any hope.

"There is always hope in these cases," he was told. "The attack may recur in a few hours, or it may not recur for a week—or it may never recur at all."

"But you think it will recur?" persisted Guy.

"Well, if you put it in that way—yes; I think so. It would not be honest to say anything else to you. But you may honestly tell Lady Luttrell that the child has rallied in a way which I should not have dared to expect half an hour ago."

So Guy took back that message of comfort, whatever it might be worth, with him.

CHAPTER XLII

MADAME DE CASTELMORON was quite unselfishly sorry when she heard that her whilom admirer had embarked for West Africa to fight with savage hordes. She had never been able to see anything interesting or attractive in tragedies, whereas a nice, bright little comedy, properly seasoned with incidental vicissitudes and terminating in a manner satisfactory to all the actors concerned, was entirely to her taste. She therefore felt that she had a genuine grievance against Miss Luttrell, whom she did not fail to upbraid.

"If only you had deigned to write two words to him, as I begged you to do, he would have been here now, and we should all have been enjoying ourselves together! But you have ruined everything by your misplaced English prudery. Do not blame me for what may happen, that is all I ask; I have done my best for you and for him, and I wash my hands of the affair!"

Madeline did not mention that she had despatched the two words in question, and that they had altogether failed to produce the anticipated result; but she disclaimed the slightest intention of blaming anybody, and expressed a hope that M. de Malglaive might come safe and sound out of the perils inseparable from a military career.

She was, however, sick at heart, and she had to call upon her whole reserve strength of pride and self-control in order to maintain the demeanor which her mother wished her to maintain, and to behave with due civility to the male visitors whom her mother was feverishly eager to

attract. If they found Madeline attractive, those male
visitors, it must have been solely by reason of her beauty.
She treated them all alike, seeing indeed no difference
worth speaking of between them; she was amiable with
them, cold with them, bored by them. From morning to
night she was repenting bitterly (for there was neither
harm nor good in repenting now) that she had sent a man
who had loved her and whom she loved to distant lands,
whence in all probability he would never return. Even if
he did return, it would not be to her; his silence proved
that he had taken only too literally the sentence which
she had pronounced upon him. "The deil gang wi' him
to believe me!" she might have sighed, had she been acquainted with the ditty which records that pregnant ejaculation.

But what is done cannot be undone, and what cannot be
cured must be endured. The weeks passed away, aided in
their flight by the customary devices for killing time;
Madame de Castelmoron, restored to activity after her
shaking, departed for Nice ; Lady Luttrell hatched schemes
which had to be circumvented by nice management, and the
Pau season drew nearer and nearer to its close. It was on
a somewhat sultry spring morning that Madeline stole out
of the house and strolled off to the shady park, hoping
thereby to escape the maternal lecture which was her due,
in consequence of her having returned home from a dance on
the previous evening at the absurd hour of eleven o'clock.
It was considered allowable, not to say advisable, that she
should begin showing herself at dances once more, and, a
friend having kindly offered to take charge of her, she had
been sent to this one. Her abrupt retreat, for which she
had assigned a headache as an excuse, had in reality been
caused by the alarming attentions of a suitor whom she did
not wish to get herself into trouble by refusing, and who
was rapidly becoming so explicit that the only thing to be
done was to turn and flee from him. Now, Madeline and
her mother, following the French custom, breakfasted in
the middle of the day, and the former generally found that

she was better able to cope with the latter at *déjeuner* than in the course of any chance previous conversation.

She was wandering along, thinking forlornly what a number of years must elapse yet before she would be permitted to claim the privileges of an old maid, when the name of De Malglaive suddenly fell upon her ear and caused her to glance with interest at the old gentleman who had pronounced it. This old gentleman, who was seated upon a bench, with his back turned towards her, held an open newspaper in his hand, and was growling out dissatisfied comments upon its contents in an audible voice.

"De Malglaive—that must be the young fellow whom one used to see from time to time when his mother was still living — I remember that somebody told me of his having joined this expedition. A pretty affair, *ma foi!* They are pleased to make light of it; but if such a disaster had befallen our troops under the Empire, it would have been quite another story! What it is to live under a government of *bourgeois* who think only of enriching themselves at the expense of the taxpayer!"

Madeline stood still, and her heart stood still also. She listened breathlessly for something further; but the old gentleman's grunts and growls became unintelligible, and she had not the courage to ask him what had happened. Presently she hastened back towards the town, and, on reaching the Basse Plante, met a newspaper-boy, from whom she purchased a copy of every journal that he had under his arm. These she carried to a bench which was screened by shrubs from the public gaze, and, sitting down, was soon in possession of such meagre details as had come to hand respecting the annihilation of Colonel Davillier's column. The papers, being of diverse shades of political opinion, magnified or minimized the importance of the news according to their several ways of thinking; but that a serious reverse had been sustained was admitted by all, and in each case the concluding paragraph—the only one that interested Madeline—was identical:

"We have also to deplore the death of the Vicomte de

Malglaive, a young officer of much promise, who fell while gallantly defending himself against a cloud of assailants."

This, then, was the end; hope was extinguished finally and forever! It is true that Madeline had long ago made up her mind to her inevitable fate; but she had not quite made up her mind to Raoul's. Besides, who knows how much he has secretly hoped until he is forced to despair?

The most crushing calamities fall upon us; we stagger for a moment under the blow, and then proceed on our way through life almost as if nothing had happened. Afterwards we are apt to wonder how it could have been possible to do this; but the truth is that it is seldom possible to do anything else. As a general rule, there is work to be done, duties, formalities which must be discharged, and are discharged—more or less mechanically. So Madeline went home to breakfast, and found her mother in the dining-room, dissolved in tears, with a newspaper before her.

"Oh, my child," exclaimed the poor lady, "what a misfortune! What a terrible—terrible misfortune!"

"You have heard, then?" said Madeline, vaguely wondering at her mother's excessive grief.

"I have just read about it. Is it not too horrible? It is enough to make one believe that we must be under a curse! Everything goes wrong with us—everything!"

"I did not think that you would care so much," Madeline could not help saying. "If Madame de Malglaive were not dead, I should understand your being unhappy on her account; but—after all, he was nothing to us."

She spoke quite calmly, and was almost as much surprised at the numbness of feeling which enabled her to do so as she was at her mother's exaggerated distress. Lady Luttrell turned upon her with sudden indignation.

"How can you talk like that!—have you no heart at all? Do you not know that it was you who sent him to that atrocious place, and that his death really lies at your door? If you have felt no remorse before, Madeline—and certainly you have shown none—I should have thought that you would be a little ashamed now!"

Madeline made no reply. What she felt was not to be expressed in words, nor could remorse be of the slightest avail. She stood like a statue and gave no sign of emotion, while her mother went on :

" The cruel part of it is that I believe you really cared for the man as much as you are capable of caring for anybody ! It was nothing but that wild rubbish which you learned from Clarissa that made you refuse him. And now it is impossible for you to make any reparation : as impossible as it will be for me to—to cease regretting your obstinacy !"

Lady Luttrell had been upon the point of ending her sentence in quite another manner, and indeed she was spurred into saying what she had been going to say, when her daughter answered quietly :

"I could not have accepted him at the time that he asked me, and, as you say, reparation cannot be made now. Why should we go back to old disputes ? I hoped that your tears were for him, not for the loss of his fortune— which you knew already that we had lost."

"Oh, I am sorry for him, God knows ! Poor, dear fellow !—it is dreadful to think of his young life being cut short ! But how can I help remembering also that his death may mean something like ruin to us ?"

Hitherto she had said nothing to her daughter, save in general terms, about her financial straits ; but now, being so disconsolate and so hopeless, she poured forth the whole story of the money advanced upon mortgage by Madame de Malglaive and of her inability to pay the interest due to Raoul.

" He was most kind about it," said she; "he promised to give instructions to M. Cayaux that I was not to be annoyed. But his death, of course, must change everything ; we shall have a new creditor, who probably will show us no indulgence, and I am convinced that Cayaux will at once begin to press for payment. We may find ourselves turned out into the road from one moment to another !"

Such prompt and drastic measures were hardly likely to

be resorted to either by Raoul's heirs or by their legal representative; but Lady Luttrell, who, in truth, knew very
little about money, except that it was a necessary thing,
and that the sources from which she had always drawn it
seemed to have run dry, was thoroughly scared. Perhaps,
too, she derived some melancholy satisfaction from demon-
strating thus convincingly to Madeline whose fault it was
that the family had been reduced to beggary.

Little could be said to comfort her. Madeline was even
more ignorant than her mother of the pains and penalties
which debtors may be made to suffer, while the futility of
confessing her own tardy sorrow and repentance was obvious. One thing, however—so she was presently informed
—she could do, and that was to betray to nobody by word
or sign how the personal misfortunes of the Luttrells had
been augmented by this check to the arms of the French
republic.

"If that man Cayaux suspects that we are frightened, it
will be the signal for him to swoop down upon us like a
hawk!" Lady Luttrell declared.

For many days the poor lady remained in constant terror of being swooped down upon; for many days she refused to leave the house, feeling unfit to face the world,
while her daughter went about as usual, with an aching
heart and a composed countenance; and although the
non-appearance of the lawyer became in the long-run reassuring, she did not cease to tremble every time that she
heard the door-bell, until she was provided with a fresh
cause of anxiety in the news of Netta's illness.

Her first impulse, on hearing of this new trouble, was to
fly post-haste to Cadogan Gardens (where she would have
been of no use and would have been very much in the
way); but once more lack of the necessary funds con-
fronted her and drew from her renewed lamentations. It
was cruel! — it was monstrous! That her grandchild
should be lying ill, possibly at the point of death, and that
she should be compelled to remain at a distance for a
reason so unheard-of, so grotesque, as that she literally had

not the wherewithal to defray the cost of a journey to
England and back ! Perhaps only those who have been
rich and have suddenly become poor can realize the sensation of indignant impotence with which the widow of Sir
Robert Luttrell contemplated an empty cash-box and an
overdrawn banker's account. We all consider that we
have a right to meat and drink, and indeed the State admits as much ; this unfortunate woman could not help
thinking that she had a right to what she had always been
taught to regard as the necessaries of life.

Nor did Clarissa's rather brief letters tend to lessen her
uneasiness. Once she wrote to Guy, and received an answer couched in far more sanguine language than his wife
had employed ; but it was impossible to place much reliance upon Guy, who always expected things to turn out
in accordance with his wishes. Meanwhile, dread of M.
Cayaux dropped into the background, and his destined
victim had almost given up expecting him when, one
afternoon, she startled Madeline by rushing into the drawing-room, with blanched cheeks, and exclaiming :

"Here he comes ! I have just seen him walking up the
drive ! *Mon Dieu!* what shall I say to the man ? Would
it be any use, I wonder, to order him out of the house ?
He was afraid of me—or he pretended to be—once upon a
time."

It would indeed have been a very timorous man who
could have been afraid of poor Lady Luttrell at that moment, and M. Cayaux did not bear the reputation of being
easily overawed ; but despair gave place to astonishment,
not unmixed with hope, when it was announced that the
lawyer had called to request the favor of an interview with
Mademoiselle, not with Madame.

Madeline hoped for nothing (because there was nothing
left to hope for) when she stepped into the room where the
sharp-eyed, gray-whiskered man of the law was awaiting
her ; but she was conscious that her color came and went under his keen scrutiny, and that his errand must be in some
way connected with Raoul she could not doubt. He bowed

low, and, after expressing a respectful hope that her mother was in the enjoyment of good health, handed her a sealed envelope.

"I have just received this," he said, "from the Governor of Senegambia, who forwarded it to me in obedience, it appears, to a last request on the part of my profoundly lamented client, the late Vicomte de Malglaive. As you see, mademoiselle, I have hastened to discharge personally the mission confided to me."

Madeline took the letter, striving in vain to subdue the trembling of her fingers, thanked M. Cayaux and hoped that he would soon go away. But he did not seem at all inclined to go. He began to talk about the unhappy affair in which M. de Malglaive had lost his life, about the treachery on the part of the native troops to which it was probably due, and the difficulty which the authorities would find in explaining away a military expedition which appeared to have had no definite object; finally, he asked permission to take a chair, remarking, apologetically, that he was no longer as young as he had once been.

"I ought not to detain you any longer, M. Cayaux," said Madeline at last, not caring very much if she did offend the man, whose frequent glances at the unopened letter which she held betrayed his motives for abusing her patience.

"I beg pardon a thousand times, mademoiselle," he returned, "but if you would have the goodness to break the seal of that envelope and look at its contents before I leave, you would do me a real service. I find myself, to speak frankly, in a position of some difficulty. The instructions left to me by the Vicomte were far from precise, and among the papers forwarded from Sénégal there is no trace of—of—in short, of such a document as one might have expected to discover. It is just possible that his communication to you may contain something which will help me to decide upon the course that I ought to pursue."

The request was indiscreet and unwelcome; but there was no valid excuse for a refusal. Madeline tore the envelope open and ran her eye over the letter addressed to her—too rapidly, indeed, to take in all that it had to say, yet with sufficient deliberation to warrant her in assuring M. Cayaux that it dealt with purely private and personal matters. "There is nothing here that can interest or concern you in the least," she remarked, as she folded up the sheet.

The lawyer raised his eyebrows, depressed the corners of his mouth and said he was sorry to hear it. "This," he observed, "forces upon me the painful conclusion that my late client died intestate and that his property must be divided among those whom the law constitutes his heirs. I had hoped, I confess, that a will might have been discovered among his papers; I am evidently not to blame if no such document exists."

"Of course you are not to blame," answered Madeline, irritated, without quite knowing why, by a certain subtle change of manner on the part of M. Cayaux. "In any case, you can hardly have expected a will to be forwarded to me. Why should it be?"

"*Au fait;* that was hardly to be expected, mademoiselle, and I beg you to accept my excuses for having intruded upon you unnecessarily. You will understand, no doubt, that I was anxious to miss no chance of making a discovery which would have saved me—and probably also others—some distress of mind."

Madeline understood nothing, except that there was a veiled impertinence in the obsequiousness of this provincial attorney, and that she was in an agony of impatience to get rid of him. As soon as he had bowed himself out she dismissed him from her memory and sat down to peruse the lines which her dead lover had penned, one hot night, in remote Saint-Louis de Sénégal.

The paper was thin, the ink had run and had already turned brown; the words read like the last confession of one who had long ago passed away from this troublesome world, with all its foolish complications and misunderstandings, its transient, irreparable miseries. The dead,

we trust, are at peace, even if they do not wholly forget;
but they retain, or rather acquire, the power to inflict the
cruellest anguish upon the living.   While Madeline read,
and while her slow, useless tears splashed down upon the
open sheet which she held, it seemed to her that she would
almost rather have been forgotten altogether by Raoul than
remembered in such a way and at such a time.   He had
not, it was evident, received the apology which she had
sent to him at Madame de Castelmoron's instance ; he had
not known, and now he never would know, that she had
repented of her arrogant, uncalled-for harshness ; still less
could he know the one thing which she would gladly have
sacrificed the remainder of her life to be able to convey to
his knowledge.   It was all so heart-breaking !—it had all,
from first to last, been so needless, so senseless, so mean-
ingless !   That was what pressed upon her most in her
natural, human revolt against destiny.   Of course she had
been in the wrong ; of course she should have disregarded
anonymous missives and the irrelevant special pleading of
Clarissa ; of course she would have done more wisely to
listen to the dictates of her own heart and her own instincts.
But why, if there be indeed any overruling and pitying
Deity who takes note of our follies and blunders, are we
permitted to suffer so horribly for the comparatively venial
offence of being what we are ?   What is the good of it ?—
to what does it lead ?

From time immemorial such questions have been asked
by despairing mortals ; until the end of time they will
continue to be asked, and never an answer has been or will
be vouchsafed ; though well-meaning people are ready
enough with answers which some (when they are beginning
to recover from their wounds) accept as satisfactory.   For
others only resignation is possible, and resignation is a
healing herb of slow growth.

Far indeed was Madeline's mother from stooping to cull
that humble remedy when her nascent hopes were dashed
to the ground by the account imparted to her of the lawyer's errand.

"A letter for you?—only a letter!" she cried, in dismay. "And there was nothing about—about money matters in it, you say?"

Madeline raised her heavy eyes for a moment. "Did you think, as M. Cayaux did, that a will had been sent to me, instead of to him?"

"*Bon Dieu!* how could I tell? When one is drowning one clutches at straws. He cannot have wished—he cannot have thought of what would happen to us in the absence of instructions! But now there is no hope — no escape! How we shall live I cannot imagine; but I suppose we shall have to seek shelter in some horrible *pension*. And who," concluded the unhappy lady, throwing up her hands tragically, "who, I ask you, will come to look for a wife in a *pension!*"

She burst into tears; she did not mean to be cruel or brutal; on the contrary, she had always meant to do her very best for those whom she loved. For the rest, great pains swallow up small ones, and perhaps the necessity of endeavoring to console her mother was a better thing for Madeline than brooding over her own incurable sorrow.

CHAPTER XLIII

IL GRAN RIFIUTO

IT was a melancholy little company that met every morning in Cadogan Gardens while the weather grew warm and the days grew long and London extended its annual costly hospitality to fashionable and would-be fashionable folk. They cheered one another up with perfunctory sanguine assurances, those anxious watchers; but there was, as Guy remarked to the nurse, "not quite hope enough among the lot of them to go round"; so the lion's share was retained by him. Neither the nurse nor the doctor did much towards augmenting that insufficient supply : the utmost they would say was that every twenty-four hours which elapsed without a return of the attack which had so nearly cost their patient her life were so much gained. They evidently did not expect the child to recover; and Clarissa, who had been reassured for a moment by what she had taken for Divine intervention, lost heart once more.

Netta herself, meanwhile, seemed to be free from apprehensions, and, although she was not up to talking much, was cheerful enough when she did talk, which her father declared to be a good sign. Between them they represented the aggregate cheerfulness of the family; and Clarissa, seeing how happy, and even merry, they always were together, was too grateful to her husband to be jealous of an affection which he had perhaps done scarcely as much as she had to earn. "Save my child !" was the one mute prayer which she addressed to Heaven and earth ; like the mother before the judgment-seat of Solomon, she was ready to forego all that she was entitled to claim in consideration of a favorable reply to that petition. Nor had she any thought of unsaying what she had said, in her terror and anguish, to Guy. She was determined to keep to her word, even though she should fail to obtain the object of her self-sacrifice—and indeed she did not feel as if there would be any great difficulty in doing so; for if she had changed of late, so had he. His kindness and gentleness brought the tears into her eyes; the quiet, firm fashion in which he took command, ordering her to rest at certain stated times, forcing her to eat and drink, whether she wished it or not, and making her drive out for a couple of hours every afternoon, was not unwelcome to her. He seemed, without making any fuss about it, to have resumed his proper position, and, in spite of all that she had preached in public and in private, she could not help recognizing the comfort of having been relegated to hers. Nothing, to be sure, had been said about his domiciling himself in her house, nor had the faintest allusion been made by either of them to their reconciliation; but arrangements for the future might very well wait; she was all the more grateful to him for the delicacy which he displayed in that respect.

At length came a day, to be marked forever in her memory with a white stone, when the doctor took her breath away by saying, coolly, "Well, Lady Luttrell, I think I am now justified in telling you that you may discard immediate anxiety. For the last week there has been a steady increase of strength, and as none of the alarming symptoms have reappeared—"

"Do you mean it?" interrupted Clarissa—"do you really mean that she will get well?"

"Oh, I quite hope so," answered the doctor, smiling; "I should have told you so before this, only it was better not to shout until we were out of the wood. Mind you, I don't say that we are altogether out of it yet; I don't say that you will not have to take very great care. But, humanly speaking, there is no reason why your daughter should not grow up into a strong, healthy woman and live to be ninety."

28

Clarissa, who had just returned from her drive—that obligatory drive which was a daily penance to her—rushed excitedly up-stairs and met her husband upon the landing. He generally left the house about that hour, and she was rejoiced to find that she was in time to intercept him.

"Oh, Guy!" she exclaimed, "have you heard? Have you seen the doctor?"

She stretched out her arms involuntarily; but he drew back a step: perhaps he did not realize all that was implied in her mingled laughter and tears.

"Of course I have," he answered, in the cool, good-humored accents which once had been so exasperating to her (but his face was radiant, all the same); "didn't I tell you from the first that it was going to be all right? You mustn't be in too great a hurry, though; it will be another fortnight at least before Netta will be fit to be moved to Switzerland, where the doctor thinks you ought to take her."

Clarissa clasped her hands joyously. "A fortnight is nothing!" she exclaimed. "Is it possible that we shall be able to travel in a fortnight? How delightful it sounds! Did he mention any particular place? But you will find Switzerland dreadfully dull, won't you?"

Guy left the last question unanswered. As to the preceding one, he said that the doctor had spoken of the Lake of Geneva to begin with and the mountains later. "And if it is fine to-morrow, Netta is to go out for a drive with you, I believe." Then he glanced at his watch, and, remarking that it was time for him to be off, suited the action to the word.

For some little time after that Clarissa was *aux anges*. She was too happy to think of anything but that Netta was unquestionably getting well, that she herself had most unexpectedly been set free from the horrible aching pain which had hitherto haunted her through interminable days and wellnigh sleepless nights, and that the gloom of the world had all of a sudden become replaced by sunshine. But she ended by noticing a marked disposition

on Guy's part to avoid chance encounters with her, as well
as the total cessation of those comforting declarations by
means of which he had latterly been wont to combat her
despair; and as she felt a little shy of asking him what this
might mean, she made a confidant of Paul, whom she saw
constantly, and whose renewed approbation she had reason
to believe that she enjoyed.

"Does he imagine that I was not in earnest?" she asked.
"Has he taken it into his head that, because I am no
longer frightened, I want to be off my bargain? Surely
he cannot think so meanly of me as that!"

"I'm afraid I can't tell you what he thinks," answered
Paul; "he hasn't spoken to me upon the subject. Wouldn't
your best plan be to apply for information at headquarters?"

"Perhaps it would; only he takes such pains to deny me
any opportunity. I would much rather that you said a
word or two to him, if you don't mind."

The Reverend Paul undertook this mission with a light
heart. The truth is that he prided himself not a little
upon his ability to deal with human perversity, and he
was inclined to claim more credit than was strictly his due
for the circumstance that Clarissa had begun to attend
week-day services at a neighboring church. He was, therefore, somewhat taken aback when his brother, in answer to
some opening observations of his, said, tranquilly:

"My dear fellow, the thing can't be worked. It would
be more comfortable for us all, of course, if it could, and I
like her for sticking to a promise which, between you and
me, she only made because she was in a blue funk at the
time. But as for taking such a promise seriously—come,
now, setting aside clerical prejudices about marriage being
a sacrament and so forth, don't you think that a man who
did that would be a little bit short of a gentleman? I
couldn't do it even if she were poor. Considering that she
is atrociously rich and that Haccombe as good as belongs
to her, I really must beg to be excused. We shall be better friends in future, I hope; we have had a rough time of
it, both of us, during the last few weeks, and I dare say we

have both made some excellent resolutions. But we aren't going to risk breaking them by becoming husband and wife again—no, thank you !"

Paul said what there was to be said, and emphasized the obvious with much dialectic force. There had been faults on both sides ; there was now, he trusted and believed, repentance on both sides. Very well, then ; nothing that he could see stood in the way of mutual forgiveness. The accident that Clarissa was a wealthy woman could not be accounted an obstacle by any reasonable being.

"Set me down as an unreasonable being, if you like," said Guy, composedly ; "all I know is that I don't mean to drive an unfortunate woman into a corner, even if she does happen to be my wife. It's a simple affair enough, if you'll just leave it as it stands. Clarissa has done a few things of late which I haven't quite liked ; I think she has burned her fingers, and I don't think she'll do them any more. I have—well, you know about that, and I also intend to turn over a new leaf. But you mustn't ask me to believe that she is really anxious to surrender her independence out of sheer affection for your humble servant."

"I do ask you to believe it, because it is the truth," Paul boldly asserted. "If you were not blinded by pride and obstinacy, you would recognize that it is the truth, and you would acknowledge that you are just as fond of her as she is of you."

"All right ; anything you please. We are a pair of sighing lovers, if you choose to call us so ; but that, unfortunately, won't help us to hit it off together. Seriously, Paul, I couldn't consent—even admitting, for the sake of argument, that she wanted me to consent. I can't see things as she sees them ; I can't stand that Woman's Rights business ; I can't behave with decent civility to her friends—"

"But don't you understand that she is sick of those silly men and women, who were never really her friends ?"

"For the moment, she may be ; but I doubt whether she will ever be able to help sympathizing with their ideas, and I am sure she would never be able to like the sort of people whom I like. No, no; let's be satisfied with what we have got and be thankful that it's no worse."

A part of this conversation the discomfited Paul felt in duty bound to report to Clarissa, who was less displeased and less surprised than he had expected her to be.

"I think there is a good deal of common-sense in what Guy says," she remarked; "he is entitled to ask for proofs, and he ought to have them. Perhaps, after all that has passed, it will be better for us both to preserve our independence; but, for Netta's sake, we should try to arrange something that will at least look like a reconciliation. Anyhow, I must do *my* share."

Although she spoke with outward composure, she was deeply mortified at heart. It had not occurred to her as probable that her husband would courteously wave aside the tendered olive - branch; she was conscious of having behaved with some generosity, and had supposed that he would be willing enough to meet her half - way. But, after all, why should he? Seeing that he had long ago ceased to love her, there was really no inducement for him to do so, save that of sharing and controlling her fortune; and if, in days gone by, he had sometimes been careless and extravagant, he had never, to do him justice, shown anything resembling greed in money matters. Nevertheless, that ostensible reconciliation ought, if possible, to be contrived, and her duty, as she had said, was to do what in her lay towards bringing it about. In pursuance of that commendable resolution—and partly, no doubt, because she resembled the majority of her sex in thinking that the more disagreeable a particular course was to her the more likely she was to discharge her duty by adopting it—she had herself driven, that same evening, to a certain Ladies' Club to which she belonged, and where, as she had been duly informed by a printed notice, a discussion was about to be held respecting divers burning questions. She had often taken part in such discussions, and she had made up her mind to take part in this one, much though she dreaded and disliked the prospect.

And when she entered the familiar room, which happened
to be unusually crowded that evening, it did not make her at
all more comfortable to descry, among other salient objects,
the aggressive nose of Mrs. Antrobus.   Mrs. Antrobus, of
course, was present as a guest (for on these occasions
members were permitted and requested to bring possible
converts with them), and that her immediate conversion
was not a thing to be anticipated was shown by the extreme
aggressiveness of the feature alluded to.   She at once recognized the new-comer and beckoned imperatively to her;
but Clarissa preferred to ignore this signal, and, as a formi-
dable-looking lady in spectacles and a stick-up collar was just
then addressing the meeting upon the question of religious
education for the young, it was easy to sink down quietly
into a chair on the opposite side of the room.

The spectacled lady was talking with great fluency and
volubility; but since it appeared that, according to her, the
young were to have no religious education at all, an impatient hearer might have thought that some saving of
time would have been effected by her simply saying as
much.   Clarissa, however, was not impatient; she herself
had something to say, and she was not sorry to be granted
a little leisure in which to rehearse the heads of her forthcoming deliverance.

When the speaker had resumed her seat several ladies
rose simultaneously; but the general voice was evidently in
favor of Lady Luttrell, who was therefore called upon, and
who was greeted with prolonged, sympathetic applause.
Clarissa's friends were aware of the domestic affliction and
anxiety which had prevented her from joining their gatherings for some time past, and — being, in spite of all,
women — they seized that occasion of conveying their congratulations to her.

As soon as their kindly demonstration had subsided and
had been gravely acknowledged, she embarked in a clear
voice upon the statement which she had to make. She did
not expect, she said, to carry her audience with her; a
complete change of views on the part of one of the leaders

of a movement never could be, and perhaps never ought to be, acceptable to any audience. At the same time, one owed it to one's self, if not to others, to be honest, and she felt she had no alternative but to confess publicly that she had altered her opinion with regard to religious and other questions. The reasons which she adduced for having altered her opinion were not, it must be owned, very conclusive, nor was her discourse by any means as eloquent as previous discourses which had brought her renown; but it had at least the merit of being unambiguous, and an occasional loud "Hear, hear!" from Mrs. Antrobus broke the silence which she might otherwise have found a little chilling.

"I still believe," she declared, "that we have done some good; I still believe that it was right and necessary to call attention to the unfair treatment which for so many generations has been considered good enough for women, and I still believe that unmarried women ought to be as independent as it is possible for them to be. But I have come to see that, in the case of married women, independence is both impossible and undesirable. There cannot be two masters in one house; other things being equal, the husband is better qualified to assume authority than the wife; and when there are children a woman is sure, I think, to be unhappy, and almost sure to be wrong, if she demands release from the vows that she has taken. Nothing compels us to marry; but it seems to me that, if we do marry, we had better accept any consequences that may follow."

Lady Kettering, who occupied the chair, here remarked that she was unwilling to interrupt, but that she really could not quite see what all this had to do with the subject upon the paper. Clarissa replied that her speech was in the nature of a personal explanation, and begged permission to finish it; whereupon a brief debate ensued on the point of order. Finally, in deference to the evident wish of the majority (who may have thought that personal explanations are apt to be better fun than theoretical lect-

ures), it was decided that Lady Luttrell should be heard;
and Lady Luttrell accordingly proceeded with her recantation, which was a tolerably complete one. Perhaps some
of Clarissa's hearers were a little disappointed; for she did
not gratify them with any revelations bearing upon her
own domestic history. But she stated in so many words
that she had become a convert to Christianity because experience had taught her that she could not get on without
it, and she added that she was now ashamed of having ad-
vocated the dissolution at will of a tie which Christianity
had emphatically pronounced to be indissoluble. In conclusion, she begged to say that if her sentiments were held
to be incompatible with those professed by the club as a
body, she would at once resign her membership."

"Best thing you can do, my dear!" called out the decisive voice of Mrs. Antrobus. "I'm all for women getting
their own way in matters which fall within their own
province, and they always have got it when they haven't
been fools. But, bless your soul! they'll only lose that
and gain nothing in its place by putting on baggy breeches
and cutting their hair short, like certain old idiots whom I
could name."

Lady Kettering, who was especially identified with a
movement in favor of improved feminine costume, dealt
promptly and sternly with this discourteous interrupter.
It must be distinctly understood, she said, that visitors
were only admitted on sufferance to that meeting; they
had no *locus standi*, and could not be permitted to take
part in any discussion that might arise. She then expressed some regret that Lady Luttrell should have selected that occasion for proclaiming a change of front
with which the actual proceedings were but indirectly
concerned, and hastened to call upon the next speaker.

The next speaker, poor thing, did not obtain the attention which she doubtless merited, and was fain to expend
the flowers of her oratory upon sparsely filled benches.
For Clarissa, who had already left the room, had been followed by a host of bewildered disciples who, naturally

enough, were eager to be informed whither their former teacher now proposed to lead them. She could only reply that she no longer proposed to lead anybody anywhere. She was no better than a deserter, she confessed, and who ever thinks of applying to deserters for guidance ?

"I had to say what I said just now ; for private reasons I was obliged to say it. But it isn't a matter for argument; I may be quite wrong, and the rest of you may be quite right."

Mrs. Antrobus was loudly of opinion that those who differed from Lady Luttrell were a pack of silly and ignorant geese, but that there was no need to be distressed about them, because they. would certainly come to their senses as soon as they found men courageous enough to marry them.

"I am glad I let myself be persuaded to come here this evening," she added ; "it has been an amusing experience, and it has set my mind at ease about your husband. My mind wasn't quite at ease about him the last time we met, if you remember; but I take it that, after the fright you and he have had, you will trot along quietly, side by side, now for the rest of your days, like decent people. And how is the small girl ? Getting strong enough to knock her parents' heads together, I hope."

Clarissa was glad to be able to give an excellent report of her daughter. She neither affirmed nor denied that she and her husband had buried the hatchet ; but to herself she vowed that Guy should hear how she had done penance in a metaphorical white sheet. It was a part of her penance that that information should be conveyed to him, and if he should misunderstand (as most likely he would) her motives, the penance would be the more complete. Even the support of the redoubtable Mrs. Antrobus could not save her from the half-compassionate, half-incredulous comments of ladies who were not all of them spinsters and who thought that her action had been, to say the least of it, uncalled for ; but she made her escape at last and returned home, with the consolatory consciousness of having left an accomplished and most distasteful task behind her.

In the drawing-room she found her uncle, who had taken Cadogan Gardens on his way back from the House of Commons—a habit which had become frequent with him during Netta's illness—and who remarked:

"This looks like restored confidence. I didn't know that you had begun to go out into the world again. Is it permitted to ask what social function you have been attending to-night?"

"I haven't been attending any function," answered Clarissa, throwing off her cloak and seating herself rather despondently in a low chair; "I have been to a meeting."

"Dear me!—a mothers' meeting?"

"No, not a mothers' meeting. There were some mothers present; but I don't think their children can ever have had scarlet-fever. Oh, Uncle Tom, if you knew what a fool I have been looking!"

"By making a vigorous demand upon my imaginative faculties, I can conceive the possibility of your having looked a fool, my dear," answered Mr. Dent. "Of course that is not the same thing as having been one."

"Not necessarily," agreed Clarissa, in somewhat dubious accents. "At any rate, I have done what I made up my mind to do; and I want you, please, to tell Guy."

"May I suggest, as an amendment, that you should tell him yourself?"

Clarissa shook her head. "I can't do that. He would only laugh, and it is so hateful to be laughed at when—when—"

"When one has deserved it? Well, I won't laugh; the comic side of things doesn't strike me as forcibly as it did once upon a time. Now let us hear what you have been about."

CHAPTER XLIV

MR. DENT OBTAINS THE REWARD OF PATIENCE

"I DARE say," began Clarissa, with a faint sigh, "you have quite forgotten my telling you, on the evening of my return from Ceylon, that in my opinion the only thing to be done after a mistake has been made is to acknowledge it and try to undo it. Well, I am of the same mind still as to that, though I have changed my mind in other ways; so, as it seemed to me that I had been leading people astray, I thought I ought to go down to the club and make a sort of public recantation."

"Well done you!" cried Mr. Dent. "And what happened? Did they throw things at you?"

"Not exactly," answered Clarissa, with a short, involuntary laugh; "that is, they didn't throw material objects. But of course they despised me, and of course they were rather disgusted with me."

"That was the least that could have been expected of them. Well, I suppose you don't particularly care."

"I can't pretend not to care at all. I was in earnest, you see, when I preached the doctrines that they have taken up; and there is so much to be said in favor of those doctrines, whereas I could say nothing intelligible in explanation of my surrender. I find that I haven't the courage of my opinions—that is the long and the short of it, perhaps."

"I have taken a tolerably active part in political life from my youth up," remarked Mr. Dent, "and it has more than once been my privilege to see leaders on both sides of the House swallowing their former utterances. The spec-

tacle isn't an altogether edifying one; still, one tries to
give them credit for being honest men, and often, I believe,
they really are honest. Only it stands to reason that every
time they act in that way they will be accused by the world
at large of a mere desire to catch votes. The world at
large is far too knowing to place faith in any other motive
than self-interest; and by the time that you have reached
my age, my dear, you will probably have discovered that
what the world at large thinks or says is of singularly small
importance. Let us take the lowest view of your conduct
and say that you have ceased to advocate female emancipation because you want to be happy, and because it has
dawned upon you that you will never be happy apart from
your husband. It seems to me that such an accusation as
that need not interfere with your sleep or your appetite."

Clarissa shook her head. "You say that you give public
men credit for being honest," she returned; "but I know
quite well that you have never given me credit for being
serious, and that you don't now."

"Oh, excuse me; all I was venturing to anticipate was
the verdict of stupid and ill-informed persons. I myself,
of course, fully understand that this concession of yours
must be regarded merely as a sort of generous sacrifice to
Æsculapius, and that your happiness cannot in any way
depend upon the companionship of such a good-for-noth-
ing fellow as Guy."

"Don't laugh at me," pleaded Clarissa, with tears in
her eyes; "you promised not to laugh at me! I want you
to tell Guy what I have done, because I think he ought to
know, and because—"

"Yes?" said Mr. Dent, after waiting a moment in vain
for her to conclude her sentence.

"Well, because I did fancy, a short time ago, that it
might be possible for us to make a fresh start and live together once more. But he doesn't wish that; he doesn't
think that we could ever get on now—and very likely he
is right. Still, I was anxious to prove to him that I was
at least willing to give up what he dislikes so much."

"I see, and I shall be happy to undertake the mission. You have no further instructions to give me?"

"Well, of course there is that horrid money question. If only he could be persuaded to do what I have wanted him to do all along and take his fair share of the income which ought to belong to us both!"

"Ah, I think you had better settle that between you. You are to be friends in future, I take it, and you are to meet pretty often, although you are to have separate establishments."

"Yes, I do hope so. And, Uncle Tom, you won't lead him to imagine—"

"Oh dear, no! How could you think such a thing of me? I am merely authorized to point out to him that you have now made every sacrifice that could reasonably be demanded of you, and that your separation is henceforth quite as much a matter of his choice as of yours. He is a sensible man, if he isn't a good husband, and I am sure he will acknowledge that."

"I am afraid," observed Clarissa, hesitatingly, as she accompanied her uncle to the door, "that you do not think me a very sensible woman."

"Shall I?" said Mr. Dent. "Yes, I really think I will give myself that little satisfaction, considering how long and patiently I have waited for it. No, my dear, it does *not* strike me that common-sense has hitherto been your distinguishing characteristic. But it is only fair to add that you show signs of amendment. Good-night."

He trotted briskly down-stairs and, as soon as he was out in the street, astonished the loitering policeman by bursting into a peal of laughter. "Heaven be praised!" he muttered, "there is now every prospect of my getting that infernal property off my hands."

It was not until late the following afternoon that Clarissa, on her return from a drive round the park with Netta, was informed by her butler—a well-trained servant, who never permitted his emotions to be legible upon his rubicund countenance—that Sir Guy was waiting for her in the drawing-room. The butler, no doubt, knew all that there was to know respecting the relations between his mistress and the gentleman who was not unlikely to be his future master; but he maintained an air of blank unconsciousness, and only betrayed his suspicion that a crisis was at hand by surreptitiously plucking at Netta's sleeve.

"You come along with me, miss," he whispered, "and I'll show you that there wonderful musical box I was tellin' you of. I think your par and your mar wants to talk business—which you didn't ought to interrupt 'em till you're sent for."

Clarissa, without noticing the discreet disappearance of her daughter or the promptitude with which the drawing-room door was closed behind her, stepped quickly forward to greet Guy, whose face had an eager, embarrassed expression.

"Have you seen Uncle Tom?" she asked.

Guy nodded. "Yes; the old fellow wired for me this morning, and I have been having a talk with him. I can't quite believe all that he says; but he has convinced me, anyhow, that I ought to beg your pardon."

"For what?" Clarissa inquired.

"Well, for a lot of things, I'm afraid. At least I owe you thanks, as well as apologies, it seems; for he told me what you had done last night, and I know you must have done that a good deal against the grain, in deference to my wishes. It was awfully good of you, you know."

"I am not sure," answered Clarissa, "that I did it altogether in deference to your wishes. I did want you to understand that your wishes counted for something with me and that I had not forgotten the promise I made to you; but under any circumstances I should have had to confess that I had abandoned my old notions. I don't think now that they were notions which any woman would be the happier for adopting."

"Nor do I, to tell you the truth," said Guy; "still, I don't wonder at your having adopted them. You had great provocation."

There was an interval of silence; after which he resumed : " Now, Clarissa, I have something to say to you,
and—and I'll be hanged if I know how to say it in the
right way !   But you'll make allowances for a man who is
honestly trying to do the straight thing.   You yourself
are trying to do the straight thing, I know, and I don't
doubt for a moment that you would take me back and forgive everything, if I asked you.   What I can't get your
uncle to understand, but what I hope you will understand,
is that I couldn't possibly ask for or accept such a sacrifice.
There isn't the least reason why we shouldn't be friends—
indeed, we are quite sure to be friends, I think, now that
we are not likely to differ about Netta's education—but
there are insurmountable reasons against my inflicting myself upon you a second time.   I needn't mention them all,
because one is enough.   I am not the man that you took
me for when you married me, and I am not the sort of
man whom you would choose for your husband if you were
free to choose.   Now, isn't that so ?   You won't hurt my
feelings by answering truly."

Clarissa surprised him a little by replying, with some
appearance of resentment : " I don't call it 'doing the
straight thing' to throw the whole responsibility and the
whole blame upon me.   Surely, if you wanted to be quite
honest, you would admit that you have been as much disappointed in me as I can have been in you, and that you
would a great deal rather be my friend than my husband."

" But I'm afraid," he observed, " I couldn't honestly
say that you have disappointed me of late—except in an
agreeable way.   As for blame and responsibility, I'm willing
to take the whole of that, if my taking it will make you
feel more comfortable ; though I don't know who has the
right to put us upon our defence."

" Oh, your mother, for one, and Uncle Tom, for another,
and—and Netta, perhaps, some fine day.   I think it ought
to be clearly understood that, if our separation is to be
final, you, and not I, have decided to make it so.   And I
think, too, that it will be rather ungenerous of you if you

persist in refusing to take your share of my money and my expectations.   You would feel as I do if you were situated as I am."

Guy smiled and shook his head.   " For that matter," said he, " I suspect that you would feel as I do if you were situated as I am.   It's a pity that there should be this complication about money ; but really it can't be helped, and, as far as Netta is concerned, I can't see that it will matter very much whether I am a rich man or a poor one.   I'm sure I don't want to be ungenerous ; but you must be aware that I should lose what little self-respect remains to me by living apart from you and going shares in your income.   Living with you as your husband would be another thing ; but that, of course, is an impossibility."

" Why is it an impossibility?" asked Clarissa, boldly, after a moment of hesitation.

" Well, for the reason that I gave you just now.   We married because we were in love with one another, didn't we ?   That wasn't a bad reason, as reasons go ; but you were only a girl at the time, and you couldn't go on being in love with a man in whom you found that you had been totally mistaken.   You won't, I am sure, pretend that you have any love for me now ; so—"

" Nor can you pretend that you have any love for me," interrupted Clarissa.

" That isn't the question."

" But it *is* the question !" Clarissa declared, vehemently. " Why should not the truth be told, now that I have no pride nor any belief in myself left ?   I have been in the wrong, and I have acknowledged it ; but I should never have done what I have done if you had not shown me that you had ceased to care for me.   It was because of that, and only because of that—"

Her voice broke ; the tears which she was unable to restrain rolled down her cheeks ; she had, as she mentally avowed with profound mortification, made a complete fool of herself, and had said more than she had ever meant to say.   Yet it is certain that, five minutes later, she would not for the world have recalled her words; for within that comparatively brief space of time she had become happily convinced that her husband, whatever his past aberrations might have been, loved her still, and more than that she neither asked nor cared to know.

"No, I don't want to hear about it," she said, when Guy embarked upon a remorseful statement respecting his flirtations with Mrs. Durand and other ladies out in Ceylon; "that is over and done with, and I don't suppose it would have happened at all if I had known as much then as I do now. Anyhow, it won't happen again."

"Well, no," answered Guy, with a sigh, "I think I may safely promise you, my dear, that it won't happen again. Perhaps I also know a bit more now than I did then, and, though I shall never be worth much, I do believe I shall be a better husband in future than I had it in me to be in those days."

"With all your faults, you will be the husband that I chose, and the only husband that I ever could have chosen," was Clarissa's satisfactory rejoinder. "It is almost a comfort to think of all the worry and vexation that I have brought upon you; because now you won't feel bound to thank me for forgiving you."

However, his method of thanking her was not so objectionable but that she submitted to it cheerfully enough for the next half-hour, nor was it unpleasant to him to hear, in return, that she had lost faith in the ability of women to stand alone. One does not abandon one's cherished convictions without a pang; but, after all, the condition of this world and its denizens, if not ideal, is perhaps inevitable, and may even be the best that can be attained, considering what our physical and mental limitations are. At any rate, there are moments when it is not unnatural to adopt that optimistic view.

Mr. Dent, who looked in late that evening to be gratified with the intelligence which he had fully anticipated, was a little provoking. He was told that he was provoking, and replied that he believed he had earned the right to be so.

29

" Haven't I kept my temper for months and months, like an angel in the skin of an elderly banker, notwithstanding all your efforts to provoke me into losing it ?" he asked. "You really must not grudge me the privilege of pointing out to you now what comes of taking the bit between your teeth. Moreover, I don't care if you do grudge it; for I have, in a certain sense, drawn your teeth by handing over Haccombe Luttrell to Guy, as your marriage portion. I have handed the place over to *him*, you will observe, not to you."

" And has he accepted it ?" inquired Clarissa, eagerly.

" I am thankful to say that he has. He is a queer fellow when it comes to the transaction of matters of business, and I doubt whether he has even an elementary comprehension of the value of money ; but at least he has common-sense enough to agree with me that control over a landed estate should always, if possible, be kept out of female hands. So when you take up your residence at Haccombe, my dear, you will go to your husband's house."

It may be hoped that Mr. Dent enjoyed being hugged and kissed on both cheeks : it will be admitted that he deserved some reward for having bided his time so patiently.

CHAPTER XLV

THREATENED EVICTION

AN English watering-place out of the season is dreary and depressing enough in all conscience; but the melancholy desolation of such resorts is not worthy to be compared with that of a Continental winter station after the swallows have winged their way to cooler northern latitudes and the last invalid has been lifted into the departing express and the pitiless sun beats down, day after day, upon dusty, empty streets. Madeline Luttrell and her mother, who had had no previous experience of what Pau could be like after everybody's outside shutters had been closed, found themselves scarcely able to endure the life which they were now compelled to lead. Escape, however, was impossible, by reason of the deplorable condition of the family exchequer; and they knew that, whether they felt able to endure the stifling heat and the unbroken solitude or not, they would have to endure these things until the autumn—always supposing that M. Cayaux and his myrmidons did not turn them out of house and home before then.

It is not, we are often assured, degrading to be poor, and perhaps it is not; but it may be dreadfully uncomfortable, and to persons situated as these two unfortunate ladies were it may be made something very like a subject for shame. Their servants, they could not help noticing, had become careless and disrespectful; tradesmen eyed them askance and with a certain air of pitying disdain; they really had no business to linger in a town which had been deserted by all its well-to-do inhabitants, not to speak of

its visitors, and it was with difficulty that they could refrain from apologizing for such unheard-of conduct.

Nevertheless, there were compensations. Poverty, says
the proverb, makes us acquainted with strange bedfel-
lows; it also, in some cases, leads us to treat our fellow-
sufferers with forbearance, and this forlorn pair did not
quarrel. The dowager no longer reproached her daughter,
for whom she was truly sorry and who was truly sorry for
her; each of them was, after a fashion, resigned, each
tried to be brave, and both were thankful for the respite
which that terrible lawyer seemed disposed to grant them.
In the course of their conversations—which, it must be
confessed, were apt to flag a little—they seldom alluded
to M. Cayaux, and never to Raoul de Malglaive. To sit
silent is better than to discuss painful or controversial
matters, and Netta's slow progress towards convalescence,
of which tolerably frequent and faithful reports were despatched to them, provided them at least with one safe and
interesting topic. Neither Guy nor Clarissa thought it
advisable to tell them how very near the child had been to
death; but they were duly informed of the doctor's subsequent favorable opinion, so that their minds were set at
ease with regard to that anxiety.

One morning, when the post came in, bringing several
letters for Lady Luttrell and a very fat one, addressed in
Clarissa's handwriting, to Madeline, the latter withdrew
into the garden to see what a correspondent by whom she
had been somewhat neglected of late had to say to her.
Seating herself there beneath the shade of a copper beech
and in view of the distant peaks which towered dimly
above a quivering, intervening mist of heat, she opened
her sister-in-law's epistle and embarked upon what appeared to be a penitent, yet jubilant, apology. Clarissa
began by stating that she was very happy — which, of
course, was pleasing intelligence—and went on to say that
her happiness was not due alone to the daily improvement
which was becoming manifest in dear Netta's health.
Then she grew apologetic, and remarked that she really

did not know what Madeline and others would think of her.

"I have been so unpardonably emphatic in laying down the law, and so absolutely certain of being in the right, that it requires almost more courage than I possess to own myself a blind guide, after all! But there is no help for it; the truth must be told; and if I have done some mischief—as I dare say I have—it is not too late, I hope, to undo it. I can't admit that I was *quite* wrong, and Guy—who, I must say, is most generous and tolerant about it all—says that he agrees in principle with a great deal of what I used to urge; still, after several long talks with him, I have come to see that, so far as our immediate actions are concerned, we can only take the world as we find it, and, when all is said, the fact must always remain that love atones for everything. Even if he had done all the things of which I so hastily accused him, what would it have mattered? I can't feel, and I don't believe any woman can feel, that the past signifies much. It is the present, and only the present, that really counts."

"Well," thought Madeline, laying down the open sheet for a moment, "that is pretty cool, considering that the supreme importance of the past was the very thing which Clarissa never missed an opportunity of impressing upon me! But I am very glad that she should have made friends with Guy; and that, I suppose, is what she is going to tell me presently that she has done."

That, indeed, was the announcement diffusively contained in three closely written sheets of note-paper, embellished with alternate expressions of contrition and appeals for congratulation. But a good deal more than that remained to be said, and her unquestionable duty, the writer declared, was to say it. "Dear Madeline, you know how afraid I was that you would end by marrying that young M. de Malglaive, of whom, you must acknowledge, we did not hear the best accounts. You will forgive my saying that I saw you cared for him, in spite of all your denials, and I hope you care for him still; because I can-

not doubt that he cares for you. *If he does* (of course all
depends upon that), I implore you not to throw your happiness away and to dismiss from your mind anything that
I may have said against him. I understand so much now
that I did not understand a year ago, and I should be so
terribly grieved if I thought that I had influenced you in
the wrong direction. Guy says—"

But Madeline had not the heart to go on reading what
Guy had said. Neither he nor Clarissa could bring Raoul
back from the desert sands where his bones lay bleaching;
the teacher might cry " As you were !" and might herself
execute a *volte-face* without loss or hurt, but the disciple
could not obey orders ; and if the past may in some cases be
treated as being of no importance, it retains, in others, the
grewsome quality of being irrevocable. Under such circumstances, the poor disciple may be excused for feeling a little bitter, and for a quarter of an hour or thereabouts
Madeline sat, with her open letter upon her knees, thinking rather hard things about the self-deposed leader of a
sufficiently silly crusade. But she ended by absolving her
sister-in-law. Clarissa did not know that Raoul was dead,
nor did she, presumably, know that he had been innocent
of some of the offences laid to his charge. What was the
use of being angry or envious or contemptuous ? The
calamity which had occurred would have occurred, perhaps, even if Clarissa had never lectured in public or in
private ; anyhow, what had been done could not now be
undone, and it was at least a good thing that two people
who had been rather unhappy were going to be happy together for the future.

The dowager Lady Luttrell, who emerged hastily from
the house at the moment when her daughter's meditations
had advanced thus far, was of opinion that this was a very
good thing indeed. She advanced, with her cap-strings
flying and her hands outstretched, to exclaim :

" Madeline, dearest, I could not think what had become
of you ! Have you heard the news ? But I know you
must have heard, for there was a letter for you from

Clarissa. Is it not a mercy! Dear Clarissa wrote to me also, and so has Guy, and so has Mr. Dent—all most satisfactory! They are to live at Haccombe, it seems, and no doubt they will be extremely well off—much better off than we ever were. One does not really know how to be thankful enough!"

It was pretty of her to be so overjoyed at an event from which she was unlikely to derive any personal profit, Madeline thought, and it would have been most ungracious on her own part to resent her mother's next half-involuntary ejaculation of, "Ah, my dear, if only you were as comfortably provided for as Guy is! Then I would take a second-class ticket for Lourdes this very afternoon, in spite of the heat, and give thanks where thanks are due!"

"You must not worry about me," the girl said; "I am as well provided for as I deserve to be."

"My dear child, you are not provided for at all!—that is just why I must go on worrying until you are. But perhaps our luck is going to turn at last; this news, which I confess that I had quite given up expecting, makes me almost hope that it is."

"Are Guy and Clarissa going to stay in London for the rest of the season?" asked Madeline, to change the subject.

"Oh no; they couldn't very well do that without exposing themselves to all sorts of petty annoyances. It is much better for them to go away until their reconciliation has ceased to be a nine days' wonder, and, fortunately, the doctor recommends mountain air for Netta. So they are to start as soon as possible for Switzerland, where they suggest we should join them. I only wish we could!" added Lady Luttrell, wistfully; "but that, of course, is quite out of the question."

"*Faute d'argent?*"

"*Faute d'argent,* as you say; but please don't mention that when you write. They evidently don't know to what straits we have been reduced, and I would rather not distress them by saying anything about it."

The excellent woman could be as worldly as another where her children's interests were concerned; but it did not even occur to her as possible to ask pecuniary assistance from one of them. Like the rest of us, she had her standard, which, after all, was not, perhaps, such a very low one. As if in anticipation of a suggestion which she did not wish Madeline to make, she went on:

" Nothing is more painful for a man who has married an heiress than to be encumbered with poor relations, and I would rather pawn the clothes off my back than let Guy know how frightened I am of that wretched Cayaux. For the rest, I quite hope that Cayaux has departed to spend his summer holiday at some distant *ville d'eaux;* I am sure he must be rich enough to treat himself to that luxury!"

It may be conjectured that he was; but some people prefer hoarding their money to spending it, and M. Cayaux, who had not left Pau, called at the Château de Grancy that same afternoon, to state — among other disagreeable statements which he found it his duty to make—that he would be glad to receive certain moneys long owing to him by the nominal mistress of the house. That doomed lady was writing a long and affectionate letter to her daughter-in-law when the enemy was announced, and she laid down her pen with forebodings which were but too speedily fulfilled.

" *Ma bonne dame,*" said M. Cayaux, after the preliminary skirmish for which he had been prepared (and it was terribly significant of what was to come that he should dare to address his former patroness in such terms)," it is not I, believe me, who desire to ruin you. I have incurred losses through my anxiety to accommodate you; it is probable that I shall lose the interest, if not the principal, of the sums that I have advanced, and, considering that I am a poor man, the prospect, I frankly confess, does not smile upon me. But what would you have ?—one is the friend of one's old friends or one is not."

" Cayaux," exclaimed Lady Luttrell, suddenly turning at bay, " you are insupportable ! If I must go to prison until I have paid my debts, to prison I will go; but never will I permit you to speak of me as an old friend!"

The man of law smiled venomously. "As you will, madame," he replied. "It is true that I have expended a great deal of time, for which I have received no payment, in striving to preserve you from bankruptcy; it is true that I have again provided you with cash, which I suppose I shall never see back; but it would be presumption and exaggeration, no doubt, to describe such trifling services as acts of friendship. You will not be sent to prison; for the law does not, in these days, allow those who have defrauded their friends — I beg a thousand pardons, I should have said their men of business—to be imprisoned: all that the law will do will be to turn you out of a house which no longer belongs to you and to sell your furniture for what it will fetch."

M. Cayaux glanced disparagingly at the faded carpet and curtains and the frayed damask of the sofas and chairs, while poor Lady Luttrell's lips trembled. However, she knew that it would be useless to appeal for mercy or pity, and it was in a tolerably steady voice that she asked:

"When do you mean to turn us out?"

"I fear, madame, that you will have to surrender possession to the rightful owners within three weeks; but allow me once more to say that you will not be dispossessed at my instance, although it so happens that I am empowered to take proceedings on behalf of the heirs. For myself, I shall probably be a loser by means which I sincerely deplore; I can but take my chance with the other creditors. At the same time, I am instructed by my clients to say that, on prompt payment of all arrears, they will be willing to renew the mortgage."

"You know very well that I cannot pay the arrears!"

"I did not know it, madame, though I must own that I feared as much. It only remains, then, for the law to take its course. That is, unless your son, Sir Luttrell—"

"Sir Luttrell, as you absurdly call him, has nothing to

do with my affairs. You can reduce me to beggary; but
you have no claim, I am thankful to say, upon him."

"No legal claim, I admit; but I understand that he has
become by his marriage a wealthy man, and possibly he
might not relish the idea that his mother was so deeply indebted to a humble provincial lawyer. Were I in your
place, I should communicate with him; being only in my
own place, and having ascertained this gentleman's address,
I may find it advisable to adopt that course."

"I forbid you to think of it! If I prefer starvation to
borrowing money, that is my affair, not yours."

"Pardon me, dear madame; it is a little my affair also,
seeing that you have not always preferred that distressing
alternative, and that you have done me the honor to accept
advances from me which I could ill afford to make. *Allons!*
you will write to your son, I have no doubt, and all will
arrange itself for the best. If you remain obstinate—*ma
foi!* I shall have to take such measures as I can to regain
my own."

Upon that, M. Cayaux smilingly bowed himself out, leaving his victim to demand of high Heaven what she had
ever done to merit such cruel afflictions. High Heaven,
in accordance with precedent, remained mute; so the poor
lady was fain to seek out her daughter and repeat the
same despairing query to one who was at least in a position
to sympathize with it.

"This is what comes of my having said that our luck
had turned! That wretch will write to Guy—I know he
will!—and if he does, he may spoil everything! It will
look as if we had only waited to make sure of Clarissa's
money in order to become her pensioners!"

"I am quite sure that neither Guy nor Clarissa will think
such a thing as that of us," Madeline declared. "Whatever they may be, they are not stingy people, and Guy, at
all events, must know that if you are in difficulties now, it
is partly because he cost you a great deal of money when
he was younger. If I were he, I should certainly feel that
you were doing me a kindness by telling me the truth."

"Ah, my dear, you don't understand! Of course they would respond to our appeal; but I should never be able to hold up my head again, and Guy, who has already had to put his pride in his pocket, would never be able to forget that he had been forced to ask his wife to relieve his family. And to think that if I could only, by some means or other, have tided over the next six months, I might have been independent! By that time, I mean, you may be happily married; and, as for me, I can live easily enough upon my little income and pay Cayaux off by instalments."

"But there is no way of tiding over the next six months, is there?" objected Madeline.

"None that I can see. Yet one never knows, and miracles have been worked in favor of people who did not seem to me to deserve them as much as we do. Let us at least go to Lourdes to-morrow and ask. I told you that I would go there to return thanks to the Blessed Virgin if I had reason to be thankful, and she will understand our errand, even if she does not grant our prayer."

Madeline was not quite sure what form of prayer her mother wished her to offer up; but there would be no difficulty about praying for release in some form from a situation which looked very like an *impasse;* so she assented. Moreover, she thought that she would like, if there should be time, to walk along the banks of the Gave to a certain spot which had associations for her and which she had often longed to revisit.

CHAPTER XLVI

BLACK SAMARITANS

In the semi-darkness of a low, stifling hut not far from the banks of the Sénégal River lay what remained of a white man, who had long been tended by black men and women with extraordinary devotion, if not with skill. How he had come to be in so strange a situation, who his preservers were, and why they had been at such pains to preserve a worthless life he neither knew nor cared ; only at intervals during the interminable period of lassitude and suffering which stretched far back into the recesses of a confused memory had he been conscious of his personal identity, and even then he had been too weary and too indifferent to ask whether he was alive or dead. But now, turning his hot, aching head towards the huge negro who was sedulously fanning the flies away, he inquired, with languid curiosity, "Is that you, Salem ?"

A double row of brilliantly white teeth responded by an affirmative grin, and from between them issued a joyful, guttural voice—"*Beau temps que je suis guéri, moi! Toi aussi, tu vas être sur pied tout à l'heure. Seulement, faut pas bouger, hein? C'est pas les blessures, c'est la fièvre qui a manqué de te finir.*"

There was little need to caution him against attempting to rise from his recumbent attitude; the inert frame of skin and bone which represented his body was not at the orders of his enfeebled mind, nor, if the hut had contained a looking-glass, would he have detected in the reflection of his haggard, bearded visage any resemblance to that of a smart young cavalry officer who had long ago been reported dead and buried. Somebody, no doubt, had been buried, and official despatches were responsible for the statement that due honors had been paid to the remains of Vicomte de Malglaive; but this bewildered invalid was becoming slowly aware that his career was not yet at an end, and that he had been snatched—somewhat unnecessarily, perhaps—from the jaws of death.

Presently he closed his eyes again, feeling unequal to the effort of interrogating his attendant, and soon he dropped off into what, had he but been aware of it, was the first sound, natural sleep that he had enjoyed since he had been removed, senseless, by friendly hands from the scene of Colonel Davillier's disaster. The remote negro village where he lay had been visited, that afternoon, by one of the terrific thunder-storms which burst over that region in early summer; and perhaps the passing refreshment which follows such atmospheric disturbances had been beneficial to him. In any case, he was recovering. His wounds had healed, though there was a bullet somewhere or other about his person; his fever had been treated after the fashion customary among ignorant savages, and the most learned and civilized of physicians could have done no more for him than had been accomplished by good fortune, or by his constitution, or possibly by Salem.

That stalwart and self-complacent warrior told him all about it, the next day, in a concise and graphic style. *"Pas mort moi—pas mort toi—parti tout le monde! Alors je me suis un peu traîné le soir, et je t'ai fait porter. Ceci, tu sais, c'est mon pays."*

The thing was easily said, but it could not have been very easily done; and indeed Raoul heard afterwards by what amazing and heroic exertions a man who was himself badly wounded had contrived to drag him within reach of assistance. But for the circumstance that he had won— without having taken any particular trouble to do so— Salem's affection, he must inevitably have perished, seeing that the people who were now giving him shelter had no sort of love for his race; but it was only by slow degrees

that he realized where he was, how long he had been lying
ill and all that had happened to him.   Swift and summary
vengeance, it seemed, had been wreaked by a French force
from the Niger upon the Touaregs; but nobody had supposed that there could be any survivors of Colonel Davillier's column, save such as found their way back to Saint-
Louis, nor had Salem thought it incumbent upon him to
undertake a long journey on foot in order to report himself and his master to the successful avengers.   It was represented to him that he had missed a fine opportunity of
securing promotion and reward by neglecting this obvious
duty; but he was inclined to doubt whether he had not, on
the contrary, exercised a wise discretion.   There had been
whispers of treachery on the part of the native troops, and
the fact that he had been half killed might not have availed
to save him (so, at least, he affirmed) from a short shrift.
For the rest, his presence by the side of a raving, feverstricken patient had been indispensable.   " *Moi partir, toi
crever bien vite,*" he observed, succinctly.

He was not unwilling, however, to return to his regiment
so soon as Raoul should be in a fit state to face the fatigues
which that return must entail.   To savages contact with
civilization has many points in common with dram-drink-
ing.   They would be happier without civilization; but
when once they have assimilated its ways they cannot live
comfortably in barbarism, and this *tirailleur indigène,* who
had been drilled and disciplined, had little inclination to
play the deserter.   He thought, too, that the officer whom
he had rescued from death would speak in his favor, and
that he might hope to escape punishment, even if he did
not obtain promotion.

The rescued officer, as may be imagined, gave him every
assurance that he asked for; although it did not seem altogether certain that the services which he had rendered
had been so great as most people would have pronounced
them to be.   Raoul, while strength and the power of connected thought came gradually back to him, felt more than
doubtful whether this tedious and painful recovery of a

life which he had made up his mind to lay down was a thing to be thankful for; he knew that he must have been reported as dead; he knew (or, at all events, believed) that not one human being in the wide world would rejoice on hearing that he had come to life again, and he was disposed to think that he had been somewhat cruelly defrauded of the release for which he had paid so heavy a price. But of course he did not say this to Salem, who would not have understood him in the least if he had; nor did he fail to express his gratitude in warm terms to Salem's hideous compatriots, who indeed deserved some thanks at his hands. They had not deprived him of his coins or his trinkets, and these he distributed among them, only reserving for himself as much as he was told would be required to defray the cost of a protracted journey to the shores of the distant ocean.

Many days had yet to elapse before he could set forth upon the first stage of that journey, accompanied and guided by his faithful servant; but at length a start was made, and at length a small French settlement upon the banks of the yellow Sénégal River was safely reached. *"C'est bon, nous avons fait le plus dur!"* cried Salem, encouragingly; but that only meant that the vast stretches of desert and forest which still separated them from their goal could now be traversed by water, instead of on foot. There was difficulty in securing a native canoe and rowers; there were difficulties about obtaining supplies; above all, there was the terrible, overpowering heat, which to a white man barely convalescent might bring death at any moment. If that indefatigable negro had saved his master's life once in the desert, he must have saved it again and again before the canoe, pursuing a tolerably swift course down-stream, arrived at Podor, where a handful of troops was stationed and where Raoul received a hearty greeting from astonished comrades in arms. Through what adventures he had passed and by what a succession of miracles he had come to be where he was he could hardly relate to these naturally inquisitive gentlemen. He was still so weak and so utterly prostrated by the heat that his experiences represented themselves to him rather as an uneasy dream than as a reality, and in his more lucid moments the one thought which kept recurring to him was, "What trouble I am taking, what a fuss I am making, to get what I don't want !"

But perhaps nobody in his sober senses really wants to die, however weary he may be of life, and Raoul, at any rate, wanted very much to escape from Africa. Some additional facilities were afforded him and some additional comforts procured for him at Podor, and during the remainder of his progress down the river towards Saint-Louis no soldier of Xenophon's retreating army can have longed more eagerly for the sight of the Euxine than he did for the thunder of the unceasing Atlantic breakers. It was merely a physical craving; but physical cravings, as those who have suffered from African fever are aware, may be desperately intense.

The silent, melancholy old town of Saint-Louis at last ! —in the far distance the sound of the sea, and at night a European bed and linen sheets beneath the hospitable roof of the commandant ! It is needless to say that a kindly reception was accorded to M. de Malglaive, and an uproarious one to Salem, who, if the truth must be told, got gloriously drunk that night with his comrades, instead of going to bed, like a Christian. As he was not a Christian, he may perhaps be pardoned for having thus given way to one of the vices introduced into his country by exponents of Christianity, and it is a well-attested fact that the eyes of those in authority over him remained closed to this misdemeanor.

The governor, it appeared, was absent on leave; but on the following morning Raoul saw and received the congratulations of his deputy, who remarked : "You have had a marvellous escape, monsieur; but, frankly, you look more like a ghost than a living man, and if I were you I would not tempt Fate by remaining here a day longer than you can help."

"I ask nothing better than to sail for France at once," Raoul declared.

"Oh, at once!—that would be rather difficult; but we will ship you off with as little delay as possible. It is your heirs who will laugh on the wrong side of their mouths, M. de Malglaive," added the official with a smile. "We have had several letters of inquiry from your lawyer; but of course we had not much information to give him. We forwarded, I believe, a document which you handed to his Excellency—ah! and here, now that I come to think of it, is some correspondence which arrived for you after your departure. It should have been returned to your representative; but the matter was overlooked. In this atrocious climate one is apt to overlook everything that is not imperatively necessary."

Raoul took the little bundle of dusty envelopes, upon which the ink had already turned brown, and soon afterwards withdrew. Not that he was in any hurry to read his letters; for the sight of them had not stirred his curiosity, and indeed the first few that he opened proved quite as uninteresting as he had expected them to be. But presently he came to one, addressed in a handwriting that he did not recognize and forwarded from Tours, which brought a sudden rush of blood into his thin, sallow cheeks. He had not changed; he had not forgotten Madeleine, notwithstanding his wounds, his protracted illness, and the lassitude which had robbed him of almost every conscious wish, save an overwhelming desire to fly from the tropics; but he had come to look upon himself as dead to her and upon her as dead to him; so that this stiff little note of apology, penned long ago, moved him to an extent never contemplated by the writer. She had "heard reports about him which she had since discovered to be untrue"; she had said things to him for which she was sorry!—was it an intuition of the truth or only his ignorance of the candor permitted to English girls that made him stagger in the blinding sunshine and clutch at a glaring white wall for support as he read those very conventional expres-

30

sions of regret ? For a few joyful, bewildering moments,
at all events, he yielded to the most extravagant hopes.
Afterwards, when he was within doors and had read Madeline's letter through a dozen times or so, he grew more
sober and less sanguine. False reports ?—well, it might
be so ; but plenty of reports which were not false could
have been communicated to her, and would, no doubt,
have led to an equally lamentable result. It was the old
story : if she had loved him, she would have understood
that these things made no real difference; if she did not
love him, she would not be made to do so by any whitewashing of his character. For all that, the fact remained
that she had cared enough about him to think it worth
while to ask his pardon, and it was well worth while to
have survived as he had done, if only because it was now
his clear duty to present himself to her and ask hers.
Such a letter ought not, of course, to have remained unanswered ; obviously, he could do no less than hasten to explain that it had only now reached his hands.

He did not, however, avail himself of postal facilities—
how was he to know, without making further inquiries,
what Miss Luttrell's address might be at that season of the
year ?—but his eagerness to embark upon a homeward-
bound steamer became redoubled, and no obstacles were
placed in his way by the authorities, who had only too
good reasons for sympathizing with him. Meanwhile,
what was to be done with or for Salem, to whom his debt
could never be discharged by a mere payment of money ?
Alas ! there was not much to be done ; for the big black
man had no desire to cross the ocean or to accept any situation, however easy and lucrative, in a strange land.

"*Toi partir, mon blanc, moi rester ici,*" Salem said, with
matter-of-fact pathos; "*c'est entendu. Puisque te voilà
content, moi aussi je suis content.*"

But he wept unrestrainedly, like the great, courageous,
uncivilized baby that he was, and nothing would satisfy
him but that he should accompany his charge to Dakar
and see him safely on board the Messageries boat which

touched at that port on her northward voyage from Rio.
Of promotion Salem was already assured, and money he
was certain not to lack to the end of his days; nevertheless,
he was a sorrowful man as he stood on the desolate height
of Cape Verd and watched the steamer which was bearing
away a friend who would never return. To this day he
continues to receive periodical letters, which are read to
him by competent persons and in which Raoul de Malglaive speaks of his intention to revisit the banks of the
Sénégal River some day; but Salem knows very well that
some day means no day. "*Pas bon pour les blancs, notre
pays à nous,*" he is wont to remark; "*moi, j'aime mieux
qu'il reste chez lui.*"

So Raoul took the news of his escape back to France
with him; for in Sénégal, as the governor's listless deputy
had told him, nothing is done that is not imperatively necessary, and to have telegraphed that one white man who
ought to have been dead was still alive would perhaps
have been a superfluous expenditure of energy. For the
rest, the idea of reappearing, unannounced, at home was
not distasteful to him. He had no particular sympathy
for his heirs, about whom he knew next to nothing; he
thought it would be rather amusing to watch the faces of
those whose duty it would be to congratulate him upon his
resurrection, and at the bottom of his heart there lurked just
the shadow of a hope that if Madeline Luttrell was not at
the Château de Grancy, she might be found at some neighboring Pyrenean watering-place. There is no harm in
hoping, and it may be that other hopes, grounded chiefly
upon the dramatic suddenness of his advent, insinuated
themselves into the meditations in which he indulged
while the steamer ploughed her leisurely way through the
long Atlantic rollers.

These last, however, had sensibly diminished, though his
health had as sensibly improved, by the time that he
stepped ashore at Bordeaux. The tall European houses,
the broad quays, and the throng of sunburnt, indifferent
passers-by had no welcome to offer him; he realized that

not one of us counts for much in this busy little world, and that the immense majority of us, from the moment that we are dead, or supposed to be dead, count for precisely nothing at all. Madeline had, of course, heard that he had been killed, and possibly she had been sorry for a few minutes or hours or days; but the chances were that she had already clean forgotten him—the chances even were that she was by now married, or engaged to be married, to some other man. Raoul betook himself to a hotel, wrote one or two letters, official and other, which it seemed to be incumbent upon him to write, and wandered out of doors again aimlessly to get through the evening as best he might; for he had decided to wait until the following day before continuing his journey to Pau. There was no such desperate hurry, he somewhat sadly reflected; Cayaux would be better prepared to receive him in the morning than at night, and nobody was likely to jump for joy on recognizing him.

But somebody who chanced to recognize him before he had wandered a hundred yards along the hot, crowded street jumped like a jack-in-the-box and accosted him with what at least bore all the outward semblance of joy.

"*Dieu de Dieu!*—is it possible! And we who have been saying masses for your soul all this time! But, my dear De Malglaive, if you did not so intimidate me with your impassive air, it is I who should permit myself to embrace you where you stand!"

The dapper little man was red with excitement; there were actually tears in his eyes; he had so far forgotten the *tenue* upon which he prided himself that he was quite capable of carrying out his threat in the presence of surprised lookers-on; and Raoul, although he did not go the length of embracing M. de Larrouy, shook him very warmly by the hand, saying:

"You give me back life! I was just beginning to ask myself whether I had any right to be alive or a friend in the world who would be glad to see me alive."

"*Eh, parbleu!*—for whom do you take us all?—we, who

have known you from the cradle ! They did not massacre you, then, those savages ? You must relate all that to me. You will come and dine with me—yes, it is positive ; I accept no excuse !—and you will tell me where you have been and why you have made no sign. I am here for a night only, on my way to Arcachon. *Sapristi, quelle chance !*"

Perhaps the worthy M. de Larrouy, who was a renowned and inveterate retailer of the latest news, may have meant that it was a piece of great good luck for him to be provided with a truly sensational narrative ; but his satisfaction at grasping a hand which he had believed to be long since reduced to dust was quite unfeigned, and when he had conducted Raoul to a restaurant, where he ordered a sumptuous repast, he rubbed his own hands gleefully.

"It is that dear and unhappy Lady Luttrell who will not be sorry to see you !" he remarked. "For I am persuaded, my friend, that you would rather lose your money than consent to her being turned out of house and home."

The explanation which Raoul instantly demanded had to take precedence of the story for which M. de Larrouy was yearning, and, as may be imagined, the agitation produced by the former was fatal to any adequate statement of the latter.

"Oh, it is quite simple," Raoul said, impatiently. "I was wounded, but not mortally ; I was nursed afterwards through a long bout of fever by some black Samaritans in a negro village, and as soon as I was well enough I made my way down to the coast. There you have the whole history. But that rascal Cayaux !—where did he find the impudence to disobey my express orders ? I will wring his neck for him to-morrow !"

"Oh, as for that," remarked M. de Larrouy, "I suppose he could not very well help himself ; and if the orders of a dead man have been disobeyed, the fault is scarcely his. Does one, I ask you, go and get himself killed without taking the ordinary precaution of executing a will ? Happily, you are here to make amends for your carelessness."

It was indeed a happy thing that he was, and now, at any rate, he was able to flatter himself that his life had been restored to him for some good purpose.   Naturally, he had a great many more questions to put, and M. de Larrouy, who doubtless had suspicions of his own, but was discreet enough to abstain from betraying them, answered him in full detail.   By way of return, Raoul consented, in common gratitude, to give a somewhat less bald account of his African adventures; so that when they parted, one of them was in a state of high gratification, while the despondency of the other had been to a considerable extent dispelled.   Madeline was neither married nor betrothed: of so much De Larrouy had expressed himself certain, and had likewise declared that the young lady might have made half a dozen good matches, had she been so minded. Well, that, to be sure, proved nothing; but she was still at Pau, and she would be visible on the morrow, and he would be in a position to bear her good tidings—what more could he have expected of kind Fortune?

CHAPTER XLVII

"BENEDICTA TU IN MULIERIBUS!"

THE department of the Basses-Pyrénées may seem agreeably cool in summer to those who have just escaped from the horrors of Sénégal; but people who would fain be, and cannot be, in Switzerland are likely to groan at the sweltering heat, the dust and the parched aspect of it. Madeline Luttrell and her mother, journeying towards Lourdes in one of the railway-carriages which the Chemin de Fer du Midi considers good enough for second-class passengers, and gazing mournfully out of the window upon scenes which they had never before witnessed at that season of the year, could not but experience the sensation of discomfort which arises from a consciousness of being out of one's proper place. It is a trifling discomfort, no doubt, to be detained in a country which all your friends have deserted, and a still more trifling one to be compelled to travel second-class, instead of in a reserved compartment; but then, as everybody knows, enjoyment of life or the reverse depends very largely upon trifles. Rich people, who can afford to dress shabbily, can also afford to economize in the matter of railway fares (and often have a rather offensive habit of boasting that they do so); but to be reduced against your will to resort to such dismal expedients is a very different thing. So Lady Luttrell bemoaned herself aloud while the train jogged deliberately on, and worded her lamentations in English, to avoid wounding the susceptibilities of her fellow-passengers.

"What heat!—what dirt! I am glad your poor, dear father cannot see us in this horrible cattle-truck. He

would say, I know, that it could not be necessary—and yet
it is of the most absolute necessity! Well, if we have any
sins upon our conscience, we are doing penance for them
now, and that ought to count for something—I do honestly think that that ought to count for something. It
is a thousand times worse than wearing a hair shirt or putting pebbles in one's shoes!"

Madeline was not disinclined to agree with her mother;
but she was thinking to herself that there are forms of suffering far greater than can be inflicted by hair shirts or
pebbles or even second - class railway - carriages. *"Nessun
maggior dolore Che ricordarsi del tempo felice Nella mise-
ria."* . . . Why had she wilfully thrown away the happiness which had been within her grasp, and of which she
was reminded by every landmark that flitted past her?
Why had she listened to Clarissa, for whom a way of repentance had been found which was forever barred against
less fortunate persons? She was willing to kneel before
the Grotto of Lourdes, since she had been asked to do so;
but not by her were the miracle-working properties of the
locality likely to be put to the test. The line must be
drawn somewhere, and even Our Lady of Lourdes could
hardly be expected to resuscitate a dead man and transport him to France from the sandy wastes of the Soudan.

Still one may plead for possible things; one may beg to
be pardoned for irrevocable follies; one may implore such
strength and guidance as are required for the performance
of one's duty; one may also add a brief, fervent entreaty
that duty shall not present itself in a matrimonial form.
Of that nature were Madeline's petitions when, later in the
day, she occupied a *prie-dieu* chair by her mother's side,
and well aware was she that, if they were granted, her
neighbor must needs be disappointed. However, she felt
no resentment against the poor lady who, with clasped
hands, rapidly moving lips, and eyes full of tears, was ham-
mering at the gates of heaven. It was a case for remorse
and regret rather than for resentment, and her mother's
yearnings were at least unselfish.

The season of the great pilgrimages had not yet begun, and the shrine was comparatively free from besiegers. There were, indeed, so few people about that, after a time, Madeline rose from her knees and stole noiselessly away, thinking that she would have no difficulty in finding her mother again when she should have accomplished a certain little secular pilgrimage of her own. But Lady Luttrell at once got up and followed her, saying, with a sigh :

"I am at the end of my strength ; I am no longer as young as I was, and this sun makes me dizzy.   I think, too, that I have been heard ; for I feel less hopeless than I did.   Shall we try to find a shady place near the river and rest until it is time for us to go back ?"

Madeline assented, and gave her arm to her mother, who leaned rather heavily upon it.   There was a shady place that she knew of and would have preferred to revisit alone ; but she wished, in any case, to see it once more ; so she bent her steps thither, and was soon at the spot where her father had once interrupted an interesting conversation. Oddly enough, some association of ideas prompted Lady Luttrell to refer to that by-gone incident.

"I remember," said she, "that the last time we were here your dear father told me he had found you sitting on the bank of the Gave with Raoul de Malglaive.   He was rather put out about it ; we were ambitious then, and we did not think that it would be a good enough match for you.   Ah, what changes in so short a time ! What would I not give now — but it is useless to speak of such things !   Only I felt almost sure at the time that you were really fond of the young man, and—"

"Don't !" exclaimed Madeline, sharply.   And then, as her mother turned an astonished face towards her, it came across her all of a sudden that there was nothing better to be done than to tell the whole truth then and there.

"I *was* fond of him," she said ; "I have never cared for anybody but him in that way, and I never shall.   I refused to marry him because I had heard stories about him—you remember that horrid newspaper story, for one. It was false, I believe; but others, I dare say, may have been true —what does it matter, now that he is dead? Only you won't try any more to make up a marriage for me, will you? I know it is hard for you; but I can't help it! Even if we were starving and if a millionaire were to cast himself at my feet, I should have to say, 'No, thank you'—I couldn't say anything else, unfortunately."

The girl laughed unsteadily. She was prepared for remonstrances and rebukes; but she received none from her mother, whose heart, after all, was a tender one, and who only said :

" My child, why did you not tell me this before? 1 would not have added to your sorrow, as I must have done last winter, if I had known."

It may be conjectured that the good lady made some inward allowance for the extravagant assertions of youth and did not quite abandon the hope of witnessing Madeline's wedding ; but for the moment, at any rate, she was touched and sympathetic, and during the half-hour that followed these two were brought nearer together than they had been for a long time past. They were both, in truth, so sad and so forlorn that they would have been less than human if they had not striven to comfort one another.

The heat of the day was over, and the shadows of the hills stretched across the valley, when they slowly retraced their steps, talking, as they went, about the manner of life which awaited them. Madeline was for leaving Pau, which is not a very cheap place of residence, and settling down in some country district, where their means would enable them to live with a certain degree of comfort and where they would not be hampered by the reputation of having once been great people ; but her mother demurred to a plan which had obvious disadvantages.

" It would be a living death, Madeline! You do not realize what it would mean to you to be separated from all your friends. An old woman like me may bury herself alive if she chooses, but not a girl of your age. However disagreeable it may be in some ways, I shall always feel that my duty to you is to be in a place where somebody knows who we are."

"Why should you feel that, when the very thing that I most wish for is to be in a place where nobody knows who we are?" Madeline asked. "I don't think we should either of us care to go back to England, and it would be miserable for us both to see strangers inhabiting our dear old tumble-down Château de Grancy. Our only chance of ever being anything like happy again is to make an entirely fresh start."

She stepped aside to give passage to a gentleman who had just appeared round the corner of the winding footpath, and who had not been polite enough to make way for the ladies. But this gentleman, instead of walking on, stood still, removed his hat, and said, in a quiet voice which betrayed a good deal of suppressed emotion, "It appears that I am unrecognizable, *mesdames.*"

It was scarcely surprising that he should be so, seeing that sickness had left its mark upon him, and that hostile bullets were supposed to have long since laid him low; but recognition was prompt, at all events, on the part of Lady Luttrell, from whose lips a glad cry escaped.

"Raoul! — ah, my dear boy, you will forgive me — I am old enough to be your mother, and I was your mother's oldest friend! It is a miracle from Heaven that has brought you back to us!"

. It was, perhaps, more agreeable to be embraced by Lady Luttrell than to be made the subject of a similar demonstration by M. de Larrouy. At any rate, Raoul did not seem to object to the experience; although his gaze, naturally enough, was directed over the head of the lady who was sobbing upon his shoulder at the pale, silent girl behind her. Madeline had spoken never a word; but her eyes spoke for her, and presently, when she gave him her hand, it seemed to him that at length the bitterness of death was past. She was very glad to see him, and she no longer despised him : that much he understood, and that, surely, was enough for a beginning.

He gave the account of himself which, as a matter of course, he was eagerly entreated to give, and was rather more circumstantial in his narrative than he had been at Bordeaux ; but he was so frequently interrupted that by the time that he had made an end of speaking neither of his hearers could have given a very coherent *résumé* of the adventures through which he had passed. One of them inwardly resolved that he should tell her the whole story again from start to finish ; the other drew a long breath and said :

" But what has brought you to Lourdes, of all places ? That is what I do not explain to myself."

" It is easily explained," he answered, smiling. " When I arrived at Pau this morning, I went straight to your house, and was told that you were here. Then I permitted myself to follow you, and, as you were not to be found in the church or near the Grotto, I walked on, upon the chance of encountering you. I was happily inspired, as you see."

" You went straight to our house — you followed us here ?" repeated Lady Luttrell. " You were in a great hurry, then, to let us know that you were safe and sound ?"

She could guess why he had been in such a hurry ; but she wanted to enjoy the luxury of hearing him say what he lost no time in saying.

" Ah, madame, it was the least that I could do to shorten your anxiety by a few hours ! I mentioned to you just now that I had run against De Larrouy at Bordeaux ; I did not mention that he told me of the annoyance to which you had been subjected through my inexcusable thoughtlessness. I ought to have remembered that, in the event of my death, you would be liable to disturbance, and I ought to have taken steps to prevent the possibility of such a thing. Most fortunately, and through no merit of my own, I have returned just in time to take those steps, and—"

"But the house is not ours," interrupted Madeline, quickly; "it has only returned to its former owner, and we must give it up to you."

"Pardon me, mademoiselle; legally, the house may be mine, but for all practical purposes it belongs to you. These are matters of business, which cannot be made clear in a moment; but I may tell you that I am absolutely bound by the instructions of my mother, who expressed a wish on her death-bed that you should under no circumstances be disturbed."

Had the late Madame de Malglaive expressed such a wish? Well, at all events, Raoul had done so, and she had assented—which was perhaps sufficient to save his character for veracity. But indeed the subject was not one which there was any need to discuss then and there, and, perceiving that Lady Luttrell's mind was at ease, he hastened to change it. He, on his side, had questions to ask; they had many common acquaintances, as to whose welfare he may not have been precisely burning with anxiety to be assured, but the mention of whose names served the purpose of giving a lighter turn to the conversation. And then he had a proposal to make.

"It is so hot, and those railway-carriages are like an oven! If we were to stay and dine here together? Then we might return to Pau by a late train and escape being grilled alive."

Lady Luttrell agreed unhesitatingly to this suggestion. "The more willingly," she added, "because I cannot leave Lourdes without acknowledging the marvellous answer that has been returned to my prayers? You do not believe, perhaps, that you are here in answer to my prayers? You will say that your life was saved before there was any question of my being turned out into the street— you were always a little of a sceptic, I am afraid. Never mind!—leave me to my faith, and I will ask that your scepticism may be pardoned and conquered. You will find me before the Grotto in half an hour, you others; I would rather be left to myself until then, if you permit."

She turned on her heel and trotted off, without waiting for any formal permission. It was unquestionably the best thing that she could do, and the couple whom she left behind her, although they may have been slightly embarrassed, did not think it necessary to call her back. Raoul spoke first.

"I have to thank you and to beg your pardon, mademoiselle," he began. "You had the great kindness to send me a letter which must have reached Tours after I had started for Sénégal, and which I only received on my return from the desert. I hope you divined how it was that I made no reply?"

"No reply was required," answered Madeline, hurriedly; "I found that I had done you an injustice, and I thought I ought to say so—that was all."

"But was it an injustice? I can't tell what you had heard about me; but I know, unhappily, that you might have heard things which, according to your ideas, would have sounded unpardonable."

"I have altered my ideas. Now that I come to think of them, they never were so much my own ideas as those of my sister-in-law, who also has altered hers. Besides, the things that you speak of happened long ago, before—before—" She broke off, perceiving that she was going a little too far, and concluded abruptly with, "Anyhow, it does not signify. I am not sorry that I wrote to you, and I am glad that you got my letter; but it isn't a subject about which there is any more to be said."

"It is a subject about which I have thought a great deal," observed Raoul, gently and tentatively.

But Madeline did not respond. She had moved from the spot where her mother had left them and was unconsciously walking back towards that for which it is not impossible that he had been bound when their meeting had taken place. No wonder her brain was in a whirl; no wonder she felt as if a genuine miracle had been worked, and threw furtive, sidelong glances at her neighbor to convince herself that she was not dreaming. Happiness, when it presents itself after so sudden and unimaginable a fashion, is apt to produce queer results, and for the moment she desired nothing more ardently than that the man whom she loved would leave her. There was so much to be considered; it was so essential that she should not lose her self-command; and she was so very uncertain of her power to retain it! Fear of what he might be going to say prompted her, as soon as he opened his lips, to forestall him with a hasty, thoughtless query.

"What made you go to that horrible country? It would have been different if you had been ordered there; but, as you were not, why could you not have remained with your regiment?"

"You ask me!" he returned, gazing at her, with uplifted eyebrows. "Yet you ought to know, if any one ought, what I went to Africa to seek—and what," he added, shrugging his shoulders deprecatingly, "I did not, as you see, find."

"Oh, glory? Well, it is not exactly glorious, I suppose, to be defeated; but I am sure you did your best to be victorious, and no man can do more than his best. Tell me about the battle; you gave us no particulars just now."

"It was scarcely to be called a battle," answered Raoul; "there was a short scrimmage, during which I defended myself instinctively. For the rest, it was not glory, as I think you know, that I coveted, but—the recognized alternative. I obtained neither the one nor the other; yet I am more indebted to my friend Salem than I thought I was, since he has enabled me, at least, to render one small service to you and your mother."

"Mamma is always in such a hurry to jump to conclusions," answered Madeline. "I don't think she can have quite understood what you said about Madame de Malglaive, and I am sure I did not. We must have some clearer explanation before—"

"Everything shall be made as clear as crystal, I promise you!" interrupted the young man, somewhat audaciously. "But we need not discuss dry matters of business now and here, need we? Do you know where we are, I wonder? Do you remember this place?"

"I remember it so well," she answered, quietly, "that I came here to - day on purpose to see it again. I do not mind your knowing that; I want you to know—and, be-sides, mamma is sure to tell you—so there would be no use—"

He caught her by both hands, crying out her name in passionate accents which did not fail to find an echo in her heart; but she wrenched herself away.

"It can't be!" she exclaimed. "Don't you understand how impossible it is? I have not had time to think; but I know very well that the more I think of it the more I shall be convinced that it is out of the question."

"Because I am not worthy of you?—because I did this and that before I knew you? But, Madeline—"

"No; not because of that. Did I not tell you that I have changed my ideas, and that even Clarissa has changed hers? But how can I accept you, now that we are so poor and you are so rich? Would not everybody call me, and have the right to call me, an *intrigante?* I had my chance, and I was too blind and opinionated to take it; it cannot be given to me a second time."

But of course it could be, and was. By pleas so feeble no lover in the world was likely to be discouraged, and Raoul de Malglaive, from the moment that he knew all he wanted to know, proved himself as masterful as he had hitherto been diffident.

"Are we to be made miserable for the rest of our lives for fear of ill-natured speeches being made about one or both of us?" he pertinently inquired. "That would be a little too strong! No; you have told now that you love me, and decidedly I do not release you from your word! Think no more about these pitiable trifles, and tell me again—tell me that you are really as happy as I am!"

Assurances of the nature requested are apt to occupy a very long time in the giving, and at the dowager Lady Lut-trel's age one cannot remain for upwards of half an hour upon one's knees without experiencing physical sensations which are not conducive to devotion. So her ladyship rose from her knees and sat down, patiently and contentedly enough, upon a neighboring bench to await the return of two people who had forgotten all about dinner. Their protracted absence did not disquiet her, and when at length they appeared, pacing along quite slowly, side by side, there was no occasion for them to tell a tale which told itself.

"What I shall never be able to understand," remarked Raoul's prospective mother-in-law at a later period of the evening, "is why all this did not happen long ago. Ah, Madeline, my child, I owe a fine crop of gray hairs to you! —and assuredly it is not to you that this poor fellow is indebted for his life."

"But I am indebted to her for everything that makes it worth my while to live," said Raoul. "Besides," he added, thinking of certain unpalatable allusions made by his betrothed to the repayment of a sum of money due to him, "there can be no more question of debts between us now, thank God!"

Lady Luttrell was ready enough to thank God, and Raoul, when the suggestion was timidly made, was not unwilling to pay a final visit to the Grotto. As he knelt there, slightly in the rear of two ladies who may have been offering up petitions on his behalf, and as he gazed at the blaze of tapers which the twilight was making conspicuous, he thought to himself that it was not, after all, such a very difficult thing to believe in Divine interference with mundane affairs. Some people become devotees when they are in despair, others when their fondest hopes have been fulfilled. It is a question of temperament and circumstances, and Raoul de Malglaive, being what he is, may quite possibly die in the odor of sanctity. It may, at any rate, be predicted with confidence that he will never, if he can help it, cause a moment of uneasiness to his wife, whose mind will scarcely be easy until she has brought him within the comprehensive embrace of Mother Church.

31

CHAPTER XLVIII

A COMFORTABLE CONCLUSION

"AND so," remarked the Reverend Paul Luttrell, "our ends have been shaped for us, in spite of the frantic efforts that some of us have made to rough-hew them."

He was lying flat upon his back on a flowery, grassy meadow beside his sister-in-law, who had established herself upon a campstool beneath a large white umbrella, and who replied:

"Oh yes; they have been shaped—I am bound to admit that. But I don't think I ever denied the existence of a Providence, did I?"

"I thought you did. You certainly denied the existence of most things which are obvious to a plain man like myself. But you have eaten humble pie now; and, besides, I am too hot and too comfortable and too tired, after the long tramp I have had to-day, to argue. What a lovely, quiet spot you have managed to discover in this tourist-ridden land!"

He raised his head a little to survey the prospect, which indeed looked charming enough on that cloudless summer day to have attracted more tourists than had apparently found their way thither. The shattered peaks of the Diablerets rose, snow-besprinkled, against a dark-blue sky; on either side of the smiling valley towered those eternal, majestic heights which neither Cook nor Gaze can vulgarize; and Paul Luttrell, himself a pedestrian tourist in Switzerland for a brief holiday, gave a sigh of satisfaction. He had only just arrived, having been summoned by his brother and his sister-in-law, who had heard of his vicinity and who wished—so they said—to give him ocular demonstration of the marvellous improvement which mountain air had already effected in Netta's health.

"Where is Guy?" he asked, presently.

"He has gone off somewhere with his gun," answered Clarissa, "accompanied by Netta on a mule and a *soi-disant* chamois-hunter whom he has picked up. There is not the slightest chance, I believe, of his finding anything to shoot; but he says it makes him feel more comfortable to carry a heavy gun over his shoulder, and it seems to be an understood thing now that wherever he goes Netta is to go. She will grow up into a grouse-shooting, salmon-catching young woman, I foresee."

"Well, that may be better for her, perhaps, than growing up into a stump-orating young woman."

"As if I had ever contemplated such a thing! But, down-trodden as I am, I mean to have some voice in my daughter's education, and as soon as she is really strong again lessons will have to be resumed. Guy thinks that the less book-learning a woman has the more likely she is to enjoy life. We should quarrel over the question if we had not bound ourselves by the most solemn vows never to quarrel again over any question."

"So that when you differ, the weaker will have to go cheerfully to the wall," remarked Paul. "That is an admirable plan, and I trust you have realized by this time which of you two is the weaker vessel. You don't look particularly down-trodden," he added, with a glance at Clarissa, whose face had recovered an almost girlish roundnesss of outline; "slavery seems to agree pretty well with you, so far."

She laid down the strip of embroidery upon which she had been engaged and turned a pair of deprecating eyes towards him. "I am so perfectly happy and contented," said she, "that I feel as if I owed a personal apology to every one of the women whom I have been trying to make discontented, and who have much better reasons than I ever had for being so."

"That would be rather a long job, wouldn't it? But

you did, I believe, burn your false gods in a quasi-public manner."

" Well, I confessed that I had ceased to worship them. I don't think I denounced them as false—not all of them, anyhow. What I wanted people to understand was that I myself couldn't any longer be one of the leaders of that movement ; I didn't mean to say that it was an entirely mistaken movement."

" You could scarcely have been more convincing, though I dare say you might have been more logical. As for apologies, one does not beg pardon for having come to one's senses. May your bright example find many imitators !"

" It would be better to wish that many women may be blessed with the chance and the power to follow my example. You must remember that I could not have done what I have done if Guy had not been Guy. Well, I have the comfort of knowing that one, at least, of my former followers, in the person of Madeline, has escaped from being led astray by my mistaken advice. By the way, did I tell you that Madeline and your mother are to arrive here this evening ?"

" You don't mean to say so !" exclaimed Paul, assuming a sitting posture. " No ; I have been out of reach of letters, and I did not even know that they had left Pau. It was only when I was upon the point of starting from London that I heard the news of Madeline's engagement, about which my mother wrote in enthusiastic language. Tell me about it—for I presume that you are in possession of all particulars."

" It has been a strange and romantic affair," answered Clarissa. " Your mother ascribes what has happened to a miracle ; but you, of course, don't believe in miracles."

" My dear Clarissa, don't I pray for rain or fair weather whenever my bishop directs me to do so ? If you were to ask me whether I believed that miracles are matters of every-day occurrence, I should have to answer that I don't ; but I hardly see how a man can go about the world with his eyes open and deny that they take place every now and then."

"Even when they are said to have been worked by Our Lady of Lourdes ?"

"I didn't come out for a holiday to be drawn into theological discussions ; I would rather listen to the history of the strange and romantic affair, please."

So Clarissa related a narrative of which the full details had but recently been communicated to her, and when she ended Paul was fain to admit that human agency had done what in it lay to convert a simple love tale into a very ugly tragedy.

"Madeline has indeed had a narrow escape—and so have you !" he remarked.

"That is just what I feel. Never again, you may be sure, will I run such a risk. All your flower-girls shall marry needy and disreputable costermongers now before I lift a finger to deter them !"

"Well, you wouldn't deter them if you lifted the whole ten at once," said Paul ; "nevertheless, I congratulate you upon a wise resolution. Is that your uncle, bearing down upon us with a newspaper in his hand ?"

Mr. Dent, who had been persuaded, not without some difficulty, to join this little family gathering in the Alps, shook hands with the new-comer and observed that the Radicals, as he had always foreseen would be the case, were rushing upon their own destruction.

"I give them less than a year to lose all credit with the constituencies," said he. "As if they could hope to carry one out of the half-dozen revolutionary measures that they announce with a patchwork majority like theirs ! Not that I complain of them for promising what everybody knows that they can't perform. On the contrary, I am infinitely obliged to them for being such geese as to go about the country proclaiming their intentions, and I anticipate that, at the next general election, we shall replace them by a fine, large flock of swans, including Sir Guy Luttrell. You will allow me, I hope, my dear, to count

Guy as a swan—that *rara avis,* a black swan, shall we say?"

"Well, he is a Tory, at all events," answered Clarissa. "Uncle Tom has made up his mind that Guy is to sit in Parliament for the division which his father used to represent," she explained to Paul. "Perhaps it would be a good thing."

"It is a necessary thing that he should have some work to do," Mr. Dent declared. "You don't think so now, because you and he happen to be living at present in a sort of Garden of Eden; but you may recollect the catastrophe which befell our first parents by reason of their idleness."

"I am very glad to hear it accounted for on that ground," said Clarissa; "I have always hitherto been given to understand that the woman and the tree of knowledge were to blame."

"It is not for me," returned her uncle, "to dispute the mischief that may be brought about by a woman who nibbles at the tree of knowledge; but, more by good luck than by good guidance, we have escaped that particular danger. Let us not run our heads against another."

They were the less likely to do that because Guy himself was quite alive to the perils of yielding to constitutional indolence. He will never be the prominent political personage that his father was; but he has made himself extremely popular with his constituents in these latter days, and the chances are that their demands upon his time and attention will keep him a busy man for the rest of his life.

He returned, with an empty bag but a cheerful countenance, from the heights just in time to welcome his mother and his sister on their arrival, and shortly afterwards a very joyous little company sat down to dine together. They had a great deal to say to one another; but there were several topics which, naturally enough, they preferred to leave out of discussion until they should have broken up into groups, and only after the sun had disappeared behind the crags and twinkling stars were beginning to show themselves here and there did the dowager, who had seated herself beside Mr. Dent on the veranda of the little hotel, remark :

"This is all very delightful; but is it quite right that Guy should accept such a magnificent present from you as a large estate and its revenues ?"

"It is absolutely right," replied Mr. Dent. "The estate, you see, must have gone in a few years' time to his wife, since there is nobody else to inherit from me; and I think you will agree that it is better for the estate, as well as for her and for him, that he should be master in his own house. For the moment, to be sure, Clarissa is as reasonable as can be desired; but my experience—pardon me for saying so—is that the reasonableness of women is not a thing to be implicitly relied upon. Therefore, if I have made Guy a present, I have done so simply because it suited my own convenience, and it isn't a case for gratitude."

"That is exactly what Raoul says about the Château de Grancy. He pretends that I shall do him a service by relieving him of a house for which he has no use, and—*ma foi!* what would you have? I am an unscrupulous old woman, I fear; but I tell myself that I should make the young people unhappy if I were to raise difficulties."

"I am sure you would; and I may add that I don't think it was very friendly on your part to conceal the fact that you were in difficulties from an old and trusted adviser. I thought, of course, that your private fortune remained intact."

"But, my dear friend, what could you have done if you had known the contrary? For all my poverty and unscrupulousness, I am not a downright mendicant! *Enfin!* —Heaven has been very good to me, and I may hope now to end my days in peace."

"Precisely my own sentiments," observed Mr. Dent. "At our age one doesn't ask for much; but one is uncommonly lucky, all the same, if one gets the little that one wants. Dear me! I believe there was a time, long ago, when I wanted to be Chancellor of the Exchequer."

They went on chatting about by-gone days and forgotten ambitions until Clarissa stepped out of the house to join them.

"I have been talking to Madeline," she announced, "and I feel even humbler than I did an hour ago—which is saying something. How near I have been to making shipwreck of my little world!"

"It must be admitted, my dear," answered Mr. Dent, dryly, "that circumstances seemed at one time to be all in favor of your fell designs; but then other circumstances arose, you see, and ground you and your designs to powder as easily as possible. Being in an optimistic mood this evening, I venture to believe that that will always be the case. The big world and all the little worlds are somewhat out of health; but human nature has a knack of asserting itself at the right moment, and so our necks are delivered from the yoke of amateur physicians. To have cured herself of empiricism is surely a sufficient feat for any one woman to have accomplished! Put that feather in your cap, my dear, and accept your old uncle's respectful congratulations with it."

THE END

By GEORGE DU MAURIER

TRILBY. A Novel. Illustrated by the Author. Post 8vo, Cloth, Ornamental, $1 75; Three-quarter Calf, $3 50; Three-quarter Crushed Levant, $4 50.

Certainly, if it were not for its predecessor, we should assign to "Trilby" a place in fiction absolutely companionless. . . . It is one of the most unconventional and charming of novels.—*Saturday Review*, London.

It is a charming story told with exquisite grace and tenderness.—*N. Y. Tribune*.

Mr. Du Maurier has written his tale with such originality, unconventionality, and eloquence, such rollicking humor and tender pathos, and delightful play of every lively fancy, all running so briskly in exquisite English and with such vivid dramatic picturing, that it is only comparable . . . to the freshness and beauty of a spring morning at the end of a dragging winter. . . . It is a thoroughly unique story.—*N. Y. Sun*.

"Trilby" suggests so much and furnishes forth such a vast deal of delight, that it is a book hard to describe or even to talk about. As regards its charm, there will be but one opinion; everybody is reading it and enjoying it.—*Hartford Courant*.

PETER IBBETSON. With an Introduction by his Cousin, Lady * * * * * ("Madge Plunket"). Edited and Illustrated by GEORGE DU MAURIER. Post 8vo, Cloth, Ornamental, $1 50.

Mr. Du Maurier deserves the gratitude of all who come across his book, both for the pleasant and tender fancies in which it abounds, and for its fourscore dainty sketches.—*Athenæum*, London.

There are so many beauties, so many singularities, so much that is fresh and original, in Mr. Du Maurier's story that it is difficult to treat it at all adequately from the point of view of criticism. That it is one of the most remarkable books that have appeared for a long time is, however, indisputable.—*N. Y. Tribune*.

There are no suggestions of mediocrity. The pathos is true, the irony delicate, the satire severe when its subject is unworthy, the comedy sparkling, and the tragedy, as we have said, inevitable. One or two more such books, and the fame of the artist would be dim beside that of the novelist.—*N. Y. Evening Post*.

PUBLISHED BY HARPER & BROTHERS, NEW YORK.

☞ *The above works are for sale by all booksellers, or will be sent by the publishers, postage prepaid, to any part of the United States, Canada, or Mexico, on receipt of the price.*

R. D. BLACKMORE'S NOVELS.

PERLYCROSS. A Novel. 12mo, Cloth, Ornamental, $1 75.

Told with delicate and delightful art. Its pictures of rural English scenes and characters will woo and solace the reader. . . . It is
charming company in charming surroundings. Its pathos, its humor,
and its array of natural incidents are all satisfying. One must feel
thankful for so finished and exquisite a story. . . . Not often do we
find a more impressive piece of work.—*N. Y. Sun.*

A new novel from the pen of R. D. Blackmore is as great a treat
to the fastidious and discriminating novel-reader as a new and rare
dish is to an epicure. . . . A story to be lingered over with delight.—
Boston Beacon.

SPRINGHAVEN. Illustrated, 12mo, Cloth, $1 50; 4to, Paper,
25 cents.

LORNA DOONE. Illustrated. 12mo, Cloth, $1 00; 8vo, Paper,
40 cents.

KIT AND KITTY. 12mo, Cloth, $1 25; Paper, 35 cents.

CHRISTOWELL. 4to, Paper, 20 cents.

CRADOCK NOWELL. 8vo, Paper, 60 cents.

EREMA; OR, MY FATHER'S SIN. 8vo, Paper, 50 cents.

MARY ANERLEY. 16mo, Cloth, $1 00; 4to, Paper, 15 cents.

TOMMY UPMORE. 16mo, Cloth, 50 cents; Paper, 35 cents;
4to, Paper, 20 cents.

His descriptions are wonderfully vivid and natural. His pages
are brightened everywhere with great humor; the quaint, dry turns of
thought remind you occasionally of Fielding.—*London Times.*

His tales, all of them, are pre-eminently meritorious. They are
remarkable for their careful elaboration, the conscientious finish of
their workmanship, their affluence of striking dramatic and narrative
incident, their close observation and general interpretation of nature,
their profusion of picturesque description, and their quiet and sustained
humor.—*Christian Intelligencer,* N. Y.

PUBLISHED BY HARPER & BROTHERS, NEW YORK.

☞ *The above works are for sale by all booksellers, or will be sent by the
publishers, postage prepaid, to any part of the United States, Canada, or Mexico,
on receipt of the price.*

By A. CONAN DOYLE

THE REFUGEES. A Tale of Two Continents. Illustrated. Post 8vo, Cloth, Ornamental, $1 75.

A masterly work. . . . It is not every year, or even every decade, which produces one historical novel of such quality—*Spectator*, London.

THE WHITE COMPANY. Illustrated. Post 8vo, Cloth, Ornamental, $1 75.

. . . Dr. Doyle's stirring romance, the best historical fiction he has done, and one of the best novels of its kind to-day.—*Hartford Courant*.

MICAH CLARKE. Illustrated. Post 8vo, Cloth, Ornamental, $1 75; also 8vo, Paper, 45 cents.

A noticeable book, because it carries the reader out of the beaten track; it makes him now and then hold his breath with excitement; it presents a series of vivid pictures and paints two capital portraits; and it leaves upon the mind the impression of well-rounded symmetry and completeness.—R. E. PROTHERO, in *The Nineteenth Century*.

ADVENTURES OF SHERLOCK HOLMES. Illustrated. Post 8vo, Cloth, Ornamental, $1 50.

MEMOIRS OF SHERLOCK HOLMES. Illustrated. Post 8vo, Cloth, Ornamental, $1 50.

Few writers excel Conan Doyle in this class of literature. His style, vigorous, terse, and thoughtful, united to a nice knowledge of the human mind, makes every character a profoundly interesting psychological study. —*Chicago Inter-Ocean*.

THE PARASITE. A Story. Illustrated. Post 8vo, Cloth, Ornamental, $1 00.

A strange, uncanny, weird story, . . . easily the best of it* class. The reader is carried away by it, and its climax is a work of literary art.— *Cincinnati Commercial-Gazette*.

THE GREAT SHADOW. Post 8vo, Cloth, Ornamental, $1 00.

A powerful piece of story-telling. Mr. Doyle has the gift of description, and he knows how to make fiction seem reality.—*Independent*, N. Y.

PUBLISHED BY HARPER & BROTHERS, NEW YORK.

☞ *The above works are for sale by all booksellers, or will be mailed by the publishers, postage prepaid, on receipt of the price.*